Praise for *The End of Yester*

San Francisco Book Review
Stacia Levy

> *There is a satisfying character arc in Analise—the mild-mannered girl who was judged too weak—mentally and physically—for nursing and chases after a fiancé who doesn't even love her matures into a woman of independent will. Overall, the story is compelling and difficult to put down.*

Portland Book Review
Norman West

> *The story has a touch of magical realism, with Mark and Analise experiencing bouts of déjà vu and sharing dreams of a past life. Their budding connection is framed to great effect by the war that surrounds them. Corbin does a remarkable job of describing the gruesome realities of conditions suffered on the front lines, both with the soldiers and the medical professionals. As such, readers overly sensitive to descriptions of gore and squalid living may want to steer clear of this book, but those who do choose to dive into its pages will be well rewarded! The book is rife with social commentary and observations about human connection that are applicable today, making this work of historical fiction wonderfully relevant. The End of Yesterday is a story that will keep you turning pages late into the night and wondering about any déjà vu experiences in your own life.*

The End of Yesterday
Copyright ©2017 E. M. Corbin

ISBN 978-1506-904-77-1 PRINT
ISBN 978-1506-904-78-8 EBOOK

LCCN 2017948995

July 2017

Published and Distributed by
First Edition Design Publishing, Inc.
P.O. Box 20217, Sarasota, FL 34276-3217
www.firsteditiondesignpublishing.com

THE END OF YESTERDAY

A Novel by

E. M. CORBIN

First Edition Design Publishing

Sarasota, Florida USA

TO STEPHANIE

For your perpetual help, and love and encouragement.

PROLOGUE

1938

It was her father on the phone.

After her ordeal in Spain, her mother had sent him to Paris to rescue her. Her parents, despite their divorce, were always agreeable where their daughter was concerned.

But Analise did not need to be rescued.

She needed to be understood. And Mark needed to be understood. And Spain needed to be understood. Yet both she and Mark knew that neither her parents nor anyone else would ever understand or sympathize with them. Still it was good to hear her father's voice. He always spoke with a youthful eagerness that lent persuasiveness to whatever he said.

"Is that you, Ana? - Thank God, you're safe! Listen, do you want to meet me here? I'm at the Ritz, or do you want me to come there? Anything you say's fine with me."

"- I'll meet you at your hotel, Papa. You can buy me lunch."

The Ritz was world famous. Her father's lavishly furnished room reduced hers to little more than four walls and a bed. He greeted her at the door with a big grin and outstretched arms and she went to him and he hugged her. He always smelled of cigars and Bay Rum shaving lotion. Then he held her at arm's length to look at her. There was a certain air about her now that he could not quite identify. What had happened to her in Spain?

He led her over to a small couch and studied her face as they sat. She smiled and gave him an account of her experience in Spain. She knew her recital was sketchy, but neither he nor anyone else would ever believe what had really happened so why bother. Nevertheless, she braced herself for an onslaught of questions.

Instead he reached into his suit coat pocket and produced an envelope. "Here," he said, handing it to her, "that's your passage on the

1

ship. We can leave tomorrow afternoon. I have to get back as soon as possible. The government wants we should get into production as soon as possible. War pictures."

"- I can't take this, Papa. Didn't Mom tell you? About Mark?"

He sat back and stared at her. His stare used to reduce her to rebellious outbursts and occasional tears. Now she stared back. He was of middle height, tanned and youthful looking with a full head of hair and mouth that suggested a friendly smile.

"- Do you know what you're saying?" he asked quietly. "You're not a child, Ana. I shouldn't have to explain it to you. For God's sake, think of your mother tearing her heart out with worry all these months. Did you get bombed? Shot? Dead? No letters, nothing but worry, now this. Such a daughter no one should have. This doctor you're engaged to – Jacob - he's a nice boy...."

"I didn't come here to quarrel with you, Papa," she said quietly but firmly. "I'm not leaving Mark and that's all there is to it. This isn't one of your movies where everything is nice and tidy at the end. I wouldn't be alive today if it hadn't been for Mark."

He saw she was determined. After a moment "- So alright. Alright, I'll give this Mark money, what he wants. What else can I do? I'll buy him a ticket home but please, listen to me, don't destroy your life, *and his.* Yes, his, don't forget. America is what it is, Ana. Germany is what it is. Better maybe he should stay here. The French treat those people well, but us - Jews?" He shook his head – "You can't stay here with war coming and Hitler...."

CHAPTER 1

1934

Analise wanted to be just like her friends Sarah and Miriam, Connie and Agatha. Their lives were spent in the warm, safe cocoon of matrimony, untouched by the gloom of the Depression or rumors of war or whispers of rape or talk of robbery. Tuesday followed Monday with pleasant regularity. Milk and bread arrived on their door step each morning and later the morning paper; they knew the butcher and the baker and the grocer by name and they in turn knew theirs. Their lives were normal. She wanted that; every girl did. Each of her friends had been rescued from the hovering shame of being *left behind* – of growing old and unmarried and unwanted and unloved.

Analise was slender with thoughtful green eyes and a young girl's open smile. By nature self-critical and anxious to please, she would seldom argue or raise her voice. Her dark hair was worn in a chignon that kept her slender neck clear and free. She was careful to follow the fashion of pleated skirts and round collared sweaters. Everyone who knew her said she was nice and considerate and inoffensive. And she was. Still, beneath it all was a hidden streak of determination that would later shape her world in a shocking fashion. She was what followed the word "*but.*"

To prepare herself to be like everybody else, she thoughtfully read the "textbooks" concerning matrimony. There was the *Ladies' Home Journal's Book on the Business of Housekeeping*, and *McCall's* and *Ladies' Companion* explaining the intricacies of refrigerators and mattresses and linoleum flooring. The "text books" quietly advised the good wife to know who Babe Ruth was and that FDR was the president and that Communists were bad and – sometimes – one might find an oblique reference to a thing called "family planning."

Girls of her class were often encouraged to attend college, not primarily to get an education, but to find a husband and when she was a sophomore, Analise was thrilled to find herself among the chosen. She became engaged to Jacob Miller. She was ecstatic. She was successful. She would soon be a married lady like everyone she knew!

Yet now, three years later, she felt him slipping away like a soapy, expensive platter. She was making an effort to catch the platter before it shattered on the floor. It seemed she could almost measure the distance growing between them. Then the diamond ring on her finger felt like someone's borrowed jewelry.

Occasionally, to persuade herself that her engagement to Jacob was not in jeopardy, she caressed her engagement ring with her thumb, treasuring what it meant – a culmination of her having grown from a little girl playing with dolls to a young woman experiencing a handsome man saying, "I love you" and making her feel especially chosen.

But she knew he was slipping away and the devastating fear of *being left behind* seemed more real now that she had had her chance.

***

When she was fourteen, in private school in Manhattan, still too young to fully understand the nuances and implications of boy meets girl, she had begun learning the intricate dance of courtship with Saul.

He was a tall, awkward boy who pretended he had friends when he hadn't any. He would stand near groups of popular kids as though he were a part of their group. They resolutely ignored him. Some of it was his own doing because he avoided any activity with the other boys that could cause him a bruise or a bump.

Analise felt he needed looking after.

Saul liked to hike in Central Park searching for odd colored stones that he collected with an air of triumph. One day he finally marshaled the courage to mumble an eye evading invitation. Would she like to hunt rocks with him?

Her first thought was, "*Ugh!*" It sounded dirty! But she smiled and murmured, "Yes," though it meant going into the woods - that domain of ugly, crawly insects that raced up your legs and over your arms and even *down your back!* They bit you and flew and beat against your face!

She scrunched her shoulders. Still she went. She wore a long sleeve shirt and hugged herself.

Determined to acquire an interest in rocks and stones, she borrowed books from the library that showed pictures of pink and blue and gray stones and she studied their names and shared what he knew with Saul. She even pointed a delicate finger to a stone or two that lay half buried in dirt, refraining from picking them up herself.

When his parents lost their money in the Stock Market crash in 1929, they could no longer keep him in private school. They drifted apart.

The summer she was seventeen, she met Manny while she and her mother were on vacation in Connecticut. He took her canoeing. She went although she was afraid of the water because she could not swim. They spent afternoons on a nearby lake. Since both of them had to paddle, she found the task exhausting and, smiling, had to beg off frequently to rest.

Manny said she would be more comfortable in a swim suit. She sensed a danger in that. Smiling, she demurred. They quarreled about it; it was more a thing of pouting than anything else but she stopped seeing him.

Finally there was Jacob, a medical student at NYU. Almost from the first, she wanted to own him. He was tall, a little stooped and he wore wire rim glasses; his hair was parted in the middle and it made him look like an artist. Jacob had a disarming, boyish smile and he didn't mind in the least that she was a little thin, slender really.

That was when she began to think of the glorious state of marriage and was surprised to feel twinges of jealousy when other girls were around. It made her feel a little ashamed; they were her friends, but still she monitored the distance between him and them.

He cared deeply for people and wondered when the Depression would end and why no one cared enough about the people who suffered and went hungry or stood in block-long soup lines and couldn't afford medical care. He almost shouted that it was obscene. She treasured that about him and adopted his pure, clean outrage as her own.

So it surprised her when he unexpectedly sneered at the victims of the German Zeppelin, *Hindenburg*. The newspapers were filled with pictures showing the huge dirigible descending in flames to the ground at Lakehurst, New Jersey.

It was all anyone talked about. To be burned alive like that, falling from the sky with no way to escape - it was horrible. She scrunched her shoulders just thinking about it.

Jacob was unmoved. "Serves them right. They're all Nazis and they're doing worse than that to Jews in Germany!" His eyes were harder than she had ever seen them. For a moment it unnerved her. Arm in arm they were on their way to see *Snow White and the Seven Dwarfs*. He paused on the sidewalk to scold her for showing sympathy for the people on the *Hindenburg*.

"I'm surprised you don't know about the Nuremburg Laws, Ana, and what those Nazis do to Jews! Hundreds, *thousands* brutalized every single day, children even!"

"I know about the Nuremburg Laws, Jacob," she replied quietly, "but they weren't all Germans on the *Hindenburg*."

"Then they shouldn't have been on it!" He was livid. "They should never have set foot in Germany. The whole damn crew was German."

It was their first argument. She strongly disagreed but did not pursue it. Would anyone say the same thing about a ship at sea? The *Hindenburg* was a ship of the air which was supposed to be the future of transatlantic passenger travel; they said that it was only a matter of time before ocean liners disappeared altogether. In the days that followed, she chastised herself for not having spoken up and defended her beliefs. He even declared that the only good German was Bruno Hauptmann because he was dead - executed last year for kidnapping the Lindbergh baby.

But mostly they laughed and did silly things at sporting events and parties to call attention to themselves. They kissed passionately in dark places and wrote letters back and forth. He told her the things he wanted to do with his life and she said encouraging things to send forth her knight in shining armor.

Once when they were parked in his father's car behind Maxwell's gas station, kissing passionately, his fingers, like an advancing army, captured her knee and then part of her thigh. Emboldened he sent troops sliding between her thighs headed for the Golden City. Alarmed, she caught her breath, snatched his hand away, pressed her knees together and crossed her ankles.

"Aw, come on, honey," he pleaded softly in her ear, caressing her face with kisses, "– we're already engaged."

"But we're not *married*, Jacob. We're not married. - Why can't we wait?"

"- That's old fashioned," he murmured with a chuckle. "Nobody cares about that 'virgin' stuff anymore. It's *1936*, honey, not 1836. Everybody does it. We're going to get married, aren't we, so what difference does it make? We're practically married already. You're going to be my wife, Ana."

"- I won't feel right about it, Jacob!" she pleaded. "I'll feel like…like a *whore*. I can't help it; it's how I was raised. And suppose I got *pregnant*! That's not 'old fashioned.' I know a girl who got pregnant. Her parents won't even speak to her anymore and another girl tried to get rid of it and died. - I'm sorry, Jacob. It's all my fault. I should have stopped letting you do things a long time ago…."

Disgusted, he blew his breath out and sat back and hit the steering wheel with the heel of his hands. Silence took a seat between them. Several minutes squirmed by.

"- I know you're disappointed, Jacob, but so am I. - What makes you think that I'm that sort of girl?"

"I don't want to talk about this anymore! It's asinine. You sound like somebody's grandmother. *'That-sort-of-girl!'* You should hear how you sound."

Silence nudged them farther apart. He was on the verge of starting the car up when she held out her palm. Her engagement ring was in the middle of it. For a second he stared dumbly at the ring before lifting his eyes to hers. There were no tears. Maybe there was anger; her eyes were steady. He tried to gauge her resolve.

"I want to marry you, Jacob. I love you and I want to give you children, and…and I'll give you the most *precious* thing I have – my body. When you give me the most precious thing you have – your name."

He shook his head as though to clear it. He stared at her in mild disbelief. After a count of three, he reached out and closed her slender fingers around the ring. "I'm sorry," he said. It was then that she cried and he took her in his arms and let her cry and then he took her home and kissed her on her forehead and on her face.

***

The first inkling that he was slipping away presented itself around the time that the *Hindenburg* exploded. But was it because of sex or socialism? Maybe it was both. By then he was finishing medical school and socialism had become important to him. When had she first noticed the slippage? Was it that time he had called during one of his rare breaks from his studies? "We're meeting again this Saturday. Want to come?"

"- The Student Socialists?"

"Yeah. It's going to be really swell. You ought to come and hear what they have to say."

He first expressed an interest in socialism shortly after she met him. She hurried to the library and researched socialism so she could discuss it intelligently with him. She came away confused. The various philosophical permutations left her convinced socialism was the stuff of dreams, and even if it wasn't, you'd have to virtually stand the world on end to accomplish anything. But she did not tell him that.

"- Nobody said much of anything the last few times we went, Jacob. Remember? We just sat around listening to people arguing and shouting each other down. I still have no idea what anybody was trying to say."

"Yeah, I know, but *Norman Thomas* is coming! He's the real deal. He ran for president last year and a lot of people voted for him. We need to get more people like him to run for office, not just for president, but mayors, councilmen, congress; it's the only way we can really make a difference!"

"– Gee, I don't know," she said with a smile in her voice. "I didn't want to go the last time; I just wanted to be with you and to be honest, I don't think I have any real interest in that sort of thing. I know you said it's not like Communism, but – I just don't have any interest.

But I'll go if you...."

"No, no, don't do that, Ana. It's all right. Maybe you'll change your mind later...."

Should she have gone anyway? And all of the times after that? Would it have made a difference had she learned to distinguish Eugene Debs from Norman Thomas? Other things played a part. Distance and time now that he was also doing work at Johns Hopkins in Baltimore. The future became even murkier when her mother reminded her that she and Jacob might not be able to get married until after he got an internship and then established a practice. Years.

There had to be a way to halt the slippage and she needed to do something to occupy the time until they could get married. He was still in school, growing, while she was finished with college and standing still. That posed other problems - there were few options for a woman with a college degree outside of social work or teaching. Doris Cortland graduated Phi Beta Kappa and was a Marshall Scholar at Oxford yet could not do better than run copy at a magazine. Everyone said it was a disgrace but that didn't change anything. You had to be a wife and a mother. Nothing else.

Then a solution presented itself. - What would be more logical than becoming a nurse?

That way she could be a helpmate to Jacob and have a realistic understanding of the hours and pressures he faced every day. She dreaded the sight of blood and even more the thought of someone in pain, but if he wanted to succor the poor, so would she. She meant to hold on to him, and the sight of blood was not going to stop her.

CHAPTER 2

Olga Stern frowned. "Be a *nurse?* For that you didn't need college!"

"I know Mama, but it's what I have to do. I'll be helping Jacob in his practice, that's all."

"What does Jacob say?"

"I've only told you so far. He'll be surprised and pleased. I know he will."

Olga's face registered doubt and disapproval.

Analise's friend, Miriam, offered a puzzled expression. "Can't you get a job in some kind of business, Ana? You went to college. That gives you a lot of prestige. Anybody can be a nurse."

Sarah, another friend, also expressed surprise. "Do you think you'll like seeing sick people every day and *touching* them....?"

Undeterred, during a rare dinner date with Jacob at Alfonso's, eyes glowing with suppressed excitement, she told him that she was going to go to nursing school so that she could be of help to him in his practice, and she'd be able to understand the things he had to go through every day.

He chewed thoughtfully for a long moment, searching for the right words. Failing to do so, he engaged her eyes and suggested she do something other than nursing.

"– But don't you want me to be able to help you?"

"Not if it means tearing yourself apart, Ana. Nurses have to be tough, not kind and gentle. That's crap you see in the movies. Nurses don't go to college; some of the older ones never finished high school. It's a lunch pail kind of job. My God, you went to *Smith!* That's like me going to Harvard then saying I want to be a carpenter or a plumber.

"This is like that boy you were telling me about who liked rocks. You followed him into the woods worrying the whole time about insects, then you get into a canoe when you can't even swim. Stop trying to please everybody and that includes me.

"You're not cut out to be a nurse. There's no room for sympathy in a hospital. You're so full of sympathy you'd be used up in a week. A nurse has to forget her feelings and her sense of propriety. And sometimes you have to inflict pain to ease pain. You're not that sort of person, Ana."

"...What 'sort of person'?"

"Tough."

They finished the meal in silence. After the waiter cleared the dishes he said, "- I didn't mean to offend you." But that was all he said.

She never mentioned nursing to him again, but she was determined to be a nurse and to help him and to understand the stresses and strains that would attend his being a physician. That was her vision. Let it be a surprise, one she believed he'd appreciate when the time came.

Nevertheless, she resented his belief that she was inadequate and could not do what other women did. Was she supposed to be a frail, perishable creature best kept in the safety of a house sorting laundry and preparing meals? She kept her feelings to herself for fear of endangering their engagement, and once she even thought of sacrificing her virginity to him, but her mother's voice screamed and echoed in her head – *KEEP YOUR KNEES TOGETHER!*

***

Nurse Kendricks, a humorless, lantern jawed instructor, was a woman who either disliked her job or disliked her nursing students. Her students grew tense under her baleful glance and they were well aware that she was convinced that, "You're half trained. What do you know about nursing, anyway? In my day we were expected to cook, serve meals, polish furniture, make beds, bathe patients, dress blisters, burns, give massages; prevent bed sores or heal them if we saw any; we gave enemas, inserted catheters and applied leeches – Yes, *leeches!* You girls today are lucky...."

"You think you're a nurse if all you do is observe urine and bowel movements or take somebody's temperature. Anybody can give medicines and monitor them. You're too hoity-toity if you ask me."

Analise was certain that "hoity toity" was aimed at her. Kendricks took a dim view of those with the dubious benefit of a college education. She let it be known that any number of nurses who had not even finished high school were "Splendid, wonderful nurses!" She'd place her life under their care any day. Who could say that about nurses nowadays?

Once, Molly, a bold individual with red hair and freckles, offered the view that she and her classmates still did most of those things. Except apply leeches which was "antique."

The room grew cold with silence. There was the fleeting temptation to turn around and stare at the red haired girl. Kendricks' color went up and her grey eyes swept the room looking for any signs of sympathy with the heretic.

"Let me tell you something, Miss Know-It-All!" she intoned between clenched teeth and narrowed eyes. "We didn't have any so-called *nursing schools*! We worked from sun up to sundown every day of the week. The only break we got was when the doctors gave us lectures. That's what we exchanged our hard work for – lectures on nursing and that was only when the doctors had the time, and it took three long years. We started out with 30 student nurses and ended up with 12.

"Three years! We learned two things that you'd better learn if you ever expect to get anywhere – when a doctor comes into the room, *stand*. And when he gives you an order, *obey it*, period! You'd better not ever *ever* contradict a doctor or you'll find yourself out on the street pronto. Nobody's paying for your half-baked opinion!

"Doctors are sick and tired of all this hoity-toity nonsense! All a nurse needs to know is how to keep a patient comfortable and take care of his or her needs. You belong *bedside*, not looking through microscopes trying to be a doctor. It's none of your business why a patient's sick! That's for the doctor to decide. Just do as you're told!"

On one level Analise could understand her hostility; Kendricks felt threatened – but there was no going back to the medieval practices of her day when nursing knowledge was divorced from medical knowledge. For Kendricks and her generation, nursing was a trade, not a profession based on science.

Out of her hearing, the student nurses excoriated both her and her heroine, Florence Nightingale. Nightingale was the one who had proclaimed that a nurse's primary reward was not for pay, but the simple satisfaction of helping others. And Nightingale believed, like the doctors, that nurses did not need medical knowledge. Everyday sanitary knowledge was all that they needed – open the windows and let fresh air in, plenty of sunshine, nutritious food, clean sheets and quiet rest.

"That'll cure cancer and diphtheria for sure," they hooted. As for no pay, Molly observed, "I'd like to see how many times Nightingale put 'satisfaction' on the dinner table. The woman was rich; she could afford to preach stuff like that!"

One day in the hospital ward, Analise balked at having to actually touch a man's penis in order to insert a catheter. To her it was akin to plunging her bare hand into a toilet and lifting out and squeezing the feces.

"You're not cut out for nursing," Kendricks fumed, scornful of Analise's slight build and "hoity toity" ways. She threatened to have her dismissed.

Upset, Analise discussed it with her mother that night. "I'm not going to do it," She declared adamantly while washing the dinner dishes. "I may have to withdraw."

Her mother said nothing as she dried and put the dishes away.

"All she does," Analise continued, "is find reasons to criticize me. – 'You're not tough enough,' 'You'll never make it,' 'You should quit now before they throw you out!' She's making me the butt of ridicule!"

After the dishes were done and Analise had finished drawing and quartering Nurse Kendricks, Olga asked quietly, "What do they call this –you know - that you put the catheter in?"

"– Penis?"

"And a child, a baby, has one, too? People are grown up babies and those you see are babies who depend on you to feed them and change them and pay attention as they whine and cry and have tantrums. This thing, the penis, is what babies have. The nasty names we give it, forget. It is a *penis*. A baby you don't mind, but it is the same thing. You must say 'penis' over and over and nothing else, Ana. It is as God intended."

Next day Analise inserted a catheter, holding her breath the entire time, and later felt justifiably smug. But one day she fainted in class. It was during an autopsy when the surgeon lifted out of a cadaver's chest cavity a purplish looking slimy thing that was a heart. But she was not the only one who fainted; Molly did, too. Another time was when she saw a seven year old child that had been struck by a car. One eye was hanging out.

CHAPTER 3

Things fell apart when Jacob completed medical school.

Analise and her mother were having a celebratory dinner for him at home. They were passing the brisket when out of the blue he announced that in two weeks he was leaving the United States for Spain.

Analise hid her shock or at least hoped she had.

Olga Stern's eyes widened for a second. Seated at the head of the table, she sat frozen, fork in one hand, knife in the other. Perhaps five seconds passed. She was a slender woman who had been a beauty in her youth. She wore glasses to read, kept her graying hair in the latest fashion, read constantly, and when she spoke, she pinned her listener with a steady, almost challenging gaze.

Finally, she registered her disapproval by placing her silverware down beside her plate.

Jacob and Analise sat opposite each other. She kept her trembling hands in her lap.

"I'm going to be a volunteer doctor for the Spanish Republic in their war against Franco and the Fascists," he explained. "The American Bureau to Aid Spanish Democracy is setting up hospitals in Spain to take care of the wounded. It's a great opportunity; I can do my internship there. A Spanish doctor has even found a way to have *blood banks* for blood transfusions!

"A lot of fellows are already over there fighting with the Abraham Lincoln International Brigade. There're a lot of international brigades, guys from all over the world – Poland, England, France – you name it. They're willing to give their lives. I can at least give a little of my time.

"The Socialists and Communists are the only ones trying to help Spain. Everybody else – the United States, England, France - its hands off! It's like watching a gang of men raping – pardon, Mrs. Stern – a woman and claiming there's nothing they can do to stop it!

"Meanwhile Hitler and Mussolini are sending troops, planes, tanks to help Franco overthrow the Spanish government that won the last election fair and square." His face was flushed, his eyes avid.

"No telling where Hitler and Mussolini will stop. They've already taken over Austria and Ethiopia. Look what Hitler's doing to the Jews in Germany – Those Nuremburg Laws are a disgrace to mankind. They're practically the same laws they have here for Negroes. He's got to be stopped and I'm not the only one who thinks that – you've got famous people like Ernest Hemingway and Dorothy Parker, Picasso, Langston Hughes –they're all going over to help!"

Time held its breath. One second, two seconds, three, four, five....

There was something in what he said, but Mrs. Stern was not prepared to admit it. "Better you should stay here, Jacob," she finally advised him. "Leave war to others. Married, you stay. Begin a practice. Plenty enough to do here."

He smiled. "I'm not a married man yet, Mrs. Stern. Besides, life's not just about making money or being successful or getting married. People are starving and being beaten, blown apart and killed every single day. Even as we sit here.

"And it's going to spread here, too. Ever hear that creep Fritz Kuhn? He admits the aims of the German American Bund are the same as Hitler's! According to him, all Jews are the enemies of the U.S and they control both political parties and must be forced out of power!

"You can't stand on the sidelines and pretend that what's happening somewhere else doesn't matter because it's not happening to us because it *will* be happening to us! I won't be gone forever. It'll be good experience. If anything, it'll make me a better doctor but I have to do something."

" - And bombs?" Olga Stern frowned. "They care? Bullets stop because you're a doctor?"

He chuckled, "Nobody bothers hospitals, Mrs. Stern. We take care of enemy soldiers, too. I'll be all right; don't worry so much. Everything'll be fine."

"– When you're married to my daughter, then everything is fine, Jacob, not before! Three years engaged – that's enough."

"Mama!" Analise exclaimed, face scarlet.

"Three years," she intoned. "It's enough." Her lips were tight with disapproval.

"…How long will you be gone?" Analise managed to ask. It took an effort to keep the catch of a sob out of her voice.

He took a deep breath, carefully inspected the ceiling and finally exhaled. "Can't say, for sure. We never discussed it."

She took a sip of water. "Do you have any idea where you're going?"

"Probably a hospital in a place called *Villa Paz*. I'll be with the American Medical Bureau. Dr. Barsky's heading it. He's real famous."

Now she knew it was not her imagination – he was slipping away, perhaps for good. He had never bothered discussing his intentions with her. Later that night, she called him.

"Jacob, do you think we could possibly get married before you leave? It doesn't have to be anything fancy, just 'I do' and let it go at that. I'd like to really spend at least a couple of days with you all alone; just the two of us. We've never done that. We've never been all alone for an entire day. It's just been dribs and drabs and I think love needs more than that. It needs nourishment like roses do. We need to be together, Jacob.

"…Jacob – do you love me?"

"- Of course. We'll get married as soon as I get back, but right now I need a few months to just breathe and finally get to practice medicine on my own and get my thoughts together. We've waited this long; what's a few more months…?"

She listened for sounds of reassurance and hoped that she had heard them. Yet she knew in her heart that she had not; she had not caught the platter.

CHAPTER 4

Analise.

Jacob was ambivalent about her. She was clearly a superior person but he did not understand in what way.

Now that he was leaving, he could appreciate and even admire her wrongheaded resistance to sexual intercourse before marriage. But his appreciation may have had more to do with his assurance that she would be untouched when he came back than with her moral beliefs. By any measure since the Twenties sex had become open and honest and attempts by men to monopolize the privilege of sexual experimentation was *passé* along with frowning on women smoking in public, drinking or raising hell.

"'Wrong,'" he had argued, "is a matter of taste, Ana, or the age you live in. People have to decide things for themselves. Our parents think one way and their parents another. Times change, but 'right' or 'wrong' – it's not even a matter of opinion. It's nobody's business."

With a skeptical smile in her voice she asked, "- Was it 'right' to burn 'witches' and 'heretics' when they did it, Jacob? - I'm just asking…."

Her mind was a labyrinth that made it unprofitable to argue with her. She would smile gently and say that there was no one more stubborn than a person who wouldn't change his mind. Unless it was the person trying to make him change it.

He decided she was old fashioned, maybe even prudish.

Would she insist on keeping her petticoat on once they were married to conceal her naked body? Or shrink from touching his penis or cringe if he touched her clitoris? Sex should be a bawdy, loud, obscene, joyful shout that moved mountains and emptied the seas. It should be sinfully nasty. It was *fucking* not "intercourse", "cock" not "penis", "pussy" and "cunt."

Would she spoil it by silent disapproval?

It was not a thing he wished to quarrel about.

Both of them, having studied the human body and having seen and touched the flesh of strangers, should be beyond modesty, but he found he had to restrain his impatience with her. Quietly, he was beginning to believe that there was something fundamentally wrong with her and that her avoidance of sex was simply a ruse to disguise it. When he decided to go to Spain, he was surprised at how eagerly he looked forward to it.

Spain was adventure. A little dangerous but not enough to be fatal. It offered the openness and the freedom one feels among perfect strangers. Spain was tomorrow and the day after tomorrow. It was running with the wind singing in your ears or turning somersaults; it was laughing with a full throat – it was the shout that he needed. It was the taste and the feel and the sound of freedom.

The night before Jacob was scheduled to leave, they met for dinner. He had booked a room in the hotel. Over steak they smiled too much and talked too much and ate too little because they both knew why he had booked the room. They toyed with their chocolate mousse until he paid the bill and they went up to his room. He kissed her and she pretended to respond but did not feel it. When he kissed her again, she fought the urge to keep her eyes open.

"Do you know when you'll be back?" she asked.

He shook his head. "I think people volunteer for six months."

"That long?"

He turned off one of the two lights. He began removing his tie. She sat on the bed and removed her shoes. She removed her blouse and her skirt and sat on the side of the bed in her petticoat with her knees pressed together. He sat beside her. She could see he was aroused.

He reached behind her and unfastened her bra and exposed her small, firm breasts. She hunched her shoulders together. He caressed her nipples; his fingers felt like sandpaper. She did not want him to do things like that, exposing her with the light on. He felt her tenseness.

"We're going to be married, Ana," he reminded her softly, pulling her back on the bed.

He caressed her thigh and moved to take off her underpants. She shrank at the thought. It was her fault; she never should have come to this filthy room to do filthy things. Trembling she pushed his hand away and struggled to sit up.

"I can't," she wept. In misery she turned her tear streaked face to him - "I'm so sorry, Jacob. I can't.... I don't feel right. We're not married. We should be married, Jacob. Please...."

He leaned up on an elbow, shaking his head in wonder. "Why'd you lead me on, Ana? You could have told me that in the restaurant instead of all this convoluted shit. *What are you saving it for?* Nobody wants virgins anymore. You won't get pregnant. Damn it – *I'm a doctor!*"

Her mascara was beginning to run down her face. "I'm so sorry Jacob. I thought...I thought I could. I know you're leaving, I wanted to but I can't. I don't feel right about it. I'd feel dirty. I love you but...."

"What's wrong with you anyway!" he cried standing up. "Are you cold natured?" He went to the dresser and shook a cigarette out from the pack. He lit it. It glowed an angry, bright red. Shit, you had no business leading me on! You knew what this was all about. You're not a child! 'Feel dirty' – the only thing 'dirty' about intercourse is the people who think that way! '*Dirty!*'" he snorted. "I thought we already had this discussion. All this shit about getting pregnant – hell, only ignorant people get pregnant! You're just scared, that's all. You're terrified!"

She put on her skirt and her blouse. "Don't yell at me, Jacob," she said, holding back tears. "You said... you said yourself since we waited this long, we could wait a little longer. What happened to that? It's already been three years. If we can't get married in a simple ceremony – what's the rush all of a sudden?"

"Nobody waits anymore! Wait for what? Don't play dumb. How's anybody supposed to know it they're even suited to each other....?"

She paused in the act of buttoning her blouse. She stared at his anger-ridged face for a moment. Then her lips parted. "- You mean like a car? Take a test drive to see if you like it and if you don't, give it back? Then it's used. How about you? Are you used, too?"

Her tears were gone. Her eyes accused him. She held her clenched fists by her side and lashed out at him. "*I'm not a whore, GODDAMN IT!* And to hell with your garbage about 'wrong,'" she said taking off her ring. "If you'd really, truly wanted to marry me, you'd have done it!" She placed the ring on the dresser.

He was not prepared for her anger or her fierce resolve.

19

Because Analise had never shown anger before. Even when they argued she had always been agreeable, thoughtful and non-confrontational, searching for compromise. Now her green eyes examined him more than looked at him. They placed a wall between them. Her lips were a thin hard line. Her nostrils flared. She was a different person. He did not know how to approach her.

"– Look, I'm sorry…."

"So am I!" she snapped and stormed out of the room, her face streaked with mascara.

He called her early the next morning. It was 5:30. "Will you come see me off, Ana?"

She hesitated, trying to control her emotions. She had not slept the night before. "– Do you really want me to, Jacob? As your future wife?"

"Yes. That's why I called. Please forgive last night. It will never happen again, I promise. Please, – will you come?"

"Yes, I'll come, Jacob…."

When he saw her on the dock, with the enormous ship looming in the background, he was reassured when he did not detect a gleam of triumph in her eyes. There was the familiar vulnerability that he knew so well; she hugged him and laid her head against his chest whispering, "I love you."

He was a little unsure of himself after last night, and might have felt a latent resentment. He repeated after her, "I love you, too." And they kissed in public. With a demure smile she accepted her ring back.

But the smart that Jacob felt never completely went away.

She watched him board the *Normandie* in the company of eight or nine medical personnel. Four were nurses. One caught her attention. She had excellent posture and cool, blonde features. There were thirty or forty volunteer soldiers who were not dressed as well as the other passengers. News photographers snapped their pictures and urged them to smile or wave.

They left for Spain.

***

It was almost eight weeks before she heard from him.

"The postal service here is virtually non-existent because all means of communication have been seriously disrupted. It is useless writing to me. If

you receive this at all, it is only because we have a friend with the American consulate who will occasionally get some of our mail out by diplomatic pouch.

"It is still possible to use the telephone, but only if you are in Barcelona or Valencia where telephone exchanges are equipped to handle international calls. I am nowhere near either and I'm afraid that Valencia will fall to the Fascists any day now. The suffering here is unimaginable. We not only have the soldiers to treat, but also the people – especially children. It takes very little to injure them. No one sleeps any more. We can only nap for an hour or so. Occasionally one of us will collapse and have to sleep for as long as 18 hours. Even then we have to be shaken awake, groggy and disoriented...."

Eighteen hours after collapsing? Then there had to be an urgent need for many more volunteers. Worse, she could not surprise him with the news that, despite his doubts, she would soon be a real nurse and that she was coming to help him; nor could she write anything encouraging like "I love you." She fantasized that together they would work shoulder to shoulder to end the pain and suffering amid the smell of alcohol, iodine, feces and urine.

Fantasy aside, her doubts about her own capabilities lingered like shadows on a wall. Could she possibly be strong enough to be of any use to him? Would she crumble in a faint when he needed her, forcing him to choose between the bleeding and the betrothed?

She struggled not to think of it, but there were doubtless women with the American Mission who were not afraid. Like the blonde nurse she had seen board the ship with him. There were those who watched surgeons cutting away damaged flesh and sawing off arms and legs, women who were brave and strong; women who could congratulate themselves because they had stood tall through it all.

The *Ile de France* would take the next contingent of volunteers sometime in June. Nothing would stand in her way. She would go to Spain.

Mom was right – it was not mere squeamishness or weakness that caused her problems, *it was her overwhelming capacity for empathy.* She could *feel* the broken bone and it made her shudder. She *winced* to see a needle plunge into flesh because she could feel the prick of the needle, and she shivered at the sight of blood oozing from jagged flesh. She truly could feel how someone else felt; she understood the need to be comforted.

Like the woman she had watched die in the charity ward.

She remembered watching the light leave the woman's eyes and knowing that she could do nothing to stop the light from leaving her eyes; impulsively she gathered and hugged the woman's frail body. It seemed the decent, human thing to do and she was not ashamed that she fought back tears. But it was a splendid thing to do and she knew it.

When the world was filled with so much hate, how could compassion be a sin rather than a holy thing?

She would leave on the *Ile de France*.

CHAPTER 5

Mark was also leaving on the *Ile de France*. At times he wondered whether or not he would be killed in Spain. But wasn't that the real reason he had volunteered to join the Abraham Lincoln Brigade?

The chances were he would never see his father again. His father was a simple man who relished his title – *Reverend Wilson*. He took comfort in his belief in God, like a child clutching his mother's skirt, and since that thing last year with Ruby, he was all the family that Mark had.

But his father had never forgiven him when Mark came home from college that summer, confessing that he no longer believed the Bible and its "ludicrous fairy tales" and that he was weary of sitting in his father's church on Sundays pretending that he did. Moreover, Mark bleated - leading a decent, pious life had nothing to do with God or religion; it was simply common sense, like cooperating with people rather than fighting with them.

The shock on his father's face had surprised Mark. Until that moment he had not realized how sincerely his father believed. It was as though he had slapped his father's face, bruising it.

And it may be that his father would have preferred a bruising slap, no matter how hard, to his son's blasphemous confession. From then on there was always a quarrelsome tone in his father's voice whenever they spoke together.

When Mark told him that he was leaving America to go to Spain to fight with the Abraham Lincoln Brigade for Spanish Democracy, Reverend Wilson's reaction was precisely what Mark had expected. He was thunderstruck. Had the reverend been eating he would have choked. He stared, slack jawed. His *Evening Bulletin* slid to the floor beside his padded rocking chair.

A bewildered stare enlarged his brown eyes. "What in the name of Jesus *Christ* is wrong with you, boy!" he exploded. "Bad enough you don't believe in God and lied about going to Ruby's funeral and had us waiting around for you like a bunch of fools and almost got yourself fired, hard as jobs is to get!

"You're letting that woman drive you *outta your mind*, do you know that? You're acting *crazy*! Walking the streets half the night; won't talk to nobody – don't shave half the time. You used to be intelligent! *BE A MAN!* Plenty of women out there *begging* for a man with a college education and a job who can put food on the table. *Plenty*! I can name six right now in the church be glad to get a good provider."

Rev. Wilson cared nothing about Fascists or Nazis or Spain or Hitler or Benito Mussolini or Hirohito or anything else that did not concern colored people going to church on Sunday and taking home a paycheck on Saturday. Truth be told, he spoke for everybody else in Mark's world, and they would all have cried, *Amen.*

His father got out of his rocking chair and confronted him. They were the same height.

"What's that foolishness in Spain got to do with you, anyway, Son? Don't colored folks have enough to worry about right here getting lynched right and left; can't even get a job with your family starving? Huh? You been to *college,* and what good it do you? Why you have to look for trouble half way around the world? You ever stop to think you could get yourself *killed?* And for what? Answer me that!"

Mark had no answer. What could he say – "I don't give a shit whether I live or die!" only to be told, "Don't talk crazy! Be a man!"

How could he not know there was injustice in America? That was the whole point. Insane injustice made a mockery of his entire life. Ostensibly his graduation from college was a momentous occasion. His parents invited a few picked relatives to witness their son's monumental ascension; they basked in vicarious triumph over their neighbors, their friends and their enemies. Their son was a *college graduate*! A feat that elevated him and them far above their awe-struck heads. They in turn were a success!

Who else could boast that their child had not only graduated from high school, but had *also attended college?* It was worth a story, (along with Mark's yearbook photograph), in the colored newspaper, the *Philadelphia Tribune.*

But news drifting back to college about the fate of colored college graduates darkened his horizons. Many graduates only found jobs as obsequious Pullman porters; a few were offered refuge in the post office and still fewer labored triumphantly as file clerks in the labyrinth depths of government agencies.

Mark, like others, took numerous civil service examinations but despite high scores, was consistently passed over. Newspaper ads sounded promising, until it was pointed out – the ads did not contain the magic words - *negro or colored man* wanted. Allen Clark managed to get a teaching position paying a pittance by taking a chance at a segregated school in Alabama. There were none to be had anywhere else.

Mark felt the injustice acutely because college had greatly enlarged his world and his expectations. Wasn't that the purpose of a college education? To give him wings so that he could fly?

Thirteen years slowly hissed away like air from a bright and shining balloon, a balloon that now lay in limp mockery for all to see, especially his wife, Ruby. His college degree aged into irrelevancy; he stopped taking examinations for the civil service and for teaching positions and had long ago surrendered hope of answering newspaper ads seeking a "bright young man…." Now dressed in a maroon uniform, he ran an elevator in a department store, greeting each floor with a smile and being ever so polite.

Ruby and their apartment had been his sanctuary, a place to hope and to dream and to believe that light always followed darkness. With her he closed out the world and felt his undisputed worth, if only in the warmth of her arms. So when her thighs had been thrust open, the door of his sanctuary had been thrust open and he had been explosively furious and bitter and why shouldn't he be when he was strangled by the sulfur smell of betrayal?

His father did not understand this or Spain or anything else, but Mark had to tell him that he was leaving for Spain on the *Ile de France* and endure his scolding. He wanted his father to know and to care if in the end, he were killed.

***

Ruby.

When she died he refused to claim her body or attend her funeral.

He left it to her parents. He despised them now for having reared a bitch who would be found dead in the back seat of a car, parked in a garage, with her thighs spread and her bare ass lover lying on top of her. Both asphyxiated by the fumes of a running car engine.

He hated his horse faced father for not seconding his rage and humiliation. Instead he had urged him to make a spectacle of himself, as though he were some tattooed circus act, and attend her funeral like "…. a decent Christian." More, he should hang a black, death wreath on his door and sew a black band around his coat sleeve.

Like shit he would! Hadn't she and that son-of-a-bitch, Thomas, both sung on the "decent Christian" choir? And after choir practice, fucked on the back seat of his car?

Attend her funeral for what? Just to let people stare at him and nod – *That's him. It was his wife they found.…* Their stares would feel like lice crawling over his body, biting and itching. He knew what they were whispering among themselves – that he was not man enough to satisfy his wife but Thomas could.

"I'll go," he solemnly promised his father, but it was only to stop his pious insistence.

It was drizzling on the morning of the funeral. He slipped out of his apartment before dawn and took the trolley car down to Dock Street. He boarded the ferry and crossed the Delaware River to Camden, New Jersey. He spent the morning and part of the afternoon, under a gray sky, traveling back and forth between Philadelphia and Camden, staring at the brownish, debris laden river. Finally the ferry's crew escorted him off for fear he was trying to get up the courage to jump into the river.

After that morning he avoided everyone. At night he walked for hours through dark streets, past houses with drawn shades and dark window panes that reflected light, like mirrors.

Why had Ruby done a thing like that?

She was modest; he'd seldom even seen her naked body. *Why* tagged along on one side of him and *How* ambled on the other. It seemed impossible she'd have the nerve. How many times had she done it? The image of Thomas's massive body between her spread thighs was like a permanent, pounding headache. Was that why she had begun to deny him sex? Because she was already satiated? Or had he become too sexually inadequate?

Ruby's infidelity forced him, on some level, to listen and to think and to observe things that he had not before. He was slowly beginning to believe that women were complex individuals who in the end did what they wanted to do just as men did, but that women just went about things differently.

On one of his aimless walks, he briefly flirted with the notion that it had all been his fault and his grievance that Ruby had been "deceptive," "cunning," "two-faced," "unpredictable" and any of a number of similar slanders was only the howling of a dog struck by a truck. He quickly brushed such treasonous ideas away. Still, like lint, they clung to him.

Their sex life together, on her part, might well have been compliance rather than surrender and the social conformities that she had strongly endorsed were really egg shells that she routinely crushed when circumstances arose that were beyond his comprehension and maybe hers.

He had to acknowledge that the reasons she did things could be murky. There were probably sensible reasons – insensible to him and perhaps even to her – for what had happened to their marriage. Her reasons were probably fashioned over tens of thousands, maybe thousands of thousands of years.

Women were forced over that span of time to be "two-faced," to be "deceitful" and to be "cunning." It was an intelligent way to survive in a world where men could, with impunity, crush their skull with a single angry blow. Women learned how to pet the lion, as it were, and live with it and sometimes tame it.

On some level, weren't women treated like slaves were treated? Slaves and conquered people learned to read the faces of the conquerors and to decipher the nuances of a master's voice. All to avoid the flame and lashing and gouging and blows of aroused displeasure.

Crossing a street one night, still another thought presented itself. - He had not listened to her.

He had dismissed her want of a life beyond having babies, cooking and cleaning. She wanted to work and with thrift, purchase property and become a successful business woman. She had not been happy. That was clear now, but only in retrospect. Their apartment had been his sanctuary but her prison.

But for the love of God! Hadn't he done everything people expected a man to do? Hell, he paid the rent promptly, put food on the table, given her a few dollars for her personal use, bought the seal skin coat she'd wanted last Christmas, saved a few pennies in the bank? Shit, what more could a man do!

On her part no babies, only miscarriages and her muted, inexplicable sullenness. Maybe she saw intercourse as a sexual assault whenever he was aroused. But then why the filthy infidelity with Thomas who provided nothing for her?

He never really understood what *purpose* meant until now when he found he had none. There needed to be a reason to live driven by purpose no matter how shabby the purpose. Else why shave or bathe or eat or care or work? For whom and for what?

Whenever he entered his apartment after trudging about the streets at night, *Why* and *How* always came in with him. They slipped in bed with him and taunted him in dreams. Would his going to Spain shut them up for good? Or was going there simply being stupid. Vomiting anger on vague enemies he could not visualize, for a people for whom he cared nothing, and for a cause that was beginning to sound like just so many words.

CHAPTER 6

Olga Stern enjoyed the quiet rhythm of early mornings when other people were preparing to go to work. She was up before six and put on a pot of coffee. She glanced over last night's *Evening Bulletin* until the morning *Philadelphia Inquirer* arrived. Newspapers were her theater. The tragedy of the *Hindenburg* crashing to the ground in flames, the Lindbergh baby kidnapping, the trial of Al Capone, the melodrama of King Edward surrendering his throne for "…the woman I love." Then there was Ginger Rogers, Lionel Barrymore, Jean Harlow….

Olga got the bottle of milk and newspaper from her doorstep and over a hot cup of coffee, skimmed the political news. Hitler, Mussolini, that Japanese emperor – all the same. What difference would it make if they were called Caesar, Kaiser, Alexander or Genghis Khan?

She was surprised to find her morning interrupted by footsteps. Analise appeared in the kitchen doorway. "Why're you up?" Olga asked. "You don't have class until noon."

Analise came into the kitchen in her bathrobe and sat at the kitchen table beside her mother, her hands clasped in her lap. Olga searched her face and put her paper down and reached over and covered Analise's hands with her own. "I know," Olga whispered, "I worry, too, Ana. Did you know? Didn't he tell you?"

She shook her head. "- I'm going to Spain, too, Mom," she said softly. "I'll lose him if I don't. I'll be old and all alone."

Startled, Olga looked deeply into her daughter's anguished, green eyes. She moved her chair closer and with her other hand, laid her daughter's head on her shoulder. They sat for a while just feeling, unaware of time.

"Europe," Olga finally said in the same whisper, "is for nobody to live. Love? Never, Ana. Believe me, I was there, and these Socialists and Communists – they have no heart, just ideas. I was afraid when you told me that Jacob was one of them. I said nothing – 'It will pass,' I said to myself and now you see – these Socialists and Communists - no heart.

Intellectuals - not for people. Not for you, Ana. For Spain they care, yes, but not for you or for children, a home and love. 'Free love,' yes and...."

Analise sat up. "Mom, I'm 24 years old. I don't know anyone who's not married. Miriam, Sarah, Connie - all my friends! They're happy. They have husbands and children and I have nothing. They talk about their kids and what's for dinner and...I hardly have any friends anymore. People ask, 'When are you going to get married? What are you waiting for?' What can I say to them? Mom, *I'll be an old maid!*"

"Tell them this weekend you will go to the Husband Store and buy one. They're on sale!"

"Oh, Mama! Think of all the years I'll have wasted if I just sit here and let things happen. Years wasted - flushed down a toilet. I'll lose him if I haven't already. I have no alternative; not one I can accept. Do you know what he told me? That I was always trying to please everyone - even him - and he's right. In another month I'll be a nurse, then I'm going to find him and make him see who I really am!"

Olga grew rigid. She took Analise's hands in hers again. "Ana, look at me! Don't you *dare* change who you are! You are kind, generous, thoughtful – who needs more? On his knees he should be begging! Please, Ana, listen to me! It will be wrong to chase him, any man; you only end up being his whore."

Analise was startled to hear her use the word "whore."

Stricken eyes met stricken eyes. Softly, almost whispering, Olga said, "To this day I never told anyone, not even your father, not even God. *To no one.* No one must hear, do you understand, Ana?"

Her steady, penetrating eyes demanded an answer. Her daughter nodded, a little frightened, but her mother's hands, still embracing hers, were reassuring.

"Younger than you – I was 19. I was a revolutionary. Yes, Ana, it's true. A *revolutionary*...Where, I won't say. Too much you shouldn't know, but this I can say – in Europe, politics is not like here or in England. Europe, people hate those who disagree. They assassinate those they believe are dangerous to them, but there *everyone* is dangerous who disagrees and the government is ruled by such people.

"The authorities are afraid of the people. Spies everywhere. They send spies to join you and the spies sometimes become your leaders.

They give orders to kill that one, to spy on this one and they themselves will assassinate even some of those they work for to convince you they believe in your cause.

"So, yes, you come to trust. With your life you trust until the police come and arrest you and your friends and sometimes your family. Your 'leader' will denounce you and you are executed. No trials and publicity. Just shot.

"Nineteen I was – in love with Boris. We were lovers." She shook her head. "Never become a man's lover, Ana, *never*. You will be only a whore in the end. I was his lover. One day he came to me. 'You must help me dispatch Anton. He is a filthy informer who will denounce the lot of us and we, all of us, will pay with our lives. Will you do this for me?'

"I was to persuade Anton – I knew him – that I was fond of him and wanted him to be my lover and together we would betray Boris. We arranged to meet one night. It was bitter cold. My hands were in my muff. I smiled at him. We turned to walk away. It was then, at that moment, I removed my hand from my muff, put a gun to his head and shot him. I only heard him fall. Look, I could not. Wild I was with terror. I dropped the gun and ran blind with fear. Boris and others caught me and led me away. They gave me wine until I vomited."

She stopped. Her eyes were tired. One corner of her thin lips quivered slightly. She stared past Analise at figures long gone on streets only dimly remembered. Analise, lips parted, stared at her mother, trying to grasp what she had just heard. There was pain in her mother's eyes. Impulsively, Analise reached out and hugged her. She felt tears in her own eyes and wanted to cry, not for herself but for her mother.

"Don't feel bad, Mama," she whispered. "It was a long time ago. It's all right, Mama. Nobody knows. It was long, long ago. We'll both forget it, Mama."

Olga made no attempt to move from the comfort of Analise's arms. She spoke, her voice muffled against her daughter's body. "I hated Boris after that. All of them I hated. They lie and deceive and murder. *This* they justify, *that* another excuse. They give reasons for everything and in the end murder, murder, murder.

"Do you know what we told ourselves? 'This is revolution and revolution is war. People die in war. We, all of us, understand this. One does not murder in war; one kills to prevent ourselves and our friends and families and Comrades from being killed. It is right to kill, for in return our Comrades hazard their lives for us.'

"I escaped and became Olga. Always afraid. Even now, afraid. It is why I left your father in Hollywood. Fame I don't need, my picture here, there. – Too much. It is a terrible thing, Ana, to kill another human being. And why did I do it? Not for any 'cause' but for love. Europe is a graveyard for those who love."

She straightened up. Her eyes were moist. She looked deeply into Analise's eyes and slowly shook her head. "You should not go to Spain, not for Jacob, not for anyone. Let him return to you. If it is to be, it will be."

Olga's confession echoed and re-echoed in the long silence that followed. It had been surreal, a thing beyond belief. Words. So many words about a man without a face. A man without a history or substance and all in a time beyond her comprehension. The shock gradually subsided. Her mother's confession must - in the end – be only words. Words best forgotten. Her words were like distant earthquakes in Tibet or floods in Ecuador - things that happen in foreign countries with vague, unfamiliar names that are soon forgotten. Her confession was a scream that must be stopped. An open door that must be slammed shut.

She looked in her mother's eyes and told her over and again, "It was a long time ago, Mama; everything's changed; it's nothing to remember anymore. It was a long time ago...."

Maybe revolution really is war. And people get killed in war. Wasn't that the purpose of war? People get killed and they become the garbage of Time. To shift the topic away from the confession, Analise said, "I'll be O.K. in Spain, Mama. I promise. I'll go and be back in no time, but I have to know where my life is taking me."

"After what I told you, you'll still go? You're such a fragile child, Analise. All alone – just you and war and bombs, bullets. Not for you." She shook her mother's head, "Not for you, Ana."

"I'm not so fragile, Mama. I'll be scared, sure, but I'm 24. I'm a woman. I can't be scared of living and afraid of dying. Isn't that what you always say? I saw other women getting on that ship; I guess they care about Spain, too. They can talk to Jacob and share things. Right now, I can't do that. I can't fight back.

"And Jacob taught me something about myself – he was criticizing me for going in a canoe and looking for stones, but you know what – I did what I felt I had to do, and scared or not, I *did* it. That's the me I have to believe in. I hate the sight of blood and pain and suffering, but I became a nurse. But *I did it.* "

They sat together unaware of time, sharing the warmth of their bodies. Sometime later Analise whispered, "…Mama… can you tell me one thing? – What's your real name?"

"– Analise."

CHAPTER 7

In June Analise took the trolley car to Grand Central Station to meet two other nurse volunteers, Irene and Clara. The three women, each wearing an identifying red rose pinned to her lapel, arrived within half an hour of the other. They laughed when they discovered that by coincidence they each wore pill box hats and white gloves.

Armed with friendly smiles, they left the station and walked toward the Washington Square address that they had been given. It was a chilly and windy day and they kept up a brisk pace. On the way they attempted to size each other up.

Analise and Irene assumed that Clara, who looked about forty, was married. Did she have children? Why would she leave them to go to Spain? Clara put Analise down as a gadfly because she did not appear to be robust enough for real nurse's work. Too, her luggage was better than theirs and so was the quality of her clothes. Why was she going to Spain?

Irene presented a frequent, nervous smile as though she were anxious that the other two would like her. She was a head taller than either of them. Clara, noting her height and plain looks, decided she would probably never find anyone to marry her.

She was twenty-eight and wore her hair in a bob that over emphasized her long neck. She wore thick eyeglasses which magnified her eyes. She hated them but it was that or spend the rest of her life in a hazy world. When she told them that she had a boyfriend and they were going to Spain together, she had their full attention.

Her boyfriend, Rex, was shorter than she was but, she smiled, she didn't mind. Rex wanted to be a pharmacist but there was no money to send him to college and truth be told, he'd barely made it out of high school.

"I always wanted to be a doctor," Clara confided. "I never minded that there wasn't enough money to send me to college, but you know what burns me up? Even if I *had* the money – so what? I had to be a man to be a doctor!

"That's why I like Communism. Everybody's equal. In the Soviet Union women sweep the streets, they drive trolley cars, they can join the army and they can be doctors, too."

"– They drive *trolley cars?*" Irene asked in awe.

Clara eyed her from the other side of Analise. "- How much do you know about Communism?"

Irene smiled sheepishly and shrugged her shoulders.

In Irene's defense, Analise offered, "- I don't think all the volunteers are Communists. I'm not. My fiancé's a doctor and he's not either; he's a Socialist. They said everybody who believes in democracy should volunteer no matter their race, creed or politics. I'm going to try to help him in some way."

Clara rolled her eyes and pursed her lips and they marched along in silence.

***

Twenty-nine volunteers for Spain milled about the bare meeting room at the Finnish Workers' Hall near Washington Square waiting to be checked in and receive their ship boarding tickets.

They discovered that this fellow was from the Young Communist League while another was a member of the Socialist Labor Party. Men from the American Communist Party and the Socialist Party of America seemed to be a little older and harder. Those from the American Student Union were barely out of their twenties. Some were idealists bent on saving the world for Wilsonian democracy.

The hall was decorated with Communist posters. Some displayed the hammer and sickle while others showed men and women dressed as workers and farmers, wielding the tools of their trade, standing resolute and facing the sun beneath the slogan *Unite!*

Long tables offered coffee, donuts and sandwiches. A few folding chairs were scattered about. Someone thought they should be offered to the three nurses among them.

That was when Mark saw Analise.

She was the slender one with her hair parted in the middle and drawn back into a bun. She appeared to be in her twenties. When she smiled and exchanged a few words with the men who brought the chairs over, her smiling lips hardly moved, as though she were whispering. The

35

tallest one of the three nurses gave a broad grin while the oldest one presented something akin to a grimace.

For some reason, he wanted to get a closer look at Analise. He found spaces between shifting bodies to catch glimpses of her. After a while, he became self-conscious. Did anyone think he was just another Negro lusting after a white woman? Well, he wasn't!

He knew he should not care how she looked or how she smiled or how she held her head. But what was he supposed to do, stand there like a mannequin, eyes forever fixed in one direction? He shifted around until he saw Willie Washington, the only person he knew. They had taken the bus together from Philadelphia where they had attended Communist meetings. Mark had so far declined to join the party.

Willie, a tall man, was laughing and talking with a group on the other side of the hall. He was from Mississippi where his attempts to organize cotton field workers had nearly gotten him lynched.

"I always knowed they was watching me," he confided in an open meeting in Philadelphia. "They didn't want nobody organizing folks in the Tenant Farmers Union 'an tellin' them that they won't nothin' but slaves in disguise. They pay you just enough to keep you owing them for the rent an' the food they give you on credit. Treated white folks the same. Boss man come near lynchin' me," he confided. "A white boy come up to me and whispered – 'Better git…. Klan be here 'bout noon. Heard 'em talkin.'

"Left my cotton bag where it was and ain't stopped till I got to Natchez. Party there got me out."

Willie made no secret that he was disappointed that Mark who "was supposed to be intelligent" hesitated for even one second to join the Communist Party. For Willie, the party was both home and family.

Mark's eyes drifted over to the girl again.

Some would call her thin but she was really slender – embraceable. But why in the name of God was he acting this way? He'd never been attracted to white women. They screamed rape just for the fun of seeing a man get lynched, like those women did with the nine Scottsboro Boys….

He sought diversion. Men's shoes, run down at the heel and probably lined with cardboard, told a story. So did frayed shirt collars and cuffs. And hats. Frayed cloth caps, and fedoras that badly needed cleaning and reblocking. Eight of the men, including him, wore decent suits and clean neckties. A few had suitcases but most carried bundles and some had only the clothes on their back. Maybe they were the smart ones; if they were going to be issued uniforms, why did they need anything else?

Later as they were leaving for the *Ile de France*, Willie sidled over, eyes amused. "Saw you lookin' at that girl…Thought you had better sense."

Mark flamed into anger fueled by embarrassment. He wanted to snarl a dozen things all at once but his words were so jumbled and incoherent that nothing came out.

CHAPTER 8

It was not her first voyage. When the women reached their cabin, she maneuvered herself in the lead so she could be the first to open the cabin door. Once in, she casually, but immediately, tossed her luggage on the single bunk to the right. Bunk beds were on the left.

Clara claimed the bottom bunk. Irene looked dismayed.

"Won't I fall out?"

"You won't fall out," Clara assured her. "There's a rail."

Analise felt guilty and was on the point of offering Irene the single bed when Clara said, "Leave the luggage till later. Let's go up on deck and watch as we leave. "Maybe," she suggested to Analise, "you can see your mother and wave to her."

They squeezed their way to the ship's rail among the press of people waving to friends and relatives below. Analise searched the crowd below for sight of her mother. She had hugged her goodbye, promising to be careful and assuring her that she would write and be all right. Irene's eye swept the view of the city and its immensity. Clara was more interested in the people around her.

Analise first became aware of Mark when the *Ile de France* began to glide away from the dock. She was inadvertently pressed against him. Disconcerted to be pushed into physical contact with a Negro, her instinct was to flinch away but to her alarm she was jostled even closer.

At some point their hands on the ship's rail touched. In that instant she was struck with an intense, eerie feeling. It crept up her neck and crawled over her scalp like a deep, tingling blush. Momentarily she was deaf.

Déjà vu. But like nothing she had ever experienced before. Those had been uncanny feelings, as sudden as light from a flashbulb. A sudden conviction of having been there or done that before. Too swift to form a lasting memory.

But this was no momentary flash. She knew she would turn to this unlikely man standing next to her and their eyes would meet and she knew that they had met before. She knew his name. She could speak to him, resuming once again an interrupted conversation.

She turned. Their eyes met as she knew they would. She saw pain in his eyes as of someone pleading – "Help me" or "Forgive me."

It passed as suddenly as sound does. Had it echoed the tiniest bit longer she would have known his name and where and when. She could have reached out over a hundred years, perhaps a thousand years, to Spain or Egypt, Rome or Greece or the Steppes of Russia – she could have reached out and spoken his name.

Time shut the door.

"Jesus, is anything wrong?" Irene frowned. "You're all white. You O.K.?"

Clara seized her wrist and pulled her away from the rail. "Come on," she ordered. "You look terrible. You need to lie down."

"– I'm fine," she insisted, glancing around. The crowd obscured him. "I just…I just had a strange…you know. *Déjà vu.*"

"Everybody has those," Clara said, putting a supporting arm around her waist. "They can be scary."

They escorted her back to the cabin. "People react different," Clara explained. Analise's bed became the cabin sofa. Clara sat on it and patted a place where Analise should sit. She felt grateful for their solicitousness.

"My gran told me she had *déjà vu* back when she was 30. She always called it a 'sighting' but that's what it was. She was 80 when she told me, but she never forgot it. People say you don't remember because it happens too fast to make sense, but Gran remembered clear as day.

"Said she went to this auction on a horse farm to get a plow horse. There was this Clydesdale. – You ever see one? You see them hauling trash trucks. Big as a truck. Gran said this one was like a wall. Anyway, the horse turned its head, took one look at her and started for her.

"People had to hold it back, but Gran said her hair stood on end and she felt this *déjà vu* tingle all over her. Said she suddenly wanted to scream, not because she was scared or anything – she couldn't explain it. Know what she said? She said it was a *joyful* feeling. She just wanted to scream and be on that horse. Then later she saw this motion picture about the Crusades. That's when she said she first saw war horses.

Monsters. There was this scene when the Crusaders and the Moslems charged each other and Gran said *she was there*. She was on a war horse and giving a war yell and she said she never felt so good in all her life! That's when she said she knew she'd been there or someplace like it. She never forgot it. Never."

There was silence. Clara's face was alive, as though she had been the one who had experienced *déjà vu*. She looked at them for validation.

Analise smiled. "She was in a fight? – A battle?"

Clara nodded. "That's what Gran said."

Irene occupied the lone chair in the cabin. She frowned. "– Was the horse there, too? And did she think she used to be a man?"

"…Gee, you know I never thought of that. But Gran said she was there."

Irene pursed her lips and raised a skeptical brow.

Clara noticed. She got up and commenced unpacking. Analise and Irene followed suit.

"Whatever happened to that man you're going to Spain with?" Clara asked while hanging up a nurse's uniform. "You see him up on deck?"

Irene colored and made a show of rummaging through her suitcase. – "No."

"Didn't he come?" Clara pursued. "You two didn't travel together?"

Irene's lips tightened. She continued to rummage. "-You ask a lot of questions," she said without looking up.

"- Ask Ben Cross," Analise suggested. "He should know. He's in charge and said to ask him if we needed anything."

Irene brightened. She left her suitcase open on the cabin floor at the foot of their bunks and hurried to speak to Ben Cross. The moment the cabin door closed, Clara said scornfully, "Sounds fishy to me. You ask me he's a yellow belly."

Analise paused, holding some cosmetics. "You don't think he'd back out without telling her, do you? That would be horrible to let her go to Spain all by herself."

Clara glanced at her before carefully stowing her empty suitcase under her bunk. She was about Analise's height, but heavier. Her hair was graying and her mouth had a set to it that made saying "no" sound natural. She fetched a bottle of whiskey from the dresser drawer that she had selected for herself and poured herself a drink. She sat in the lone chair and crossed her ankles.

"You got a lot to learn," she advised in a matter-of-fact tone. "Can't tell what men will do. 'Me first' is all they know. A bunch of selfish bastards. She's sappy enough to go to Spain just to suit him, but dollars to doughnuts he'd never do the same for her. They're all like that. Lord, God and master until they get sick. Then you've never seen such a bunch of whining, scared, piss pots!"

Analise was shocked at her indictment. She struggled not to show it. She'd never heard such harsh words spoken about men before and guessed that Clara had had her heart broken in a terrible way. Clara took out a cigarette and lit it. "You don't drink, do you? Naw, I could tell. Know what I think? I think when we get to France, you ought to forget about going to Spain. Go home. A place like that'll be the end of you. You're too skinny and 'genteel' to make it.

"No offense, Analise, you're kind and considerate but," she shook a doubtful head, "in war, that's not enough. You'll go to pieces. Seen it happen in hospitals back home and what's that compared to war. I know. I was over there during the Great War."

Analise smiled because she did not know what else to do. She continued putting her cosmetics away. "You were there during the war?"

"Got there in 1918. Just about your age."

"I'm not planning on staying long," Analise said. "Maybe a month or two. I know it'll be messy and I won't like it, but I'll do what I have to do. I can try anyway."

Clara shrugged and put the bottle away.

***

Mark, Willie and Danny Wilcox had never been on a ship before. Their cabin contained a single bed on one side and bunk beds on the other. Danny, 20, the youngest tossed his belongings on the single bed. Willie glanced at the upper bunk and placed his brown paper package on the lower one. Mark inherited the upper bunk.

"You can't see out," Willie observed, looking around. "We must be under water."

Curious, they tested the water spigot in the wash basin that sat against the wall facing the door. Fresh water came out. Mark and Danny opened suitcases and began making use of the clothes racks on either side of the wash basin. Willie did not bother untying his package.

"Les go see what it look like upstairs," he suggested. "This stuff ain't going nowhere."

The deck was crowded with people in a holiday mood forging animated friendships that would last for the voyage and end with bright smiles of "Hope we meet again!" The volunteers stood out in their cloth caps, scuffed shoes and frayed cuffs among a sea of well-dressed men with shined shoes, starched white shirts, navy blue blazers and white trousers who smiled easily and tipped their fedoras or straw hats to fashionably dressed groups of ladies in soft colored gloves and wide brimmed hats.

Mark felt stares directed at him and Willie. He met curious eyes here, hostile ones there and turned away from challenging stares. It was then that he saw the girl from the meeting hall. He was confused and stunned by the unexpected thud in his stomach.

He wanted to examine every inch of her face, her lips, her eyes and her hair, her small shoulders and her smile. He wanted to discover why she had such an effect on him. Especially since he had spent a life time despising black men who lusted after white women simply because they were white. He dreaded having anyone even *think* he was one of them. He still smarted from Willie's sly smile back at the meeting hall that implied Mark was doing just that.

He forced himself to pay attention to the group of volunteers around him. Many of them were drawn to Willie who was open, loquacious and friendly. Mark feigned interest in what they were saying, joining in their bursts of laughter, watching their faces to see whether or not they were aware of his interest in her. As the men joked and moved about, he shuffled among them so that he eventually faced in her direction.

She probably smells of something clean. Her face is open and her voice is probably clear and friendly. What would it be like to stand before her and look into her eyes and speak to her?

Had Ruby felt this way about Thomas?

Of course not. Her betrayal was another thing altogether. Yet he found that he could not conjure up the same anger against her. Anyway, what did it matter? He felt nothing that could have any meaning for this girl. How could he? Should he forget the lynchings and the burnings, the castrations, the Scottsboro Boys, the midnight whippings for not saying "yes, sir", or "no, ma'am," and the wholesale raping of young girls as a rite of passage that produced millions of mulattos?

"We're moving!" someone called out.

There was a surge toward the ship's rail. He was jostled toward it and was surprised to see water between the ship and the dock. The expanse of brownish, sudsy, debris-dotted water widened, turning bluer and cleaner. Someone was pushed against him. He glanced to his side. Incredibly it was her. His hand was pressed against hers and just like that, he felt a sudden hot flush of shame. Not because he was attracted to her but for some other elusive reason and for a fleeting second, he actually felt like crying. It vanished. He felt his heart pounding. It was almost hard to breathe. Then another woman drew her away.

In their brief encounter he saw that her eyes were green. He controlled his breathing.

"You coming?" he heard Willie say as from a distance.

"– Sure."

They were on their way to Spain.

CHAPTER 9

The last faint smudge on the horizon of America disappeared; the ship left a straight, white, creamy wake on the sparkling sea of sun lit silver, and Irene reported that Rex had not gone to the meeting hall nor was he on the ship. She stood in the middle of the cabin and recited this in a bewildered tone that suggested Rex was a little boy who had not come home from school and everyone must rush out to search for him. Analise exchanged glances with Clara but saw no sympathy. Finally, Irene slumped on Analise's bed and covered her face.

"– You got enough money to get back home?" Clara asked, seated in the lone chair.

Irene shook her head, wiping her nose on the back of her sleeve. Her face was red. "The only reason…the reason I came was so we could be together…."

Analise put her arm around her and Irene leaned her head against her shoulder.

"– What am I going to do? I don't want to go to Spain. Not like this…all by myself…."

Analise hugged her and looked at Clara hoping the older woman could offer some solution.

"In four days," Clara said in a flat voice, "we'll be in France. Take the next ship back."

"She doesn't have any money," Analise reminded her. "They paid her way over."

"Why'd the two of you decide to volunteer?" Clara asked in the tone of an inquisitor.

Irene sat up and tried to compose herself. "Rex always had rotten luck – like me. He was a clerk in a drug store when I first met him. He lost his job and when his landlady put him out of the boarding house he didn't have any place to stay. I used to steal food from the hospital so he'd have something to eat." She paused to wipe her tears and steady her voice.

"A lot of us work in hospitals now. It's the Depression. Nobody can afford to hire private duty nurses anymore. Women are even having babies in hospitals now. I used to work in a settlement house helping poor people and immigrants, but it was supported by some rich lady and when she lost her money…"

"Where're you from?" Clara broke in.

"Akron."

Clara said, "I used to work in a settlement house, too, for unmarried women. I left after a month." Her tone suggested disapproval of either the house or the women.

"At school," Analise offered, "they told us that in the future there won't be any more private duty nursing; people will go to hospitals and nurses will work for hospitals. If you're lucky, you may be able to get a good job as a stewardess on an airplane."

Clara shook her head. "I'm not getting on anybody's airplane."

"A lot of us don't have any choice," Irene explained. "Some private duty patients expect you to work all day but they won't give you room and board. After you pay to stay at a boarding house out of your own pocket, you end up working for free."

"What do hospitals pay?" Clara pursued.

"Nothing. Room and board and sometimes laundry."

Clara stared at her in disbelief. "Just room and board?"

Analise came to her rescue. "Not all hospitals, but a lot are like that because of the Depression. They can get regular nurses to do the same work that nurse trainees were doing. If there aren't any jobs, what can you do?"

Clara digested this. "I was private duty for years. Room, board, good pay, time off. When they went on vacation, I'd go too. I've tried working in hospitals on and off - anesthetist, instrument passer, taking care of surgical patients - lots of things. But they never offered anything permanent. I've been helping the Party run free clinics the last couple years.- So you stole food from the hospital?"

Irene nodded. "He tried sleeping in train and bus stations but the cops won't let you do that. One day he got fed up and tried to rob a store by pretending he had a gun. The manager fought with him but

Rex got away. Somebody recognized him, though, and with the cops after him, we figured this was the best way out for now...."

"Can't anyone in your family help," Analise asked, concerned.

She shook her head. She and her mother did not get along. Anyway, Irene didn't like her mother because her mother didn't like her. "If it weren't for Aunt Mindy I never would have become a nurse. She sold her insurance policy for the $350.00 and that paid my way. Only Aunt Mindy ever cared about me and she's dead."

Analise could not imagine anyone admitting *that she disliked her own mother* or that her mother disliked her. She found it difficult to offer a sympathetic face. What sort of person was Irene anyway? And what about Rex who couldn't keep a job and ditched her without saying a word?

Clara took out her bottle and poured whiskey into a glass. She gave it to Irene.

"I know all about family," Clara said, pouring another glass for herself. "My father beat my mother for no other reason than that he could do it. She'd try to get on his good side by being meek and subservient and would never answer back. But that just...I don't know. The more she tried to please him the more he'd beat her. Knocked her bottom teeth out.

"I wanted to hit him over the head with the frying pan and knock him out but I was too scared. Figured if I missed or didn't hurt him enough he'd beat the holy shit out of me and break every bone in my body. And know what? - I knew my mother wouldn't help me."

She shook a cigarette from a pack and lit it. The end glowed an angry red. "She was stupid in a way. When he got the flu, he was too sick to get out of bed. Laying there in his sweaty, gray undershirt whining and pissing himself. To this day I don't know why she didn't let the son-of-a-bitch die!"

Analise could no longer make a pretense of not being shocked. She had never heard such hatred directed toward parents in her life. She knew people could be cruel. The newspapers were full of murders and crime, but people did not tell you that they hated their mothers or fathers or wanted to kill them. She needed to get out of the cabin.

She rose abruptly. "I'm going to speak to Ben. Maybe he can think of something."

Clara snorted shaking her head and blowing smoke from her nose. She pursed her lips in a grim smile and said disdainfully, "You're not a Communist and neither is she or you wouldn't bother asking Ben anything like that. We think Spain's important and so do a lot of other people. Important enough to die for or get an arm blown off or suffer in other ways. I can tell you now, Ben's not going to give a *shit* about her or her boyfriend. You're either with the Party or you're not!"

She leaned forward; her impassioned face looked years younger. "Know what he'll say? 'Spain's more important than Rex or twenty people like him!' He'll say she had no business signing up. Neither did her boyfriend or you either for that matter!"

Analise flared, "I had every right! They told me I didn't have to be a Communist; it was better if I weren't...."

"Yeah, yeah, spare me the bullshit. I know - 'Let the world see that it's not just Communists, but people from all over the world – every race and creed.' I know, but when you get down to it, that's just a crock of shit. Only Communists *really* care." She crushed her cigarette out in the wash basin.

"If the Fascists win, it's the beginning of the end of democracy, decency, freedom – every Goddamn thing! *Nobody gives a shit except us.* These so-called democratic nations all signed a so called 'non-intervention' policy that Hitler and Mussolini wipe their asses with. They're *giving* Franco anything he wants - planes, pilots, tanks, soldiers while nobody'll even *sell* arms to the legitimate government of Spain. Nobody. Except the Soviet Union!

"Everybody who came with us made a commitment. Those who couldn't pay their passage on the ship, the Party paid with money that other people donated. Nobody's asking you to spend the rest of your life in Spain – just give us a little of your time. Others are prepared to give their lives. Nobody said this was a free ride or some kind of 'adventure' or a convenient way to escape the cops. You can go see Ben if you want but don't say I didn't warn you."

She looked twenty years younger and glowed with purpose. She had been pretty once.

Irene sat, hands lying loosely in her lap. "Let it go for now," she said. "I have to let it sink in."

Clara was on her second drink. "How come you two didn't travel together?"

"– He said if the cops caught us together, they'd lock me up, too, so it'd be better to travel separate."

"That's probably what happened," Analise offered, glancing at Clara for support. "He was right; he got arrested and you're safe."

Irene brightened. "You figure that's what happened?"

"He wouldn't just leave you," Analise assured her. "He was looking out for you."

Irene let this sink in. She looked to the ceiling and sighed deeply. "Poor guy. He always has rotten luck...."

CHAPTER 10

Seasoned travelers were fortified with novels or fashionable magazines. Some devoted time to keeping journals that they were never likely to read again. In the men's smoking rooms, passengers held forth on Joe Louis's recent conquest of the German Max Schmeling in the heavyweight title fight. And what about that son-of-a-bitch, the Duke of Wales, giving up his throne for a piece of ass? Jesus, talk about stupid!

Conversation escalated to volcanic anger at Congress's outrageous imposition of the 25 cents an hour minimum wage for a 44-hour work week. And what about that goddamned Roosevelt permitting workers to go on sit-down strikes! Jesus! Amelia Earhart? Hate to say it, but serves her right. Shoulda stayed in a woman's place. Too damn many women wanna act like men but wanna be treated like ladies. Next thing you know they'll want to come in here!

Thoughts turned to Europe. Who among them had been there and which of them could say what to do and what to say? Bernard Larson could and he was on board. He was a well-known and well-traveled newspaperman who wrote for the *Journal*.

And there he was. He had set up court at the rear of the promenade deck where the semi-circular curve of the ship's stern formed a natural theatre. He sat, legs crossed, his back to the sea, calmly smoking a pipe. The ship's creamy wake spread out behind him like a magnificent cape. Deck chairs were pulled up around him; those without chairs stood in respectful silence.

Larson had a longish, genial face. He was often told that he resembled the late President Wilson which he took as a compliment. Mark, Danny and Willie paused at the gathering; Analise, Irene and Clara were already there. When Mark noticed Analise, he felt his heart thump. Danny nudged them to move on. "He's a Fascist," he whispered. "They mentioned him back in New York."

"We oughta know what he be tellin' folks," Willie pointed out. "We gotta prepare folks for the truth."

Mark agreed, not because of what Willie said, but because Analise was there. They stopped and listened. Mark managed to maneuver so he could look at her without seeming to stare.

***

Until Danny Wilcox arrived in New York, he had never personally seen a Negro. Ben Cross had deliberately assigned him to share the same cabin with Mark and Willie. A junior at a small college in the Midwest, Danny accepted the cabin assignment without hesitation; it was an opportunity to show his total commitment to the Communist tenet that espoused the equality of all people. Barely twenty, he was of medium height with blondish hair and intelligent brown eyes.

At first Willie intimidated him, especially when Danny noticed the scar that began below his left eye and coursed down near his mouth. Too, at first, he had difficulty understanding Willie's thick, Mississippi dialect. But Willie's soft voice and easy smile dispelled Danny's concerns and he began to realize that the big man's slovenly speech disguised a good mind.

For his part, Willie was immensely pleased to find that a white man was going to bunk with them. Sharing the same room with Danny made him feel like a true Comrade, and it gladdened his heart when Danny, without hesitation, extended his hand to shake his. Too, he owed the Party his life; they'd helped him escape from being lynched.

Danny found Mark a different story; he displayed none of Willie's open friendliness. Their handshake was perfunctory. This demonstrated one simple fact – since Mark was not a Communist, the Party had to be suspicious around people like him.

Mark saw Danny as just another white guy like those with whom he had been surrounded at school in Philadelphia. A lot of them were great guys one-on-one, but you could be deeply hurt once they were joined by their white friends. Then a steel, white door closed in your face with a solid *thump,* and you were excluded even from eye contact.

Mark met Danny's innocent brown eyes and only saw in them another great guy like Paul Ogden, Timmy O'Brien, Greg Wahlberg, Wally Polanski, and on and on world without end. It was a white door he never wanted to face again.

***

THE END OF YESTERDAY

Analise saw Mark and the others approaching Larson's "theater" and when they stopped to listen, she knew Mark would see her. She did not look in his direction but she felt his presence as though he stood behind her breathing on the nape of her neck. She turned once when someone behind her moved and in that instant their eyes met. She refused to wonder why she cared that he was looking at her, yet her stomach flurried. She quickly turned back to Larson.

Bernard Larson, the journalist, had helped inform the world of events in Germany during the Austrian Anschluss back in March; he had quietly assured his readers that the Austrian people were delighted to be incorporated into Hitler's Greater Reich. Then he had been dispatched to London to memorialize the aftermath of King Edward's abdication in order that the king might marry "– that Simpson woman." If a thing were to be known, Larson would know it.

"But why," a thin woman with a Southern accent asked, leaning forward from her deck chair, "are the papers portraying Herr Hitler as a bad man. Is he really such a bad man?" Her expression and tone urged him to say no.

"Communist rubbish!" interjected a large man with a British accent who stood somewhere across from the thin woman. He was dressed in white trousers and a blue blazer; his full face was crowned with a straw hat. "Good friends in Germany. They adore him," he informed the group. "Nothing but nice things to say about him."

"But why is he supporting that awful General Franco?" the Southern woman persisted, darting nervous eyes between Larson and the large British man. "What's the point of the Spanish holding elections if anyone can come along and overturn the results? It's an exercise in futility."

Larson displayed a tolerant smile. "Do you believe things would have been any different had the Spanish Conservatives won the election?"

"Blood in the streets!" the British man grumbled with certainty. "Jews, Communists, anarchists – whole bloody lot throwing bombs, assassinating government officials. Utter chaos."

Larson paused. Once assured he was free of interruption, he puffed his pipe and continued. "In Spain, no one listens to anyone. Each political party has its own narrow point of view. You have the anarchists, the Socialists, Communists and that's just for starters. On the other side the Carlists and Falangists support the king, the church and the aristocracy. – All of them believe the other side is loathsome and represents the end of civilization as they know it. They think they have no option other than to destroy them or how else can they 'save' Spain?

"I'm afraid Spain badly needs someone with an iron fist like Generalissimo Franco to sort things out. So, yes, you're correct. Elections are useless. The Spanish have never understood them. South America is all the proof you need - one coup after another.

"The present Spanish government, or what's left of it, wants the world to help them fight Franco. They want the world to believe that they're democratic just like we are and that they're fighting for freedom, equality and human decency. It's hog wash."

"Aren't they Communists now?" someone asked.

Larson puffed acknowledgement. "Some, but Socialists mostly. To hear them tell it, oh, no, they'd never do away with private property; the banks are safe, so are factories and large estates. Yet when you read their local newspapers it's a different story.

"There the government is assuring the peasants and workers that the large estates *will* be broken up and distributed among them, and yes, the factories will be turned over to the workers. They promise to do in Spain what the Communists did in Russia."

A woman's quiet voice filled the thoughtful silence. "Is it true that they've murdered thousands of *priests* and…and done unspeakable things to *nuns?*"

"Of course, it's true!" the Englishman glared. "Why on earth would anyone say it if it weren't?"

The quiet spoken woman glared a full second of rebuke before returning to Larson for affirmation. He paused, drawing thoughtfully on his pipe. "- I can't speak for the nuns; but both sides are guilty of murdering priests. The people supporting the government have committed the majority of the atrocities."

"Rubbish," the Englishman contradicted. "Only the Communists are murdering priests. They're atheists; they don't deny it. Everybody in Spain is Catholic!"

Danny called out from the edge of the group, "Isn't the real reason that France and England and America won't get involved is they're too scared of starting war with Germany?"

"No," Larson said with barely a glance and immediately turned to address someone seated close to him.

Rebuffed, Danny glared for a moment then motioned to the others to leave. Mark turned to look back at Analise. He was stunned to see her face turned in their direction. She immediately averted her eyes. Only faintly did he hear Danny declare, "I told you he was a Fascist."

Mark followed along only half listening and partly seeing, remembering the face of the girl who had looked at him. What was her name? With an effort he listened to what Danny was saying.

"You call the back of the ship the stern," he informed them. "The front's the bow. We're on a ship, not a boat. A boat can be lifted out of the water. The direction we're walking now, toward the front of the ship – we're going 'forward.' When we go back toward the stern, we'll be going 'aft.'"

Mark roused himself. "What do you call the middle of the ship?"

"Midship. About where we are now. And those aren't 'walls.' They're 'bulkheads.' Floors are 'decks,' stairs are 'ladders.'"

"Sign don't say that," Willie pointed out mildly. "It say stairs."

Danny conceded that every nautical term was not used so that people would feel more at home. "But see that sign? *Starboard cabins*? You need it. When you're going forward toward the bow like we are, the right side is always starboard."

Willie looked at him in wonder. "How come you know so much?"

"I knew I was going to Spain so I looked up stuff about ships. Since the *Titanic* sank, a lot of stuff's been written about ships. Ocean liners want people to feel like they're safe in a first-class hotel. Everything's made to look like a hotel. Pictures on the wall, carpets, wood panels - look around. It's a hotel. Barbershop, hair dressers, stores, laundry, dry cleaners, entertainment...."

"Better watch out," Mark smiled. "That's for the bourgeois."

"Who told you that?" he challenged. "Communists don't have to dress in rags and live in huts. Everybody should enjoy a good life, not just a handful of greedy capitalists. Sure, I like this; it's a good life."

Though there was a nip in the air, most of the deck chairs were occupied. Curious eyes watched them. When they came upon a vacant deck chair Mark stopped. "You guys go ahead; I'm going to sit here a while and relax."

He told himself he wanted his turn staring at passengers, but he was praying she would pass so he could look at her again. The others hesitated a moment before Willie declared, "I'm gonna see what this Bingo thing's all about. Supposed to be fun."

Danny wanted to explore the ship; they went their separate ways. Mark was framed on either side by other couples who confided quietly about things he could not hear. A minute later first one couple and then the other got up and left. He was not offended. He would have been surprised had they stayed. Even some of the volunteers kept their distance.

He thought of her. He wanted to touch her and to hear her speak. Would he see her again? But why did he even *contemplate* seeing her? It was beyond ridiculous. Why not walk into a police station with a pistol and announce it was a stick up. Nevertheless, he waited for her to glide past his deck chair while drawing hooded stares from others who passed.

The day passed.

***

Willie shook him awake. Willie's face was a dark moon staring down in wonder to see tears fresh from a dream.

"You dreamin' out loud and sound upset…!"

Mark turned away and faced the wall, hugging himself and curled into a fetal position. He wanted to cling to his dream, to his feeling of immense sadness. He wanted to keep his tears because they were what was real, not Willie or the cabin or the ship. He fought to return to his dream which, like smoke, thinned and drifted out of existence.

Yet it was not a dream just as *déjà vu* is not a dream. It was a remembrance of her. A remembrance of familiar things from another time and another place when she and he were not who they were now. It was remembrance of an overwhelming shame because somehow he had failed her horribly. How? Yet it was a remembrance of someone he never actually saw in his nightmare and a voice he never heard, but he *knew* it was her as you know someone if only from the sound of their footsteps.

The shame he felt was like his skin being torn in strips from his body. He wanted to return to the tears, to hear and to know and to touch and to witness the shame, and to do what it was he had not done in that time and place of remembrance.

"- You alright?" Willie asked.

He would not uncurl his body or look at him; he nodded and quietly wiped his nose on his sleeve. He wanted to cling to remembrance but could only cling to fragments of blurred, disjointed sights and sounds. He knew he had loved her a hundred years ago or a thousand years ago. But where and when?

CHAPTER 11

The next day he made eight slow circuits around the ship hoping to bump into her, all the while trying to convince himself that she did not matter to him; he was simply curious. He scolded himself for even thinking of her. After all, she was white, but remnants of his nightmare convinced him that there was something strange and inexplicable between them. Passengers sunning themselves in deck chairs or playing shuffleboard or reading or talking stared at him as he passed.

Suppose he did see her? What would he say to her? "Good morning"? How would she respond and would that provoke startled stares and red faced indignation from onlookers? But even so – what did it matter? Chances are he would remain silent. She was not only white, but probably *rich*. In the here and now the social mores on the ship consisted of marble-hard eyes, flared nostrils, tight lips and heightened color. Just as in America. So why even *consider* anything pertaining to her? He might as well try to lift the ship out of the sea.

He'd heard that her name was Analise and she was already engaged to be married; she was traveling half way around the world to be with him. Wasn't that sufficient to end all fantasy born of a stupid nightmare?

Then there she was.

Splendid in light blue, reading alone in a deck chair. Several empty chairs were scattered nearby but they were as distant as the moons of Jupiter and before he could even get close enough to say hello, her two friends arrived, pulling chairs close beside her.

He passed them, his heart pounding. He found a chair some distance away and turned it so he could see her unobtrusively. He was like a little boy with his nose pressed against the window of a candy store wishing and wanting. He watched her lips move in her smiling manner and his scalp tingled with an eerie sensation that had nothing to do with desire; it had everything to do with the strange nightmare.

He felt no craving for her body; he hardly noticed it except to note that she was slender. What he felt was a strange, almost urgent need to hover over her, to *protect* her. But from whom or from what? Maybe if he could just speak with her long enough, undisturbed and unafraid, it would all become clear.

Analise felt him staring. She didn't see him but she was certain that if she turned their eyes would meet. She fought the urge. "I'm engaged," she said to herself. Then she was joined by Irene and Clara. They were no sooner settled when an older, stout, pleasant looking woman approached. She was carrying a straw bag from which protruded the tops of several magazines.

"Beg pardon," she smiled, motioning to an empty chair, "is that occupied?"

Assured that it was not, she carefully lowered her body until she was comfortable. "Am I mistaken," she asked soon after, "but aren't you young ladies nurses?"

"Boy," Clara frankly mused, "gossip sure does travel."

"You'll find that happens on a ship, young lady. They're small villages, really – even the best of them and I've been on most.... Permit me to introduce myself. I'm Leah Moss, but you mustn't mind me. You young ladies have more to do than fuss with an old lady."

They knew that she did not believe what she said. Her eyes, behind spectacles, were too alive with curiosity; her manner too confident and her tone too cultured for her even for a moment to consider herself a nonentity and never a nuisance. They assured her that they did not mind her intrusion and introduced themselves.

"And I understand you're bound for Spain," she smiled. "I've never been there though I've seen most of Europe."

"- Have you ever been to Germany?" Analise asked.

She shook her gray head. "Not since before the war, 1913, really, a quarter century ago, but horrible things are going on there now. This man Adolph Hitler's responsible. I once met a man – I suppose you'd call him a spiritualist – who told me I'd go back there one day to live in a village, but it never happened...However," her face expressed surprise, "now that I think of it, we did indeed have a little place in a village. Not in Germany, though. In Holland. Not all that different from Germany. Can you imagine that?"

"Somebody predicted this?" Clara asked. "Remember who it was?"

"I certainly do. Edgar Cayce. It was years ago, 1924 at least. You've probably never heard of him, but he's world famous. Even President Wilson has consulted him."

Clara's eyes were alive. "President Wilson?"

"What did he do, tell fortunes?" Irene asked, suppressing a smirk.

"Certainly not!" Mrs. Moss's jowls quivered with indignation. She fixed her inquisitor with eyes that glowed behind her spectacles. "President *Wilson* consulted him. Edgar Cayce is a spiritualist. He can place himself in a trance and his sprit leaves his body and travels into the past or the future.

"*Everyone's* heard of Edgar. The man's been written about *extensively*. He even predicted the Depression five years before it happened! Three years ago, he predicted that there would be revolutions and wars and he was right. Mussolini invaded Ethiopia, Germany invaded Austria, the Japanese invaded China, King Edward abdicated his throne and you have this thing going on in Spain as you well know. Edgar *predicted* it!"

With skeptical eyes Irene asked, "– You say his spirit leaves his body and goes somewhere else?"

Mrs. Moss gazed at her for a long, level moment. Then as she looked down in her straw basket to search for a magazine she resisted the urge to say, "Try not to be ridiculous." Instead she murmured, "That's what they say," and opened her magazine to end the discussion with this uncouth person.

"Let's go see what this new game Bingo's all about," Clara suggested in the silence that followed. Once they all escaped the daunting Mrs. Moss, Analise took the opportunity to fetch a book from the cabin rather than play Bingo. She found a small table in the lounge near a porthole overlooking the sea. It was an area where people were constantly passing.

***

She had been aware of Mark watching her. She was careful not to give any indication.

She felt like a ballet dancer, lovely and almost ethereal floating upon the stage seemingly unaware that anyone is watching or desiring her supple, sensual body. But she was experiencing an undeniable interest in him. Hoping to see him, she glanced around as she settled herself next to the porthole and prepared to read Daphne du Maurier's *Rebecca*. She was dragged from chapter two by – "Ah, Miss Stern, I believe?"

She looked up once again into the bright spectacles of Mrs. Moss. Analise smiled politely to hide her annoyance. Why did people interrupt you when you were obviously engrossed in reading a newspaper, a book or a magazine? What made their desires more important than yours, especially when they did not know you?

"Please," Analise invited," won't you join me?"

The stout woman made a show of hesitating but took the seat on the other side of the table, again resting her bag of magazines on the floor beside her chair. Analise glanced up in time to see Mark pass. She knew he had seen her and she knew he would have stopped. She suppressed her further annoyance at Mrs. Moss.

"I hope I'm not disturbing you," Mrs. Moss smiled. "What's that you're reading?"

"– *Rebecca*."

"Oh, my!" she beamed. "– Daphne's new book. I know her and her father, Sir Gerald du Maurier. They live in Cornwall. Lovely people. You mustn't think I simply go about dropping names of famous people and pretending that I know them, but actually I do. My husband, when he was alive, and I spent a lot of time traveling and one does get to know people. Some, of course, are only acquaintances but over the years some become friends.

"I'm accustomed to travelling first class. My dear, you have no idea the difference. There was a time when I wouldn't *dream* of traveling tourist. Actually, it used to be called third class. Now it's 'tourist' or 'second class' and some lines have the audacity to claim there are no classes on their ships.

"Nonsense, of course. You get what you pay for. Even your seating at dinner is determined by class. But since Mort, my husband, passed and then with that awful Wall Street crash, life really isn't the same. It went topsy-turvy overnight. Some of us were able to salvage enough to get by on, but barely.

"Still, tourist class or not, I must travel. It's really all I know but most of the people I know can't even afford tourist. A very few still go first class. Of course, we aren't allowed in their lounges or on their deck. You get what you pay for.

"So there," she smiled brightly, "you know all my secrets. Now tell me, Miss Stern, how on earth did a nice girl like you come to be a *Communist?* One can tell by your manner and clothing that you come from family."

"I'm not a Communist, Mrs. Moss." She explained why she was going to Spain.

The older woman processed this, her eyes alive with interest. She motioned to a passing waiter and ordered tea for the both of them. "I understand Spain is a dangerous place. I'm surprised your father would ever permit you to go."

"It wasn't my father's decision. He's busy producing pictures in Hollywood."

Her eyes widened then narrowed to a beaming focus. "Not *the* Mort Stern! Is Mort Stern your father?"

She nodded, wishing she had kept quiet about her father. Now she was trapped in a morass of speculation.

"…But I don't understand," Moss frowned. "Dare I ask, my dear, why you are traveling tourist rather than first class?"

They waited while their tea was placed before them. "I'd rather not go into that but it's strictly my choice." She sampled her tea. "You said something yesterday that I've thought about almost constantly – about a man whose spirit leaves his body." She went on to relate her strange experience when Mark and her hands touched. She described him only as "a man."

"Have you ever heard of anything like that, Mrs. Moss?"

The world traveler sampled her tea before replying, disappointed in not being able to pursue Analise's private affairs. She shrugged. "It seems like *déjà vu* but that only lasts a few seconds and one has trouble remembering anything about it. Strange. If Edgar were here, my guess is he'd say you actually knew this person in a previous life. What did he look like?"

"I really don't remember; it happened so fast."

"Do try to remember. If you knew him before, perhaps he'll remember something about you. Maybe you can meet together in the lounge. There is the possibility that you'll have that feeling again, only stronger, enough for a name to emerge, a face, a town, a road. Oh, if only Edgar were here or we could go see him!"

"– But what I experienced had nothing to do with the dead...." Analise protested.

"My dear, don't you see? There is much more to existence than we can possibly know; it isn't a question of *im*possibility but always possibilities."

Analise was disappointed with her answer so she did not tell her that she had been having strange dreams ever since. They seemed to be about a place she had never seen and a time that was strange. She seldom had dreams. These dreams were fuzzy and filled with shouting and noise. Trying to remember them was like looking through a window smeared with Vaseline.

Mrs. Moss reached over and patted her hand where it rested by her tea cup. "We meet as bodies but we can also meet as souls. Imagine the possibilities when those souls are buried, imprisoned really, in other bodies, struggling to get out!"

"– You really believe that, Mrs. Moss?"

"Of course I do. Why else would I say it? Young people today don't believe in spirituality, but in my day we all attended séances. The best people were certain to have a medium attend their parties. One also went to mediums, by appointment of course, to have a reading.

"I preferred Madame Zachary. She spoke with an accent I could never identify. She gave a reading to Biff and Carol Harkins, the steel people. She told them to beware of fire in the sky. Of course we all laughed it off; it sounded so preposterous at the time; that was 1927, the same year Lindbergh flew the Atlantic and landed in Paris. But do you know," she leaned forward as though prepared to impart a secret, "they died in the *Hindenburg* – a fire in the sky!"

They drank their lukewarm tea in silence.

"Everything that becomes fashionable becomes vulgar once the public takes it up," Mrs. Moss complained. "You can't imagine the charlatans that came crawling out of the ground with ridiculous turbans, crystal balls, horrendous looking robes."

Her chubby cheeks glowed with well-mannered outrage. "Horrible cheats pretending to be in contact with spirits! Tables rising, knocking on doors, lights going out, hollow voices – oh, I can't think of it!"

She revealed herself to be a woman who longed for a time long past and mourned things and people she could no longer touch or see. Who could tell how much of what she said was truth or how much was fantasy? She could have known Daphne du Maurier if only for a fleeting moment. In the end, did any of it matter?

CHAPTER 12

He no longer wanted to throw his life away.

Not since the day he first saw Analise. And suppose Larson was telling the truth? What would be the point of going to Spain?

"Aw, he's just full of shit!" Danny said, waving his arm dismissively.

But how could Danny know? He'd never been to Spain; he was still a kid in college. Still what was the point of going there to help dogs fighting over a bone.

After Ruby died he needed a new rhythm to his daily existence beyond long brooding walks, indifferent dinners, unmade beds, unwashed laundry and incessant anger. *Time* stumbled along, pausing here and there and at times it seemed to stop altogether. *Why* and *How* – his constant companions - woke him at all hours shouting things he half remembered and often driving him back into the streets.

He began attending Communist meetings the way bums enter churches for shelter and inadvertently find Christ. Attending the meetings was a distraction, a way to force *Time* to stop loitering and move along. Besides, Willie had asked him to come. It was at the meetings where he heard of Spain.

At the Communist meetings, the cry went up that civilization as it existed was in imminent peril and that whatever happened to Spain would happen to the rest of the world just as the Ice Age had happened to all people in the world. And it would be as brutal and as long, an endless age of unimaginable cruelty.

Hitler and Mussolini hovered over each meeting like low, dark clouds blocking out the sun. And there were the other petty bastards that everybody else ignored - the Black Shirts of England, the Blue Shirts of the Irish Free State, the Green Shirts of Brazil, the Iron Guard of Rumania, the Cross of Fire of France, the German American Bund and on and on, stretching out to the crack of doom.

Impassioned speakers exposed the deeds of these mobs of frenzied men masturbating their emotions and ejaculating hatred on every man, woman and child who was not like them. And in America, economic and social injustice was spread out like maps on a table and he saw that the Communists included colored people along with white, spirit-broken factory workers, Southern sharecroppers and Midwestern Dust Bowl refugees.

He drew closer.

He followed the bright light that they shined into dark places where evil danced and swayed undisturbed by a numb populace. What would have happened, speakers demanded, had Communists not shined a light on the dark, horror of the Scottsboro Boys? Nine black boys would have been lynched simply for riding in the same box car as two white female hoboes. What of Emma Goldman, the San Francisco Bloody Thursday....? The list was endless. The light inexhaustible.

Now on the ship he wondered, did the light include Spain? What was the truth about Spain? He counted it good luck when he spotted Larson alone in a deck chair with a bottle of beer on the deck beside him. He was bent over a writing tablet on his lap.

Sensing Mark's hovering presence, Larson looked up. He was showing gray at the temples like Professor Miller at Grizzly State who taught Elizabethan Drama. Miller, too, was tall, trim, wore glasses, a bow tie and seemed faintly amused by what went on around him. Mark and Prof. Miller had held a number of lively discussions in his office. Larson seemed just as approachable. Mark remembered hearing Larson say to someone, with an easy smile, "Call me Bernie."

When Bernie lifted his pleasant, inviting face, Mark, in a nervous rush, blurted - "Excuse me, but could I ask you a favor?"

Bernie inspected his face, squinting slightly as though trying to place him. When he decided he was not part of the ship's crew, he did not bother to answer; he lowered his head and without a word returned to his writing.

Mark stood a little distance from his chair, waiting for the journalist to finish what he was writing. He was nonplussed when Larson's face reddened. The man gathered his hat, left his drink, stood up and without a glance stalked off. A short distance away he paused briefly to accept a brief greeting from a heavyset man who turned to watch Larson retreat into the ship.

Evidently put off by Larson's abruptness, the heavyset man's demeanor seemed to say,

"What was that all about?" He carried a fan in one hand and a handkerchief in the other although it was not that hot. With a shambling gait, he approached Mark. He stopped and cast suspicious blue eyes on him. He jerked his thumb behind him and demanded, "What'd you say to him?"

Mark's first thought was, "None of your business." Yet there was something about the man's bluff manner that aroused his curiosity. As the stout man lowered himself into the deck chair vacated by Larson, Mark explained that he knew Larson was a reporter and wanted to know what he could tell him about Spain.

The stout man emitted a derisive hoot and began fanning himself. "Mr. Larson can't tell you anything about Spain worth hearing. Too concerned with Hitler, King Edward and Mrs. Simpson! – You must be one of those tom-fool 'volunteers.' Want my advice, boy, you'll carry your ass back where you belong."

Mark looked down at him undecided what to say. He squatted. They were at eye level. "Don't worry," he smiled without humor. 'I won't bite."

The man snorted with amused contempt. He contemplated the sea for a moment then growled, "What's Spain got to do with you people anyway? Just get your balls shot off and," he turned back with a grin, "that'd be terrible, wouldn't it?"

"– Maybe. Not as terrible as being lynched by a mob of cowardly motherfuckers or being burned alive by moronic church-going crackers. I figure this way, at least I get to shoot back."

Their eyes met. The heavyset man gave another derisive hoot. "La-de-da...Didn't take you long to get uppity, did it? Just remember, boy, there'll be plenty of rope left when you get back."

"Maybe enough to drag some white son-of-a-bitch down the street behind a car."

They engaged in a long mutual glare. Mark said just above a whisper, "You ever see the face of hate? - Not because some stupid shithead didn't like somebody else's religion or nationality or politics or color, but because you murdered, burned alive and tortured their fathers and

65

brothers and sons and husbands and then raped their mothers and sisters and daughters and wives at your depraved pleasure and made you watch while they did it and crushed your soul.

"You see, O, White Lord, God and Master, I can understand hate because I can feel it, too. – Surprised? And you and your kind could never in a million years match *justified* hate and righteous hate with your flimsy, filthy ignorance."

They examined every inch of the other's face. The large man had a mole on his jaw near his left ear. He was not the least offended. He fanned himself. "You hate everybody?"

"That would be stupid. But then I'm not white. I only hate people who hate me. People not races. Like that pile of shit who was just sitting here. He wasn't a pile of shit until he spit in my face. Until then, I liked him. Now I despise him because for a moment he reminded me of a good and decent man."

The stout man consulted the sea for a moment. "Why don't you pull up that chair? - What'd you say your name was? - Mark? I'm Tank Maynard. Maybe I can tell you a little about Spain."

What Tank Maynard saw in Mark's face was the same malevolent look of cruelty he had seen in China when he was covering the Boxer Rebellion. He'd been twenty-three when the Chinese guerillas captured him and twelve others outside of Canton in 1900. They had forced the English man, Lieutenant Logan, to his knees and one of them remorselessly hauled off with a sword and decapitated him, dodging the explosion of blood as Logan's body toppled over. They lifted Logan's puzzle-faced head and tossed the thing back and forth, finally stomping it into a misshapen mass.

One of his captors who spoke English came over and squatted before him. Tank prayed to himself, *"Not me. Please, God – not me!"* The Chinese man engaged his eyes. "You see, Englishman – this is a terrible crime when it is an English head, but when they did this to my uncle, it was righteous, joyous punishment. Is this not true?"

Tank nodded yes because it was true. His captor's eyes had not been wild or harsh. They were like brown buttons. Like Mark's. Brown, steady and accusatory. Tank had later written a book about his experiences in China in which he claimed he had courageously escaped rather than admit that he had been shown mercy along with five other captives.

"Spain's not what most people think it is," he began. "I've been there. Going back to report on the end of the war. The country's mountainous, almost like Switzerland, and it's not one country. You have regions. At least four - Aragon, Catalonia, Galicia and Castile. What side of the war you're on depends on what part of Spain you're from.

"People like Larson don't know that. People in Aragon are Basque. They speak a different language. Nobody knows what to make of them or where their language comes from. In Galicia they speak Galician. Catalonia – different language, too. A mixture of French and Spanish. They all want to be independent countries. The rest of Spain speaks Castilian."

He grinned. "Head spinning yet? Add the Catholic Church, the monarchy, the aristocracy and the military. They're interbred. They're one family. Everybody else – they're the people. No government stays in power without the military's approval and that means the church's approval, too. All the officers and Catholic higher ups are from the aristocracy. Larson never mentioned that, did he? Course not.

"And guess whose side they're on?"

"– The people revolted?"

He shook his head. "They had an election. Wasn't a landslide; the Cortes – that's their legislature - ended up something like 51 to 49 but enough to give the Communists, anarchists and Socialists the win. Mostly the Socialists."

Refusing to speak Larson's name, Mark said, "That other one said they can't get along with each other."

"He's right for once. The anarchists and Socialists are divided into a dozen splinter groups each yelling at the other. They even have their own flags." He started enumerating on his fingers - "You got the United Socialist Party, the Spanish Communist Party, the Workers Party of Marxist Unification - they're Trotskyites - the Republican Union, National Confederation of Labor - they're anarchists - and they may be responsible if the government loses the war.

They revolted in the middle of the war – demanding absolute, Russian style revolution *now* while the rest were trying to persuade them - wait until we win the war. But no. They tried to form a separate state in Catalonia. Government had to waste time fighting them which gave Franco time to capture all of northern Spain.

"Communists would never tolerate anything like that. They believe a mind of your own is a dangerous thing. You blink at the wrong time," he made a fist and pointed a finger to his forehead, "you're automatically a 'Trotskyite' or just as bad, an anarchist. As far as Stalin and his crowd are concerned, either one makes you a Fascist."

"Wasn't Leon Trotsky a big time Communist?"

"He and Lenin pulled off the Russian Revolution. Lenin died and you had a power struggle. Stalin won and declared Trotsky an enemy of the state and anybody who supported him."

They talked until it was time for dinner. When they stood they glanced around and seeing no witnesses, surreptitiously shook hands.

"Still hate me?" Tank asked shambling away.

"Never in a million years. – Thanks."

CHAPTER 13

Ben Cross was embarrassed by the behavior of the volunteers.

Compared to previous contingents, they looked poor and shabby which was magnified whenever they were in a group. It was certainly no sin to look shabby but looking shabby and also acting loud and rowdy was a lot different. Then, damn it - in addition to calling attention to themselves, some had committed the stupid *faux pas* of requesting seconds like somebody out of Dickens! He had never expected that.

Seated among them, he quietly fumed when their requests elicited smirks from some of the other guests. For meals they were assigned seats in the rear of the huge dining room. The nurses were somewhere among the other guests.

Ben was forty. A sergeant during the Great War, he was the only one among them who had ever been shot at or seen men gassed or killed. He had been wounded during the Battle of the Marne. His full head of curly brown hair was streaked with grey. Bushy eyebrows gave him an owlish appearance. He spoke with a Brooklyn accent.

As for this crew, he'd been disappointed with them from the beginning. Fifty-two signed up for Spain; twenty-nine showed up. Twelve were Jewish. Over a third. It had been the same with the previous contingent – a third were Jewish. Yet Jews were not a third of the U.S population. Not even close. Where the hell were the others? More disturbing, a lot of these people weren't even Communists. A bunch of barroom Socialists. Three or four characters had no political leanings at all! So-called "intellectuals" and "idealists." Unemployed bums most likely. What could you expect from people like that in a pinch?

Comrades came back from Spain wounded or shell-shocked and told him what had happened to them and to other Comrades. Al Burris had been blinded and committed suicide. Carson, the fat guy, deserted; a bomb hit the truck Phil Novitsky was riding in and nobody ever found a trace of him.

Basically, he disliked filling the ranks with those who had to die. He had known both the living and the dead. Not just Spain. He remembered the Battle of the Marne and the faces of men who would die. Faces. Cheeks creased in grins, mouths moving in speech, eyes roving, lips compressed in fear or anger or disgust.

Pistol in hand, he had led them out of the muddy, stinking trench and when Bobby Farrell refused to come along, he had snarled, "Die here or there, dammit!" and he shot Farrell in the head. When the Germans threw them back in wild retreat to the muddy, stinking trenches, Bobby Farrell was lying where he had fallen, having saved himself the trip.

Most of these men would soon be dead, too, torn apart by angry explosions or lying in contorted positions with disbelieving eyes and puzzled expressions. Or mouths open in mid-screams of horror. Danny, Kellerman, Willie, Walter, Callaway, the kid, Dana Andrews, only 18, Kahn, Winters, Wilson. Who among them would survive? Danny was only twenty and probably hadn't had his first girl yet. Ben was good at sizing up men. He had been selected by the Party to shepherd contingents across and keep a close eye on them. That kid, Danny, was an up and comer, so was Willie. Once they cleaned his grammar up he'd be a good recruiter. Ben had serious doubts about the other colored one, though. He could be Willie's first project.

After being embarrassed, Ben went among them, encouraging them to stand tall, to be defiant and to present themselves as proud proletariat. They must *never* appear to be crude or ill-mannered or uncouth in front of these smug bastards.

"That's all they wanna see! It helps 'em justify all the shitty crap they pull; they wanna believe you're dirt so they can treat you like dirt. Don't make these Fascist sons-of-bitches feel superior! And for Christ sake don't ask for seconds, and watch out for reporters. They're the worst. They'll write stuff that'll make us all look like saps. I'd like to see the bunch of them tossed overboard."

There was the late night complimentary buffet that the ship offered the passengers. The men descended on the tables and stuffed their pockets with apples and oranges, cookies, cheeses and dried sausages until Ben's furrowed brows put a stop to it.

***

Mark kept to himself. Sometimes while Danny was out of the cabin, Willie would quietly urge Mark to "act like people" and join the rest of the fellows. Mark smiled and put him off. He said he needed to spend time in the ship's library reading up on Spain since they were going there. But faced with Willie's continued blandishments, he finally admitted the real reason was that white people had no interest in anything a colored man had to say outside of boxing or jazz or the weather or sometimes sports; never anything like literature or politics or science. But no matter what, you were expected to grin and agree with everything *they* said but they never believed you had anything to say that was worth their time.

Willie snorted and accused him of being "spoiled" because he lived in the North. "You ain't never see nobody git beat to death or hangin' from a tree an' nobody gonna take your side; ain't no law for us. I been smacked in the face by little boys an' couldn't even raise my hand! You ain't see how ugly they can be or you wouldn't be worryin' 'bout nobody listening to you!"

Mark had been lying on his bunk. Angry, he raised up on one elbow and shot back that it wasn't being "spoiled" because somebody couldn't beat, rape or murder you whenever the hell he felt like it. Besides, his grandfather had fought in the Civil War in a colored regiment, so there.

Willie stared at him undecided. "We ain't gonna talk about all that old-time stuff; we here now. We both different or we wouldn't be here. These people different, too. They *decent*. You gotta give 'em a chance, man. When the las' time a white man shake your hand? They real people. Talk to 'em. Man for man, they *different!*"

Unwilling to create bad feelings with a man who had nearly been lynched, he rested his hand on Willie's shoulder for support, and jumped down from his bunk.

"O.K," he said. "Like the man said - 'Once more into the breach.'"

***

It was true; there was an easy camaraderie among the men. At lunch somebody said, "Pass the rolls."

"Not until you say, 'Please,'" Danny scolded.

"Don't give 'im any," Willie added. "He already had three."

"Let him eat cake," concluded a third.

They all laughed. But cracks in their camaraderie were beginning to show, maybe because of Walter. He was an agitator. Mark liked Walter because Walter made eye contact with him when he told a joke or made a comment. He poked fun at everyone including Ben, but some of his remarks were barbed, and he tended to single out three men in their forties who had left college positions to volunteer - Ralph Kellerman, Norman Kahn and Cecil Winters.

Ralph was heavyset, balding and had red lips surrounded by a grey streaked beard. Norman wore wire rim glasses that magnified his eyes. Cecil was a thin man who favored a pipe and had a superior smile that was perceived as a smirk. Walter called them "the old guys" behind their back and the "professors" to their face which they accepted with good grace. Others found their conversation tedious and shied away so the three tended to keep to themselves. But like bees, if disturbed, they could offer sharp stings.

Walter invited a few barbs when he asked, "What made you guys come anyway?"

Had Ben been sitting at their table, he would have squelched the question, but he alternated sitting at the three tables that the men occupied. A long moment of offended silence followed. Kellerman turned a bearded face to Kahn who glanced at a frowning Winters. Turning gleaming spectacles to Walter, Kahn replied, "There is the man who faces punishment because he dared protest that he and his family are hungry, cold and in rags. And there is the well fed, comfortable man who faces punishment because he protested that his *neighbor* is hungry and cold and in rags.

"Which is the better man?"

Dramatically he rose, followed by his two companions.

Ben was livid when he heard about it. Lately, by the third day at sea, contingents began to bicker, grew tired of playing cards or shuffleboard or throwing darts. They had exhausted meaningful conversation. Innocuous statements led to arguments. Someone would commence drumming his fingers and another tapping his toes in pursuit of the elusive "something to do" all to the annoyance of others.

It was different in '36 and '37. Then they found time all too fleeting. Those men were great readers and activists; they had little time or inclination for games or amusements. They studied maps of Spain and books on military strategy; they schemed and planned for the day after tomorrow when they would help re-make the world. For them today was already spent, tomorrow too short. They wanted to say that they had fought the good fight and wrestled monsters down.

Now he had to hover over these people like a kindergarten teacher lest they misbehave or call each other names.

But maybe it was Professor Kellerman, not Walter, who had broken the unity of the men. Previously, at dinner, Jasper Morgan made an offhand remark to which Kellerman took exception. Jasper said that when he got to Spain he wanted to see one of the ancient aqueducts.

"What for?" Kellerman challenged, wiping his bearded mouth with his napkin.

Jasper looked puzzled. "What do you mean, 'what for'?"

"Don't you know those things were built with slave labor?" Kellerman scolded.

Jasper bristled. "Nothing wrong with *looking* at 'em. Hell, people come from all over the world to see the Coliseum and Pantheon and stuff like that. It's just history!"

Kellerman was silent for a moment. He sat at the opposite end of the table from Jasper. The seven other men at the table were hoping that Jasper would put Kellerman in his place. Few liked him. He was impatient and imperious. Worse, he was one of those intellectuals which translated into soft, muddle headed and unreliable.

"-It's not 'just history,'" he explained in a gentler tone. "People come to see them because they're ignorant. They don't say, 'How awful,' they say, 'How wonderful,' 'How marvelous!' As long as it's in the past they don't give a shit. But they're looking at human misery. Each and every stone represents some man's agony, day after day after day, year after year until he drops and another man or boy is put in his place like a horse or mule.

"Freemen were soldiers. Even Greek and Roman senators were soldiers. Who was left to tend the fields and mind the sheep, build

73

roads, go into the mines, load ships, carry shit? - Who'd you fuck when you wanted to whether it was male or female? *Slaves.*

"Armies didn't just burn cities to the ground," he lectured. "When Caesar defeated an army, he'd chop off the right hand of the captives. They took the women and children as slaves. Hundreds. Six, seven hundred, sometimes more. Africa, Asia, Europe, Britain – all slaves. Caesar brought back *a million* from Gaul. You can't even imagine that many people. Slaves were money. Pieces of gold. Brand them with hot irons; castrate some to make them eunuchs – Sell them like fish at a market.

"You want to fight back or run away? – Ever hear of Spartacus? Led a revolt. Lost. They crucified him along with *6,000* others who joined him. Strung them along the Appian Way. Don't kid yourself. It wasn't uncommon. Christ wasn't the only one crucified. It was to teach the rest a lesson. And women? What chance do you think they had? The whole idea was to make people so scared they'd surrender rather than risk making you mad."

He paused in the attentive silence to let what he said sink in.

Kahn added, "When you see those monuments, think of Hitler and the 'master race' who're too superior for the rest of us. What's that make us – animals to work in their factories, farm their land, carry their garbage, work their mines, serve as whores for his armies? Son-of-a-bitch thinks he's another Caesar.

Maybe he is. People are just toys he can play with any way he pleases. Heil, Hitler, Hail, Caesar, what the hell's the difference? When we change the way we look at things, the things we look at change."

Winters, Kellerman and Kahn rose leaving behind a chastened silence. Mark was moved by what they said. He wondered why the mention of Romans suddenly made him remember his nightmares. He needed to see her; she had become very important in his life.

CHAPTER 14

He met her that night.

She was behind him at the night buffet, waiting her turn while others served themselves. Their eyes met briefly. His voice was almost inaudible as he stepped back. "Ladies first."

She had already seen him standing in the late buffet line and quietly maneuvered until she was standing just behind him. She needed an excuse to touch him. If she did, would she experience *déjà vu* again and perhaps remember more about him? Who could say what that might be. She was hesitant.

When he said, "Ladies first," she smiled and selected the things that she wanted and offered to help his plate, too. He accepted, heart pounding, wondering who was staring and what they were thinking. He felt hot and uncomfortable.

"There's a seat over there," she said, pointing delicately to an empty table.

He followed her. Each step that he took seemed to pound like a bass drum, reverberating throughout the room, echoing and re-echoing from the walls. He felt forty pairs of eyes crawling up his back. His scalp felt hot. The room suddenly seemed tiny and completely silent. As she prepared to sit, he self-consciously held her chair for her. Her dark hair was in a chignon which emphasized her slender neck. Her voice was a girl's voice – young and innocent and honest.

He remembered the photograph in the colored newspaper that he had seen as a child. He had not understood it at first. The photo showed a mob of white men in white shirts and suspenders and fedoras surrounding two colored men who were hanging by ropes tied around their neck. The mob turned jubilant faces toward the camera. Some had raised arms pointing toward the two victims. The paper was suddenly snatched away from him and he was told to mind his own business and to go out and play.

After she was seated he sat down facing her, wondering what he could use to protect himself if anyone, insane with anger, attacked him.

He let his breath out, surprised that he had been holding it in. He was afraid to look at her. His mouth was dry, his stomach tense. He wanted to look over his shoulder to detect signs of danger. He imagined he could hear angry breathing, and if he looked he would see nostrils flaring, faces flushed and marble-hard eyes. He realized he was holding his breath again.

"You look so serious," she smiled. "By the way, my name's Analise."

"- Hi. I'm Mark. Are your friends going to join us?" He wondered how that would compound the rage he felt in the room.

"They went to play Bingo."

She sensed his discomfort and she began to be conscious of the silence in the room. Her stomach felt tight. She took a deep breath and talked, almost rambling at times. She told him she was from New York and was an only child and she had been on a ship before, twice. Once when she was sixteen and again a year later.

He was dismayed. That meant she was rich, not that it made any difference of course. They could never, ever be friends. "Where'd you go?"

"France. Everybody went to France. I think I was too young to appreciate it, though. The Louvre and Notre Dame and the Arc de Triomphe didn't mean all that much to me. I wanted to do ordinary, everyday things like meet a French girl my own age who I could talk to and write to when I got back home but we only met the French people who waited on us and for some reason I don't think they liked Americans very much. Everybody we knew got the same impression. I hope it's not that way now."

He noticed again how her lips seemed to smile when she spoke. She felt him staring at her lips and lowered her eyes and looked away and in that moment he felt a strong surge of sadness; he fought off the tears that suddenly stung the back of his eyelids; it was the same sadness he had felt during the nightmare. He collected himself but failed to conceal his emotions.

"Is anything the matter?"

He had to tell her. He wanted to. "I had a nightmare - no, it was more like remembering. I don't recall much but I know it made me feel awfully sad, and for some reason just now something about you made me feel sad again.... It's nothing bad, I think...." He shrugged. "It was just a dream."

Their eyes met and lingered. Her face registered concern. Impulsively she started to reach for his hand where it rested by his plate but quickly withdrew it as though she had touched a hot pot on a stove. Then she wondered what would have happened had she touched him as she had planned.

He sensed that she needed to know who he was. He told her he was from Philadelphia and that his father was a preacher but he lied to her when he said he was going to Spain to fight for democracy.

"I went to college, not that it's done me any good. You probably never heard of Grizzly State. It's a small colored college in Pennsylvania. I wanted to study archaeology but they didn't offer it so I had to settle for English, and where I come from," he smiled without humor, "when it came to a thing like college, you went any place you could afford and any place that would accept you. It was a big deal."

"Your family was poor?"

He thought for a moment. "You know something – I don't really know. Everybody seemed to be in the same boat. I think it depended on how large your family was. You know – if everybody's bringing home seven or eight dollars a week, the family of three will do better than the family of six."

"– *Seven dollars?*"

He smiled at her astonishment and picked at the food on his plate. "That's supposed to be good pay for certain people. It's a thing called discrimination. It can be sneaky sometimes and at other times bold and obnoxious."

She colored and sat further back in her chair. "I know about discrimination. I'm Jewish and we aren't allowed in a lot of places. We aren't always welcome in certain neighborhoods or law schools or medical schools or hotels or nursing or dental schools and we're hated in lots of places...."

"...*But aren't you white?*"

Her smile was ironic. "We're a breed apart as far as a lot of people are concerned. Haven't you heard that I killed Jesus? And of course there's

Adolph Hitler, Fritz Kuhn and his German American Bund and the KKK...."

"They're stupid!" he snapped. He wanted to reach for her hand but knew he could not.

She smiled. "Don't look so angry. People will think you're angry at me."

Just then she nodded to someone behind him and rising, smoothed her skirt and prepared to leave. "I have to go but I'm glad I met you, Mark."

He rose and saw her two friends waiting for her by the exit. Their faces were blank; neither looked friendly. He turned to her. "I'm glad I met you, too, Analise."

He wanted urgently to add - *"May I see you again?"* but he knew the impossibilities. He left the lounge soon after she did, looking to neither right nor left, plowing through a thick sea of indignation, expecting at any moment to hear a shout ring out or feel some thrown glass strike his back. His hands were sweaty and he held his breath until he was out of the door and into the passageway.

***

Over Mark's shoulder Analise had seen Clara and Irene signaling to her to leave. Not much was said on the way to their cabin. Analise was aware of tension; an icy wind spreading frost on spring flowers. They had barely closed the cabin door before Irene swung around, eyes blazing and enlarged behind her thick lenses. *"Do you know what the hell you're doing!"* she hissed.

Analise chose innocence as her defense. "'Doing'? What are you talking about?"

"Don't play dumb with me! That nigger you were talking to in the lounge, that's what! What was that all about?"

She bristled not only at her tone but also at her referring to Mark as a nigger. Irene glanced at Clara for support before continuing. "People didn't like it. It was embarrassing! You two had an awful lot to say. What's the matter with you anyway? You can't be that dumb!"

Clara made herself look busy preparing for bed. Analise, struggling to conceal her resentment at being taken to task, chose her words carefully.

"I don't see anything wrong with talking to another Comrade. Aren't we supposed to treat everybody the same or do we just talk about it? Is it only when nobody's looking? He's going to Spain, too. We're all in this together in case you haven't noticed."

Neither cabin mate offered an immediate reply. Analise turned down the covers of her bed; she made an effort to control the tremor of her hands and the anger within her. Irene found her tongue. "I'm not a Communist. I don't go for that 'we're-all-the-same' shit. Neither does anybody else. It's one thing to be courteous to those people but you're making a fool of yourself and what you do reflects on me and Clara! That's why we got you out of there."

"Well, Clara's a Communist," Analise reminded her. "Ask her to explain it. Communists don't discriminate; it's one of the first things I was told. Since we chose to come along, I think we have to respect their point of view."

Clara maintained her silence and avoided eye contact. Analise began undressing for bed. She had not intended saying what she had; she was only parroting things that Jacob had told her. Had her tone been too confrontational? Confrontation made her tense and gave her mouth ulcers. Besides, she was alone and far from home and everyone she knew; she could not afford to alienate Irene or Clara.

Facing the mirror over the wash basin, she commenced combing her hair, still hoping to conceal the tremor in her hands. When she had mastered herself, she held out her hand. "I guess you didn't notice I'm engaged. I think I told you the day we met that the reason I'm going to Spain is to be with my fiancé. He's a doctor with the American Mission."

Irene came closer to inspect the ring. "Where are you supposed to meet him?"

"I'm not sure," she responded with a smile. "Either the hospital in Villa Paz or the one in Gastellijo. We'll all probably end up in the same place. If you like, I'll introduce you when we get there."

Clara finally found her voice. She was in her nightgown. "We weren't trying to butt in but we both heard some ugly things being said. That's why we gave you the high sign to leave."

She was tempted to ask, "What 'ugly things?'" but it might be better not to know. When she sat on her bed and began removing her shoes, Irene sat beside her. There was a curious gleam in her eyes. "– Can I ask you something? - How'd you find anything to say to a *negro*? What could you possibly talk about?"

"– I don't know; just regular stuff. About his college and how he wanted to be an archaeologist but had to major in English instead...."

"*College...!*" she cried, in disbelief. "He went to *college?*"

She nodded. "And we talked about France. Stuff like that. He's really a nice person, well-spoken – just like anyone else except that he's colored instead of white."

Clara produced a cigarette. "Is he a Communist?"

"I didn't ask."

"Still," Irene frowned, "maybe you shouldn't do it again. We heard people talking about throwing you both overboard."

Analise's green eyes widened, but she displayed no other emotion though she felt a sense of dread. Clara noticed the color drain from her face. "Maybe in France or Spain," she suggested mildly. "Not here. But anyway, what's the point?"

"That's right," Irene added. "What's the point? This should be the end of it - period. You already gave the boy something he'll remember the rest of his life."

Analise smiled agreeably and slipped into bed. They would be in France in two more days.

CHAPTER 15

Dear Mom,

So far the voyage has been smooth and uneventful.

Remember the two nurses you met before we left? Irene was the tall one and Clara was the old one. She's a Communist and seems disappointed that we're not. I think she's in her forties and has had lots of nursing experience. I can learn a lot from her.

She hates her father because he beat her mother and Irene hates her mother because she says her mother does not like her. I've never personally known anyone like them, but I'm beginning to wonder whether or not they are all that unusual. Have I been living in a cocoon?

Irene's boyfriend was supposed to accompany her but got cold feet and ditched her without telling her. It was a dreadful thing to do. She doesn't want to believe it and has to go to Spain all alone. She's very upset but tries to hide it. Clara brought a bottle of whiskey with her and maybe she drinks too much. They both can be a little too outspoken, but I have to get along with them because I don't know anyone else and I don't want to feel that I'm alone.

Most of the men who are coming with us are poor. All you see are frayed cuffs and collars and worn out shoes. Their pants don't have creases and some don't even have hats or caps. A few can be very bitter and sarcastic but not to us. They all like to talk to us. I guess we're the only show in town since they can't even approach any of the other women on board.

They come from all over. One is from Cuba. There is a colored man who everybody likes to kid with, a boy who is a know-it-all and Walter who looks chubby but insists it's all muscle. He likes to tell corny jokes. He said a man went to his doctor and said, "Doc, I got a trick knee." The doctor said, "Join the circus." All the men thought it was hilarious; I didn't. Maybe they're nervous.

To be honest, a lot of the passengers are hostile. You can tell by the way they look at you. At dinner no one at our table wants to talk to us. On the first day some reporter named Bernard Larson (you have probably heard of him) was telling everybody how terrible the people are who are fighting for Spain and against Franco even though Franco is the one who's trying to overturn the last election which was fair. Larson makes it sound as though people who are volunteering are stupid.

Love, Me

* * *

Hi, Mom,

The more I see our men as compared to the other passengers, the more I realize how unequal society is. I don't think I am seeing anything I have not seen before; it's just that everything is so much more magnified, and I am part of it.

Clara has been quite a revelation. She is what you'd call a man-hater even though she's been married twice. I think a big reason she hates them is she wanted to be a doctor and she blames men for stopping her. She said she will die without ever being all she could have been. She's impressed with some woman named Emma Goldman and quotes her a lot like, love has nothing to do with marriage. Marriage is just an economic arrangement where women sell their bodies for support, and men want to keep women barefoot, powerless, pregnant and ignorant.

Clara said men love to idolize themselves judging from all of the statues of themselves on horses and grand monuments like the Arc de Triomphe, the Washington Monument, Trafalgar Square. She can go on for days. She wants to know where are the monuments to women because without women no one would even exist.

Clara says that Emma Goldman is right; that a woman should be intimate with any man she pleases because that is what men do. If people can idolize Don Juan and Casanova and "playboys" for being intimate with whomever they please, so can she because men are no better than she is.

Actually, some of the things that she says are food for thought. Why do Chinese break the feet of little girls so that they can totter along on crippled feet for the rest of their lives just because it looks attractive to men? She said that in Muslim countries a woman is stoned to death if she is raped, and in India, when a husband dies, his wife is burned alive at his funeral because without him, she has no purpose. This is called suttee and guess who lights the funeral pyre? Their oldest son! In Africa they mutilate a girl's private parts so she will get no pleasure from intimacy.

The funny thing is Clara can sound romantic though it sounds funny coming from a woman her age. She says she agrees with Emma Goldman that love is the strongest and deepest element in all of life and that love will defy any law or custom and it really determines your destiny. Maybe love does defy all laws and customs. Isn't that why I'm going to Spain?

I wish you could tell me what you think of all of this and whether or not she might not be right about some things. I need to have fresh thoughts that are filled with hope and love and all of the things that life should be about.

Love, Me

CHAPTER 16

What had seemed impossible had after all been possible.

If only they could have spoken longer and exchanged little pieces of themselves that could germinate and flower. Yes, there had been tension among the other passengers but if she had had the courage to speak to him, his courage must match hers despite the lynchings and castrations and hot hatred.

Again he roamed the deck searching for sight of her and not knowing what he would do if he saw her but knowing that he must do something. He noticed more intense scrutiny as he passed deck chairs and small groups of passengers, some of whom deliberately forced him to step around them.

He left the deck and found a small table near a window in the lounge outside the dining room where he could sit and watch the deck and the sea. Moments later he was rewarded. Her slim figure slipped past the window and entered the lounge. But her two friends were with her, and at that moment someone sat down heavily in the chair he was saving for her.

Tank Maynard set his glass of scotch on the table with a click. A little surprised, Mark greeted him, losing sight of Analise. Tank did not respond immediately, regarding him with shrewd blue eyes.

"- I wouldn't get too interested in her if I were you."

Mark flushed. He felt a mixture of anger and shame at having his thoughts revealed. The big man leaned forward and continued quietly, "There's talk - and you didn't hear this from me – but there's some grumbling about a certain 'fresh nigger' disappearing overboard because of last night." He leaned back and crossed his thick legs.

Mark saw that he was serious. "– Thanks," he murmured, his heart pounding. "Thanks a lot…. We were only talking. I guess, maybe I thought things on the ship would be a little different."

Tank snorted. "Where do you think the passengers come from, Mars? People take their habits with them. Surprised you wouldn't figure that out."

"I wasn't expecting anything crazy; I know she's already engaged and…I mean it's like you can look but don't touch…."

"You forgot – speak," Tank added, lifting his glass.

Analise was alone, speaking to an older woman outside of the dining room. At the same time, he noticed Ben and Danny head for the men's lounge next to the dining room. He brought his eyes back to Tank.

"Speaking of overboard," he said, "the guy in charge of us thinks a lot of reporters are Fascists; we're not to talk to you guys and it wouldn't hurt if one of you ended up overboard."

Tank's eyes widened, his lips formed an O. He nodded his head several times as though to say, "We'll see about that."

Analise was gone. Tank followed Mark's eyes and gave a sympathetic shrug. They talked of other things, revealing glimpses of their lives. With reportorial skill Tank made interrogation sound like conversation and Mark told him more about himself than he would ordinarily have. Then it was time for lunch and Tank lumbered away toward the dining room after telling Mark that he still thought going to Spain was a mistake.

***

Later when Mark returned to the cabin he felt tension, as though he had interrupted something private. Willie was the catalyst among them; he always found something to talk about. Now he was strangely quiet, straddling a chair turned backward, his large arms resting on the top of the chair back.

Danny sat cross legged on his bunk, his back resting against the wall. Neither said anything. Smiling, Mark started to leave when Danny said, "Mind if I say something?"

He turned, curious. "-Sure."

Danny glanced at Willie as though not certain who should speak. "-You may not like what I have to say," he began, "but I'd like to be frank if I may."

Willie adjusted his weight on the chair. Mark glanced at them, sensing some sort of ambush. He leaned his back against the door, crossed his arms and waited. What in the name of God could this twenty-year-old boy say to him that was relevant?

Willie, waiting for Danny to continue, grumbled, "Say it, man. He grown. Truth don't hurt nobody."

"- The reason I'm in the same cabin with you guys is Ben wants to prove that Communists don't discriminate. We see people as people, nothing else matters. Willie and I want a chance to explain what we believe."

"I already know what you believe."

Willie shook his head. "Naw, or you be with us. You ain't got the right attitude. Any man - woman, too, for that matter - be with us 'cause if you ain't, you don't mind being kicked in the ass – in the balls more like it. You sayin' you *like* it. You sayin' you won't fight back for your own self-respect. I don't hear you sayin' anything – speakin' up for things."

His tone was matter-of-fact, as though what he said was self-evident. Danny smiled, "He's not saying you're wrong to hold back and think it over, Mark. People like to walk around a new idea, sort of touch it and see if it's going to hurt. We all went through that. But you can see for yourself that men and women from all over – Germany, Italy, Bulgaria, Puerto Rico, England, Ireland, France, America – are coming right out and saying, 'O.K., I might get killed and never see my friends or family again; I might get badly hurt but this is worth it!'

"Why would they do that, Mark? They can't all be crazy. We're talking about college professors, college students, doctors, nurses, ex-soldiers and people like Ernest Hemingway, George Orwell, Martha Gellhorn, Paul Robeson, Miro!"

"Wait a minute!" Mark cried, holding up a hand, eyes closed. He shook his head as though to clear it. "Does that mean I won't get killed, too, or get my head blown off? You mean I've been wasting my time worrying about nothing? Sounds good to me."

Danny and Willie exchanged glances to see who was going to respond.

"We ain't sayin' that," Willie explained patiently. "We sayin' there ain't no real reason you here. – Why you goin' to Spain? You ain't never said you believe nothin'. Why you goin'?"

"You said yourself," Danny pointed out, "you're not a Communist or Socialist."

Had Ben put them up to this? Did they suspect that he was some sort of spy because he'd been talking to Tank?

"- The last I heard, you guys wanted to prove that everybody in the world was on your side – men, women, Catholics, Jews, red, yellow, black, cats, dogs – everybody! - What're you saying now? That everything you said is just a bunch of crap? That everybody has to be a Communist or a Socialist for the privilege of losing an arm or leg?"

"We ain't sayin' that, either," Willie answered. He took time to choose his words. "We sayin' when the shit go down you gotta be with us 'cause unless you believe real down deep, you may's well go back home."

Danny took it up. "We're talking about people who crossed oceans like we did, crossed mountains like we're going to do but they had to *escape* to do it. Over 40,000 men from *fifty two different countries!* And they're asking for nothing in return!"

"Ain't nobody ever did what we fixin' to do. All kind of races mixed in together…We ain't out to take nobody's land…We just wanna do what's right an' stop all this evil."

Silence. They looked at him and he looked at them. Mark controlled his anger. *'They're asking nothing in return'* as though he were. They did not want his body, they wanted his soul.

Tank Maynard was right – for Communists, having a mind of your own was a dangerous thing to have.

He remembered the Communist meetings back in Philadelphia and how much they reminded him of his father's church. People testified at the Communist meetings just like the congregation testified in his father's church. Following one of his father's passionate sermons, men and women stood up from the pews, arms uplifted, swaying, eyes raised to the ceiling weeping and confessing to the church their sins and begging Jesus for forgiveness; they begged Him to save them from a life of adultery, from thievery, from lying and from evil of every kind.

Women fainted and white uniformed ushers rushed to their aid; men danced in tight circles in the aisle, possessed of "the spirit" and in the end, faces streaked with tears of redemption, they all felt relieved of their burdens and safe in the bosom of Christ.

People testified at the Communist meetings, too.

Willie gave thanks to the Communist Party for saving him from being lynched; men confessed to crimes committed against women, they told of misery, hunger, depression, suicide attempts all due to the soul sapping evils of capitalism. But they had been saved by Communism, and safe in the bosom of Communism, they raised clenched fists and shouted, "Power to the people!"

He was coming to believe that over time they gave away pieces of their soul and replaced it with obedience until they had nothing left for themselves.

"It's not just Spain, Mark," Danny assured him. "People are in trouble all over because of capitalism and exploitation. Did you ever ask yourself, how can a couple thousand capitalists keep 20 or 30 *million* people on their knees in country after country? How can they have all that power? They have all the *money* – they control the law, the police and the armies. We have to break that to pieces like they did in Russia. They broke the police and the army!"

"I don't know what you guys expect me to say or do," Mark rejoined, "but if taking a chance with my life's not enough…." he shrugged and turned to leave.

Danny got off his bunk. His eyes were alive with the pure conviction of youth – brown and piercing and holding in righteous anger. "Let me ask you something – what's wrong with Communism? Especially since you're colored and you can see that we treat you with dignity and respect!"

"He right," Willie growled. "You been to college and you running a damn elevator."

He was stung and felt betrayed. He and Willie had worked in the same department store. Somehow the Party had gotten Willie hired in the warehouse. He and Mark started eating their lunch together. It was Willie who persuaded him to attend the Communist meetings with him.

His back still to the door, he lashed back. "Nothing's wrong with Communism. - Why're you looking surprised? Nothing wrong with religion either. Or dictatorship for that matter. The thing that's wrong is the *sons of bitches running things!*

"You can't butcher two million kulaks –*two million men, women and children* with all of their hopes and ambitions and desires – you can't butcher them and say it's all right because they're not *goddamned Communists!* All those boys and girls who never had a chance, and then you call it just and necessary. What gives you the *right?* You didn't just kill them. You murdered all of their children and grandchildren and great grandchildren!

"Sure, everybody deserves a job, a decent house and food to eat and clothes on their back, everybody deserves a real chance to be somebody – we all agree on that but *people* get in the way, Danny! *People.* They *always get in the way!* They burn people alive because they're 'heretics,' they sacrifice innocent children to so-called 'gods,' they put out people's eyes and cut out their tongues, they cut off the balls of boys so they can sing like girls and they do any god-damned thing they please to girls and women just because some psycho son-of-a-bitch said do it!

"People set up a democracy then butcher Indian men, women and children so they can steal their land and then they pray to God while they're doing it! They make animal slaves out of us so they can rape our women anytime they please and castrate us if we just look at theirs. Nothing's wrong with all of these ideas and theories, Danny. – 'Be kind, love your neighbor, do no harm.'

"But *people are the shit factor!* Ideas and theories, like wholesome food, become shit once *people* get through with it and it stinks like shit. Every man with his head torn open, his teeth knocked out, every woman raped and tortured with a bayonet rammed into their stomach…"

Unexpected tears overtook him. At the mention of the bayonet he was seized with a wave of overwhelming shame. His chin crumbled and he stood against the door fighting for his dignity. He was ashamed as he had been the night of his nightmare. He fought for composure and then angry that they had seen him that way again, he cried out in a muffled voice, "Goddamn it! Goddamn it!" as though profanity would lend manliness to his tears.

He wiped his sleeve across his nose to clear the snot away. He avoided looking at them as he got control of himself. They watched, puzzled and embarrassed, uncertain what to do. Danny had never seen a grown man cry. He had heard Mark having the nightmare but had not seen him.

The sight of him now was like that time he saw Eric Lars in the throes of an epileptic fit in the dormitory. He had felt helpless; what should he do for a flailing, convulsing person whom he was afraid to touch? Should he try to restrain his thrashing limbs? What about his tongue? If only the mythical *somebody* would appear. And like with Lars last year, he could only stare at Mark.

Willie had seen Cassius cry, begging in a pitiful, hoarse voice, promising to suck their dicks, anything, please have mercy. That only excited the lynch mob to a joyous, almost erotic, flushed-faced frenzy as they dragged him away while Cassius called on "God, please, sweet Jesus, please…!"

Willie was puzzled. Mark's tears had not been those of self-pity or anger or fear; nor for friends or family, but for people he did not know; for the *idea* of universal, unremitting cruelty. He was crying for everybody but himself. Willie shouldered past him. "You stay here an' get yourself together," he said softly. "We be back." He ushered Danny out of the cabin.

Mark wiped lingering tears away with the heel of his hand. He could not understand the sudden surge of overpowering emotion. He went to the wash basin and leaning over, splashed cold water on his face and then looked at himself in the mirror. His eyes were red and puffy, his mouth held the posture of misery. The surge of overwhelming emotion had been accompanied by sudden flashes of memory.

He remembered that the surge of emotion began the instant he mentioned bayonets thrust into the stomach of women. One flash after another of vivid shame, of pity, of rage and of impotence – helpless, unable to move his arm.

The flashes of memory faded like wind driven smoke just as they had the morning of his nightmare.

Again, they left a faint trace, enough to make him wonder – had he existed in some distant past and had he in some way failed Analise? Could she possibly have been tortured with swords or bayonets? Because now he knew that she was inextricably connected to his life and it was for her that he wept because of unspeakable cruelties in an impenetrable past.

Turning from the mirror he shook his head as though to clear it, perplexed by what it was he had done or failed to do.

CHAPTER 17

Clara said, the night before, with a hint of understanding, "Maybe France or Spain. Not here."

Of course, Jacob was the overriding goal in her life. There was no question about any of that. Her purpose was to reunite with him and to get married and to have wonderful children for him, and she was letting no obstacle stand in her way by taking control of her own destiny. But what had she been to Mark and what had he been to her? What harm could the answer be? Nothing would come of it, but she needed to know how or why, where or when Mark fit into her life.

Olivia Bright, the medium who gave readings in the evenings, was a possibility. But weren't mediums people with crystal balls at carnivals telling the gullible that they would meet someone to love or that there would be important changes in their lives in the next twelve months?

With whom could she discuss this? Mrs. Moss would have been the logical choice had it not been for her behavior earlier in the lobby. Analise had seen her seated alone outside of the dining room just before lunch but had not seen Mark seated with Tank Maynard. Irene and Clara hurried ahead to avoid having a conversation with the talkative old woman. "I'll catch up to you," Analise said and approached Mrs. Moss whose head was bent over a magazine.

"Good afternoon, Mrs. Moss," she smiled. "How's your day going so far?"

Mrs. Moss neither answered nor looked up. Instead she bent her head further as though by doing so it would make the words more intelligible.

"…Mrs. Moss?"

The woman reached down for her bag where it sat beside her chair. She hauled herself up and as Analise stepped back to give her room, prepared to lumber in the direction of the dining room. Analise, flushed with embarrassment and wondering whether or not other people had witnessed the scene, asked, "– Mrs. Moss, is anything wrong? Did I offend you in any way?"

Mrs. Moss offered a cold stare. "Yes! You offended me and every woman on this ship! *The idea!* Sitting and eating with *a negro!* You look white, but are you? Are you one of those negroes who *pass for white?*"

Suddenly she looked stricken. She reached out and took Analise's wrist in her hand. "Oh, my dear, my dear, you must forgive me! What a cruel thing to say. Don't be angry, but my child you really, *really* must be careful how you *behave!* Europe is different from America, but this ship is composed of *Americans.* You absolutely shocked the life out of people. Everyone is talking.... Please, for your own sake...." Then she was gone.

Analise quickly glanced around and then moved away, telling herself that no one had noticed because there was nothing to notice. It was not as though they had quarreled or created a scene.

Embarrassment turned into anger. She joined Irene and Clara in the dining room. Both women sat opposite her. She quietly explained what had happened. When neither expressed surprise, she realized it would have been better had she said nothing. To hurry past the odor of the incident, she asked, "Did either of you ever go to a *séance?*"

As expected Irene shook her head, mouth turned down. She had taken no pains to conceal her impatience with anything that was not tangible. It was only after she understood the extent of Clara's hostility in reaction to her disbelief regarding Clara's grandmother's experience that Irene diplomatically conceded that, yes, there might be some validity to such things.

Clara said, "We went to a few *séances.* I'm talking years ago, before the war, 1915, maybe even before that. I was eighteen."

She said that over time people compared their experiences with mediums and noticed that when mediums described your previous life, you were supposed to have been Queen Elizabeth, Joan of Arc, Caesar or some other illustrious person. The trouble was only one person in the world could ever claim that distinction.

"Nobody was ever a thief, a midwife or a butcher, baker or candlestick maker," she grinned. "Just Christopher Columbus or Napoleon."

Irene admitted she had read about spirits speaking to people. "The funny thing that I noticed," she smirked, "was the 'spirits' always had wonderful things to say but for some reason, before they could get it out, they were 'called away.'"

Clara chuckled. "They always managed to 'come back' as long as you kept paying the medium to contact them."

Analise made up her mind. She would sound Clara out in private about going with her to see Olivia Bright. The problem was getting Clara alone. The three women tended to move as a group except when Clara and Irene played Bingo.

***

An opportunity arose. She and Clara found themselves on deck chairs watching Irene and the men horse around. Walter had attracted Irene's interest; his corny jokes made her laugh at a time when she needed to laugh. They were having fun playing shuffleboard.

Analise took a deep breath. "Can I tell you something in private?"

Clara took a last drag on her cigarette. "- Maybe you'd better not." She ground out the cigarette on the deck beside her chair. "If I know your secrets, you might not like me later. That's how we women are."

When Analise hesitated, Clara grinned, "So tell me."

"When you told us about your grandmother and the horse, I believed her. You do, too. You remember the first day when I said I'd experienced *déjà vu?* That was only part of it. It was because I was standing next to Mark and our hands touched. That's what did it. It was more than *déjà vu.* It wasn't a flash of something. I still remember it.

"I *knew* him, Clara. From another time and place. I almost spoke his name but it wouldn't come out; it was like in a different language. I wasn't afraid of him. I felt comfortable. All in a few seconds and I had a strange dream, nothing I can put my finger on, but I know it was about him.

"I've been trying to figure it out. To me he's not black or anything. He's just him. It's his eyes. I've seen them before– that look of…sort of pain. Does that make any sense to you?"

As Clara took time to light another cigarette, Analise thought of something Mrs. Moss had said. *"It's what's inside us that counts, not our bodies."* Was that why you see people and wonder what they could possibly see in each other? Is it all inside?

Clara blew out a long stream of smoke. The grey in her brown hair was more noticeable in the sunlight. She was neither thin nor fat but sturdy. Analise waited.

"- Know how many times I've been married? Yeah, and I've been around the block a few times, too. After a while you get to know a couple of things. Especially about yourself. Know what I hear you saying? That your 'soul' and his 'soul' are meeting, not your bodies. Is that what you think?"

"– I don't know to be honest, Clara. I guess so. I don't know enough about anything to know what I think. It's just a possibility. I need to know more, to at least talk to him I guess…."

"All I can say is you'd better know what you're letting yourself in for. What about that guy you're engaged to? Look, I've been in your shoes, Analise. Lots of times. Telling myself one thing and doing another even when I know it's stupid. That's why men think we're inferior; we go by emotions too much. You'd best leave this thing alone. *Think* about it, don't *feel* about it. That's the trouble with us girls – too damn much *feeling*. Anyway, we dock tomorrow and then we'll split up, so forget it."

Analise regretted having said anything. Her purpose had been to ask Clara to go with her to see Olivia Bright, but things had gotten off track.

Clara gave her a friendly nudge. "Don't look so glum. These things happen when you get away from home. We do things we'd be too ashamed to do back home. You're *free* now; nobody's going to tell on you. I discovered that during the war. Nobody would ever know or tell on me.

"I could do any damn thing I pleased. Walk down a road naked, get drunk, get screwed and I did all of that. It's just being away from people who can scold you or shame you. That's what you're going through. Back home you'd never in *a million years* even *dream* of sitting down and talking to a Negro. Even if you knew him. Think about it. Would you? Have you? You have to be honest with yourself. This 'soul' stuff is just an excuse.

"Your hands touched? Sure. Now tell me this - when was the last time you were close enough to a Negro to actually touch him? - It was a shock, that's all. Somebody else might have jumped or made a noise."

Clara took another drag on her cigarette before she leaned over and stubbed it out on the deck. She tried to read Analise's face; she continued in a tone tinged with sympathy, "Be honest, Analise – do you still love this man you're coming all this way to see? *No, don't tell me!* No, I don't want to know. You're the only one who has to know. You're free – do what you want but remember tomorrow's the last time you'll ever see him."

CHAPTER 18

"Don't you get tired of sittin' around doin' nothin'?"

Mark eyed Willie's face beside his bunk. After the confrontation with him and Danny earlier in the day, he wondered whether or not the question was a challenge or an attempt to make amends. With mixed feelings he replied, "I'm not doing 'nothing.' I'm reading. It's a new invention."

Willie smiled, "That's like doin' nothin'."

"I guess you're bored and you want me to be bored, too, right?"

His face broadened into a slow grin.

Once the ship got underway, it occurred to Mark that he had never been free to do nothing. Even as a school boy his summers were never his own. To thwart the dark threat of idleness which would allow his hands to become the "devil's workshop," his mother's imagination discovered tasks for him lest he find a spare moment of his own.

To earn nickels and dimes he scrubbed his neighbors' front door steps to a clean limestone white; he carried groceries, swept sidewalks, hauled coal ashes from cellars on trash days, ran to the drug store for Mr. Carter and washed Mrs. Finkelstein's dog.

After college there had been those awful times of unemployment when he had been free to do nothing. It was then that he realized - not having anything to do and not having to do anything were worlds apart. He cherished these few days of not having to do anything without feeling guilty or anxious. The days were vanishing like the wake behind the ship. There was no time for boredom. The ship would dock tomorrow. He treasured the time that was left.

Willie's smile melted. His face became serious. "You know that reader they was talkin' about at lunch? – Let's go see her jus' for fun."

"– You're serious? You expect me to go see a fortune teller?"

He nodded. "My momma use to read folks. Couldn't do family 'cause it won't work, but I know one time she told Mis Eula Mae from down the road that she was gonna see Jesus soon an' Mis Eula Mae died that night."

"– Was she sick?"

He shook his head. He didn't know anything about grown folks' business, but other things his mother told people in Mississippi came true.

"Why don't you ask Danny to go with you?"

"He was making sport about her right along with the rest of them."

"That stuff's for ladies, Willie. Men don't believe in that. At least they don't anymore."

"Oh, yes they do! A whole bunch of men use to come to my momma worried about they wives an' girlfriends an' crops an' things!"

After further blandishments, Mark reluctantly agreed to accompany him, but it was mainly because Mark did not want him to feel alone and vulnerable since he would be the only colored person in the room as he himself had been the night he sat with Analise.

"But if you involve me in anything," he warned, "I'm leaving. I'm just keeping you company."

Olivia Bright (please don't call me 'madam') was set up in one of the lounges at a table that sat behind a screen decorated with a Japanese dragon. She was a tall, sturdy woman with pale gray eyes that appeared to look through you. Her eyes, combined with her blank face, suggested disinterest.

She eschewed the flamboyant, flowing robe and turban which had become *de rigueur* for mediums. This and her lack of a crystal ball may have disappointed some of those who waited to see her. She merely offered herself as a vehicle for the spirits.

Twenty or more people sat scattered about chatting quietly as they waited to go behind the screen when their name was called from the list that had been handed in. Mark and Willie had little to say to pass the time. When it was Willie's turn, Mark held his breath hoping the woman would not humiliate him by refusing to read him.

Willie said she motioned to him to sit down. She stared at him real hard then reached for his hand. She held it and commenced shaking her head like she was saying, "No."

"Then know what she said? Said, 'You not Mark.' I told her, 'I ain't never said I was.

You ain't asked me.' After that she was looking puzzled. Then she asked me who Mark was and I told her it was you, but you ain't havin' nothing to do with her.

"Then she said to tell you that she has another reading later on before the band and singers perform. She want you to come but said for you to wait so you be the last one. She said somethin' about you have to return to Spain. I told her that's where we goin' an' she said that wasn't what she mean."

They were strolling along the deck. Gently, Mark tried to address Willie's gullibility without deflating the big man's enthusiasm and sense of satisfaction. "Everybody on the ship knows we're going to Spain, Willie."

"– Well how come she know your name? Tell me that."

"We're the only two colored people on the ship. People are always staring at us and after what happened at the buffet, everybody damn sure knows *my* name."

Willie thought this over. "Well, the way you keep gettin' upset, somethin' on your mind deep down. You oughta see her. She told me stuff I ain't never told nobody an' don't nobody know. They ain't gonna know either."

They lapsed into silence and stood by the rail looking out into the crinkling silver sea.

"You oughta go see her, man. She ain't got no reason to lie to you. Ain't like you got to pay her. I seen her face. She ain't lying. Go on. I'll go with you if you want. Normally you have to go to a reader; they don't come lookin' for you."

Mark was beginning to feel annoyed. He cast around for a polite way to discourage his cabin mate when Willie said as an afterthought, "Oh, yeah, an' she said somethin' about you deeply ashamed of something.'"

***

Olivia Bright was a little taller than he was. Her eyes searched his face as though to verify who he was. She motioned to him to sit opposite her. He guessed she was about forty.

"You are a skeptic," she began, "but you came so you are prepared to listen. I never do this, but this is unusual. The spirits are clear. We must let them know you understand."

"Understand what?"

"That they are spirits. Do they approach you in your dreams?"

"– I don't know. I have dreams...nightmares – where I'm in agony and feel very ashamed."

She took his hands in hers. "Hush," she said. Moments passed. "This shame concerns a woman, a girl, long, long ago. What other dreams?"

"Just that. I know it concerns a woman on this ship. In my dreams I never see her – a girl, a maiden I guess, but I know it's her. It's like when you recognize somebody's footstep though you don't actually see the person. Something in the dreams tell me it's her and that we're very close and the shame that I feel – it's so deep and real...I can still feel it." Watching his eyes water, she nodded understanding. "Now, you can begin to understand. This woman or girl you speak of would know you instantly. This dream is from the past; you are seeing what happened long, long ago but what you must understand..." she paused as though listening then released his hands. "...What it is, the shame - you failed to do something."

She sat back and released a sigh. "This woman, El, See - I can't make out more, is in your dream. You and she are like this." She held up two fingers pressed together. "Who you are now is a mask or she might recognize you. The spirits accuse. – They say you did not save her...."

He rubbed his arm across his eyes.

"You must erase the shame...redeem yourself. In the past this girl was destined to be saved for another purpose.... Things are destined. Caesar's mother was destined to give birth to him. Had that not happened – who can say?"

"You keep saying 'in the past.' When you die, don't you die? I don't believe people are born over and over and can become pigs and goats. I know what I dreamed, but...." He shrugged, at a loss for words.

Her lips tightened. Her gray eyes were like ice. "– How did I know your name? I know you wish to dig in the earth. It is to find things you have lost in the past – a sword, a ring....?"

He tried to frame an argument but words eluded him.

"You will learn, my friend," she said tersely, "that there are those who return, in what form, what sex, who can say, but some return as a punishment while others must accomplish a mission. Some wish to complete a cycle after which they believe they will be free from this life of flesh that decays. Still others are incomplete, a part of someone else, as an apple cut in two. They must rejoin to become one.

"You may have your own opinion, but you are one of those." She shrugged, "Which one – who can say? Believe as you wish. No one can see air, but it is there and leaves traces. Just as with spirits. You cannot change destiny. You disturbed it too long ago to remember. That is why 'Rue E' freed you."

He was startled. Ruby?

She took satisfaction at his startled expression. "Yes," she nodded, watching him closely. "A name - Rue E." She stood to indicate that the session was over.

"This has drained me. Most unusual, though. I understand better. We all wear a mask. None of us is who we really are. The soul is who we really are. This," she pinched her wrist, "just a mask."

On his way back to the cabin he wished he had someone in whom he could confide his encounter with Olivia Bright. He needed someone more intimate than Willie, someone to whom he felt comfortable baring his soul, someone whose first allegiance was not to Communism. Willie was bound to ask what had happened but just as Willie would never divulge what the medium had told him, Mark would assert the same privilege. He knew to whom he wanted to bare his soul but could not.

Analise.

CHAPTER 19

He returned to the lounge where hours earlier he had seen Olivia Bright. He guessed that there was a chance that Analise might come for the last band performance of the voyage. He stood in the back and waited.

Then he saw her. The two other nurses were with her. She felt his stare and turned and met his eyes. He prayed she would not sit between the other two. She was the first to enter the row of chairs. He hurried from the other end and was able to get the chair next to her. His heart was racing. Clara and Irene leaned forward to look at him. The taller nurse's stare was indignant while the older woman seemed faintly amused.

"Evening, Comrades," he smiled, aware of the sudden silence in the row behind him. Heart still racing, he became aware that his brow was perspiring. He had never sat among a white audience.

Many public places were segregated in Philadelphia. There was no law as in the South mandating segregation – it was just the way things were. There was no mandated segregation in France or on their ships, but from habit he was alert for a hostile reaction. He waited until the performance had begun before he allowed himself to breathe normally. He wondered whether or not he could surreptitiously touch her hand. No. Her hands rested in her lap. He could not even touch her elbow. He was still the little boy with his nose pressed against the window of a candy shop.

He sat close to her yet far away - longing and wishing and knowing that, yes, he loved her and somehow he had loved her before he had ever seen her.

A strange coincidence occurred. The woman with the band was singing the new Broadway tune, "Where or When." He listened to the words; his scalp tingled. He felt Analise move when she heard the words: "...it seems we've met before, but where or when...." And later, "...we looked at each other in the same old way, but where or when...."

It described precisely how he felt. When the performance was over, she turned to him and smiled. "Did you enjoy the show, Comrade?"

"Very much, Comrade," he murmured. "Thanks for asking." And while rising – just for a second – placed his hand on her back as though to steady her. He felt a sudden movement from her body that he could not identify, but touching her felt natural and he had known how it would feel before he did so. He felt hostility emanating from someone behind him but he did not give a tinker's damn.

As she turned to go up the aisle, she looked at him and he knew she wished he could openly speak to her. Analise suggested to Clara and Irene that they go out on deck for some fresh air. He followed at a distance as the ship plunged into a wall of quiet darkness, but near enough to hear her marvel at the sky bright with encrusted diamonds.

"Look – over there!" she pointed. "A shooting star. There's another one. All those stars; you can't see this anywhere else...!"

Though she implored them to stay, they rolled their eyes and headed for the cabin. The sky was just the sky. She watched them go. She didn't mind being alone as much as she did feeling abandoned. Some moments were meant to be shared. She lingered a little longer, watching the white, creamy, sudsy water spread out from the bow and disappear into the darkness beside the ship. Someone snickered. It sounded like a man. She glanced over her shoulder.

Two men stood conversing but not near enough for her to hear. Just then two strollers passed blocking them from view. Feeling uneasy she decided it was time to go. She hesitated for perhaps a count of ten.

The attack was sudden.

She sensed more than heard their movement. Shocked by how quickly they had moved, she barely saw their faces. One was stocky, the other tall. A third man rushed from the shadows yelling something as the men, without a word, stooped, seized her ankles and up-ended her - head first - over the ship's rail.

Screaming in horror, she desperately seized the rail with both hands as she was somersaulted over the side. Her back slammed against the side of the ship. The impact loosened her grip on the rail. In terror she saw the creamy onrushing water beneath her. Then she was afraid to scream, reserving every ounce of her being to holding on. Everything else was a blur – except the terror and darkness and the sea below rushing and splashing away.

A hand grabbed one of her wrists and with her other hand she desperately grabbed the person's sleeve.

She was clutching Mark's sleeve.

Other hands were on her body. She was being pulled up. A vision of Mark sitting astride the rail flashed past her. Others came to her rescue and tried to elbow him aside but he clung to her until she was safely back on deck.

She was crying and trembling from the horror; bewildered and vulnerable from shock. She heard him ask, "Are you all right?" and another voice answered for her. Their eyes met briefly and she longed to have him hold her and comfort her but she knew he could not.

He asked again, "Are you all right?"

Between sobs she nodded. Several women were trying to comfort her.

A fat man with a face purple with rage suddenly began punching him. Somebody else suddenly had him in a choke hold. As he struggled, kicking and flailing blindly, a woman screamed, "Not him! Not him!" She had helped Mark pull Analise back up. "It wasn't him, damn it!" she shouted. "Let him, go. He was helping!"

She elbowed them aside but a few of his assailants were reluctant to let him go. He shrugged himself free, angry, frightened and bleeding from the mouth. He felt dizzy. But he was more concerned that Analise was all right than he was with his reeling head.

Clara appeared. Feeling guilty for not spending a few minutes with Analise, she had returned bent on patronizing her and watching a few shooting stars with her. Her jaw dropped in astonishment. What could have happened in so short a time that Analise was sobbing and nearly hysterical? Seeing Clara, Analise hurled herself into the comfort of her arms.

A curious crowd had gathered.

- Anybody see what happened?
- Who'd pull a stunt like that?
- That's *murder*.

Apologetic ship's officers arrived. They escorted Clara and Analise to the infirmary. A woman took Mark by the arm.

"He's going, too," she declared. "Let them look at him. He got hurt." Dazed, he let himself be guided along, vaguely aware that the woman at his side was the same one who had helped pull Analise up and put a halt to the attack on him. He murmured his thanks and then he waited his turn in a tiny anteroom while the ship's doctor tended to Analise. When the doctor was finished, a ship's officer and Clara hurried Analise back to their cabin. The woman who had come to his aid disappeared soon after delivering him to the infirmary.

***

In her cabin, a ship's officer wanted to know what had happened. Analise, on her bunk with Clara on one side of her and Irene on the other and still trembling from the memory, her voice faltering now and then, told him how she had been attacked by two men for no reason at all. And no, she had no enemies on board to her knowledge and she could not identify the men; she'd never really seen their faces.

He wrote everything down. "- Please, *mademoiselle*, I must inquire. Were you the young lady who was dancing with a Negro passenger?"

Clara's eyes flashed. "Certainly not! Who told you that? We were with her the whole time - both of us." She indicated Irene. "She wanted us to stay with her up on deck but we left. If we'd have stayed none of this ever would have happened."

He nodded, fiddling with his pen. "– But, *mademoiselle*, you *were* friendly with him?"

For a moment, Analise was disconcerted. "If being courteous is 'friendly,' yes. What of it?"

"Tonight did you meet him up on deck? You seem to have been together and the captain thinks that may have precipitated the attack on you. I understand he was also attacked."

"- He was attacked?" Momentarily she was at a loss for words. Then with color returning to her face she said evenly, "Is your captain implying the attack was my fault? Is he? What right does anyone have to murder somebody else because of who they talk to!"

Clara was furious. "Who she knows or talks to is not the point! - *Attempted murder is.* You got any more questions?"

He politely bowed himself out of the cabin.

"Son-of-a-bitch," Clara fumed. "They were out to punish you. You didn't stay in 'your place.' Bastards think it's alright to punish you because you're a just woman and they figure you're a Communist, too, so anything goes! Any way you look at it, it's because you're a woman! I told you that's how these men are."

Ben arrived, brows furrowed in concern. They told him what had happened. He slammed his fist against the side of Irene's bunk. "Cowardly sons-of-bitches!" He peered at Analise and asked how she felt. She said her back was still sore from where it had struck the side of the ship. He shook his head. "Shows how low those capitalist bastards can get! You women stick together. Don't go anywhere alone. I'll post somebody outside your door."

A multitude of thoughts and emotions swirled through her mind. The horror of hanging over the ocean and the fear of being dropped into the sea and watching the ship's lights rush away into the darkness; Ben's remarks, the ship's officer's insinuations and Clara's outburst.

And Mark had been there and he had been hurt. But why had he been there? Coincidence or had he followed them from the lounge? Now there was the ironic and preposterous suspicion that they had been secretly meeting because he happened to help save her life.

***

Another ship's officer with gray hair and a trim beard interrogated Mark. Mark sat on Danny's bunk with Danny beside him and said he could not identify anyone.

"He got jumped, too," Danny reminded the officer.

"Yes, we have received apologies from some of the men involved."

"Anybody going to apologize to Mark?" Danny persisted.

"It was a mistake...."

"Yeah, but nobody's come here to thank a passenger for preventing a murder on your ship and for almost being murdered himself!"

The officer turned away, murmuring that he had no control over events.

Mark had not once considered it necessary for anyone to thank him for helping to save Analise. It would be obscene to think so. And who in his right mind would expect an apology from a lynch mob?

"How did you happen to be there at that particular time?" the officer asked Mark.

Resentment flamed up. "That's none of your business!"

Undeterred, he asked, "Were you two together?"

"He's not answering any more questions!" Danny said standing up. "Come back with 'Thanks' and 'We're sorry.' Anything else is an insult. Are you're trying to say those slimy bastards had a legitimate reason for trying to murder an innocent girl? - *Are you?*"

"The man want an answer," Willie growled in the silence that followed.

"Come back with an apology!" Danny repeated.

"Time for you to go," Willie said with menace, rising from his chair.

For several seconds they all tried to stare the other down before the officer left the cabin with a smirk.

"Capitalist sons-of-bitches," Danny fumed. "They're saying that we're just Communist scum and anything that happens to us doesn't matter!"

Willie turned a grim face to Mark. "You liked to got yourself killed messing around with a white woman!" he scolded.

"What are you talking about! I wasn't *'messing around'* with anybody! I spoke to her once."

"But how come you were there?" Danny persisted. "People already think something's going on."

"I ain't gonna tell you what to do; you a grown man – but I seen how you be lookin' at her so don't make me out to be a fool. You be lynched and burned alive where I come from after they cut off your privates and that ain't no maybe so!"

"All right!" he yelled, getting to his feet. "What do you want me to say? If I'm willing to get shot up in Spain for people I don't even know, I'll talk to anybody I please! Anybody doesn't like it can kiss my ass!"

Someone knocked on the door. It was Ben, face disgruntled. They explained what had transpired. He stood with both hands in his rear pants pockets. He looked at Mark for a long second. "You OK?"

He nodded.

"Don't leave the room by yourself. I'd post somebody outside the door but I figure you got all the protection you need. – I want it straight, Comrade Wilson. Were you two meeting or was it just coincidence?"

"Not that it's anybody's business, but just so you know, I was there because I wanted to see her. After the performance, I followed her and the other two just so I could get a chance to speak to her. Willie's right – I like her. She never saw me. But yes – I like her. Period. And I don't care who doesn't like it!"

Willie shook his head, disappointment on his face; Danny turned away and threw up his hands. Ben's face was inscrutable.

The captain decreed that Analise and Mark were to have breakfast in their cabin. Ben was going to object but everyone in both cabins preferred to stay in until the ship docked the next day.

CHAPTER 20

The *Ile de France* edged into Le Havre on a June morning filled with bright sunshine. The ship's crew marshaled the passengers onto the appropriate departure gangway according to their passenger class. Led by Ben, the volunteers trooped ashore. The signs on the dock were printed in French, but the dock workers looked no different from anyone else. The night before, Ben met with them in small groups in his cabin. "I don't want you guys bunching up when we get there. Spread out. Pretend you don't know each other or people'll get suspicious.

"Everybody knows what's going on in Spain and they know we're not allowed to go there. There're plenty of Fascists here like everywhere else. Use your head. *Don't attract attention and get the police involved.*"

As they disembarked, Mark looked for Analise. He didn't see her. Had she left ahead of them? Was she behind? Would he ever see her again? Port personnel moved everyone along in a steady, uninterrupted flow into a huge shed where they had to present their passports. All American passports were clearly stamped INVALID FOR SPAIN OR CHINA.

"Why have you come to France?" each arrival was asked by uniformed Frenchmen seated at tables.

They answered as Ben had instructed. "I am a tourist. I've come to see France."

Then they held their breath.

Despite skeptical stares at both their paper bags holding their few belongings and their impoverished appearance, they were passed on and once through customs, they bunched up on the pavement outside the terminal. Soon a short, chubby man who wore a blue beret sidled up to Ben. He smiled. The two men greeted each other with a quick hug that caught the men's attention. They were not accustomed to seeing men hug. Ben and the Frenchman moved to one side where they could confer in private.

Mark, his attention diverted by watching Ben and the Frenchman, glanced around just in time to see a tall, smiling man usher Analise, Clara and Irene into the train station across the street.

"I thought I told you to guys to spread out!" Ben scolded in a hushed voice. "Walk up and down. Nobody's going to be left behind." He was tempted to add that they'd make lousy soldiers if they couldn't follow simple orders.

Some of them shuffled a few feet from the man next to them, keeping Ben in sight, but most remained slouched against the wall clutching their belongings. The Frenchman and Ben, still conferring, strolled away toward the end of the terminal. After a while Ben came back and instructed the men to go across the street to the train station in small, separate groups.

Mark was among the first to cross. Analise was in the train station. He was anxious to see her again. If not on the train, he would see her when they arrived in Paris at the Gare du Nord, the North Station. There he would speak to her openly, one human being to another.

***

He did not see her in the station and once the men boarded the train they were not permitted to wander from coach to coach. Later when the train pulled into the Gare du Nord, Ben quickly directed them to a cadre of socialist cab drivers who were waiting to drive them to a reception center in the 9th Arrondissement of Paris. There was no time for anything else.

The cabbies drove with heedless speed, at times maneuvering through narrow, winding streets. Now and then the men glimpsed sidewalk cafes and once bright but now faded carts in open air markets; they saw awnings over shops advertising merchandise in French and they often felt the rumble of cobblestones beneath them.

The reception center was a bare meeting hall located above a print shop on a side street. As they filed into the building, wind blew paper and bits of debris around. A man and a woman, looking noncommittal, stood at a table set against one wall. While Ben took a head count, the man and woman, with occasional smiles, began distributing packs of cigarettes to those who wanted them. There were no chairs; they sat on the floor.

A dozen others were already there. One was a stocky woman who wore slacks; she appeared to be in her thirties. She sat cross legged with her back against the wall, smoking a cigarette and flicking the ashes onto the floor beside her. The men noticed her not only because she was a woman but also because she wore slacks. There were knowing whispers, nods and assurances among them that she was "funny."

Two men vanished into a small room at one end of the main room. One emerged with a cardboard box from which protruded long, brown, crusty baguettes; the other man carried a box with a whole wheel of cheese from which several knives protruded. They were placed on the floor; the men were invited to break off pieces of bread and cut slices of cheese. Unfortunately, there would be no wine.

As they ate, Walter nudged Ben, "Who else is coming?"

"- Guys from all over. Bulgaria, Germany, Poland – lots of places like the guys who brought out the food."

"How many we talking?"

He shrugged, poker faced. "We'll see when they get here." He got up and strolled away to the table where the man and woman sat. The man was in shirtsleeves. He had thinning, brown hair, wore glasses and looked meek. The woman's black hair was parted in the middle and pulled back. She had heavy, stern features that permitted a bare flicker of a smile now and then. Ben addressed her as Comrade Svetlana. The three obviously knew each other.

The meek looking man addressed them with an upper class British accent; he stood on one side of the table and gave instructions. His voice, belying his meek appearance, was surprisingly clear and assured. Small groups of the volunteers would be assigned to hosts who would shelter them until it was time to leave for Spain. Those who could not be accommodated - he pointed to an indistinct mound of blankets in a corner - would stay in the meeting room and make do.

The three prepared to process the men to see whether or not they were worthy enough to take the chance of losing their lives or limbs in defense of Spain.

"After we speak with you," the Englishman said, "pick out a beret that fits. Wear it so you will look more French."

Walter led the derisive hooting. They hadn't come this far just for a chance to look stupid. The meek looking man was not amused.

"The French pretend not to notice us because they have a Socialist government. But at times they must act and make arrests. They cannot shake their finger at the Germans and Italians for sending so-called "volunteers" to Spain then openly allow us to do the same. We understand that. We are not here to debate.

"It is useless to point out that the German Condor Legion and Italian "volunteers" are really regular army men who are *flown* in by the Germans and Italians. The German and Italian navies patrol the coast ostensibly to enforce the so-called nonintervention policy of the other nations. It becomes a game, Comrades. One must learn the game and go by the rules. If you are arrested, go quietly; say little and we will assist you later.

"*Wear your berets*. You will look no more 'stupid' than tourists who come here wearing cowboy hats. Be as inconspicuous as possible for the little time you'll be here. – Now come to the table when your name is called so we can process you. Then get a beret."

The three at the table made no attempt to keep their voices down. Ben stood behind the table like a sentry examining each person with critical eyes. Hannah Goldblatt, the lone woman, was the third person interviewed.

"We thought you were a nurse," Comrade Svetlana frowned.

"I came to fight not wipe asses!"

The four of them entered into a spirited exchange in English, French and her native Polish tongue. Hannah's facial expressions and passionate hand gestures were a marvel to watch. It was clear she was insisting that she could handle a rifle as well as anyone there – probably better.

Ben shook his head, but his tone was sympathetic. "Comrade, I assure you I believe you can fight. We believe you. I fought beside women in Madrid. So did," he indicated the meek looking man, "Harold. Together we all helped save Madrid and we were all inspired by the courage and the words of *La Pasionaria*...."

"Yes!" she cried. "Delores Ibarruri, the passionate one! She is the soul of resistance. We have all heard her cry, *'They shall not pass....'*"

"And they didn't!" Harold declared, face aflame. "Madrid still stands!"

"- It is for her I come. We women can fight and win!"

There was not a sound in the room. The sympathy in Ben's voice and Harold's passionate outburst that matched the passion of Hannah took them by surprise. Both men had seemed bloodless.

Svetlana spread her hands in a helpless gesture. "We women are no longer in the trenches. We have proved we are brave and strong and we do not fear death, but …." She shrugged.

"Help us with the wounded," Harold urged. "There are many ways to win the struggle. Men drive ambulances and they carry the wounded from the field and they are nurses, too."

Her mouth formed a sneer. She stared at them with venom before gesturing some final obscenity. She turned to stalk off.

"- Wait, Comrade," Svetlana called out. She rose and leaned forward, resting her hands on the table. "You have come so far, Comrade, the dangers you faced. Go forward, Comrade, not back to the shit you left! Go back to what? Like many others," she indicated the men in the room, "you have no country, now. *We* are your country.

"There you are a criminal to be shot. You, they rape first. Many times. That is how women are punished. I know, Comrade. I know. *We* are your country, Comrade. Come with us.

"I, too, was a soldier in the war for the Motherland and I fought against the Czar. Many women fought. We carried shells and ammunition, we did reconnaissance, we helped the wounded and we were in the trenches. I know. I was in the trenches."

Ben added hopefully, "Women are still fighting, Hannah. Guerillas in the mountains. Come with us. It's a slim chance but take it."

She paused, her back half turned to them, and then she turned and in a gentler tone, in her native tongue, said something to Svetlana. Svetlana came around the table and the two hugged. Svetlana reached into the box by the table and took out a beret which she carefully placed on Hannah's head.

***

"Where'd the nurses go?" Mark asked Danny.

They were sitting on the floor with their backs against the wall. Willie sat between them.

"You mean Analise, don't you?" Danny replied. His tone was not as friendly as it had been.

"- I guess so, yeah."

"They ain't comin' with us," Willie said. "They got different passports. They ain't got to sneak in 'cause they like the Red Cross or something."

Mark was annoyed that they knew things that he did not as though he were not part of the group. Truth be told, they were probably right.

"They stayin' at the 'lay-say' somethin' hotel," Willie added.

Mark looked at Danny, silently questioning 'lay-say' something.

"Gone an' tell 'im," Willie urged. "We all Comrades."

"- Les Saisons," he said reluctantly, and then he got up to join another group.

A moment passed. "Thanks," Mark said. "I never said what the medium told me, but I understand now about your mother. That's why I have to see her."

A pleased look crept over Willie's face; he slowly nodded I-told-you-so. "I'm gonna get somebody to write down that hotel 'cause can't nobody half pronounce that stuff."

"Wilson," Ben called.

Svetlana examined him from head to toe as he approached. Ben and Harold looked non-committal.

"You are not a Communist?" she asked with accusatory eyes.

He shook his head. She pursed her lips. "– Socialist...Anarchist? *Non, non, non?*" She glanced at Harold who sat beside her.

He stared at Mark with unblinking eyes. "You're not needed," he stated loudly enough for all to hear. "We're after chaps with guts and conviction to go up against dedicated Fascists."

Mark looked to Ben for support. Ben ignored him and called Norman Kahn, the last man to be processed. Mark was both surprised and embarrassed. As Kahn, adjusting his glasses, approached, Mark gathered himself, placed his hands on the table, leaned over until he was nose to nose with Harold and stared directly into his calm, meek looking face.

"Don't you *dare* talk to me about 'guts and conviction!' I paid my own way over here to offer my life. – You Communists are a bunch of lying hypocrites. And that goes for you, too," he glared at Ben. "You're all a bunch of *liars*! Your sanctimonious crap that 'the whole world is on your side regardless of race, creed or politics' are lies. Just make sure you're a Communist, right?

"But, oh, no - we're all just 'fighting for Democracy.' Well, *prove it, damn it because that's why everybody's here!*"

None of the three flinched. The volunteers sat as an audience watching a drama unfold. Like a door suddenly slamming shut, someone cried -

"The man's right!"

It was Walter. Others nodded. Walter looked around for support and then added, "He's like this guy they're taking to the electric chair. On the way, he passes one of his pals who yells out, 'More power to you, buddy!'"

There was a roar of laughter though Walter's joke, like most of them, had nothing to do with the present situation. "Give him a hat!" somebody else yelled. "Yeah", others said, "Give him a hat." Mark was flabbergasted. Somebody walked up to the box beside the table, reached in and plopped a beret lopsided on Mark's head. The others applauded.

Ben shrugged as though he did not care one way or the other. They turned their attention to the last man, Norman Kahn and after they were finished, Harold stood and announced everyone was free to tour Paris but only until midnight. He discouraged them from going as a group because they would attract attention. They might even get arrested. No more than three together, preferably two.

Montmartre was not too far. There they would find a lot of cafes and clubs - the Moulin Rouge, Pigalle, Le Chat Noir. The Metro would take them there. Of course, they would need money. "And if you take the Metro, there's first class coaches and second class. Don't sit in first class by mistake. You'll get arrested.

"The two main streets to keep in mind," Harold continued, "are the rue La Fayette and the Boulevard Haussmann. They're that way," he said pointing out the window. "They'll take you to the heart of Paris and bring you back here. Don't be late."

They would leave from the Gare d'Austerliz no later than noon tomorrow.

"Where're we going?" Walter asked.

"Near a place called Perpignan," Ben answered. "From there we'll sneak over the Pyrenees into Spain."

"Wouldn't it be a lot easier to go to Marseilles?" Kahn objected. He had been a professor of geology at Temple University. "You can get a boat that'll take you right to Barcelona. Beats the hell out of climbing mountains." He looked around for support.

Encouraged, he continued, "You wouldn't have to worry about slipping and falling off a mountain path or freezing to death."

A loud murmur of agreement. Ben waved for quiet.

"Forget Marseilles. We did that back in '36, '37. We'd hide under cargo and get off the boat in Barcelona but that's ancient history now."

Harold broke in. "The Germans and Italians will sink any vessel headed there. Spain's blockaded."

"And they don't take prisoners," Ben added. "Any more advice? O.K., make sure you have your passport at all times. No passport, we can't help you. – Got any more comments for us, Walter?"

"What did Paul Revere say after his famous ride? – 'Whoa!'"

Temporary hosts began arriving. Mark and twelve others could not be accommodated. Harold gave them blankets. They chose a space on the floor and dropped their belongings.

CHAPTER 21

The Hotel Les Saisons was his only link to her. He tucked the slip of paper with the hotel's name on it that Willie had given him into his wallet. He meant to see Analise and take his chances on her reaction.

"I'm going to try to say goodbye to one of the nurses if I can find her," he confided to some of the men. Everyone knew he'd caused a stir by speaking to Analise and then saving her. He told them where he was going because of their show of support for him.

Outside bits of debris and paper still swirled around. He felt a sense of newness and hope. And he felt free. He walked in the direction of the rue La Fayette, through a labyrinth of narrow streets and past store fronts and houses. After a while, every place he passed seemed familiar. Would he end up back where he had started?

He passed people some of whom nodded. How strange it was to be surrounded by other human beings with whom he could not communicate enough to ask directions. After some minor miscues, he reached rue La Fayette, a broad street with tall, massive block-long buildings. He walked along the boulevard, stopping occasionally, waiting hopefully for a cab to appear. At last a taxi drew up. The driver wore a full mustache and regarded him with curious eyes. He waited for Mark to speak.

"I don't speak French," he said, only he rendered it as, *"Non parlay francis"* rather than *fran say."*

The driver suppressed a grin. "To where?" he said in accented English.

"Les Saisons." He repeated it several times. The man shook his head, staring at him. Mark took out the slip of paper and handed it to the driver. In the end, the driver could understand Mark's English better than Mark's attempt at French. The driver put the cab in motion, then in accented English asked, "Internationale Brigade?"

They had been warned about looking obvious. "– How did you know?"

"You are not French and you are here."

After the enigmatic reply nothing more was said for several blocks. "It is bad in their republic," the driver informed him. "The Fascists are to the sea. Spain – split in two. Valencia gone today, tomorrow; who can say?" Ignoring the traffic, he turned his head to glance at Mark. "Go home. Feel no shame." He turned back and watched the road.

"France has bled enough," he offered a block further on. "France alone has sent thousands to the brigades and thousands more and even then thousands. More than any other country. Noble, brave Comrades. Of those who are alive," he turned again to explain, "they deserted, and lucky for them. Desert and be shot by the Spanish or be captured and be shot by Franco." He faced around in time to slam on his brakes. "Worse, Comrade – worse are you who are not French." He turned another serious face to Mark. "When they desert, they may end in Perpignan. "

He faced the road again. "There you will find St. Cyprian and Argeles-sur-mer. French concentration camps for those escaping from Spain – soldiers, women, children, old men. The Senegalese soldiers keep the prisoners. Better a bullet in the head, my friend, than those African devils. A bullet – pouf! Done. Go home, Comrade. I myself was in Spain briefly."

"- I will consider what you say," Mark replied wondering whether or not Spain could be any more dangerous than the cab ride. But he knew that his decision had already been made even though he had heard nothing encouraging about the battle for Spain. Had he been able to read French, he would have bought a newspaper for some news of Spain.

***

Les Saisons was a small hotel several blocks from rue La Fayette. Standing before the establishment, he realized that he did not know Analise's last name in order to ask for her. Undeterred, he entered the hotel and approached the bespectacled desk clerk whose raised brow was a mixture of surprise and curiosity.

Under the Anglo-American impression that everyone would understand English if it were spoken carefully and slowly, he said, "I – came – to – see – the - nurse. We – are – on – a – medical - mission."

The clerk again raised an eyebrow and shook his head. Mark repeated himself several times until the clerk frowned a definite, *"Non!"*

Mark took out the piece of paper that Willie had given him. On the back he printed his name, and then pointed to himself. A nod. He printed Analise's name and drew a crude red cross and pointed to the ceiling. The clerk brightened and nodded. He said something in French, summoned the bell boy and wrote out a message and sent him with it. He smiled at Mark and indicated the chairs in the lobby.

He sat where he could see the elevator. He crossed his leg and sat back in a relaxed position but he was holding his breath. His palms were sweaty. He rubbed them on his trousers. Five minutes passed. What would he say to her? If she came at all, would she bring the others as some sort of protection? Girls did that. Safety in numbers. Was she still too shaken to see anyone?

Fifteen minutes passed. He re-crossed his leg. If another fifteen minutes passed, he would leave. - Well, maybe a bit longer.

***

Analise, Irene and Clara shared a single room in the hotel because they were not staying the night. They had no idea where they were going or how they would get there. Charles, their guide who had met them at the ship, presented a bland face and professed ignorance before disappearing with a promise to return in several hours. They decided to freshen up and relax during the short time they would be in Paris.

Analise suggested they see a tiny bit of Paris. They left the hotel, being careful not to stray too far. Within two blocks they found an outdoor café where they drank coffee, relishing the experience. Analise was telling them a little of her experience in Paris as a girl, when a trim, well-dressed man in tan spats approached, politely removed his hat, smiled and said something incomprehensible in French. They laughed and Analise replied in English, "You're a nice man but we don't need company."

For a moment he looked puzzled, recovered his poise, bowed and walked away. They were laughing about it back in their room when they heard a knock on the door. It was the bellboy with a written message.

They understood him to say "Awn nuh lee." Analise took the note. It read simply, *Mark – Analise.*

"Is it for us?" Irene asked.

"I think it's from Mark."

119

The other women exchanged glances. Irene was alarmed. "The colored boy from last night? You're still going to see him after last night?"

"He's not a 'boy,'" Analise said quietly. "He's the man who saved my life."

"What's he want?" Clara asked.

"How should I know?" She was aware that her tone was sharp, but she was annoyed that Clara should ask that. After all it was she who had suggested, "Maybe in France..." She had hoped that Clara might be her ally in some capacity, and that she understood, especially after last night.

"*.... He saved my life for God sake!* If somebody else hadn't helped him, I'd have pulled him over and we'd both have drowned. I intend to have the common decency to thank him and anybody who thinks that's wrong can...."

She hardly believed she had almost said, "kiss my ass." She'd never said anything like that in her life. More, she was aware of a distant but growing anger within her that she could not identify. It had started with Clara's belief that her assailants had wanted to punish her for violating their sacred rules.

"We'll go with you," Clara decided.

She was on the point of protesting, "Why? I trust him." But then she knew they had a right to be concerned. Attempted murder was not a casual affair. Too, she was still raw and though she trusted Mark, she still needed and wanted the comfort of knowing that they cared what happened to her. They offered that additional layer of societal protection that had been stripped away. She said yes, but could they stay in the background and not be too obvious?

She went to the bathroom and closed the door, trying to sort out her flood of mixed feelings. She knew that a crowd had attacked Mark for helping to save her. Was he still hurt? How did he feel? How could she not say thank you?

Irene and Mrs. Moss's intolerance was but the tip of the iceberg when it came to race in America. Yet Analise realized that her vague ideas about Mark and her connection in some other life were suitable only in the land of *IF* and *Imagination*. She could *IF* herself to death but it would all come to the same thing - he was colored. Period. Colored was a nice way of saying Negro which in itself was a nice way of saying nigger.

And it would always be that way.

As Clara had correctly pointed out, had Analise been in America, there would never have been a discussion of Mark. America was the world of reality and all else smoke and mirrors.

And it would always be that way. Until the end of time.

She began to wonder whether or not she was being incredibly foolish, and in just five days. If the road in America led nowhere, what was the logic of taking it? It would be the equivalent of deliberately walking into a brick wall.

She looked in the mirror. Her lips were pressed together; tiny frown lines appeared on her brow. She tried to relax them. She owed Mark more than thanks for her life. In the end what was more important, her life or what people thought of her life? She washed her face and carefully applied what little makeup she used. Under no circumstances could she refuse to leave the hotel room or give Mark a half-hearted, thank-you-goodbye.

It would mean that the Mrs. Mosses and Irenes and the ones with marble-eyed stares had beaten her down and that their narrow vision of the world was the only one by which she must abide. A world in which a cowardly Rex and snickering, murderous sons-of-bitches were somehow superior to a brave Mark simply because they were white.

***

She stepped out of the elevator. She did not see him at first and felt a moment of panic. Had she taken too long? Then he stood up and she felt her stomach flutter. She smiled and he met her halfway, his heart pounding. He resisted an impulse to hug her and swing her around. Self-consciously, she looked away from his glowing eyes.

Yes, she knew him and felt she had loved him. She was sure of it. He was who she could not remember, but those were his eyes and his glow of love. Through a haze, a distant foreign name came to mind, but not one she could pronounce. But from where or when? They faced each other as though from opposite sides of a glass door that neither was able to open.

"– I hope I'm not out of line by coming here," he said, savoring every feature of her slender face.

"Oh, God, Mark, no! How *could* you be? I'm so sorry I didn't get a chance to thank you but they wouldn't let me out of my cabin but I'm so very grateful. I wouldn't be here if not for you. – Thanks for saving my life, Mark. – Were you hurt?"

"I'm all right. What you went through was a lot worse. You don't know how glad I am that I was there. Anybody who could do that to you...I wish I could have...." He was frustrated because he could not say cut off their balls and jam them back down their throat, and he wanted desperately to take her hands but dared not. "...If you're free, maybe – I mean could we go for a little walk? You don't have to. I understand. It's OK."

She glanced around and saw Irene and Clara in the lobby.

"Yes," she murmured.

They went out into the sunlight of a clear, warm day and without a word started walking slowly toward the corner. He turned to her. She met his eyes. He could not believe he was actually walking beside her, but here she was, her green eyes soft and embracing. He wanted to hold hands with her but was afraid she might think he was taking advantage of her because of last night.

He found something to say. "When do you have to leave?"

"In about two hours, I guess." She could see he was disappointed. "I wish you luck," she managed to say though it sounded awkward and foolish. "Lots of it." She offered to shake his hand though she had been taught that ladies did not shake hands.

He took her hand and in that moment of physical contact, she experienced an eerie feeling that tingled her scalp. She watched his expression change, too. Puzzled, each stared at the other. She opened her mouth to speak but there were no words. He shook his head as though to clear it.

"– I *know* you, Analise. I realize that it doesn't make sense, but..." He shook his head again in frustration. "I don't know what else to say."

Her eyes glowed. "– Oh, I'm so glad to hear you say that, Mark! I've felt that way, too, and it doesn't make sense to me, either! I feel like...I don't know, like I know your name but for some strange reason I can't pronounce it."

"Do you remember," he said, "when I said there was something about you that made me feel sad? Well, the first night on the ship, I had something like a nightmare only it was more like remembering. Whatever it was, I had the impression that somehow and somewhere I had let you down in a terrible way. I felt a terrible sense of guilt.

"And since then, I don't know, I'm convinced we knew each other before but I don't know where or when or how that can be. I mean, it's not anything anyone could believe. I think in my dream," he smiled and looked away, "I was in love with you. From the moment I first saw you at the meeting hall in New York...."

"– New York?"

"That's when I first saw you and I couldn't keep my eyes off you. I've thought about you constantly ever since. I can't get you out of my mind even though I've tried to talk myself out of it because I'm not crazy enough to think...." he refused to say any more.

They walked a short distance in silence.

"- I had an experience of *déjà vu* the first time I saw you– it seemed I'd met you before, but I don't see how that's possible. Still, I remember how I felt. And I've had fuzzy dreams full of shouting and anger, but I knew it was about you...."

They reached the corner. She saw the same outdoor café in the distance that she'd visited earlier in the day. She glanced behind her; Clara and Irene were trailing them.

".... Maybe we met before in another life," he suggested hopefully.

She smiled. "Anything's possible, I suppose, but...do you believe such a thing is possible?"

"- I'm not sure what I believe anymore, Analise. How do you explain the two of us?

She answered his hopeful stare. "The trouble with reincarnation is we could have been brother and sister or mother and child – anything. We could even have been different sexes. Animals even. There are no rules, are there?"

When they reached the outdoor café she said, "Let's not talk about this anymore before our heads explode."

They ordered cheese and sausage and bread and wine. She noticed his disappointment.

"Maybe some things aren't meant to be explained," she offered with a sad smile. "They just are. We're away from everyone we know. We can feel free to do things we wouldn't normally do because things are so much different from...you know what I mean. I've never even spoken to a colored man in my life."

He smiled. "I can say the same about white women. – This is different, though. To me you're not white – you're just *you*. That's the only way I can explain it. I even saw a medium on the ship...."

Her hand flew to her face. *"Olivia Bright? You went to see her?* Oh, I wish I could have gone but I didn't want to go by myself! Tell me - what did she say?"

"That we knew each other long, long ago and that I had to make up for letting you down. I don't remember any more than that, but I'm supposed to 'redeem' myself, but don't you see – she said we actually knew each other in another life!"

He shrugged at her skeptical eyes, wondering why she did not fully embrace what he said. They sipped wine and sat quietly with their private thoughts. Clara and Irene sat several tables away. Mark smiled and nodded to them.

"– I wonder if I 'redeemed' myself last night? If you'd fallen in, I'd have gone in after you. I hope you can believe that."

"Of course I believe you, every word. I just wish this weren't so surreal. I don't know - can you really love somebody after just two or three days? But please don't think I don't believe you, I do, but what's real, Mark, is that I'm engaged and in the real world we shouldn't even be having this discussion."

"– What's real is how we feel, Analise. People are telling us we're not allowed to *feel* what we know we feel. It's like telling somebody who's starving that he's not allowed to feel hungry. Maybe you can tell people they shouldn't steal or kill anybody or burn people's houses down but...."

She leaned forward and said softly, "Hate, Mark... You forgot hate. You also can't tell people they're not allowed to hate. If you can say that, you can say people aren't allowed to feel love, either. And people do hate and love and sometimes I have to wonder which is stronger."

He looked down for a long moment. She wanted to reach across the table and take his hand and comfort him, but she did not. She did not want to know what she would feel if she did because the only life they could live was the one that they had, not a life they imagined.

Jacob sat at the table, invisible, like wind rustling leaves.

Clara and Irene rose from their table as a signal that it was time to leave. They rose, too, and trailed slowly behind the two women. "My mother," she began softly, "always said she was Ukrainian, not Russian and when I asked her weren't they the same she said people are never the same because of hate. Those who want to rule don't understand that or they don't care; they lump everyone together for their own convenience like so much dust swept in a pile.

"She said the Russians who ruled over them were hated by the Cossacks, but in their turn, Cossacks herded Jews like cattle into places called 'Yiddish towns' and Jews were forbidden to live anywhere else and the Jews hated the Cossacks.

"Hate seems to last forever but love doesn't. People remember hate much longer. Still, even now, I think my mom misses the Ukraine. Life can be bearable even living in a hovel so long as friends and neighbors and family care about you.

"I asked her if she'd ever return. She said it's impossible. Nothing's there. Stalin destroyed whole villages, towns, farms. All gone. The Cossacks were never as cruel; at least the Jews survived, but this is almost beyond imagination - to destroy generations - not only the present but the past and the future.

"My mother didn't come to America to find a new home; she feels she was forced out by insane people who were warmed by hatred. Once she was a ballet dancer in Kiev; she was young. Only 17."

He savored her slender face, turned a little to the side; her green eyes dreamy as though watching that far away slender and graceful ballerina and he felt he had to say something to her that was deeply personal and that made him vulnerable.

"– What your mother told you is true," he said quietly. "You can live in a hovel and put up with all sorts of garbage as long as there's somebody to share it with – somebody who really gives a damn what happens to you. You can shut the world out and laugh and dance behind closed doors.

"When I was married," he noticed her stir, "– before she died, it was like that. It wasn't a hovel; we had a nice place, but it was more a refuge, and the minute I left, it was like a lynch mob was waiting to grab me and burn me alive."

"– You were married?"

"For almost three years."

"And your wife died? Did you have any children?"

He shook his head and told her about Ruby and Thomas and his father. He confessed he had not come to Spain because he cared what happened to Spain but because he did not care what happened to him; there was nothing for him to look forward to in America anymore or in life.

She was thoughtful in the long moment that they walked back to the hotel in silence. "That's an awful way to feel, Mark. Awful. I'm so sorry. Do you still feel that way?"

"- With Ruby I more or less decided to settle for 'a crust of bread and a corner to sleep in' but whatever the reality," he looked at her, "- I mean between you and me - you've made life seem such a thing of possibilities. Even now with all the impossibilities," he shook his head, "just thinking of you now I feel I can challenge the world – lose most likely – but it's better to be a fighter than cringe at every frown. I don't want to say 'I love you' yet be an ordinary man."

She treasured the concern in his eyes, and she loved the way he glanced at her from time to time as they retraced their path, matching their steps to each other.

"- After the war," she asked, "do you know what you'll do? Do you think you can stay here where you can be a real person like everybody else?"

He shrugged. "– If there is an 'after.' I can't go on living in somebody else's house where I have to tip toe around afraid to touch anything, wondering when they're going to put me out or hang me. Especially now that I know I had a real past, that I existed, that I was a real person...."

They were at the entrance to the hotel. "– I believe we two are here for a purpose, Analise, and all this was meant to be. This can't be a coincidence. Last night wasn't. It could be an adventure finding out who we were and where and when, and set things to right because I know one thing – I loved you before we ever met so it wasn't one day or two, and I believe one day we'll be a vermillion streak across the sky!"

She flushed and her scalp tingled. Seeing the earnestness in his face, the burning in his eyes, she held back tears. She held his eyes with hers, examining his face for some clue, anything that would help her confused emotions. He spoke of love. Could she speak the same? And what of Jacob? Was she to abandon the reality of him in search of fantasy in a land of *IF?* She saw only the thick glass door of here and now separating them.

Tears came and for one brief, sobbing moment she reached through the glass door and hugged him. She was gone before he could react. But she felt it, the same thing she had felt on the ship. A past reaching out for her. But the devil she did not know was more frightening than the devil she knew.

He stood before the hotel wondering what else he could possibly have said to convince her that they belonged together and that their race had nothing to do with it. What had reunited them after hundreds, possibly thousands, of years was far beyond mere imagination. It was the essence of life itself, yet he must now stand before a mute hotel and know that hundreds, perhaps thousands of years, had been wasted. When, if ever, would they meet again? He had redeemed himself by saving her life last night and that would put an end to his nightmares but he preferred them to knowing that she was beyond reach.

***

After refusing to be sent home by Ben because he must be where she was, tomorrow he must sheepishly say he had changed his mind. He cringed at the thought after the way the men had rallied behind him. But why go to Spain now? He no longer wished to make an end to his life.

The next day, in the pale light of dawn someone in the room above the print shop shook him awake as he lay on the floor. "Hey. You're having a nightmare…."

He wiped away his tears and hugged himself; he welcomed the overwhelming surge of shame. He had not redeemed himself. It meant he must follow her to Spain. He would see her again and she would, one day, remember his name that she could not now pronounce and he would remember her and who they had been. They would one day be that vermillion streak across the sky.

CHAPTER 22

Dear Mom,

We'll be in Spain tomorrow. I'm glad I came. I have a better idea of how other people live and think and feel. I've gotten to know a lot of the men, and they all have interesting things to say. Three are college professors who have given up a lot to go to Spain. No one can become a professor just because he wants to; it takes years. Most of the fellows have tragic stories. None of them except Ben and two of the professors is married, but that is mostly because they couldn't afford to support anyone, not even themselves.

But I think, if men are suffering so badly, aren't women suffering just as much, maybe more? Is selling your body just to survive irrelevant? Yet, a couple of the men say that they have relatives who have had to do that. Is their suffering irrelevant? And what about the children? You told me once that I have too much empathy but I believe that empathy is the only thing we have that will ever get mankind out of the trenches and the mud and filth that hatred breeds. Hatred sees murder as some sort of self-satisfying, glorious and acceptable option. Love, though, is only for weaklings.

I know it has only been a few days, but I've discovered that there is a lot of injustice in the world. That is not news to you, I know, but I guess it's something you have to see or experience in order to appreciate how vile and pervasive it is. It almost has a smell. I can understand now why you were a revolutionary when you were young. I am so proud of you because it seems a crime to do nothing when doing nothing makes you complicit. You were noble, Mom, and now I understand better why Jacob had to leave.

As a nurse I'll help the wounded but I shouldn't have to; they shouldn't be wounded in the first place, and what of all those who never went to war to harm other people but are wounded, too? Do I sound fanatical? I feel that way and know what? I want to shout, I AM! But I don't know how to yet.

Love, Me

PS:

The show the last night on the ship featured a tune from the Broadway musical, Babes in Arms. It's called "Where or When". Have you heard it on the radio? I'd like to hear it again. It is very evocative and in a way, it concerns me.

***

Analise, Irene and Clara were driven from place to place in a van here and a tattered bus there by Spanish men who had little to say. At meal times the drivers stopped long enough for them to take meals in villages of white washed houses where all the women wore black and barefoot children stared at them in innocent curiosity. Men led sad faced mules down narrow, dusty streets. No one spoke English.

On their way south to Tarragona, Clara wondered why she saw so many Germans. "I thought they were helping Franco."

"They're not Germans," Analise explained. "A lot of Spaniards are blond. They're descendants of the Visigoths who invaded Spain. They think their blood line is 'purer' than everybody else in Spain and not mixed with that of Moors."

"- How come you know so much?" Irene wondered.

She shrugged and smiled, "I probably read it somewhere before we left." Once Jacob mentioned Spain, she had hurried to the library to research Spain. She knew it began in history as Iberia and had been invaded by Carthage, then Rome, the Moors and finally the Visigoths.

They sped through Barcelona and never glimpsed its eight sided squares or the Ramblas or the ancient Gothic Quarters. Madrid, the heart of Spain but farther to the west, was besieged by Franco's forces. It had been reduced to mounds of smoking rubble, resulting from the confluence of exploding artillery shells and unyielding human resistance.

The Madrid of lore, stripped now of colorful Flamenco dancers, toreadors in skin tight suits of gold, beautiful senoritas and distant church bells, existed only as a place on a map; her vibrant people, *Madrilenos*, in Franco's death grip.

Tarragona.

The women had exhausted conversation and had taken refuge in private thoughts when they arrived at Tarragona. Built upon ancient Iberian ruins, it looked down on the blue Mediterranean. Tarragona had the feel of a city with its street corners, restaurants, shops, and men and women going about the day's business. When they drove past a sign proclaiming *Aquaducte roma*, an ancient Roman aqueduct, and later the remains of an ancient Roman amphitheater, Analise had been seized with an inexplicable, eerie feeling of unease. She instinctively hunched her shoulders as against the cold.

Their bus pulled up in front of a hotel. The driver motioned to them to get off. They climbed down from the bus, stiff and relieved and feeling a little irritable; they felt dirty and grimy; their hair had not been properly combed nor their teeth brushed. They smoothed the wrinkles from their dresses. Uncertain, they stood before the hotel and looked around at their new surroundings.

A uniformed officer stepped out of the front door of the hotel. He was trim, erect and appeared to be in his fifties. He affected a chevron style, clipped grey moustache and for a moment he stared at them as though wondering who they were.

"Where are the others?" he demanded, from the steps of the hotel.

"- We're all there are," Clara responded.

He came down and turned his attention to the bus driver and shouted something in rapid Spanish. The driver shrugged, replied in rapid Spanish, got on the bus, closed the door and drove off.

The officer surveyed them before announcing that he was Major Raymond Owens. He wore a shiny Sam Browne belt that supported a heavy holstered gun. Obviously dissatisfied, he motioned to them to follow him into the hotel. His office was just off the lobby. The room held a bare table, a single chair and wooden file cabinets standing against the wall to the right.

He stood behind the table. For several seconds he idly fingered some papers. They stood before the table clutching their luggage. Finally, to disabuse them of any false expectations, he said, "Don't get too comfortable. You'll be going to the front very shortly."

Analise detected an edge to Clara's voice when she asked, "Do you mind if we put our stuff down?"

He flicked his hand to indicate they had permission.

"Tarragona is for recuperation, rest, and therapy. It's not a division hospital for casualties. This was once a summer resort for the bourgeois. It's for the soldiers now; here they can enjoy the beaches and the sea air. We even have a library and a café."

Analise timidly raised her hand. "Do you know where I can find Dr. Miller? - Jacob?" To his startled stare she added, "He's my fiancé." She showed him her ring. "We're engaged."

His face reddened with annoyance. "He's at the front!" His tone discouraged further questions or comment. "Our medical teams are supposed to have five doctors, eight nurses, two drivers, a pharmacist and a lab technician. We're down to half that. You'll do your best. The wounded are transferred from the front farther back to the classification posts where you will assist the surgeons in any way they deem fit. Later, the men are put on hospital trains and sent to hospitals behind the lines."

"Can we stay together?" Irene ventured to ask.

He flicked a glance in her direction. "Need comes first and of course experience. You'll be given your assignments in the morning. Wait here. Someone will escort you to your quarters."

He consulted his watch and without a further glance in their direction, strode past them on his way out the door.

Irene, miffed, whispered, "I wonder if he realizes we're volunteers? He acts like he thinks we're slaves or something and he's doing us a favor!"

Clara was dismissive. "He's a typical S.O.B. Full of himself. You'll find a lot like that."

A Spanish nurse appeared. She smiled and led them down the hall to the hotel's ornate ballroom. Crystal chandeliers hung from the ceiling and the walls were papered with gold colored flocking. The room had been converted into a dormitory. Three rows of cots lined the ballroom. Many had already been taken by a group of young Spanish nurses who had arrived before them. Their eyes were curious. Most of them smiled – the common language everyone understood.

Analise pointed to three cots that were together. They dropped their belongings and plopped down, exhausted. Analise thought that soon there would be the sight and sound of wounded men. And Jacob. She must start asking where to find him. For a fleeting moment Mark's face appeared in her mind. She refused to see it clearly.

Shortly after, Clara roused them. "I'm washing up." They followed her, taking turns in one of the hotel rooms. They washed their hair and brushed their teeth and felt clean again. When they returned to the dormitory they saw that the young nurses were excited and crowded around the same nurse who had escorted them into the ballroom. With the help of two others, she was handing out uniforms that they took from boxes sitting on the floor.

The uniforms were dull green and resembled men's clothing. The Americans balked at having to wear trousers. They had never even worn slacks, people said they were "mannish" and would wonder if you were "funny." But the Spanish nurses were putting on the *pantalones,* laughing, joking and trading sizes. Reluctantly, the Americans followed suit.

"With all the mud and dirt I guess it's better than a dress," Clara grumbled.

They were issued Red Cross armbands. The shoes were heavy brogans. Everyone traded for size. The nearly empty boxes had hardly been carried out of the dormitory door when Major Owens strutted in followed by several men in dirty, greenish colored uniforms. The men looked tired and they all needed a shave. They slouched and had guns strapped to their side. They wore Red Cross arm bands.

The Major, speaking in Spanish, set the nurses into a flurry of motion. They began gathering their belongings and shortly after were formed into groups, assigned to a *chofer* and marched from the dormitory until only the three women were left. Analise and the others figured that *chofer* meant driver.

"That was fast," Irene remarked. "I thought they just got here."

"Those men didn't look too savory," Analise noted. "Why are they so dirty if they're just driving?"

"Guess we'll soon find out," Clara said, taking out a cigarette.

In the nearly empty dormitory, they felt an air of uncertainty. Irene and Analise found themselves sitting on a bed facing Clara. "I don't know," the older woman began, flicking ashes on the floor, "We'll be lucky if we end up in a real hospital. I remember France during the war; we took over any place that had a roof over it and painted a red cross on the side."

Analise wrinkled her nose. "What about sanitation and hygiene?"

Clara blew out an amused stream of smoke. "How many beds did you have in your hospital? Eighty? Even if you had three times that – in France - especially during the Battle of the Marne – we used to treat over 800 men a day, sometimes more.

"They'd unload them, lay them down anywhere there was space and head off to get some more. Half died right there on the ground. Nobody gave a shit about sanitation. Any building was a luxury."

Irene said hopefully, "Maybe they don't need us anymore. They have a lot of Spanish nurses now."

Clara drew on her cigarette. "They're not nurses. They're – *chicas*. Sort of like aides. They told me before I left that Spain never had nursing schools. Nuns did all the nursing and they weren't trained. I'm supposed to be here to help set up community hospitals and help train nurses when the war's over. They need us. Volunteers from other countries are the only ones with nursing experience. We have to do the best we can."

Analise had her doubts about her ability to teach anyone anything. A funny thing about Clara was her ability to sound like a died-in-the-wool Communist and idealist at the drop of a hat. At other times, it was apparent she deeply cared about her profession.

***

Later, in the dining room, they helped themselves from the steam table; Clara also helped herself to red wine from bottles that sat on a table next to it.

"If we can't stay together," Analise worried, "how will we stay in contact? I don't like feeling I'm here all alone."

"Me neither," Irene admitted. "I never figured on anything like this. You feel like you're lost somewhere."

"We'll think of something," Clara promised.

Later when she left to refill her glass, Irene said, "I wonder if the guys are O.K."

"– You thinking about Walt?"

Through her thick lenses, Irene held her eye for a moment. She nodded. "– He's fun. Not just those corny jokes. I already heard half of them, but - I don't know, he sort of knows how far to go so I still feel like a lady."

Analise nodded understanding. Irene buttered a piece of roll. "How about you? You must really be worried, too."

"– Sort of. Not like you, though. Nobody's shooting at him or dropping bombs, but he must be a zombie by now. They're so short of doctors."

Clara returned with her wine. Neither Analise nor Irene wanted to continue their conversation in her presence because of her animosity toward men. "Before I forget," Clara said, resuming her seat, "wherever you go, don't be afraid to steal things."

Analise and Irene looked at each other. Then Irene chuckled, "Like taking things that don't belong to you?"

Clara regarded them with a tolerant expression. "It's not really 'stealing,' Irene. It's not for you. It's for your patients. Like gloves for instance. You get a chance to get an extra pair, take them or would you rather infect somebody because your hands are germy?"

Neither woman was convinced. Clara reminded them, "We're here to save lives; nothing else matters. What's worse than a doctor or nurse standing around empty handed-saying, 'I can't help you'?"

"- Steal what kind of things?" Analise asked.

"Like I said. Gloves, morphine, iodine, alcohol, even gauze and syringes...."

"Where in the world would you keep all that stuff, Clara?" Irene asked.

"Cram it in your nurse's bag. Keep stuff in your pocket. Try to be a walking first aid station...."

CHAPTER 23

At four in the morning they were awakened by another Spanish nurse. She managed with gestures to make them understand that they must get dressed and be ready to leave. She held up a piece of paper that read 4:30.

They were still gathering their belongings when stretcher bearers brought in the first wounded man they had seen. He was placed on the first empty cot. His eyes were closed. A cast covered one arm from shoulder to wrist. Bandages covered his chest and one foot was also in a cast.

The nurse led them down the hall to the lobby. It was crowded with men lying on the floor on stretchers. There was something unsettling about the sudden influx of these men to a supposed rest facility. The drivers who all seemed to be weary, unkempt and unshaven, milled about, smoking cigarettes and talking. The war up until then had seemed distant.

The nurse led them outside. The street had been transformed. Ambulances and trucks now lined the curb on both sides of the street from corner to corner. Some were painted in camouflage – green, yellow, black and gray. Several had mattresses tied to the roof. The nurse signaled to someone and then she smiled good bye and went back into the hotel.

A man in dirty clothes approached. He wore riding breeches that were torn at the knee, scuffed brown boots, an army shirt stained with something dark that might have been blood; a visored cap was angled on his head. He appeared to be in his forties.

His face relaxed into a big, easy grin that softened his tired eyes and unshaven face. He announced that he was Barney Turner and he would be their driver. He smelled. None of them knew what to make of him.

"C'mon," he said and led them down the middle of the street, past vehicles with their lights on and engines idling until they reached a large vehicle with a red cross on the side. "This is brand new," he said, proudly. "It's an *autochir* – that's French for mobile operating unit. Two of you can sit up front but somebody's got to sit in back. Won't be able to see anything but you'll be comfortable. There's light back there and an operating table."

Hesitant, they exchanged glances. "I'll take the first shift in back," Clara volunteered. "We'll change every couple of hours."

Analise sat by the door and rolled down the window.

"I know I smell like hell," Barney admitted. "You will, too, in a couple days. No showers where you're going. You get used to it. And by the way, nurses don't bother wearing armbands. You go by that patch on your shoulder. The ladies just stuff 'em in their bag."

The mobile operating unit was part of a convoy making a return trip to the front. Barney waited for a signal to go. No one said anything. He took the cigarette that was tucked behind his ear and lit it. He leaned out of his window and held a conversation with one of the other drivers who stood beside the *autochir*. Truck engines began to roar to life.

After a while they lurched forward. Analise felt a twinge in her back. Memories flashed back of the horror of having been almost thrown overboard into the vast, dark unforgiving sea and having to watch the ship recede remorsefully into the night.

It brought back memories of Mark, too, and their strange attraction to one another. She had deliberately suppressed all thought of him and the disturbing questions from the *Land of IF*. With an effort she conjured up life as a married lady like her mother and Mrs. Arnold and Mrs. Muller. Max, her mother's butcher, would solemnly promise to reserve only the prime cuts of brisket for her and chickens freshly killed. Max knew the married ladies by name. All of the merchants did…. She recited, Jacob, Jacob, Jacob, Jacob…. we're going to be married like them.

She heard Irene from a distance: "…How long have you been driving ambulances?"

"…First time for this baby, but been driving since '37. Lost 8 or 9 of them…."

"Lost them? How?"

"Shot up. I don't wanna scare you ladies but that Franco bastard don't give a – They send planes out to shoot up ambulances and bomb hospitals on a regular basis."

"– *Hospitals!*" they cried in alarm.

"*They're not allowed to do that!*" Analise protested. "It's against the Geneva Convention!"

"Yeah, try telling them that. See all those guys we're bringing in? That's 'cause their planes machine gunned and bombed the hospital. Before that it was – can't think of the name now – Valverde or Castellar - but we keep falling back. Hell, if I had a dime for every time I had to jump out and dive in a ditch to keep from being machine gunned, I'd be rich as Rockefeller!"

They rode in worried silence. "– When you have to do that," Analise asked, "…jump out - what happens to the people in the ambulance?"

It took a count of five before he answered. "Depends. Look, I don't wanna scare you, but somebody oughta warn you." He reached under his seat while keeping his eyes on the road and produced a strange, egg shaped object. "This is a hand grenade. I see I'm gonna get captured, I pull this thing here and there goes the vehicle and everything in it. Simple as that. Medical personnel are allowed to carry weapons for self-protection or to protect patients, but gun or no gun, you get captured you'll wish you were dead. Doctors, nurses…."

"But *why?*" Analise cried. "*Why?* We aren't trying to hurt anybody! Don't we take care of their wounded, too?"

He concentrated on his driving. She thought he was not going to answer.

"The Great War, yeah," he said. "This war it's kill everybody. Civilians, too. Started with that bombing raid on Guernica. Wasn't a soldier in miles of that place. German air force trying out new tactics. Murdered damn near the whole town with incendiary bombs, machine guns - It was in all the papers. Didn't you read about it?

"Some reporter asked a rebel officer how they were treating our wounded men. Know what he said? 'What for? Why waste medicine on people we're going to shoot anyway?'"

Barney seemed to collect and disseminate only information that he claimed was not meant to upset anyone. Despite his big smile and friendly demeanor, he seemed only to see the dark side of events. He had complained that drivers often got by on only two or three hours sleep for days at a time. Predictably, the result was accidents. He assured them that he had never fallen asleep while driving. However, Analise and Irene noticed that each time the convoy came to a temporary halt for any length of time, they had to nudge him awake.

The convoy made a "comfort" stop by the side of the road. Analise was appalled by the notion of squatting beside a highway. She resolved to hold it. Clara scolded her. "Pride will cause more bladder problems than anything else. Come on. You don't know when we'll stop again. We're all in the same boat."

When it was Clara's turn to sit in front, she suggested that Analise go in back next so she would not overtax her back. The vehicle compartment was a compact operating room with bright lights. Several mattresses were stacked on the floor. She sat down wondering what would become of her and Clara and Irene. Barney made the war seem a thing of mass, mindless executions. And hospitals were bombed.

There was one encouraging thing. Barney knew all the doctors and nurses past and present. He'd been making runs since '37. "Do you know where I can find Dr. Miller? He's my fiancé. Is he all right?"

"Probably. You always know when a doctor gets hurt."

Analise told him of her encounter with Major Owens and his dismissive attitude.

He smiled. "Don't take it personal. He's under a lot of pressure. When we first got here, the American Medical Mission was only assigned to the Abraham Lincoln and George Washington Battalions, but you might as well say they don't exist anymore. Shot to pieces. Now they want Owens to treat half the Spanish army with less than half of what he needs just for us. He's all over the place. Be lucky if you ever see him again.

"When we got here in '37, we had about 1000 Lincolns. We got cut to pieces at the Battle of Jarma. We figured it out. The International Battalions were being used for all the dirty work - like shock troops - instead of using Spanish soldiers. Almost had a mutiny. But we saved Madrid. We gave the government time to re-build their army since most of it deserted to Franco.

"We got slaughtered again last March. Our two hundred mile front just collapsed! Everybody running for the Ebro River and getting jammed up like a thousand people trying to get out one door of a burning building. There were two or three iron bridges near Mora la Nueva, and once they went down, we were sitting ducks. All you saw was burning trucks, ambulances shot to hell, guys jumping in the river and planes picking them off...." He lapsed into remembrance. Neither Analise nor Irene asked him how he escaped or what became of the wounded men in his ambulance.

"Now we're back across the Ebro," he said with satisfaction. "Surprise attack. Bastards thought we were done last March. We'll show 'em."

Early in the war, he had been wounded in the legs, shoulder and head. They wanted to send him back home, but he refused. He figured that if a woman like Evelyn Hutchins could drive an ambulance, he could at least do that.

CHAPTER 24

Mark believed that neither he nor Analise should be involved in Spain's war.

They should be together in France, perhaps at the outdoor café where they had talked. There in the softness of evening, they could hold hands across the table and reveal hidden corners of their lives that exposed those vulnerable places where only those we trust without reservation may witness, and come away flushed with the magic music of love.

He had said, "I love you." She had not. He told himself she did, but she was engaged and couldn't say it; he was sure she did. He hoped she did.

They must depend on chance to place them together again. The nightmares had strangely elevated him because he knew that his existence had meaning tinged with whispers of immortality. What was true for him was also true for her. Did she realize that, or would she ever believe that both of them embraced meaning beyond what anyone could imagine?

In Spain seated next to a Czech he could not understand, he looked out at the countryside and felt an eerie sensation that tingled his scalp and coursed down his spine. The land was strangely familiar. Having only lived in a city, he knew nothing of mountain roads or green valleys, yet looking down at the broad valley from his seat on the bus as it crept around narrow mountain roads, things looked familiar; he knew that eventually he'd look up from the valley below to where the snowcapped mountains met the blue, cloud tinged sky, and they, too, would be familiar.

**

At midday the busses squealed to a halt at a camp near Tarragona. The camp was surrounded by a high wooden fence. The flag of the Spanish Republic hung limply from a pole. The sky was overcast but that did not dampen the curiosity and enthusiasm of the men as they clambered off the bus, stretching, chatting and looking at the collection of makeshift buildings and an old, unpainted warehouse.

An officer with Slavic features and a Spanish officer accompanied by five Spanish soldiers were on hand to greet them. Their uniforms were an indistinct greenish brown. The officers wore dark blue berets and a belt supporting a heavy, holstered pistol. With hand signals four of the soldiers marshaled the men into ranks; the fifth was an interpreter. The Spanish officer waited until they were assembled, then he turned and whispered something to the soldiers. They hurried off and inspected each bus. When they returned, the Spanish officer looked at the men before him.

"Are there no more?" he asked with a heavy accent.

The men shook their head. For the first time, Mark felt trapped. He glanced around as though seeking a means of escape. Until this moment, he believed that he could choose whenever he wanted to walk away and return to America. None of them any longer had that freedom. He realized the irony of fighting with Ben to be allowed to come.

The Spanish officer introduced himself. "I am Comrade Jorge Centuria. I will be your training officer, but first…." He deferred to the Slavic officer, a short, stocky man who spoke with a Russian accent. Whatever he said in English, the soldier interpreter repeated in another language for the non-English speaking contingent.

"I am Comrade Ivan Rykov." He welcomed them to the 35th Brigade of the Republican Army. "I am your commissar. For problems – come to me. I tend to your needs. Often men in war do not understand why certain orders are given and why they must be obeyed." He shook his head, a distant smile on his lips. "Orders should be explained. You are Comrades, not tools as in Fascist armies. You are men who reason, Comrades, or you would not be here. Come to me when you have questions. Any man who is prepared to die must know the reason why."

Unexpectedly a youthful voice cried out – "We are prepared, Comrade Rykov!"

Danny's right fist was raised in the salute of defiance. He swung around and glared behind him. "Comrades?" he demanded.

Other fists appeared and other voices were raised until there was a ragged cry of, "Power to the people!" Comrade Rykov, grinning broadly, had the men escorted to their barracks which was a converted warehouse with few windows. It was dark and reeked of urine and feces. Debris lay scattered over the dirty, mud-colored floor. Young Spanish recruits lounging on wooden bunks stared curiously as the newcomers entered.

"Holy shit!" exclaimed Walter. "Are we supposed to sleep here? Place smells like shit!"

"That's 'cause there's shit all over the floor," Willie told him.

To their amazement brown piles of fly-covered feces were scattered between the bunks throughout the barracks. It soon became evident that no one went outside to the latrine, but defecated and urinated on the floor and endured the swarms of flies.

"We're not staying here with all this shit on the floor," Mark protested.

Indignant, Kellerman declared, "We're sleeping outside." He stomped out. Kahn, Winters and a few others followed him. Irresolute, the others milled around. The Spanish soldiers were at first amused by their fastidiousness. The volunteers glared at their laugh crinkled faces. To everyone's surprise, it was Mark who suggested, "Let's find some shovels and buckets and show these jokers how civilized people live."

They hesitated and then set out to find buckets and water and anything else they could find to clean the piles of excrement from the floor and chase the rats away. The Spanish recruits stared in wonder, but a few stepped forward to help. When they finished, the barracks still smelled and smears of excrement still clung in places but they felt they had made a statement.

Walter approached Mark, eyes curious. "That's the first time I heard you open your mouth."

Mark smiled. "– The less you say sometimes, the more people listen."

Walter regarded him for a moment. Mark was expecting another corny joke. "Has anybody listened to you folks for the past hundred years, Wilson? Know why? You been quiet all that time. You want something, something that shoulda been yours in the first place – you better start yelling and screaming. I know you think nobody'll listen, but speak up. You'll see."

He liked Walter and knew the big man was earnest so he nodded and pretended to agree, but privately he wanted to say: "Ask Willie what had happened to him when he spoke up in Mississippi."

Over several days they were issued an assortment of equipment required for the art of killing the enemy – canteens, knapsacks, shovels, cartridge belts, bayonets, rifles, bullets and dull green uniforms. Hand grenades would be issued at the front. More Spanish recruits arrived, boys who looked either puzzled or smug; boys who should have been playing at whatever Spanish boys played at instead of being taught to kill on a dusty parade ground.

Kellerman approached Rykov while Rykov was making an inspection of the barracks. "I thought we were supposed to be with the Abraham Lincoln Brigade," Kellerman said. "What's this stuff about the 35th Brigade of the Republican Army?"

Rykov replied with a polite smile. "Your leaders like to speak of yourselves as a 'brigade,' but you are a battalion. A brigade is composed of several battalions; we speak of 5000 men or more. Unfortunately, your comrades have suffered very heavy losses. A battalion requires 800 men. There are not 200 of your comrades left. We must add others to fill the ranks. It is the same with the British and the French battalions. Spain offers her sons."

Kellerman reported to the others what Rykov had told him. Walter was puzzled. "What – are we in the Spanish Army?"

"That's what it sounds like," somebody else grumbled. "I ain't signed up for no Spanish Army."

They were left asking each other, "If the battalion's mostly Spanish, who's gonna be in charge?"

– "What are we supposed to do?"

Mark only wondered how he could be sure of finding Analise.

CHAPTER 25

Spanish drill instructors issued orders that the Spanish recruits obeyed, but for the other men a version of fractured Spanish became the language for battle. They came to understand the words for "attention," "silence," "forward," "obey," "fire" and "nurse." By pantomime and gestures they were taught to crouch, to move forward, to discharge their weapons and to dig trenches.

No one noticed the two trucks at first.

They began arriving in the morning. Around twenty Spanish recruits armed with rifles and in full uniform would climb aboard. The trucks headed down the dusty road in the direction of Tarragona. They returned in the afternoon. Rumor had it that there was a prisoner-of-war stockade in that direction and the recruits had guard duty.

Kahn was the first to notice that when the recruits returned, they seemed shaken. A few were near tears. Cavalierly the other volunteers attributed it to "Spanish ways." Then Kahn, the teen, Andrews and eighteen Spanish recruits, all armed, were ordered to board the trucks.

When they returned in the afternoon, Kahn himself was shaken. He refused to speak to anyone. Andrews' silence included anger. Finally, burly Walter using the approach of the friendly lion beguiled Andrews into talking. Andrews, seated on his bunk and surrounded by some of the others, mumbled while looking at the floor, "...We were a fucking *firing squad!* Supposed to 'toughen' us up." He looked at them with moist eyes. "*We were killing prisoners of war!* If we do that to them, what about us?"

Kahn was confronted for verification. Removing his glasses and wiping his eyes, he nodded and turned away. Andrews grew more expansive. "They said this one guy was a deserter. He just stood there. Never said a word. And we shot him." He lowered his head in the loud silence that surrounded him.

Mark asked, "Was he one of us – American?"

Andrews shrugged. "Might have been."

Bearded Kellerman, one of the intellectuals considered too soft, confronted Rykov when he appeared the next day. With Walter beside him, he sternly protested that they had not come to Spain to murder men protected by the Geneva Convention.

Standing resolute, hands clasped behind his back, Rykov permitted his face to register disapproval. The Russian carefully examined Kellerman's face. Then raising his voice - speaking to those who were looking on as much as to Kellerman - he said, "Executions are necessary, Comrade. It is the fate of such men in all armies throughout time. Each man has chosen his path, aware of the dangers. The things he fails to do jeopardize us all – his Comrades, his nation, his family. Think about that. This is war, Comrades, not a soccer game. We must not retreat; we may not surrender.

"Believe me, we take no pleasure in executing men. Many are mere boys, but if soldiers are permitted to advance or retreat or surrender as they please, you have no army at all. You have a disorganized mob. My orders are to enforce discipline. We have no time to imprison men or waste soldiers guarding them when every single gun is not only needed but hardly enough. And must we feed them while men at the front and families at home go hungry?

"Each of you must serve your turn on firing squads, on guard duty, latrine duty – whatever the need. We, all of us, are expected to do our duty. Do you agree, Comrade?"

"And what about *us?*" Kellerman objected stubbornly. "If we're killing their men, what's to stop them from doing the same thing to us?"

There was a shout of "- Yeah, what about us!"

"- The Fascists take no prisoners, Comrades."

Kellerman's brows shot up. Rykov's clear blue eyes did not waver. There had been vague rumors but this was the first time anyone heard it officially. Mark already knew. Tank had told him that Franco's forces murdered their prisoners. Rykov's word spread. Others repeated, almost in disbelief, "The Fascists take no prisoners!"

The executions continued. After his second turn, someone asked quietly, "Why don't we just say, no?"

"Then you'll be the one executed," Kahn told him, "for disobeying orders. We have no choice. Just pick up your rifle and go."

Kellerman grumbled bitterly when he was selected; he went reluctantly like everyone else. They all sought comfort and validation when they returned. Some spoke casually of the executions while others mumbled with empty eyes. At first the officers in charge loaded their rifles for them with a single bullet. Condemned prisoners were led to the wall in the hot sun and unless they refused, they were blindfolded. Each was permitted a few seconds to speak. The officer gave the order to fire. As the men were shot and fell, they released their bowels and urine. Other prisoners were used to carry away the soiled corpses.

After each execution the officer inspected each rifle. If the bullet had not been discharged, the man was immediately arrested for disobeying orders and led away. He was also charged with being a Fascist spy. That is what happened to Ernesto and Hector. What happened to them next, no one could say.

After three or four executions, some of the executioners were not as bothered as before. At some point, the officer in charge no longer loaded the rifles nor did he come to inspect them later.

Mark was ordered to the truck along with a group of Spanish recruits. His lips were dry. So were those of the Spanish recruits who went with him. The wall against which the condemned prisoners were placed was pock marked with ragged bullet holes, a few too high and a few too low. The ground where the men had fallen was a moving carpet of shiny, green flies feeding on thick, purple blood.

The first prisoner, a man in his thirties, was dressed in civilian clothes. They said he was a deserter who had been apprehended by the Assault Guard as he attempted to cross the border into France. He refused a blindfold and spoke to them in a clear voice in a language Mark did not understand. Before he was finished, the officer gave the order to fire. Mark aimed above the man's left shoulder, closed his eyes and pulled the trigger.

When he opened his eyes, he did not look at the fallen man. He understood why those who had preceded him in the firing squads had returned numb, silent and changed. It was not easy to murder a man. He had no way to express what he felt nor was there anyone to whom he could blurt out his incoherencies.

Except Analise. Why did men need the comfort and validation of women after their most vicious deeds? He wanted to confess to her; he wanted her to place reassuring hands on him and whisper forgiveness. He was sure she would.

And he knew he could not stay in this army.

How murder people because someone he neither knew nor cared about told him to do so? If a spy were a woman, must he murder her, too? Could he be ordered to rape, to rob, to beat, to maim, to blind, to decapitate? Because of the "sacred word" – *orders*? No, not sacred – obscene.

There was the soldier who had to be dragged to the wall. The front of his pants was wet with urine and the back was soiled down the legs where he had let loose his bowels from terror. He had to be tied to a post by three men. He promptly slumped over moaning and begging – "I came back, Comrades! I will fight with you, Comrades, *I swear, I swear...!*"

The officer gave the order to fire and they did.

Murdering these men did not toughen him. It toughened his resolve to leave this Godforsaken war at the first opportunity. Let others call him by any name they chose – deserter, gutless, cowardly, lily livered, effeminate, sissy, faint hearted, chicken hearted, scared, yellow. He didn't care, feeling above their contempt. Murder was indefensible. Murder could not be ignored; curses could.

Sure, there were cowards, men driven by rigid terror that insanely screamed *me first!* at any cost. For such as those, desertion was never a humane or common sense reason. They were simply roaches trying to escape being stepped on. He was not one of them. He was prepared to redeem himself in any way necessary. Die if he must, as on the ship, but only for Analise. How long had she had been withstanding the ravages of war while he was safe in a training camp? He must find her.

***

Three Spanish recruits deserted in the dead of night. The next morning men on the drill field nodded to the fence and whispered among themselves. Mark was considered a source of information since he had been one of the guards on duty. He shrugged. The only thing that occurred at his post was Rykov stopped to chat and Danny had suddenly appeared. For some reason, Mark's suspicion of them had been aroused before the two men dashed away when the cry went up that some men had escaped.

"They'll catch them," Walter predicted with certainty. "How far can they get on foot?"

Winters disagreed. "They're Spanish. Don't forget this is their country. Somebody like you or me wouldn't even know which way to go."

"Yeah, but you're forgetting one thing," Walter rejoined, "the Civil Guard know just as much. They're like the state police back home. They catch 'em. They're only kids. Hope I don't have to be one of the guys shooting them."

"You shoot 'em if you have to," Willie reminded him grimly.

Willie's lack of empathy was a little surprising but then he had not been called on to murder men who stood helpless on blood soaked ground. Nor had Danny. Mark had decided that the eager, fresh faced young man viewed those opposed to Communism as obstacles, not people. He was content to let "history" judge events.

Mark had contemplated simply walking away during his previous tours of guard duty. At other times he wondered if it were feasible to hijack the motorcycle of one the couriers who arrived from time to time. He went so far as to stop and examine one to see how different it was from the one he had learned to operate while at college.

Ironically it was Analise who prevented him from leaving; staying with the volunteers gave him his only chance of finding her since she was part of their contingent. But Walter was wrong that none of them would know which direction to take to reach the French border. Mark knew, but he did not know how he knew.

CHAPTER 26

Barney pulled up among a jumble of dusty Red Cross vehicles parked near a large mansion that displayed a limp Red Cross flag. There was a scattering of other buildings. On both sides of the road leading up to the mansion, white bandaged men lay on the ground like sacks of laundry dropped off for delivery.

"This is it," Barney Turner announced.

They got out with their belongings and followed him, picking their way around men lying on the ground, some moaning. Analise wondered how long they had been lying there and how much longer they would have to lie on the ground. She resisted wondering whether or not this hospital would be bombed, too. Barney greeted other drivers and exchanged brief bits of news. The drivers all bore the same unshaven, dull eyed, weary expression.

The odor of urine greeted them at the door of the mansion. Inside, chandeliers hung from the ceiling of large, formal rooms; wainscoting, thick rugs and polished floors reminded her of the hotel in Tarragona. Barney led them past rows of damaged men, swathed in white bandages, lying on cots; many had their limbs encased in plaster casts. Spanish faces with red rimmed eyes stared up at them. There was an orchestra of sound indicating various degrees of suffering. Someone spoke in Italian and there was a blond boy of not more than sixteen. Analise averted her eyes.

Barney led them to a room that had once been a pantry. A squat woman with black hair parted in the middle was unpacking iodine and peroxide. She was Comrade Juanita Aquilas, the Commissar. She handed the bottles to two young Spanish women who set them in various places on the floor. Barney addressed Juanita in Spanish. She glanced at the women briefly then turned back to her boxes while continuing the conversation with him.

When Barney turned back to them, what he said made Analise's heart sink. Clara and Irene were leaving for the operating and triage units in another building on the grounds. Clara sensed her dismay.

She unexpectedly gave Analise a brief hug. "We'll be in touch. We're not that far away." Irene's hug was quick and awkward. They left, following Barney past rows of worried eyes and pain-filled faces. Alone with Comrade Juanita, Analise felt abandoned and vulnerable like a little girl lost in a noisy amusement park. Comrade Juanita surveyed her with flat, brown eyes devoid of warmth or interest. Her squat, solid body seemed to personify an immovable boulder.

She spoke a version of English as she unpacked boxes, interrupting her discourse from time to time to instruct the two helpers.

"– You Communist? They say not Communist. Not Socialist."

"Does it matter? I came to help as a nurse. I don't care for politics."

Juanita's nostrils flared. She paused in her unpacking to examine Analise more closely. "Here you *Communist*," she declared. "Socialist, Anarchist – all Fascists."

"I am with the American Mission. I never said I was a Communist nor pretended to be one when I volunteered!"

There followed a rapid conversation with one of her assistants. "Go with her," Juanita ordered, nodding her head in the direction of a thin woman with a solemn face. Analise followed her to the second floor that housed the medical staff. Bare mattresses and folding army cots were scattered among several rooms.

The woman, whom Analise guessed to be a *chica*, a nurse trainee, pointed to a bare cot and indicated that this was Analise's. She would have protested but was beginning to understand that the men lying on the ground outside were a symptom of a war gone bad. Any of them would have preferred a hard, wooden bench inside the building rather than the bare ground where they were at the mercy of sun, wind, rain, crawling insects and flies.

This was not a hospital, she decided; it was a dumping ground. These men, if they were fortunate, might be sent next to the cots in the "dormitory" of the hotel at Tarragona. She struggled between anger and dismay. Following the woman back to the little office, she took her nurse's bag with her. There was a longer Spanish exchange between Juanita and the woman. Eventually, the woman motioned to Analise to follow her.

Scattered throughout the rooms, there were chairs among the cots with holes cut in the seat. A bucket was under them. They were toilets. They reeked. Flies crawled over the seat and the rim of the buckets. The woman slid a bucket out from under a toilet and waving the flies away, motioned to Analise to follow her. Guessing what was coming, Analise, waving angry flies away from her face, recoiled from both the stench of excrement and the very thought of carrying buckets of it. Nevertheless, she followed the *chica* out of the building and over to a huge latrine in back where the woman upended the bucket to a dull, splashing, stinking conclusion.

Thousands of flies the size of bees, rose in clouds of protest and beat against her face and arms and body. She staggered back, flailing her arms and ducking her face. Smiling, the woman trudged back to the mansion followed by a distressed Analise.

After replacing the stinking bucket, she moved to the next chair. She pointed to the bucket and then to Analise and finally to the door. Rigid with anger, Analise drew herself up and stared at the woman's smiling face. "No!" she hissed. *"No!"* She stormed back to Juanita's carton filled office.

The commissar, not the least distressed by the furious, insubordinate American, snapped, "Orders, not debate! Men here helpless. Have no compassion?"

"Yes, I have compassion!" she flared. "A lot more than you have! Why do you think I left a comfortable life to come here? I didn't travel 3000 miles to empty shit! I'm a trained nurse, not an orderly. Let orderlies do that – choose what you want, a professional nurse or a porter. Don't talk to me of 'compassion' when you have men lying on the ground who I could help whether they're Communists or not!"

Juanita's flat, brown eyes observed her closely. Her face held one expression – disinterest. She was not surprised by the outburst. People like Analise had an air of superiority and entitlement. They always thought they should be in charge.

"No other work," she said, opening another carton.

Analise stared, wondering what monstrous insanity was causing this. Surrounded by wounded, even dying men, and 'No other work'?

"Who's the doctor in charge here? I want to see him!"

"No doctors yet. I am commissar."

Analise had heard that commissars were fanatical, political officers assigned to military units to make certain the wishes of the Communist Party were absolutely carried out. They outranked everyone, but why extend it to medical units?

"Very well," she said as coldly as she could manage. She left the small office and picked her way past the men on the floor. There must be those above this woman, someone sane. She would find a doctor and let *him* tell her there was no work for her. Once her chin almost crumbled but she caught herself. She stepped outside the building and stood in the sun trying to compose herself.

She was completely on her own some place in Spain where nothing was recognizable. How could she even find her way back to America? God only knew where Jacob, Clara and Irene were. Was she at the mercy of that woman? She fought back panic. Certainly there were doctors, but strangely she could not recall having seen one or even a nurse.

To regain control of her emotions, she took several deep breaths and held them. Among the vehicles coming and going maybe someone would know where Clara and Irene's triage unit was. Maybe it was within walking distance. Someone could take her there. She searched the faces of the drivers for likely prospects, but the drivers who were not leaving were sprawled in the back of their vehicles dead asleep.

Her eyes widened and focused on one driver. Was that a woman? Was she the one of whom Barney had spoken? Analise waved to get her attention, and then because shouting over the incessant engine noises would be futile, she rushed down the steps to catch up to the vehicle but her way was blocked by an arriving convoy of three trucks. Two were packed with a jumble of things; one held people. Angry and close to tears, she was left staring as her lost opportunity roared away.

The first truck promptly eased into the vacated spot. Doctors and nurses tumbled out from the rear and the front seat. None of the nurses had on a clean uniform. The doctors wore uniforms with pistols strapped to their side. One nurse was limping on swollen feet and walked with the help of another nurse. They all looked exhausted but relieved as they slowly headed toward the mansion chatting among themselves.

Suddenly she put her hand to her mouth; she stared in disbelief. She hurried closer to the truck, her heart racing.

"- *Jacob?*"

He was speaking to the driver. He turned around. His face was haggard, his eyes bleary and his tired expression seemed to say, "What now, damn it!"

He badly needed a shave and a haircut. Squinting, he looked at her. His mouth opened, incredulous. His mouth worked but no words came out. Finally, he blurted "– What…What the *devil* are you doing here? – Is that you, Ana?"

She ran up to him, glowing. She would have flung her arms around his neck but his obvious shock – almost dismay – made her pause. She stood beaming before him.

"Yes, it's me! I'm a nurse!" Now she was safe. Jacob was here beside her. Let Juanita tell *him* that she could only carry buckets of shit. Still, nothing about his posture or his expression or even his voice eased her pang of disappointment that they had not flung themselves into each other's arms. They drew curious stares from those still milling about. One was a blonde nurse who stood some distance away and seemed to be waiting for him.

Jacob, more astounded than anything else, frowned, bewildered as though she had materialized out of a puff of white smoke. He asked her again what she was doing there. She saw no light in his eyes, heard no lilt to his voice - no sound of welcome. She flushed with embarrassment. With others looking on, in particular the blonde nurse, she smiled bravely. "– I came because you're here, Jacob. *I'm a nurse.* 'Where you go, I go' – remember?"

He shook his head and flung out his hands in exasperation. "I can see you're disappointed, Ana, but for *God's sake* - what did you think war was all about?" He swept his hands to indicate the wounded lying on the ground. "People are getting *killed* and maimed and dying every minute we stand here. None of us has been to bed in two days. This isn't the time or place for romance or silliness!"

One, two, three seconds passed.

She lowered her voice, her eyes pinning his. "Oh, I'm so sorry, Jacob. Forgive me. I didn't know there was a war going on. I was wondering why all these men were lying on the ground bleeding with bandages and why the building smells like shit and urine. I'll try not to be as 'silly' or 'romantic' as the blonde watching us!"

He looked in the blonde nurse's direction and she turned and entered the mansion. Analise watched his face. "Are you telling me," she said," that other women – super goddesses, I suppose, can volunteer to be nurses, even *chicas,* but I can't because I'm so inferior? You told me I wasn't 'tough' enough, remember?"

He turned his head away, running a hand through his hair. "Let's not discuss this here, Ana, but I told you that you weren't cut out for this. There's no time for headaches, your mascara, your hair, lipstick.... You're not used to this. Here nurses carry buckets of shit, cook, and wash filthy, shitty sheets when there's no one else to do it. It's like nursing was in the 1890's. You can't do those things. I wouldn't want you to.

"We've been bombed! Ever hear a bomb go off? You'd go *crazy.* Please, Ana – go home. This isn't Hollywood. You're scared of blood. That's all there is here. See this?" he pointed to stains on his shirt and pants. "Blood. Men have sores full of maggots and insects. This is a place with roaches as long your little finger... What can you do but faint?"

She examined his hair, his eyes, his nose, his lips and his stubble. He was out on his feet. No, this was no time to talk; it would be cruel to do so. At some other time she would tell him that she could not simply go home. She would remind him that this was war. That there were no commercial planes or buses or ships she could take. Not even a cab. She would tell him she did not come to be in the way; she had stuck it out through nursing school and had come because he was here and it was where she wanted to be and if it came to proving that she was the equal of other women, only time would tell.

But this was not the time for talk. "Go get some sleep, Jacob; you're dead on your feet. You're right, we shouldn't discuss this here. Get some rest. But can you do me a favor - Tell that bitch commissar that I'm your fiancée and I am not here just to carry buckets of shit. She told me that's all I could do here. Will you do that?"

He looked puzzled but nodded. "I'll try to bum a ride to a village," he mumbled. "Maybe we can have dinner or what passes for it. I can't say when, but then we can talk provided we're not bombed out again."

She watched him shamble away in an attitude of mental and physical exhaustion. She felt crushed. He had slipped away. Why? What could she have done differently? He saw her as a spoiled, weak woman concerned only with lipstick and mascara. After all of these years, why didn't he know those things were only for him? They were trifles, things many women largely abandoned once they were married.

She fought off the comfort of tears. She felt lonelier than she had ever felt in her life.

CHAPTER 27

After Jacob arrived, a steady stream of camouflaged vehicles bearing the salvaged contents of the hospital that had been bombed arrived. They brought pots and pans, folding canvas cots, mattresses, operating tables, oxygen, medical supplies, and a number of *chicas*. A small contingent of soldiers set up tents on the grounds with red crosses on them and carried additional cots into the mansion.

Juanita, aware that Analisc and Jacob were engaged, assigned her the normal duties of a nurse. Analise approached the first few days with a dread that never went away. She had dreams of naked men with open wounds screaming – "Nurse! Nurse!" And when she tried to go to their aid she found she was paralyzed. It was the horrible feeling of being paralyzed that woke her up in a mild panic.

She did not know any of the staff. She sat on her army cot in the morning, gathering the resolve to walk into rooms filled with pain and horror. She scolded herself for being weak. What would Jacob say - "I told you so." Had she come all this way only to creep back home having ceded her self-respect and dignity? And perhaps encouraged Jacob's admiration for someone else? She knew that she needed a loving eye and a welcome voice and a warm hug to erect walls against her fears, but they weren't there so she must leave her cot and like the king in Shakespeare's play, go "once more into the breach."

She had never been in charge of anything before; now she was in charge of part of a ward because she was one of the few real nurses on the premises. Work in the wards was mocked as "bed pan duty." The "better" nurses were considered too valuable and were assigned to the surgeons or to triage. In the ward she fought through the pervasive, heavy smell of feces and urine that stung her eyes.

However, when Miguel looked up at her, lying on his cot helpless with both arms in casts and worse, paralyzed from the waist down - it was the look in his eyes that told her that he was a person imprisoned in his own body, staring from behind the merciless bars of immobility. She was his only door to the world. He depended on her humanity.

"What do you need?" she asked in broken Spanish.

He smiled at her awkwardness and made her understand that he wanted water. It was so simple a task as helping him drink that made the difference for her. She wondered about the next time he needed water. How does one drink whose arms are immobilized? How does one urinate? Clouds of other "how's" conquered her fears; she was compelled to help these men. It became more an obligation than a duty.

She never saw a doctor who was not harried. One or two strolled through the ward without really doing anything. They barely read the charts, seldom listened to anyone and saw everything through desensitized eyes. Time, not medicine, was their master.

Within a week the *chicas* - a collection of ill- prepared girls and women – grew to admire her. She taught by example how to properly administer an enema, insert a catheter, take blood pressure, temperature and how to use the single spare stethoscope to listen for vital signs and more importantly, how to understand what they meant.

Chicas must help the men with urinals and bedpans, chase the flies from their face, and wash the upper parts of their body. The men suffered from pneumonia, jaundice, diarrhea and constipation. The messiest cases were those with diarrhea. She remembered that in the early days, nurses like Kendricks had been trained like this.

The *chicas* marveled that Analise wore gloves. The gloves saved her. Heeding Clara's advice to appropriate things, she chose gloves. She steeled herself against the sight of jelly-red wounds but it was the maggots and multiplying insects crawling over the wounds that unnerved her. In the beginning she was afraid she would faint and fall on the open wounds, adding excruciating pain to a soldier's agony.

The gloves insulated her from the feel of feces and vomit and men's penises. With gloved hands she closed her eyes and brushed away the insects, instructing the chicas to kill them which they did by squashing them between their fingers. This made her shudder, especially when they squashed the squirming, white, fat maggots.

Juanita expressed outrage when Analise instructed the *chicas* to gather and separate the patients' uneaten food. Analise then gave it to hungry refugees who came to the door, in exchange for their performing tasks around the ward. She set children to work chasing and catching flies that not only carried disease but tormented the patients.

"You feed children garbage!" Juanita accused with hard, brown eyes and flaring nostrils.

"What you take us for?"

"They already pick from the garbage cans!" she shot back. "If I care for your people, why shouldn't you?"

Being irritable and vindictive did not equate to stupidity; Juanita understood that what Analise was doing would reflect well on how well she ran the hospital. She resigned herself to a sullen, tight lipped glower.

***

Then there was Hannah Goldblatt, the only woman soldier. She was in serious danger of losing a leg to gas gangrene. It had ballooned to over twice its size and had turned black; it was oozing yellow pus where the swollen skin had split open.

Analise had never seen a woman soldier. She had seen photographs of women in Madrid with raised fists, brandishing rifles and shouting slogans but the pictures had seemed posed, a thing of make believe. No one knew to which military unit Hannah belonged and she claimed, since sustaining a head injury, she could not remember. But everyone knew there were no longer any women soldiers. Yet here she was.

She had to be placed with the men since there was no room to spare. Analise felt a personal sense of shame at her being there, as though she herself were on a toilet when a man walked in. Hannah was a solidly built woman with strong, Slavic features though she was a Polish Jew. Juanita detested her. "She full of hate," she complained. "She 'funny.' Never shut up. Pain in ass!"

Analise smiled agreeably but, without thinking, offered the view that, "Women like to talk. There're nothing but men in there."

Juanita's face indicated that she was not pleased with being contradicted by someone who was not a Communist or even a Socialist.

Though Hannah never complained, Analise saw pain in her eyes when she wanted to move. An exploding shell had thrown her violently against a truck, severely damaging her leg and back. It continued to bother Analise that Hannah had no privacy. Once when Hannah made her way painfully to the chair-toilet, Analise held a sheet up around her.

Hannah looked up and laughed. "Who cares what they see. I would feel shame if for one moment I cared. I have nothing they have not seen. You are not married; I can see you know nothing of men."

Analise smiled agreeably, helping the larger woman back to her cot. Grimacing, Hannah slowly settled herself, breathing heavily. For a quiet moment, she seemed undecided. Softly she spoke: "You should know - I am not a woman. I am not ashamed. I cannot tolerate men.... I was not born with hatred. I learned to hate at the university. You would, too, had you my eyes and my mind but you lack both."

Later, when Analise saw Hannah asleep, she saw the girl she had once been and wondered whether or not she felt isolated and alone. How could she not?

"What did you study at university?" she asked her several days later after helping her into bed. Her face relaxed.

"Many things. Philology, history, literature. I wished to be a professor and I might have been, but it was pointed out that I was a Jew and we were barred from teaching. Even before the Nazis, it was pointed out that I was a woman."

When a satirical smile curled her lips, she reminded Analise of Clara. "Over time it was 'correctly' pointed out that from the beginning of time, we women have been the principal cause of all the evil in the world. We must be suppressed. Yes. As you know women alone are witches and Jezebels and Eve cursed all of mankind and introduced sin into the world.

"Think about it," she continued, the satirical smile hardening. "Helen alone caused the destruction of Troy by 'allowing' herself to be overpowered, kidnapped and raped. Even Grendel was a monster to be hunted down for attempting to avenge the murder of her only child. You see, only men are permitted vengeance.

"Remember Pandora? She opened the box to release plagues and evils on the world. Read your history - women's armies have butchered more millions of people than Genghis Khan, Alexander, Caesar, Vlad the Impaler and Napoleon combined. But unlike them, we have no monuments to glorify our 'butcheries.' No statues of us on horses, no Brandenburg Gate or *Arc de Triomphe*. No granite fingers pointing to the sky in memory of us.

"It is even a misfortune to be born. A useless, female child. In China they are abandoned. Surely you know that you are shallow, unbalanced, credulous, childish and have a tendency to rebel against noble man's efforts to correct your behavior?"

The smile was gone. Though her voice had been tinged with anger, Analise noticed her eyes glisten. Analise reached over and took her hand in hers. Hannah was surprised but did not pull her hand away.

"– It is the reason," she continued, "that we were not permitted books, denied entrance to university and the professions and why we 'undisciplined children' cannot vote, divorce, own property or have final say as to the children we risked our lives to bear. But that is only a part of the reason for my hatred. Another day when I am not tired... – I wonder - would you be able to bring me a cup of tea? I have not had tea since I got here...."

Hannah occupied Analise's thoughts at odd moments during the day. Why was a highly-educated woman choosing to be a soldier? She was throwing her life away. As it was, she would lose her leg and be a cripple for the rest of her life if she even survived.

Analise brought her tea one afternoon and finally asked, "- Why did you choose to be a soldier, Hannah?"

Hannah was able to sit up now and move around by holding on to things. She was a sturdy woman but she was losing weight, and pain often streaked across her face like lightning. She did not answer at first as though considering whether or not it was anybody's business. She sipped her tea, and then looked at Analise for a thoughtful moment.

"– I chose to be a soldier because my war is with men and I care only to kill them. This is my opportunity. I care nothing for who they are; there are scores I must settle. I was raped once. I was twenty-two. They said I was too 'independent.' Three of them. They took turns all night. It was an act of vengeance against me. They called me filthy names. They stood over me and peed in my face. I remember their faces but I never saw them again.

"I smothered the child I bore and I am not ashamed. It was conceived in evil and would be their final victory. I smothered it to kill them, so let it be. I have only killed eight men so far of which I am certain, but still it warms my heart...."

***

Another nurse, short with worried looking eyes, was assigned to the staff. "I am Dulce," she said in accented English. She was Puerto Rican. Analise could have hugged her. Here was someone with whom she could speak and she was friendly. "Thank God!" she breathed to herself. "I am Analise," she smiled. "Come with me; I'll help you get settled."

Dulce was a few years older but she was of little help. Analise was grateful for her friendly voice and for her presence, but though they had agreed to divide their duties, Dulce spent most of her time by Analise's side. At some point, Dulce let it slip that she herself had never been a mere ward nurse. It was then that Analise noticed that the other woman's hands trembled and at times her mind seemed to wander.

"Have you been here long?" Analise asked, after they had struggled carrying a patient who had fainted back to his mattress.

"- Since April."

"That's a long time to be in a war isn't it?"

She nodded, her eyes fearful. "The bombs." She shuddered, hunching her shoulders and hugging herself. "I was not prepared. I thought I would be safe. No one told me they bombed hospitals. I am to leave soon and return to Cuba. I am no use in the operating room anymore." She held out her hand so that Analise could appreciate the tremor. "The noise is …is like *death*; each time like death and it goes on and on…. If we must retreat again…." She shook her head. Her eyes were mournful. Analise hugged her and could feel her body tremble. It took a moment or two for Dulce to collect herself. She brushed away a tear with her sleeve.

Analise asked, "How often have you done that – retreated?"

She smiled ruefully and held up three fingers. "It is always a panic and confusion. We leave men on the ground…"

"– You leave patients?"

She nodded. "If there is room for fifty and there are one hundred…" she looked off into the middle distance. "That is the worst. We must move everything almost immediately – the men, the equipment – everything and start all over again, like now. I am afraid; it will never end …."

***

Analise discovered that there was no healing in the mansion. Most of the men had not seen a doctor beyond the first cast or bandage. They might wait for as long as ten days for the occasional doctor to appear and render further treatment. Every day new patients arrived and every day a dozen or so were transported to hospitals across the Ebro or to the division hospital in Barcelona.

The most she could do was move through the ward demonstrating technique by example and sign language; she gave a nod here, a frown and a shake of the head there and perhaps a smile somewhere else. She welcomed Dulce's help interpreting.

No one got time off. "Free time" was spent collapsed on a cot. When someone on the staff got injured, or requested to be sent back home, it created shortages that were rarely addressed. Clara, Irene and she were replacing the loss of eight nurses.

And Jacob. How odd that he was within walking distance in the surgical building yet she never saw him except on the few occasions when he hurried into the ward to discuss something with Juanita before rushing away again. It was as though he and she had been lowered into different lifeboats from a sinking ship – so near and yet so far away. And the volunteers? What life boat were they in? Had they joined the fighting? Were any of them wounded, perhaps mortally? Could Mark be one of them?

***

"-I can meet you later if you can get away," Jacob said.

She looked up, surprised. She had not heard him approach. He still looked tired. Her impulse was to fly to him and hug the tiredness away but she knew she could not. She smiled, examining his face. "I'll get away," she promised, "at least for a little while."

Several enterprising villagers provided wine and food in their kitchen and did laundry for anyone willing to pay. Analise and Jacob managed to meet in one of the crowded kitchens. The food did not matter; they both knew that. He appeared in a military uniform with a red cross on his arm. He was noticeably thinner. For a moment they sat in silence, almost strangers.

"I hope you were able to get some rest, Jacob. You looked so exhausted."

"We're all exhausted. – Are things any better with the commissar?"

She nodded. "Thanks for speaking to her." She told him what she had been doing at the hospital and searched his face for signs of approval. He listened and nodded and seemed interested.

"- Are the field hospitals close to the fighting?"

"Close enough. We have to rotate with the other staff there. We have to go back in two more days."

"The nurses, too?"

"Nurses aren't required to go but some do if they're up to it."

"The blonde one who likes you, too?"

Annoyance crossed his face. "We're just Comrades, for God's sake. I'd like to have ten Giselle's. You have absolutely no idea what we have to go through or what it's like doing what we have to do day in and day out hour after hour and there were times, far, far too many when I couldn't even wash my hands! Surgery should be performed within eight hours; we don't see some of these men for twelve hours or more! God! Do you know what that means to me? I'm *killing* men, Ana. Killing them."

"- I think I have an idea what it's like, Jacob. Anyone can tell from the men here. As soon as you're done with two, they drive up with ten more on top of the ones you already have waiting; you're always running up a slippery hill and falling farther behind. And I know what it must mean to have somebody there to help!" She reached across the table and took his hand.

"*It's why I came, Jacob!* It's why I'm going to ask to be assigned wherever you are because I want to be the one helping you."

"-Assigned?" He shook his head sadly. "– You really have no idea what this is all about, do you? Most of us last about eight months. I'm overdue and I can't last much longer. None of us will. If I didn't care about you I wouldn't care where you went. Stay where you are, Ana. Please.

"We're so understaffed there's no telling where you'd end up. The American Medical Bureau is not serving the Lincoln Battalion anymore. There aren't enough Lincolns left to justify a separate medical unit. We've been taking care of Spanish, French, the British...Ask yourself -

how many Americans have you seen? I'm the only American doctor on our staff."

"What do you mean you can't last much longer?"

He removed his glasses and rubbed his eyes. "Your nerves get shot. What good's a surgeon with shaky hands, Ana? I can do other things, but I'm not sure I want to stay here. It's nerves but I can't let it get worse. We're supposed to have five doctors on our team. We're down to two. Out of eight nurses, three are left. I think I've done my bit. Even Major Owens thinks so."

"Major Owens? – What does he have to do with it?"

"He's in charge of everything."

"We can leave together, then?"

"Of course, if it's possible."

"– 'Possible?'"

"We may not both be able to get a safe conduct pass from the major at the same time. It's up to him when you can leave and he's not stationed in any one place; he's all over the front and even takes a turn operating. It's going to take a bit of luck getting to him.

"– And I know this may sound funny, Ana, but we shouldn't be seeing each other socially - let me finish – because officers aren't supposed to 'fraternize' with non-officers. It wasn't that way in the beginning of the war. Everybody was equal. There were no officers, no stripes, ribbons, no distinctions. Everyone was just *comrade*. – Everybody ate the same food, no saluting…we were equal, but a lot of things changed since we were incorporated into the regular Spanish Army."

"- Am I supposed to pretend we're not engaged, Jacob?"

"No, but it can't be blatant. Everyone knows or will know but it can't appear that separate rules apply. "

She was silent, trying to digest everything he had said and what it meant. She resolved to parse it another day so she smiled and they reminisced about the things they had done and the things they had seen but did not mention the things that they wished to do. They returned to the hospital late that night where they engaged in a tentative kiss.

CHAPTER 28

One afternoon, trucks arrived to transport the men to the front.

They assembled on the drill field in a large semi-circle. Centuria, with Rykov beside him, stood on a box to address them. Silently, Centuria held up a wine bottle. He turned it upside down. He spoke slowly so that his message could be interpreted.

"You," he shouted, "together with our other Comrades, are the cork!" He removed the cork. Wine spilled out. *"The blood of our Comrades!* You, me, all of us are the cork." He replaced the cork. The wine ceased flowing.

"We are the cork, Comrades. We must stop the Fascists. I must be honest. We face grave times. The Fascists are aided by Germany's Condor Legion and Italy; they send tanks and artillery to our enemies. We were defeated early this year but we have regained ourselves; we have gone *back across the Ebro*. Together we say – TO THE EBRO!" Led by Rykov everyone shouted, - "TO THE EBRO!" They boarded the trucks for the journey to the Ebro River which divided the government forces from those of the insurgents.

"Where's Kellerman?" Cecil Winters asked. He was saving a seat for him. Along with Kahn, the three always stayed together.

"Maybe on one of the other trucks," someone guessed.

Kellerman had drawn guard duty the night before. Winters was preparing to look for him when the truck lurched forward. With an oath he resumed his seat.

After they were in motion, Willie turned to Mark. "You nervous like me?"

He nodded, wondering how in the world he was going to find Analise and get out of this stupid war.

"Reckon we all nervous," Willie continued, making no attempt to keep his voice down.

Others mumbled agreement. "But," Willie continued, "you know somethin'? It feel down right good to fight back." More voices were raised in agreement. Waxing to the subject he declared, "Half the time all you can do is let 'em beat you worsen a mule. When you a Communist," he said directly to Mark, "you part of something big, you protected."

"Well said, Comrade," Danny called out. He had become Rykov's favorite from the moment he had shouted, "We are prepared, Comrade!" Rykov instructed Centuria to promote him to corporal to the amusement of the more mature men. Mark considered Danny the most dangerous Communist of the group because Danny held no personal grievance against the government or society.

His family spent vacations by the sea at Cape Cod. Had they lived in Russia just ten years ago, they would have been cast out of their homes, stripped of everything of value and would have counted themselves fortunate at not having been shot outright.

But Danny was on his way to evolving into the sort of ideologue for whom the end justified the means as he pledged his life to eradicate the evils of a flawed and mangled capitalistic system that was inherently unjust. Let history, like the grass and trees of nature, cover with diminished memory the sights and sounds, screams, protests and anguish of the means. At age twenty, like others his age, he was supremely confident in his knowledge of men and morality and the world.

Astride a snorting, white stallion, brandishing his youthful sword of fairness and justice in one hand and holding the banner of equality, decency and compassion in the other, he charged into the fray, convinced beyond all reason in the cause of Communism. Like the intellectuals, he was one of the few who had not personally suffered injustice, yet protested because his neighbor suffered.

The other volunteers had drifted, like fall leaves, across wind swept fields of grievances, gathering into piles. The swirling leaves were the indictments of the impoverished, the unemployed, the disillusioned, the beaten, the broken, the wounded, the emasculated – all the tinder for all of the blazes for the past, the present and the future.

They gathered in piles. One pile was the Young Communist League, another was the Socialist Labor Party and there were others. Occasionally the leaves were set aflame and roared into strikes accompanied by fists, bottles, bricks and bullets until the leaves –

consumed – smoldered angrily into yells and imprecations. There was the belief that there would come the day when the flames would spread and become walls of red and orange, burning away family illness, suffering, hunger, degradation and humiliation.

"My sister's a whore," Renfro told them. "We all knew it except mom." He uttered an abrupt, barking laugh. "Mom didn't want to know, either."

Most of the men had been knocked about over the years. They knew real hunger for themselves and for those for whom they cared. Walter had been persecuted and jailed for being a hobo riding the rails; again for being a persistent union organizer and agitator; the police denied Clarkson's family entry into California after the Dust Bowl had destroyed his family's livelihood; Steiner was shot in the thigh because he was in a picket line; one or two said they had been a part of the Bonus Army that marched on Washington and that had been beaten and shot at by soldiers led by officers with whom they had fought with during the Great War.

Mark could understand why some of them could look at him askance. He at least had had a job making twelve dollars a week and that, to them, seemed adequate. Hell, twelve dollars was more than the twenty-five cents an hour minimum wage for a 44-hour week that Congress had just passed. The only people making any real money were the guys at US Steel; they were going to start getting five dollars a day *minimum*.

Mark sometimes felt under subtle attack on the ship. Once at breakfast Willie pretended to be perplexed. For the life of him, he complained to the table, he could not understand why so many people were scared to be Communists when they were already lying flat on their back too weak to stand. "Don't make no kinda sense," he declared, chewing ham and eggs. Mark was certain his remark was aimed at him. He pretended not to notice and concentrated on his pancakes.

"'Cause they all wanna be rich, that's why!" Walter snapped. "They wanna live the 'good life.' Know what that means?" He surveyed the table, fork poised in one hand, knife in the other, shaggy head thrust forward. "– Having more than the next fella. You and me. That's what it means. A car, a big house, fur coats…." His outburst took them by surprise. They were used to his quips and jokes.

Willie took it up. "They wanna be middle class; boarwashE."

Walter seized on this. "Damn straight. Know what's wrong with that? Know what's wrong?" he glared around the table for signs of dissent, "– I'll tell you what's wrong. You can't be 'middle class' unless you got a *lower class* just like you can't have aristocrats without peasants!" He turned to Ben who sat at the head of the table with his arms folded. "Am I right?"

Ben shrugged and replied mildly, "Takes time, Walt, and patience."

Walter continued, "Way I see it, a fella'd rather starve and watch his family starve than join us. I've seen it with my own eyes. Guys whining that they don't want people telling them what to do, when that's all they been used to all their lives! - How about you guys - any of you seen it?"

Callaway, a former butcher, came forward. "Fella told me Communists won't let you own anything. I said, 'What the hell do you own *now*. Nothing.' Don't have a pot to piss in."

Walter screwed his face into a contemptuous sneer. "They don't wanna be called 'workers' or 'proletariat.' Hell, I seen men wouldn't even join the union when it's for their own damn good!" He turned to Ben. "We can't be 'patient' and wait for people like that to do the right thing…."

Ben motioned to him to keep his voice down. Leaning forward, he said just above a whisper, "We have to *seize* power first like they did in Russia! Seize it! That means take it from the police and the army."

"He right," Willie rumbled quietly. "Don't need no phony election. They fix 'em any which way they want. I seen colored folk trucked to town an' told who to vote for with white folks standin' right over 'em! I was one of 'em. Rounded us up like hogs. Ain't no difference if we take power. Least it be for they own good."

Looking grim and nodding, they all agreed with him. Danny said softly, "Power to the people!"

Mark remembered that day clearly; he did not know what his face had revealed, but today, sitting in a truck next to Willie on the way to the Ebro, he knew he had no business being among these men. They were prepared to die for Spain, while he thought only of a means to find

Analise and escape. Ben's instincts had been right in Paris when he tried to exclude him from the contingent, and before that Willie and Danny had confronted him. Had it not been for Analise, he might have gone back home.

***

And Rykov was suspicious of him, too.

The day before the three men had deserted over the fence, Rykov had sent for him. His office was a small bare room in the warehouse with a large crate that served as a desk. When Mark presented himself, Rykov pointed to a smaller crate and indicated, sit.

"- You are a Socialist, Comrade?" he began.

Damn it! First Danny and Willie and then Ben and now him. Concealing his exasperation, he shook his head. "No, I'm just a volunteer."

For a moment Rykov looked away. He lit a cigarette and offered one to Mark who declined. "So are we all, Comrade, but we are not children. Your country – we all know how you are persecuted there. Why are you here? Shouldn't you be manning barricades in your own country? Those who are starving do not feed others."

"Sometimes they do. Volunteers are from – what, fifty-two different countries? Shouldn't they be 'manning the barricades,' too, in Poland, Rumania, Belgrade, Germany?"

Rykov leaned forward, his blue eyes eager, "Yes, yes, but each is a *Communist*. They are *committed* and because of their commitment, they have been persecuted. They have *escaped* to join us. But you? Why are you here?" His eyes were serious.

Had Rykov not been an officer, Mark would have lashed out in anger. But he spoke calmly. "What difference does it make? Everybody here's not a Communist. Some are Socialists…"

He waved a dismissive hand. "Let's speak of you…."

"Good. If you think I shouldn't be here, give me a *salvo conducto* so I can leave. Why keep me here if you don't trust me? Give me a safe conduct pass and I'll leave."

They exchanged stares. Crushing out his cigarette, Rykov said in a flat tone, "You may leave now, Comrade." His eyes held the same steady expression they had the day Kellerman questioned him about executing prisoners.

Remembering that day on the ship, he had inwardly cringed. Walter and Willie were criticizing people like him – bourgeois, therefore untrustworthy. Now it's what Rykov was saying.

Truth be told, they were right. He didn't want to be referred to as the proletariat, and yes, he wanted very much to be middle class. While cars did not appeal to him, and like most of the men, he had never owned one, he did want money in the bank, and he did want to own a nice house with a lawn and a fence. More than that, he wanted to consider himself as good as, if not better than, those white people who were convinced that a colored doctor was inferior to a white convict. He saw no harm in wanting to feel better than other people. People were not equal; it was fantasy to think otherwise. Equality was impossible in either a Communist state or a democratic one.

Ruby had pointed out to him that while he had a college degree, Mr. Mosley over on Princeton Avenue – who could neither read nor write - had far surpassed him by using his natural ability. Mr. Mosley had parlayed collecting junk on trash days with a rickety homemade pushcart into collecting junk with a hired horse and wagon. Mosley eventually elevated that into his own junkyard and persuaded other scavengers to bring their items to him; he paid a higher price. He now owned a 1936 Nash and several rental properties.

Mosley would have been dumbfounded to learn that he counted as a capitalist. Mark did not begrudge him his success nor did Mark believe that what Mr. Mosley had should be redistributed among those who had less or nothing. So, no, he was not a Communist. But yes, he believed that no one should go without adequate food and shelter and no woman should be forced to sell her very flesh and soul to survive. Why should one man live under a bridge while another lived in a mansion? And who should watch loved ones go through life crippled or die for lack of medical care? Why didn't the earth belong to everyone equally?

In short, why wasn't there a bright line between ordinary human decency and Communism?

As the trucks rumbled, lurched and crept along through the night, Walter broke the silence. "Guy's on his deathbed. He's an atheist.

Preacher leans over him and begs him to renounce the devil. Guy looks at him and says, "This is no time to be making enemies."

There was laughter and the usual groans.

CHAPTER 29

At dawn the convoy passed a mansion that was surrounded by ambulances and camouflaged vehicles. Tents with large red crosses painted on them were scattered about the grounds. Once past the mansion, the convoy pulled up among the trees to partly conceal the trucks from Fascist planes. Rykov said they could rest until further orders. The men got out of the trucks, glad for the chance to stretch their legs and relieve themselves.

A little later, Callaway cocked his ear, staring into the distance. "You hear that? - Listen." There were faint sounds like distant thunder. "Are those guns?" he wondered. Their eyes surveyed the hills; they saw nothing that indicated war, but agreed it was probably cannon fire. Once that was established and the field kitchen was being set up, Kahn and Winters approached Rykov.

"We can't find Kellerman," Winters told him.

He stared at them for a moment apparently at a loss. "Kellerman? - Oh, yes. He is in the infirmary. He became ill on guard duty."

"What happened to him?" Winters asked.

He shrugged. "Why he is sick, I cannot say. He will come later but with another group."

"– Another group?" Kahn asked.

"Only when transport is available." Rykov drifted away.

"Who else was on duty with Kellerman?" Winters wondered.

"None of our bunch," Kahn said. "I remember him saying he wouldn't have anybody to talk to."

They looked at each other, dissatisfied, not knowing what else to say. Both had the same disquieting feeling that something did not seem right.

After the field kitchen was set up, they were served the omnipresent garbanzo beans prepared in olive oil with slabs of bread. They had not been served meat since the first two days of training camp. They ate sitting on the ground or on the running board of the trucks; some sat on the back of the trucks with their feet hanging down. Mark and Willie preferred the ground. Willie spoke with his mouth full. "Reckon this is it?" He indicated the distant hills with his fork.

"Not yet," Walter replied.

"– "How can you tell?" Mark asked.

"The smell. My uncle said battlefields smell like shit mixed with vomit, piss and garbage. Worse after dead horses start stinking."

Willie noted, "We musta just missed a fight. You see all those ambulances? There was a bunch around that mansion we passed."

"It's a hospital now," Danny informed them. He was surveying the area with field glasses he had borrowed from Rykov. "Mansion's being put to good use now," he said with satisfaction.

Mark wanted to borrow the glasses but he and Danny had barely spoken since Mark had made it clear that he rejected Communism. Mark forced himself to wait thirty minutes before he casually asked Willie, "You up for a walk?" They strolled toward the mansion and on the way there peered into abandoned huts with dirt floors. Mark wondered how anyone could live among fleas, flies and filth.

"I seen worse," Willie grunted. "Down home, places jus' as bad. Folks poorer than poor."

They reached several large tents with faded red crosses painted on the sides. They saw bandaged men lying on the ground. Most had their eyes closed. A few were propped up on an elbow watching them. One addressed them in Spanish. He was a boy. His left leg was in a cast; his left arm was bandaged.

Willie squatted beside him and cocked his ear. The youth repeated something in rapid Spanish and then he pursed his lips and put his fingers to them. Willie dug his cigarettes out of his pocket and carefully placed one in the boy's mouth. He lit it for him. The youth smiled; his brown eyes were soft and curious.

"Guess I'm gonna give up smoking," Willie grinned as other wounded men, placing two fingers before their mouth, called out – "*Cigarillo.*" Squatting and moving from man to man, he gave them a cigarette, followed by their "*Gracias*" or "*Camarada.*" Finally he held up the empty pack. "Ain't nobody got cigarettes," he complained to Mark. "Can't buy 'em or steal 'em."

Mark's roving eye caught movement over Willie's shoulder. He tensed and focused his eyes on a figure. It was Analise. She was struggling out of a side door of the mansion with a bucket that she held with both hands.

"I'll be back," he told Willie and tried not to run toward her as he picked his way through a sea of helpless men. She saw him hurrying toward her and her mouth opened in surprise. He reached her and immediately grasped the bucket. It reeked of feces and urine. He recoiled from the stench. She flicked a finger – "Over there. Empty it over there."

She directed him to a shallow ditch near the back of the mansion. The odor rose in a wave that made him twist his head away. Flies swarmed his face. Waving them away and squinting, he emptied the bucket and then hurried away with Analise beside him.

"Why are you doing that!" he demanded, indignant.

"I try to set an example," she replied. - "We take turns." Then she looked at him closely, eyes filled with concern. "Are you hurt, Mark? Is that why you're here? What happened to you?"

He stopped and stared at her. "I'm here because you're here. I know it doesn't make sense but…." he shrugged. "How about you? Are you all right? You look awfully tired." For the briefest second he saw her chin crumble. He wanted to gather her in his arms and hug her and he might have but she started back to the mansion.

"Are there any more buckets? I'll carry them for you."

"The others will get them."

"How've you been?" he asked again, searching her face but seeing only weariness; her slender face thinner.

"- O.K., I guess."

They stood facing each other. He was looking for clues as to how she felt. Several times he noticed the tell–tale crumpling of her chin. "You're not alone, Analise. The only reason I came is because of you. - They wanted to send me back, but I fought against it."

"- But I *am* alone! I'm all alone here. Where will you be tomorrow or the next day if you're even alive, Mark? Where will I be? I don't have any control over myself; neither do you."

"– I'll always find a way to be near you, Analise. It's just the way it is. I'm here now because I just took a chance. We both have to believe that. It's fate or something. I'll stay as long as you're here, but neither of us should be here. Can't you ask for your release?"

"– I don't know. Anyway, it's not that simple. I didn't come here just for the fun of it. I came because of Jacob. You came because of me; he didn't ask me to do that, and I didn't ask you to come. Can't you see how complicated it is?"

The unspoken fact was – he had placed himself in competition with Jacob. He wanted to know whether or not she had found him and how things stood between them, but he did not feel he had the right to ask. More importantly, where he himself was concerned - how did she feel? But here, too, he did not feel he had the right to ask.

"Please believe me, Analise, you're not alone. I know you don't believe in…in things the way I do, but you're not alone and nothing's going to happen to me. We're both here because we're supposed to be here. I'm convinced I've been here before. I can feel it."

She looked at him, not knowing what to say. That feeling had happened to her, too, but in a frightening way. It was the time the bus passed the ancient aqueduct and the amphitheater in Tarragona. She had felt a sudden sense of dread that made her cringe. It scared her. Searching his face, she wanted to ask - "What did you feel?" But Juanita appeared in the side doorway. *"You are on duty!"* she barked. *"Why are you here?"*

At that moment, Willie approached. "Gotta go, Wilson," he shouted.

Juanita's oppressive presence forced them apart. He reached out and rubbed the back of his hand against hers. She turned her hand over and gave his a quick squeeze. They parted under Juanita's glare and Willie's bemused smile.

"You damn-sure persistent," Willie said with a tone of admiration. "How you find her way out here?"

Mark, dejected at having been interrupted by Juanita, shrugged. "Fate I guess."

Later the trucks took them as far as they could over war torn roads so rutted that further passage was impossible. They disembarked and marched over stony terrain toward the angry grumble of war. An airplane watched them from above. They eventually reached the frontlines where Rykov surrendered his command and returned to Camp Tarragona.

CHAPTER 30

They were not welcomed by the men in the trenches.

Those witnesses to death, to blood, to sweat and tears looked with jaded eyes at the newcomers' clean uniforms and clean shaven faces. The men in the trenches were filthy. They had holes in their uniforms, their faces were grimy, their eyes were tired and they all needed a shave. Dirt from the trenches clung to them like lint. They stank with a strong, ugly, acrid odor.

Nor did the veterans like being called "Comrade." The rookies had not earned the right. The veterans' eyes, if they deigned to look at them at all, were filled with secret knowledge and contempt. Disillusioned, the volunteers clung to each other.

The enemy attacked a week later. The sound of war was an ugly, hoarse threat; menacing beyond anything they had ever heard before. War was fear. Their instinct was to cringe and bolt to safety. But they could not. Machine gun bullets spun men around like rag dolls. Everyone crouched lower in the trenches or clung to the ground. Exploding artillery shells flashed red and orange in the air above them or struck the earth sending geysers of dirt, blood and men into the air. And always the suffocating smell of sulfur.

The sudden heat from explosions sucked up the air, creating a vacuum that lifted men from the ground and slammed them down again, and then the force of compressed air pushed down on them like a collapsing elephant. At times Mark could hear nothing, deafened by the explosions. Bursting shells sent white hot, razor sharp shrapnel spinning, slashing men and gouging the earth. He heard the slap of things near him as they struck the earth. Sometimes they were bloody parts of someone's body.

Only after the newcomers had shed blood and surrendered lives were they permitted to share a cigarette and say "Comrade." Only when they could mourn their dead – among them – young Andrews, Callaway and Professor Winters, could they complain about the war and say "Comrade."

And through it all he worried about Analise.

He could not imagine what a bombardment would do to her. The screaming approach of artillery shells, the pause, the sudden deafening explosion and the oppressive press of air, the pressure on the ear drums. The suffocating smell of sulfur. Collapsing walls and fire and smoke. Over and over and over again. Men got shell shock and lost their minds. What about her? How could he possibly protect her from all of this? She was no more than ten miles away, yet it might as well be a thousand.

She had looked worn down and weary and believed she was alone. So where the hell was Jacob? He didn't seem to be of any help even though she had come to Spain because of him. Surely each additional day did not make things better for her. He knew in which direction escape to France lay. He eyed the motorcycle couriers who came almost hourly. When chance presented itself, he was determined to get on one and roar away to the mansion and to Analise. The longer he waited the chances of death or capture increased.

He had urinated in his pants once while hiding behind rocks while on reconnaissance, too frightened to move, as Franco's elite Moorish cavalry probed, peered, poked and passed on speaking their foreign language. Their skin color ranged from white to black. They were Muslims and wore distinctive fezzes. The veterans said Moors delighted in sodomizing prisoners and gang raping women.

The other night he groped his way to a shelf in the trench and threw himself on it, glad to be out of the mud from a recent rain. He pulled his blanket over his head, turned his face to the wall and fell asleep. Dimly at first, he heard murmuring. Faint daylight mixed with the murmurs came from above the trench. The lookouts on duty spoke softly yet in the stillness their words floated down.

"…one of the Spanish guys…."

"…Waste of time. – Where's he think he's going? A lot of guys'd skip if there was some place to go."

"Probably got relatives somewhere. Different with us. We got nowhere to go. Remember Dutch? Got shot at Belchite?"

"Oh, yeah, but he came back on his own didn't he?"

"That's what I mean. He *had* to come back. Went to the U.S Consul in Valencia. Told them he wanted help getting back to the States. Know what they told him? Had no business in Spain in the first place! His passport was stamped 'Invalid for Spain' so he was in the country illegally. Claimed they couldn't help him break the law and they called him a commie."

"– Christ, you sure about that?"

"Hell, yeah, I'm sure! Why else you think he'd desert, then come crawling back?"

"– Even if he knew they'd shoot 'im?"

"Guess he figured it proved he was ready to fight and they'd let it go after that stink they caused when they shot White."

"– Shit, he shoulda known better. Fuckers don't let nothing go. Remember Levitz? Saying stuff like the Communists only send supplies to Communist commanders. You can't say stuff like that even if it's true."

"I forgot all about Levitz. Wasn't he a captain or something? What happened?"

"They claimed he got sick supervising guard duty one night. Nobody's seen him since."

Mark sat up. - *Kellerman*. He "got sick," too, while on guard duty. Suddenly, Mark understood. He remembered the night Rykov materialized out of the dark, the night the three Spanish recruits went over the wall. Rykov had smiled and asked if he wanted to be relieved. It seemed odd. There was no reason for it and the last time Rykov had spoken to him, Rykov had been displeased that Mark wasn't a Communist. Anyway, who was supposed to relieve him?

Mark remembered smiling and eyeing the Russian's round, muscular face. "Thanks, but I don't mind guard duty. It gives me time to think. Anyway, some of the guys might get sore. Like you said, we all have to take our turn. Guys keep track of things like that." His last remark was a veiled reference to Danny and Willie who had never been assigned guard duty.

Rykov smiled again and seemed surprised that he would refuse. He stood with his hands behind his back. It was then that Danny materialized from out of the dark, but he did not carry a rifle. What was he doing out of bed at this hour?

Suspicious, Mark casually lowered his rifle and held it so that his finger was on the trigger. Rykov held his eyes as Danny approached. Suddenly a shout interrupted: *"Three men went over the fence!"* With an oath Rykov swung around and raced away in the direction of the breach. Danny chased after him. Mark watched their retreating forms disappear in the dark. He was surprised to find his heart racing. Somehow he had sensed menace a moment before.

Remembering that night, the smoke of uncertainty drifted away. Kellerman and probably Levitz had been killed for asking inconvenient questions. And he suspected that had Rykov not been interrupted by escaping recruits, he himself would have been disposed of, too, for not being a Communist.

Was it paranoid to think so and even more insane to do such a thing? But Tank Maynard had warned him - "They think a mind of your own is a dangerous thing to have."

CHAPTER 31

He deserted in the heat of battle.

In five weeks the volunteers had been reduced from twenty-nine to thirteen. Of the volunteers Mark knew best, only Walter, Danny, Willie and Professor Kahn remained. Losses were heavy all across the line and they had not won a single inch of ground nor possessed any artillery to reply to that of the enemy. The government air force seldom arrived to drive away the strafing German pilots who came and went as they pleased. The men blamed their heavy casualties and lack of weapons on inept leadership.

Morale was rotten. The Americans and Spanish had little to say to each other and there was little effort to bridge the language barrier. When one of the Spanish recruits was wounded in the left leg and left arm, Walter had quipped, "He's all right."

Some officer somewhere, looking at maps, made the decision to have the men move out of their trenches and silence the enemy artillery in their front and then somehow get to the rear of the enemy. They would, of course, be supported by invisible airplanes and elusive artillery.

The attack force would comprise the Abraham Lincoln Battalion with the French International Battalion on their left and the Italian Garibaldi Battalion on their right. In reality, the three battalions were 80% Spanish. Comrade Pena, a colonel, commanded the Lincolns.

"Artillery will shell the area ahead of us," Comrade Pena assured his men, "and then our planes will roar in and strafe and bomb the enemy like the Germans and Italians do to us. At two o'clock when I give the signal, rise up and charge; silence all signs of resistance. Be *ruthless! Take no prisoners!*" he ordered. "If you are wounded, do not surrender. They will shoot you anyway. Fight to the death! If you have no bullets, use your bayonet. Better to die with a brave heart than to be slaughtered like squealing pigs!"

He issued his orders in Spanish and then in English. Mark was convinced, based on past experience, that these orders were senseless but he was trapped like animals in a cattle chute. He had to go. Walter who seemed unconcerned, quipped, "This cannibal says to another cannibal, 'Here, let me give you a hand.' The second cannibal says, 'No, thanks. I just ate.'"

The men laughed louder than they usually did.

Comrade Pena, who stood some distance behind, was puzzled by the laughter, but he was grateful for their spirit. He consulted his watch again, and frowning, scanned the target area with his binoculars. It was three past two. He waited another two minutes; his orders said two o'clock. At five minutes after two he cried out in Spanish - "Advance!"

The order was repeated down the line. The Lincolns and other battalions crouched forward, forming long wavy lines. Peering anxiously ahead, they picked their way around rocks and over craters. The Nationalists waited patiently before opening up with artillery. Again the orange-red explosions and razor sharp shrapnel. Again cries of pain, terror, blood, again limbs shorn off and hurled across the field. Again this was followed by machine gun fire. They flung themselves to the ground as angry, whining machine gun bullets searched for them. No one stood up. No one charged.

Now and then they tried a furtive crawl forward, often blocked by a mangled, blood soaked body sprawled across their path. Here and there a small outcropping of stone offered protection from which a few dared lift their head to launch wild, aimless return fire.

Pena, viewing the failed charge through his field glasses, was aware of impending disaster. Where the hell were the artillery and the planes he'd been promised? It was not the first time the artillery had not hurled a single shell at the enemy and everyone knew that all too often the government air force was more a myth than reality.

Who would be blamed for this disaster? The usual "spies" and "fascists" and a "fifth column," of course. Yet who would be shot for this failure? Surely not the sons of whores who had orchestrated this fiasco, but him. They were stupid, using the tactics of the last war; employing one or two tanks at a time that were immediately disabled while the Germans massed their tanks into a solid gray wall of steel backed by airplanes.

He must halt the retreat - his life or theirs. Pena removed his revolver screaming, "Back! Back!" and fired at the face of the man closest to him.

Men in battle must fear their commanders more than they feared the enemy or every battle would be lost. "Back!" he screamed.

The French were still holding, so were the Italians. That indicated the rebels meant to destroy the center where he stood and split the defenders in two. Every school boy knew that meant encirclement and destruction. He watched as one by one the Lincolns fell back, hugging the earth, sliding on their bellies. By now they were a mob. When they reached a favorable drop, they came back toward the safety of the trenches where they were pounced upon by roaring airplanes flashing death from machine guns and swooping so low that they raised swirls of dust.

***

Mark saw Willie on his left. The big man was doubled over, thrashing around, clutching his leg in agony. Mark squirmed over to him, his head rubbing the ground. They were amid green clad bodies suddenly burst apart in red surprise or pierced by bullets or sliced by razor sharp shrapnel. The deadly airplanes swooped down again and again strafing the prone bodies, determined to account for each man.

Willie, gasping deep sobs, lay in a huge, red puddle of spreading blood. His right leg from the knee down was missing and blood poured out freely. His left foot was a bloody stump. His face was distorted, glistening black and red. When Willie saw him, his eyes were a mixture of wonder, pain and despair. "Help me!" they pleaded. "Help!"

Mark had no idea what to do. He took his off his red neckerchief and tried to fashion a tourniquet but the pain was too much for Willie. He uttered deep sobs and words that Mark could not understand.

"Hold still, Willie, I'm trying to help you!"

Insensate with pain, he could not hear. Mark, in the midst of trying to hug the ground and tie a tourniquet, saw Willie's head suddenly flop. Blood gushed from his nostrils. His terrified eyes accused Mark. For a moment Mark lay still, his head resting against Willie while all the world bellowed with insane, hot hatred. He repeated the Lord's Prayer and found Willie's wallet. He had no thought what he would do with it, but someone should know that Willie had died.

He squirmed back, feeling something under him that turned out to be a wet, severed arm. He saw a broken rifle there and heard cries for help everywhere. Finally he was close to the trenches. He was below the direct line of fire. The lull in the battle was sudden, like summer rain that stops to let in sunshine.

The French and Italians closed the gap left by the collapse of the Lincolns. Though the furious attack suddenly subsided, he heard a shot from the trenches. The enemy had gotten in their rear! They were surrounded.

He crouched nearer. Another shot. But each only a single shot. Puzzled, he edged closer to the trenches. Some of the battalion were there. Pena was standing behind Santiago and Raoul. Pena held a pistol. Two other men lay sprawled on the ground bleeding from the head. Others from the battalion, amid the angry sounds of war, were watching, crouched. A few were crawling forward again toward the enemy position.

Incredibly, Pena, shouting something in angry Spanish, raised his pistol and shot Raoul in the head. As he dropped, a geyser of blood spurting from his head followed him to the ground. Mark, mouth agape, could not believe his eyes. Santiago suddenly bolted. Pena aimed his pistol at the fleeing man, but suddenly Pena stumbled and fell at the sound of a shot. Everyone swung around at the sound. They stared at a blood streaked Mark and then at each other, dumbfounded. Mark had shot Pena. Mark saw Estevez and motioned to him.

"Interpret," he ordered.

Estevez nodded and began interpreting: - "'We did not come all the way here, at great danger to ourselves, to be murdered by people we came to help….'"

A Spanish soldier interrupted and Estevez interpreted - "'It was to teach us a lesson because we retreated. We must learn that there is no sanctuary in retreat.'" A number of his companions murmured verification; veterans eyed Mark suspiciously.

"'Tell them,'" Mark said, "that those who need to be taught a lesson are the ones who make stupid plans that can't succeed. They are the ones who should pay. Today they committed murder. You should not be forced to pay because you have sense enough to realize that.

"'If I have the courage to face death, then I have the courage to kill those who want to kill *me*; I do not care who it is. Only I can put a price on my life!'"

As the men milled around uncertain, Danny spoke quietly to Walter and Walter had Estevez interpret for him that nobody should kill a commanding officer. "'We are still in battle; who will follow us?'" Most of them, determined to put distance between themselves and this terrible act of insubordination, were willing to follow Walter and Danny.

"- How about you?" Walter asked Mark. "You coming?"

His position was impossible. "I quit," he said. "I don't mind dying, Walter, but not for something I don't believe in. - And Danny, next time you see Rykov, tell him better luck murdering the next guy who has guard duty. Like Kellerman."

Danny stared with a stone face. Mark, holding his rifle in one hand, backed away, pointing it in the general direction of Danny's head. "Good thing I'm not a Communist, Danny. They don't leave enemies behind."

Walter looked puzzled. "Better get going," Mark told him, "before they change their mind."

While they were forming up, Mark stripped Pena of his pistol belt, pistol and binoculars. Moments later, the Nationalists, unhindered by either Republican artillery or airplanes, came howling down in a hurricane of exploding shells, choking sulfur and slashing shrapnel. Over the renewed attack, somebody yelled, "Tanks!"

They heard the squeal, clank and the grating sound of gears changing and saw the huge mass of crawling beetles advancing toward them. Rebel soldiers advanced, crouching behind the tanks. The tanks would mercilessly roll over men lying in their path leaving bloody, elongated, crushed red smears. They would pass over the trenches and the rebels following the tanks would shoot down at the men crouching there. Wherever there were tanks, supporting German planes were sure to follow, churning the earth with bombs and stitching the ground with relentless strafing.

Armed only with rifles and machine guns and facing an advancing wall of steel belching cannon and machine gunfire, like panicked patrons rushing for the exits of a burning theater, the men fled the tanks and the angry cannon and the steel birds of prey. Walter and Danny led men in one direction; Mark and others sought safety in another.

They ran, glancing anxiously to the sky, flinging themselves to the ground to avoid the planes that gouged quarter size holes in human flesh without let or hindrance. Panicked soldiers flung away their rifles and ammunition and mess kits and they abandoned heavy knapsacks and blankets. Had it been the least helpful, they might well have stripped the clothes from their back.

The cork was out of the bottle.

CHAPTER 32

Though Mark fled like everyone else, trying desperately to stay ahead of the tanks that were hindered by trees, clogged roads and bridges that had been destroyed by the fleeing army - he was not running blindly. His goal was Analise. Had the mansion been evacuated? If so, where would he find her? He could not leave her behind.

Like Caesar, he had crossed his Rubicon; he had killed his commander. No one would ever care why or validate his reasons. He had committed heresy against an army's holy commandment– *Obey Orders.* To satisfy the gods of war, he must be burned as a heretic. As the brigades fled, no one wanted to be identified with him for fear they too would be burned at the stake for not having butchered in righteous outrage this filthy, godless creature.

The Republican generals finally managed to scrape together enough artillery to make the rebels pause. Still the rout was unabated. Every man was for himself. Those officers who stood before them with drawn pistols, ordering them to halt and make a stand were ignored, and surrounded by hordes of frightened men, they only fired their weapons into the air.

Fleeing vehicles inched forward loaded with men and burdened with others who lay along the fenders and stood on the running boards and even lay tenuously on the roof. Olive groves by the side of the road offered some protection from the searching planes. Exhausted men, sweating from the heat, sprawled on the ground beneath the trees. They asked for water from those who passed.

Mark had water. Unlike other panicked soldiers, he had not thrown anything away, keeping his rifle, bayonet, and Pena's revolver. Both his blanket, crisscrossed against his body, and his knapsack might absorb stray shrapnel or spent machine gun bullets. The very first time he heard a request for water, he had hidden his canteen in his knapsack.

Everything that he had and everything that he did had a single purpose. To find, protect and save Analise. She would need water and food and shelter. His thoughts were not only of their escape, but the means to survive the journey to the French border.

He did not pause among the trees. In the trenches he had heard tales of the Great Retreat in March when the Republican forces had fled headlong for the Ebro River leaving behind mountains of equipment and thousands of prisoners and casualties. This might be another such retreat.

Another man attached himself to Mark. It was Estevez, who had interpreted for him. He had also kept his rifle, blanket and knapsack. They forged ahead at a steady pace, using their forearms to wipe sweat from their face. Neither spoke. They came to the end of a grove. It was still daylight. Ahead lay the mansion and far to the left, north, was France. Tired, Mark sat down near the edge of the grove. Estevez followed suit. Both were filthy with mud and dirt. They rested against their knapsacks and blankets.

"– It required courage to do what you did," Estevez remarked after a while. "We are always defeated because we are led by stupid and selfish officers," he said with disgust. "General Lister hates General Modesta and neither will support the other so when we get butchered, they blame it on 'spies,' 'Fascist saboteurs' and the 'fifth column.' Even when we win, we give it all back the next day! Belchite, Zaragoza, Brunette. Good Comrades slaughtered for nothing…Now Gandesa."

"– Why do you keep doing it?"

Estevez shrugged. "You cannot quit. Spain is not my country but it is my heritage. You do not realize the things these people have suffered, not just today, but throughout history. Peasants work for two to four pesetas a day and then only for the three or four week harvesting season. No more than 30 of your dollars a year.

"They are the *hambrientos* – the starving ones. They eat grass." He nodded, eyes narrowed – "Yes, *grass*! When you treat people like animals, they behave like animals. I myself have murdered more than one priest. The world does not know the unspeakable crimes of which they are guilty. I put my rifle up the ass of one and shot him."

Mark shuddered.

"Once we had good officers, but they were pushed aside by Russian commissars who wanted their own people – incompetent asses. Yet without the supplies the Communists give us, we are helpless. In return, they insist on control." He suddenly looked around fearful of having been overheard. They were alone.

"- Many comrades quit. They are called 'deserters' but they became disgusted to give so much for so little. I do not blame those who are not Spanish."

"How long have you been here?"

"From the beginning."

"Still going to stay?"

He took his time answering, drawing circles in the dirt with a twig. "...It is pride. Maybe stupid or stubborn. How will it matter? We have already lost. There is a rumor that Prime Minister Negrin intends to make peace with them. It is a matter of time. They have captured all but Catalonia. Madrid still stands – surrounded and alone. Still I would rather be defeated than quit."

He raised his head from the circles and stared at Mark for a moment. "I am not judging you...."

"It's O.K. - I believe only I should control my destiny."

They regarded each other in silence. The logic of war and the logic of love were inimical.

There came a time when Estevez pushed on to his war and Mark pushed on to Analise. They parted with a wave of good luck. Neither said, "Comrade."

Alone again, he thought of Willie. He saw his big grin and heard his earnest voice asking why everyone wasn't a Communist. His tomorrow had been shortened as had all of the others. Estevez spoke of pride and stubbornness. They each dueled with God or Fate or Time or Common Sense. Yet all they stood to gain was what they already had – their lives.

But this was no more than a strangled rationale for killing Comrade Pena. The real rationale was Analise. Simply put he had to choose between charging senselessly uphill and being destroyed as Willie had been or engaging his real enemy which was anything or anyone that stood between him and her. She was less than ten miles away. All along he had planned to leave or quit or desert - what did it matter what the word was - the only question had always been *when*?

He had become mired deeper and deeper in the war, in day after dreadful day of bombs, shells, the smell of sulfur and shit. They ate, drank, slept, quarreled, scratched, complained, urinated, defecated, grew beards, stank and eventually got shot. The odds of being killed or wounded increased exponentially He had had to make a move.

***

When night fell he continued walking east, keeping clear of the road that was jammed bumper to bumper with slow moving vehicles taking advantage of the night when enemy planes did not fly.

He came to a small stream and undressed and lay in the water to soak the filth and stink from his body. He threw his clothes in the stream and rubbed and swished them back and forth to wash away the grime and Willie's blood and he put them back on wet. The heat of his body would dry them.

He rushed on through the night, swatting away mosquitoes, stumbling and blundering into things. On the road far to his right, he heard the heavy rumble of trucks and their shifting gears as they blundered through the night. Now and then he saw a flash from headlights. He could have moved faster on the road but he risked being rounded up at some checkpoint and forced to join another line of resistance that would only separate him further from Analise.

It was near dawn when he saw the dim outline of the mansion appear in the distance like a castle emerging from the fog.

CHAPTER 33

The morning of the rout, Dulce and several *chicas* were observing Analise prepare to insert a catheter. Dulce raised her head and stared past Analise's shoulder; Analise turned to look. Her eyes met Jacob's. He was dressed in a clean officer's uniform, a holstered pistol on his hip.

She handed the catheter to Dulce. "Here," she said, "show them."

She resisted the urge to throw herself into his arms. Moving aside, they smiled self-consciously, their eyes examining the other. He was clean shaven and did not look as exhausted as he had been.

"I've been relieved," he said quietly." Major Owens agrees I should call it a day but he'd 'appreciate' it if I'd stay a little longer to help look after the men in the wards."

She clapped her hands together with joy. *"Oh, Jacob!* I'll be able to help you! You'll be here, won't you?"

He hesitated. "–First he wants me to locate additional medical sites across the Ebro. I'm afraid we're pulling back again. There're more casualties than we can possibly handle on this side of the river. You can see how bad it is – it's a lot worse around Gandesa where the heavy fighting is. And this is just between us, but you'll be pulling back real soon. Maybe even today."

Her disappointment was palpable. "–I don't want to stay here by myself, Jacob. What's going to happen to us? How will we keep in contact? It's bad enough now when we're both in walking distance and never get to see each other!"

"Don't worry – Maj. Owens knows where everybody is; he has to...."

"That's not the point, Jacob. *Together! Together.* That's why I came. So we'd be together. How many times have we even seen each other?"

"Ana, it's not that easy. Let's just concentrate on going home. When I see him again, I'll get that straightened out. Is that O.K. with you?"

She wanted to say no and made no attempt to hide her disappointment. "I guess it has to be O.K., but you don't know where you'll be?"

He shook his head and looked at his watch. "I've got an ambulance waiting, Ana. I told them I'd only be a minute."

She walked him to the door hoping they could manage a quick kiss but they had to settle for a surreptitious squeeze of the hand. She watched him leave in a dusty vehicle that appeared to have rusty bullet holes in the driver's door. She had a feeling of foreboding.

Later in the day there came the first sound of distant thunder. Dulce shook her head.

"That's not thunder. They're guns. If it gets too close, we have to pack and leave again." Her hands did not tremble as much as they had, but her eyes looked worried. "If we wait," she said, "the roads get too bad. Nothing can move."

Twice there had been the unnerving roar of a German plane hurtling directly at the mansion. At the last possible second it tipped up and rushed over the roof. The noise and air pressure shook the building. The threatening roar seemed to linger.

A brass cow bell sat on Juanita's table. She rang it whenever she had an announcement. Just before noon the bell rang. Analise, Dulce and the other staff assembled around the door to Juanita's office. She addressed them in Spanish. Dulce, whispering, interpreted for Analise. They were to prepare the men to leave at once. Ambulances would arrive for them. From a sheaf of papers Juanita read a list of names that did not include Hannah's. Analise started to point out the oversight but Juanita's hostility toward her made her hesitate.

Analise left to help the men dress and gather their belongings. She pinned their medical records to their clothing or placed them in a pocket of their uniform if they still had one. Some uniforms had been cut off to prevent dirt from rubbing into open wounds and precipitating gas gangrene. Later she approached Juanita as she was supervising the move.

"– How many convoys do you think there will be?" she asked.

"Who can say?" she snapped. "Follow orders. They know best."

Analise did not pursue it but she was disturbed. The menacing grumble of cannon in the distance decided her. She prepared Hannah for evacuation and braced for Juanita's wrath in case her deception was discovered. She saw Hannah safely helped into an ambulance and turned away with a sudden, sad feeling. Hannah would probably not survive her massive infection. Later, a second convoy accompanied by a French doctor made a noisy appearance. The doctor and Juanita held a conference before the cow bell rang out again.

Evacuate the medical and support staff. Following that, evacuate any wounded for whom there was room. Those remaining would wait for other transport. Analise immediately thought about Irene and Clara. Where were they? There was no time for questions. Under Juanita's glowering command, the evacuation trucks were being loaded with X-ray equipment, operating tables, oxygen tanks, laboratory equipment and a panoply of boxes, bottles and cans. Nurses, *chicas,* medical technicians, kitchen staff were crowded in wherever there was space in vehicles that waited impatiently. Once loaded they pulled away with heavy truck sounds until only one truck remained.

Smoke hung in mushroom clumps on the horizon in the direction of the battle. Planes roared by so low that their pilots were visible. The black "X" insignia on the tail proclaimed them to be German. Dulce and Analise waited to squeeze into a space in one of the vehicles. Both women were glum and apprehensive. Dulce voiced her fears in a whisper. "Suppose they shoot at us? What can we do?"

"They're not supposed to...."

"But they do! They do. I know."

"- Dulce, it's much worse when you think about it. Think of the others. I hope they come back for the others. I have a feeling that they won't. What'll happen to the men?"

Several moments passed before Dulce whispered, "...They help those who are Communist first. I noticed it first at Val Verde, then at Castellar. There is no mistake. It is happening again."

"But the others...."

"They are left to God. Since they say the Holy Father is a myth, they are left to the Devil. There will be no other transport. Always when doctors and nurses are evacuated, it is the end."

"...But that doesn't make sense. Are you sure?"

Dulce looked exasperated, then her face softened. "I have been here longer than you. Who was left behind? In addition to those with stomach wounds whose lives are already forfeit – who was left?"

"Well...Hannah for one. She's a Communist."

"Juanita hates her. She says Hannah's a Trotskyite, but we know the real reason; she's 'funny.'"

Analise said nothing. She had no idea what a "Trotskyite" was but she was glad she had saved Hannah. But what of the others who were waiting and trusting people who were lying to them? And the fellows who were with her on the ship – were any of them being left behind? And Mark. He could be wounded, too.

Dulce climbed into the remaining truck and Analise was about to follow when Juanita barked, "You. – Go see my desk. A box," she spread her hands about two feet apart, "heavy. Bring quick. *Quick!*"

"Save a seat," Analise said and was about to hand Dulce her nurse's bag but changed her mind and hurried back into the mansion where she was met with anxious eyes of damaged men waiting to be evacuated. Some propped themselves up on their elbow shouting angrily, "*Evacuarme!*" Others who knew her name called, "Analise." One or two who did not know her said "*Enfermera*" - nurse. She hurried past them and entered Juanita's room. There was no box on the table that Juanita used for a desk.

Quickly, she looked under the table. There were no shelves, or doors leading to another place; she did a deliberate tour of the room to forestall Juanita's caustic criticism. There was nothing in the room except random scraps of cardboard. As she turned to leave, something struck her as odd and out of place.

Suddenly, she realized what it was. No noise from outside. All she heard were further pleas of, "Evacuate me!" from men in the ward. Feeling a sense of rising panic, she hurried to the front entrance.

There was no truck. There was nothing.

She saw the back of the truck in the distance receding down the path leading to the road. She would never catch up to it by running.

Juanita had deliberately abandoned her. She must have known about Hannah. She was punishing her for saving Hannah. It could well be a death sentence.

Her face colored with anger. "You miserable, *miserable bitch!*" she yelled at the top of her voice. She wanted to cry from sheer anger and despair and frustration. She swung her head this way and that searching for some possible solution, maybe a vehicle still on the grounds.

She was hardly better off than the men left behind pleading, "Evacuate me."

She refused to weep though her chin crumbled and tears escaped her eyes. Gripping her nurse's bag she prepared to head down the path to the road leading to the Ebro. There were men lying on the ground on both sides of the path, some brought in an hour or so ago by the very vehicles that had been commandeered for the evacuation.

She averted her eyes from the looks of disappointment and betrayal on their faces as she passed them. She deadened her ears to their pleas and when she was far enough away from them she dissolved into tears and wept openly for the men as she stumbled along, running her sleeve across her nose. She wanted forgiveness but there was no one to forgive her.

She hated herself for pretending she did not see or hear their pain, their fear and anguish. And she hated Jacob for causing her to be there and she hated the war and its utter contest of insanity. Most of all she hated The Bitch who was what Juanita had become. Once she reached the road she would hitch a ride to the next medical facility. She was sure to come face to face with The Bitch there and she would let her know the color of hate.

***

When she reached the road, she was shocked. It was choked with an endless parade of weary, dusty soldiers shuffling along among mobs of anxious refugees fleeing the Fascists. The refugees carried what possessions they could in their arms or on their back. Some led slow moving two-wheel donkey carts loaded with pieces and shards of their lives, and sometimes sad looking, aged relatives seated with their legs hanging down from the back. Other refugees pulled loaded hand wagons as best they could.

The refugees were mostly women dressed in traditional black and old men and children. Some women carried a child in one arm and led another by the hand. Others helped hobbled old men and blind women who could only creep, their faces filled with sorrow and pain.

There was no way for Analise to hitch a ride. The crowded road slowed military vehicles to a crawl. Soldiers stood on the running boards of the vehicles or lay along the fenders or sat on each other's laps in the back of the trucks. A few lay tenuously on the roof. No one offered to surrender his place to her.

She was thrust among people each of whom carried a sorrow, some more visible than others. She could not step around them as she had the men lying on the ground at the mansion, nor could she avert her eyes; sadness was everywhere. She remembered Clara saying that there was nothing worse than a doctor or nurse standing around saying "I can't help you."

She had difficulty moving ahead among refugees struggling to pull their loaded carts and slow moving vehicles. Women recognized the patch on her shoulder and they came to her with eyes that only other women recognize and though fearful of the coming night and what would become of her, she stopped and smiled and offered to help them. She gave aspirin to alleviate this child's fever and iodine for another's scratches and once she set a child's broken arm though she knew that what she did was inadequate and then there was the woman with cancer to whom she administered morphine.

She felt a growing anxiety. She had never for a second contemplated not being able to hitch a ride. What would become of her tomorrow and the day after all alone on a road in Spain where not a sole knew her or cared about her? The only food she had was several bars of chocolate. Still, she felt a vague sense of safety in numbers.

She passed fire blackened vehicles pushed to the side of the road. Some had huge gunshot holes and jagged, shattered windows. Just before nightfall she stopped by an ambulance dotted with bullet holes and littered with shattered glass. She opened the driver side door. Her mouth flew open. A thick coat of black, dried blood covered the seat, the dashboard and the floor. Large, green flies beat against her face. She slammed the door shut and searched the ground but did not see a body. She went around to the other side and after chasing the flies away, sat in the passenger seat. She tried to ignore the blood on the seat and floor beside her and the flies that crept back in.

Tired and discouraged, she closed the door and watched the never-ending traffic pass until it was night. She felt the vehicle sway slightly from people climbing in the back. She went to sleep hugging her bag to her body as though it gave her warmth and comfort.

CHAPTER 34

Mark reached the mansion at dawn. Approaching with caution, he noticed that there were no ambulances. Soldiers moved aimlessly around the grounds. He took out his pistol. Crouching closer he saw that they were not armed. Probably deserters ransacking the place. Bandaged men lay on the ground. He could tell that some were dead. He heard cries of *"Enfermera!"* (Nurse) and pleas for water. Creeping closer he was startled to hear – "Got a cigarette?"

On the ground, over to the left - one of the men from the trenches. His abdomen was heavily bandaged. Mark remembered the time Willie had given away all of his cigarettes and after that, though Mark did not smoke, he accepted the rare package of cigarettes that was distributed in the trenches.

He knelt by the wounded man and dug into his knapsack for the cigarettes and gave him one. He lit it for him as he had seen Willie do.

"- When are they going to move you guys out of here?"

" – Soon I guess. Convoy didn't come back yet."

"Are the doctors and nurses still here?"

"Naw – left already. I keep hearing trucks and things but they keep going…."

Others asked for cigarettes. He moved among them as Willie had done until the two packs were empty. By the side of the mansion he stumbled upon a heap of discarded blood soiled uniforms, knapsacks, canteens and weapons that had been removed from the patients. He rummaged in the pile and found another pistol and some ammunition. He found a strange looking pocket knife which he guessed was a Swiss army knife. He put them in his knapsack, and then he selected several canteens. He put one in his knapsack and went into the mansion.

The Spanish soldiers regarded him with suspicion. Only officers wore binoculars hanging from their neck or had pistols strapped to their side.

"Any water here?" he asked. "The guys outside need water."

They stared, silent. Using gestures and pantomime he made them understand. A blond boy no more than seventeen nodded and led him to the kitchen where he filled the canteens. Outside he went among the men giving them water and brushing away insects. He was aware that the time he spent here increased the distance between him and Analise but he also felt it would be obscene to turn his back on men lying helpless and discarded like items in the trash pile by the mansion.

After three trips to refill the canteens, several others helped him. In between times, he managed to find some cans of Russian beef and, in an oven, a loaf of stale bread. There came a time when he left. He took the road, trusting to chance that he would not be rounded up. He needed to catch up to Analise. He made his way past rusting vehicles that had been pushed off the road along with several smoke blackened tanks. They presented a medley of shattered glass, ripped tires, dried blood, twisted, rusting metal and the odor of stinking bodies.

After he passed thirty slow moving vehicles, impeded by a damaged road and hordes of refugees, he realized that it would take a vehicle close to an hour to cover a single mile. He could walk faster than that. It meant he could catch up to her medical convoy.

***

An hour later, planes appeared. Drivers dived into ditches, men clinging to the truck jumped to the ground and fled or squirmed under them. Mark and others scrambled into the olive groves; those in ambulances could only pray. He ran until he felt he had put enough distance between himself and the road. Still, he could feel the pressure from the concussion of exploding bombs and he could hear the impersonal, rapid stutter of machine gunfire. He kept going in a direction parallel to the road.

The veterans had warned them that the rebels bombed clearly marked hospitals and ambulances. He'd been skeptical. People said anything they wanted about the enemy; they had four horns and ten tails and ate babies for breakfast. However, even before the attack, he saw more than one ambulance pushed to the side of the road with shattered windshields and huge bullet holes gouged in their sides. In one a dead driver, eyes and nose eaten, sat slumped against the black, blood smeared door. Patients in the back, still on stretchers and torn apart by machine gun fire had been gutted by rats.

Analise was a target just like any soldier with a rifle.

***

After the attack, he took to the road again but soon saw the futility of trying to shoulder through crowds of people; he was a man trying to sprint through an ocean to the annoyance of everyone around him. Yet it was urgent that he catch up to her. Off the road, he had to cover twice, if not more, the distance. Exasperated, he looked behind him as though that offered a solution.

He froze. Shocked. His mouth open.

A figure farther back had an arm raised, frantically signaling.

Jesus Christ! *It was Analise!*

Without apologies he rushed, pushing his way back to her. She rushed toward him and they met. He instantly gathered her in his arms and again she felt that she knew him; she felt safe.

"I tried calling," she said near tears. "I thought…I thought you'd leave me…."

"Oh, my God, Analise –*never!* I'm so very sorry! What a horrible thing to happen! I've been looking for you. I thought you were ahead of me." He stared at her almost in disbelief. "I went to the hospital but you'd already gone."

She simply nodded, glad, near tears; to think that she had seen him so near and so far and he could possibly have been gone forever while she watched, leaving her on that road.

"God, I'm so sorry," he repeated.

"It wasn't your fault," she murmured.

They moved into the olive grove while traffic struggled past them. He offered to carry her bag but she smiled and said no. Then she told him what had happened and watched his expression of outrage; she rejoiced when he snarled – "That god damned *bitch!*"

"We were attacked with tanks and planes," he said. "All we had were our guns. Willie's dead and I'm afraid I sort of disobeyed orders."

"Willie's dead? What about the rest – But what did you do? Won't you get in trouble?"

He hesitated and then he told her what had happened. She was a little confused.

"I didn't come here to be killed for something stupid… Maybe at first I did, but right now you're the only reason I came."

He led her further into the olive groves away from the clogged, dusty road.

"Where are we going?" she asked, glancing back at the road. "Is this the right way?"

He heard doubt and perhaps a little fear. He stopped. "I was listening to the guys in the trenches. Last March they had to retreat across the Ebro. The bridges were blown up so there was no way across. The army got jammed up trying to get across on pontoon bridges; they just became a gigantic mob, easy targets for the planes and then it was every man for himself...."

Analise remembered. Barney Turner had described the nightmare of that retreat and she remembered his unspoken confession that he had abandoned his ambulance and the men in it and had swum across the river to save himself. What was the difference between that and abandoning the men at the Mansion? In the end, everyone was disposable.

"...The same thing's going to happen this time," Mark said. "There's still no bridge, just pontoons and their planes will have a field day. I want to go farther north and cross that way, away from where everybody else is going. We stand a better chance. At least I hope so. There're bound to be boats along the river. But if you don't want to go, I promise, I'll go wherever you go. I won't ever leave you."

She understood his logic. She remembered the night club fire in Boston the year before. Over two hundred people panicked and rushed for the front door. Most were trampled or burned to death trying to squeeze out of it. Two people went into the kitchen and out the back door and into the street to safety. Still there was Jacob. How would she find him? On the other hand, if she stood a chance of being taken prisoner and most likely raped....

"– You're sure this is the best way, Mark?"

"I'm sure of one thing - we'll be trapped if we follow the crowd. All I can say, Analise, is I'm here for one reason. You. I know you didn't ask me to come, but that doesn't matter. I'm dedicated to one thing – keeping you safe. That's all I care about."

Embarrassed by the naked vulnerability in his eyes, she colored and looked away. "I...I have to try to find Jacob...Do you understand that I'm engaged to Jacob?"

He nodded. "Sure, but we'll be part of each other no matter who you marry. Nothing's going to change that. I let you down once. I won't do it again. We both know there's something between us that we can't explain, so sure...I mean let's find Jacob, but it won't be among a mob of refugees and whatever happens happens. – Does that make sense?"

She searched his face and found what she was looking for. She nodded and they began their journey together to the Ebro.

CHAPTER 35

They rushed along at a pace that exhausted her. She was afraid he might leave her and struggled to keep up until finally she sank to the ground. Her face was white. Breathing hard, she said apologetically, "…You're going too fast…I can't keep up. I've got a stitch in my side…."

He immediately knelt beside her his face a picture of concern. "I'm sorry. We'll go slower – as slow as you want. I'll carry you if I have to. Here, let me carry that bag for you. It'll be easier…."

She sat slumped, cross legged, taking deep breaths. But once she heard the degree of concern in his voice and saw the anguish in his eyes, she knew she need never have to be afraid that he would ever leave her. She suddenly felt valued that nothing mattered to him except her. She presented a weak smile. "– I think I can carry it… I'll be all right. I know we have to hurry. I just need a little water, but I don't think we can trust these streams…."

He hastily dug in his knapsack and handed her a canteen. "I've been saving this for you."

She drank deeply and then caught herself and handed it back to him. She was embarrassed. "…I'm sorry. I didn't mean to drink…"

"It's yours. I've got another one. – Are you hungry?"

She nodded. He took out one of the cans of Russian beef and opened it with the can opener on the Swiss army knife. They ate with their fingers; he stole long glances at her. Embarrassed, she looked away. They rested a while among the trees and then continued along narrow ascending trails bordered by rocks and scrub vegetation. The sky was an enemy. They took turns using the binoculars to scan for signs of danger. She saw a plane in the distance.

"– Do you think we should get off the road just to be on the safe side?"

He knew that the pilot could not see them at that distance. He hesitated for a moment.

"– O.K." he said. Then he felt a twinge of guilt because he knew he would not have said "O.K." had Ruby suggested something with which he disagreed.

Now he said, "O.K." because of the nights he had rushed in pain through the streets of Philadelphia, and because of the nights of remembering while on guard duty at Tarragona, and because of the nights of reflecting during watches in the trenches. Night had infused him with thought and remembrance and intuition and introspection of all the wrong things in his life that had brought him here. So he said, "O.K."

It was not *that* Ruby had betrayed him – it was *why*. And the word betrayal was - in the end – too simplistic. It spoke of self-pity. What she had done had been for something he had not fully understood, but now he had the intimation that it had been an act of defiance or of revenge or of resentment; an assertion of her personhood that he had somehow suppressed. Who could say how or why or when?

Could Ruby herself have found her way through the labyrinthine paths of reason and self-justification? And did it matter that she had refused to be what the times and the mores demanded that she be? He emerged from a hundred nights of pounding thought and he forgave her. So he said "O.K." when Analise suggested an alternative course because he realized that his own instincts and will to survive were no more vital than hers were. Later as they sat among the trees, the plane growled over them much lower than it had been before.

"Do you think he saw us?" she whispered.

"– I don't know; he was pretty low."

"He won't land will he?"

"No, but he'll probably radio back if he saw us. Most of their army's not here yet. We'll have to watch out for their reconnaissance units, though."

"What are they?"

"Small groups of soldiers that go ahead of the army to gather information. They're like the eyes and ears of the army. They use airplanes, too. It's like sneaking around trying to find out where our forces are, how many and what they can expect from us. They try to take prisoners. They'll torture them for information."

Eventually they dusted the dirt from their clothes preparing to continue on. First, he rummaged in his knapsack and produced the pistol he had found at the mansion. "I got this for you," he said, offering her the pistol.

She stared at the proffered object. "…What am I supposed to do with it? I'm a nurse."

"Medical personnel are allowed to carry weapons to protect themselves and their patients."

Barney Turner had said the same thing; Jacob had a side arm the last time she saw him. She shook her head. "It doesn't seem right. I don't think I could ever shoot anyone – ever. Can you understand that? Thank you for thinking of me though…."

Reluctantly he started to replace the gun but paused. "Do you mind if I show you how it works?"

She sat smiling politely as he demonstrated how to hold the pistol and shoot it.

They continued in the general direction of the Ebro. They took turns using the binoculars, looking for signs of ground movement and listening for the sound of motor vehicles. Toward evening they stopped and when he spread his blanket under a tree, she looked up at the tree and wrinkled her nose. "Won't something drop on us?"

"– I don't think so."

She remained skeptical, focusing her attention on a number of large black ants going about their business on the ground, but she didn't say anything. It was not just the ants; it was the vulnerability of going to sleep next to a man for the first time in her life, and a strange man at that. And she was alone – literally in the middle of nowhere.

He noticed her discomfort. "There are bound to be bugs," he explained, watching her face. "I don't like them either. I've never slept on the ground before."

She looked around, hugging herself. Finally she pointed a delicate finger to something in the distance. "Do you think it might be better over there? See that ledge? That way we can see somebody coming a lot better."

He was on the verge of objecting. The ledge would be harder to get to and it was a good distance from the road. But then, truth be told, it was a far better vantage point and if nothing else, it was that much closer to France. She helped him roll up the blanket and tie it diagonally across his body. When they were ready, she searched his face and smiled. "Thank you. I'm sorry if I'm a nuisance, but…"

"Don't ever say that. You're not a nuisance. You're more safety conscious than I am, that's all. That's a good thing. You see and hear things before I do. It's going to take both of us to make it. We can't do it alone."

Night had fallen by the time they climbed up on the ledge. They could not see well enough to determine whether or not any bugs were present to welcome them.

CHAPTER 36

On the ledge they shared the blanket; he was acutely aware of her and longed to put his arm around her and draw her close to him but he knew that would frighten her and destroy her trust in him. Yet sometime during the night, their bodies seeking warmth, huddled together.

It was then, as they slept, that they remembered the mornings and the evenings of a distant past.

They were carried along on a river of dream-remembrances of everyday life and everyday things that had been their distant reality in a place shrouded in the fog of time.

They shared a dream-remembrance.

It was dawn when they were awakened by voices. They were lying together, their bodies touching. Self-conscious, she would have moved away but they both lay motionless, holding their breath. Below the ledge, horsemen were passing speaking a strange language. They heard occasional laughter. He guessed they were elite Moroccan cavalrymen wearing fezzes, and from the sound of horses' hooves there were twenty or so. The smell of horses drifted from the road.

They lay still until they could no longer hear them. Cautiously, they sat up and saw them in the distance spread out, searching through the olive groves. "That's a reconnaissance patrol," he whispered as though the patrol could hear. "They would have found us if you hadn't had us move."

She demurred. "I just hate bugs."

"It's funny," he said, "but I dreamt about horses last night…."

"You did? I did, too, and you were in the dream! You were on a horse – you had a spear and a sword…."

He was speechless for a moment. "– I dreamt about you, too! And you were on a horse; you had a bow and arrow and soldiers were hailing you and calling you Elissayah!"

"*Hanno! That's who you are. You were Hanno!*" she cried, "but the funny thing is, I don't remember what you looked like or how I knew your name but I knew it!"

"Do you remember what I told you about my nightmares? That I never actually *saw* you or heard you but I knew it was you? Was it like that?"

"Yes – it was like that… I could almost hear you…."

They examined each other's face as if for the first time. They probed each other for details that were rapidly fading into the mist of dreams until only the salient facts remained.

"How could we both have the same dream?" she wondered. "That's not possible."

"But we did, and I'm sure you were the leader even though you were a woman…."

"- I remember it seemed like we were going to fight the Romans. It must have been here – in the dream I mean. Back then Spain was called Iberia. How long ago could that have been?"

"I don't know. B.C something. I never heard of women fighting before except for legends – you know, like the Amazons…."

"The Iberian women did. They were cavalry. Don't ask me how I know that, but they were. Did we both really have the same dream? - I think I remember hearing 'Elissayah.'"

"Remember that medium I told you about? She said my nightmares involved somebody named 'El, See'. That's was all she could make out."

Their memories faded like steam from a pot. Except for the names Elissayah and Hanno. Their feeling of wonder remained. That they should both have the same dream and yet not know what the other looked like. A thought occurred to her. "- Maybe it's not that we both had the *same* dream, but maybe we both dreamed about the same *thing*. Does that make sense?"

He looked at her serious green eyes and slender face and nodded. "Either way we still knew each other, so what happened is still true; we both share the same past and memories and I know I loved you and you loved me. Does that make sense?"

She was cautious but said, "Uh huh."

They shared the last can of Russian beef with pieces of stale bread and lingered on the ledge in the warm sun with their backs against the wall of the ledge, their shoulders touching for the sense of comfort that it gave them; they looked out over the vast expanse of green and grey and purple land. In the distance, near the horizon, there was the haze that marked the Ebro River. Neither wanted to leave.

After a while she sighed. "We'll sound delusional to anyone but ourselves. Not so much because we had the same dream, but because we believe it wasn't just a dream. Everyone will say it's preposterous and how could you blame them? It could have been some sort of psychic experience."

They were stiff from sitting on the ledge and after peering about in all directions, they cautiously stood up and came down and walked around knowing they would have to continue their journey soon. Then one or the other said, "Don't look," and left to answer nature's call.

They lingered on the ledge and spoke of things from their lives and listened more carefully to the sound and substance of each other's voice, trying to fill in the blank spaces of the distant past. Night crept up and then it was dark. They lay side by side and looked up at the diamond encrusted sky sprinkled with blue sapphires, red rubies and green emeralds.

"Look!" she said with suppressed excitement. "Did you see that shooting star? There goes another one. I love looking at the sky; it never looks this way in the city. I've been waiting to see a vermillion streak."

"When I was a boy I wanted to be an astronomer and one Christmas my mother bought me a telescope, only it was just a toy. I wanted to see planets like the ones in magazines but I could barely make out the craters on the moon. I forget how old I was, nine or ten, but I knew enough to pretend I liked it; she was so pleased to give it to me. I knew she meant well."

"What was your mother like?"

"– My mother was small, kind of like you. She always wanted to be somebody and she wanted me to be somebody. I remember her saying over and over that I had to get an education and be respectable and if I did I'd meet people who would 'open doors' for me. I don't know how many times I heard that expression.

"When I graduated from college she hugged me so tight I can still almost feel it. I remember the look in her eyes; she forced herself not to cry, but her eyes glowed with tears.

Mom worked every day doing housework. Sometimes she would come home with little packages of leftover food that the people she worked for gave her, but it was food we could never afford."

"Didn't your father work?"

"Sure, but he never made enough. Nobody we knew did. Everybody had to work, especially if you had a family. That was the way it was. Still is. Nobody knew any other way. A man would put on airs if his wife didn't have to work. Mom would take me places whenever she could. I can't remember them all but I'll never forget the Wagner Institute on 17th Street.

"Wow! That's where I first saw fossils. My eyes must have been as big as saucers. When I was finally allowed to leave the street by myself, I can't tell you how many times I went back there. There was a friendly white guard with white hair who started calling me 'professor.' I thought he spoke funny; Mom said that was called an Irish brogue."

"Is that why you wanted to be an archeologist?"

"Still do, but what the heck – I'd like to be rich, too."

"Were you an only child?"

"No, I had two sisters and a brother. My sisters died of diphtheria when they were babies and my older brother," he shrugged, "we don't know where he is. He left home in 1919 and just lost contact."

She spoke of her mother who had once been a ballerina and was still beautiful and regal and she missed her. "Some of the other nurses have terrible things to say about their mothers. I can't imagine anyone ever feeling that way. Even when I was young, nine or ten, when my parents had an argument – nothing violent - but I was always on my mother's side. Sort of protective.

"She always knew how I was feeling; she could just look at my face and tell even when I tried to hide it. The wonderful thing was, I could tell her what was on my mind because she would listen to me. *Really* listen. I felt safe telling her things. She never tried to convince me that her way was better, but she would say, 'A forest looks different from the *outside*. Try to go in, Ana. See how it looks then.'"

They went to sleep with his arm around her, and they hoped they would dream of that other time and place that they had known - a place where they had loved each other, where they had a shared remembrance of Carthaginian invaders who had crossed the sea from Africa.

Then later the Roman invaders. Both invaders contested with each other, like snarling dogs, as to who would be entitled to subjugate and rape Iberia. Both came howling with gleaming shields and swords and swift horses. They employed cruelty as a weapon, intending that everyone would tremble and fall to their knees when they but heard their approach.

They drove terror stricken people from the coast and rivers and plains, always slaughtering, burning, pillaging. They seized virgins and young boys and demanded that gold be laid at their feet. Many who were spared were dragged away into slavery.

Not all Iberians submitted. Many stubbornly remained, always out of reach, filled with hatred, but sensibly retreating year after year, forming armies that fell upon isolated groups of Romans and occasionally contesting them in battle. Women sometimes proved the better generals and tacticians. Elissayah was one.

***

When he awoke from his dream-remembrance the next morning, Analise was sitting a little distance away from him. She was hugging her knees. Her head, resting on them, was turned away from him. By then, both knew the horrible, shameful reason for his nightmares.

Together on a cool dawn, prepared to fight the Romans who stood shoulder to shoulder in neat ranks behind their shields, spears thrust forward and on either side of them, mounted horsemen. Arrayed against them, the stubborn Iberians were a mob ignorant of military tactics or formations or maneuvers. Even when they were two to their one, hurling themselves forward in frenzied anger, they were still overwhelmed, pierced by showers of spears and arrows, and when the Iberians attempted to ward them off, they left themselves exposed to charges on both sides by Roman horsemen. Then followed the methodical charge in front by their soldiers who thrust their short swords into Iberian bellies, spilling their guts out upon the ground.

Yet the Iberians fiercely prevailed that time upon the Ebro River and Decius, the Roman general, never forgave them for he had been routed by a woman – Elissayah - who took command after her father, great chieftain Hambro, was hacked to pieces.

The Romans were contemptuous of Iberian men because they gave voice to women; they even permitted them to fight as cavalry and to sit on their councils. The Romans worked themselves into insane and murderous rages that women would dare contest arms with them and actually kill them, thus depriving them of all manhood.

Decius, his manhood humiliated by his defeat by a woman, could not return to Rome. He vowed to Rome that he would seize Elissayah and after he personally violated her repeatedly, he would let his soldiers have at her and then he would personally slash her from her crotch to her breasts, feed her entrails to the dogs, then carry her severed head attached by her hair to his saddle back to Rome. And to teach those Iberian she-dogs, and all women, never to raise their hand against a Roman, they would be violated in every way known to man, hacked to pieces and their flesh strewn over the fields.

Thus would Decius restore his manhood and proudly return to Rome.

Like hunting dogs sniffing the ground, he relentlessly followed the Iberians as they retreated toward the Pyrenees, their number diminished by desertion and battle. He followed month after month after month until they were cornered, and outnumbered thirty to one. They fought a hopeless battle. Roman soldiers spared her, under command to seize her alive though she slashed and slew all those within reach of her. They attacked her horse and when it fell, they rushed and eagerly seized her. Hannno had promised her that he would not let them take her alive and when he turned to save her by killing her, he saw his arm, still gripping his sword, lying upon the ground and then a spear plunged into his belly, pinning him to the ground and they were carrying Elissayah off with shouts of joy.

He had failed to save her. And now they both remembered.

When he awoke, he saw her sitting apart, hugging her knees and wondered whether or not they had had the same dream; he knew that they had but hoped that they had not. He said tentatively, "– I think I know why I have those nightmares…I failed to save you. I let them…."

Her head jerked up; she went white. She clapped her hands over her ears and vigorously shook her head. *"NO!"* she screamed. *"NO! I don't want to hear it! Stop talking!"*

Taken aback, he murmured an apology and reached for her but she almost shouted, *"Don't touch me!"* She covered her face.

Without another word, they later gathered their things and left the ledge and took the road to the Ebro, moving as rapidly as they could. She spoke only when necessary. He carried her bag at times and they stopped frequently. Later he stood before her and pleaded, "...Analise, I need you to say that you forgive me... Please."

"Oh, for God's sake!" she shouted, "*I don't want to think about it!* It was a thousand damn years ago!"

He wondered if their bodies would ever touch again. Much later, her tone was softer. "– I forgive you, but I don't want to think about it. I forgive you forever and a day. Satisfied?"

***

They took turns using the binoculars for signs of the patent leather hats of the para-military Civil Guards. Analise saw a bombed-out village ahead. The houses had burned to the ground leaving heaps of rubble and ragged smoke blackened walls. "There's somebody over there," she said. "No – there're three - six of them. I think they're from our side." She passed the glasses to him.

They were unarmed, prowling the ruins. Even unarmed they could still be dangerous. They were sure to want food and he would not trust them around Analise. It seemed prudent to wait until they left before they continued through the village where they hoped to find a well to replenish their canteens.

They spent part of the afternoon waiting. For some reason, after searching the ruins, the six men loitered. Mark and Analise decided they could no longer wait. He reached into his knapsack and removed the pistol that he had offered her before.

She accepted it and he showed her again how to use it; she held it awkwardly at first but soon felt confident enough to offer to shoot it. He said they should do nothing to attract attention so she stuffed it in her pocket. Cautiously, they approached the village. When they were close enough to make eye contact, they noticed that three of the soldiers were still in their teens. Mutual curiosity was palpable. They were less than six feet apart when Mark and Analise heard the ominous sound of fast approaching motorcycles behind them. The six soldiers were startled. They stared down the road, spoke rapidly in Spanish and dashed away to hide.

"Reconnaissance! Quick!" Mark said to her. "Hide in one of the houses...."

"That's the first place they'll look!" she protested.

"We'll cover ourselves with debris. Hurry!"

They scrambled to find houses with sufficient debris. He quickly covered her with fallen boards and charred remains but left space for her to see. He ran to another house and covered himself. One of the six men noticing what they were doing attempted to emulate them but his companions pulled him away. They raced away on either side of the road.

Minutes later they rushed back chased by three Moroccan cavalrymen right into the arms of the motorcyclists. A shot rang out. One of the six soldiers seemed to stumble, tried to keep his balance, then fell twitching. The others raised their hands in surrender. The three horsemen were laughing, one waved the discharged rifle.

There were two motorcycles with side cars. An officer with blond hair stepped from one side car; the other side car was empty. As the five prisoners sat on the ground, their captors stood in a loose circle eying and discussing them. A Moroccan went over to one of the older captives, a man in his thirties, and stood him up in front of his companions. He then carelessly raised his rifle with one hand and pulled the trigger. The prisoner's head jerked backward. Blood spurted out like an oil well as he fell, trailing blood at the feet of his fellows.

One of the men sitting on the ground suddenly leapt to his feet and dashed headlong toward the burned-out houses. They could easily have shot him; instead two of the Moroccans chased him down and dragged him back. They found the incident vastly amusing. The took turns beating him with their fists, the butt of their rifles and once on the ground he was repeatedly kicked in his groin and stomped on his head until it was a misshapen mass with dead, bulging eyes.

Only three were left.

One of the young recruits, no more than seventeen, was yanked to his feet. As he pleaded for his life, he wet his pants. His captors roared with laughter, pointing to the boy's shame. They made him remove his ragged dirty trousers and then ordered him to remove his filthy underwear.

The three Moroccans forced him to the ground. One of them lowered his pants and proceeded to sodomize the boy. The others cheered him on as they restrained the screaming victim.

Mark shut his eyes but he could not shut his ears. Later, fearing for Analise, he hazarded another glance and saw the boy lying in a fetal position, holding his stomach, bleeding from the rectum and uttering deep, guttural sobs.

Ignoring him, the Moroccans looked at the other two who stared back with round, petrified eyes. The motorcyclists stood apart, watching with detached curiosity. Another of the Moroccans was loosening his belt. He playfully beckoned to the younger of the two survivors who immediately began babbling in Spanish. One word stood out. - *Senorita, senorita!*

The blond officer was suddenly alert. He approached the prisoner and listened to what he was saying. The prisoner then vigorously pointed to where Analise was hiding. Mark remembered one of the six had tried to emulate his and Analise's tactics and hide among the ruins when he was pulled away by his companions.

The blond officer, followed by the other two cyclists, marched over to the ruins and began pushing aside the debris until they discovered Analise cringing among the ashes. A shout of joy went up. They roughly pulled her, clutching her nurse's bag, out from the wreckage and half dragged, half marched her away. She did not call to Mark but he heard her cry out, "I'm a nurse! I'm a nurse!"

He made no move to interfere. Three men wrestling with a woman presented too much confusion. But he knew with certainly that he was going to blow a hole in the blond officer's head. He saw them snatch her bag away from her and then fling her to the ground. The officer pulled his pants down as his companions held her arms stretched out over her head. The officer was trying to pull her pants down and force her legs apart. She resisted, crossing and re-crossing her ankles and twisting her body in a silent, desperate struggle.

Now that he fully understood how he had failed to save her from unimaginable agony at the hands of Decius, he knew now how he must redeem his ancient failure. There were six nationalists. Three Moroccans were ahead of him and the three cyclists were to his right. They were three car lengths away. He had to kill Analise before they had a chance to kill him.

They might meet again five or fifteen thousand years from now. Would they remember any of this in dreams and nightmares as they now dimly remembered Iberia and the Romans? He gathered his feet under him. All at once he thrust himself up like a whale rising from the sea. His eyes were only on Analise; she was terrified by both the past and the present horror.

The six nationalists swung around to face him. In seeming to be in slow motion as he charged forward. He saw that *only... one... Moroccan... actually... held... a... rifle* - the one guarding the prisoners.

The other two had put their weapons on the ground in order to help sodomize the boy; the two cyclists had done the same thing in order to restrain Analise so that the officer could rape her.

The second Mark exploded from the rubble and distracted the nationalists, the two prisoners of the Moroccans, instantly made a dash for the rifles that the Moroccans had laid aside.

Mark, holding his gun straight out before him, shot the rifleman in the face just as their eyes met. Instantly he wheeled to his right. Charging desperately to Analise - he jammed the gun against the startled officer's forehead while the officer was frantically trying to swing his gun around. He blew a bloody hole between his surprised eyes. The officer, still on his knees, slumped at Analise's feet.

The other two cyclists had let go of her wrists in order to snatch up their weapons. One swung around on Mark but immediately after shooting the officer, Mark swung his gun around and shot him in the head. It took slightly more than one second.

There was a flash of *déjà vu*. He had done this before. And had failed to save Analise.

Now he knew that it was too late to kill the other cyclist.

A shot rang out.

CHAPTER 37

Hiding in the burned-out debris of the house, Analise saw the men coming for her. Terrified, she had reached for her pistol but she was lying on it and by the time she reached her pocket they had grabbed her arms and were dragging her out with whoops of joy. She remembered Barney Turner declaring that the nationalists did not respect medical personnel. Still she shouted, *"I'm a nurse! I'm a nurse!"*

She had resisted calling to Mark for help for fear of his being captured, too, but after they flung her to the ground and were pulling her arms above her head and one of them was trying to pull her pants down in order to force himself between her legs, desperate, she opened her mouth to scream his name.

A shot, like a scream, froze everyone. Looking wildly about, her captors leapt for their weapons. There were other shots from the direction of the Moors.

Suddenly she was free.

Mark appeared with a savage expression on his face and thrusting his gun against the head of the officer trying to rape her, shot him. Flesh flew out from the other side of his head. Instantly she reached for her gun, even as the officer fell across her ankles, jerking with spasms. She immediately pointed the gun up at the other man on her right side, closed her eyes and pulled the trigger. Shot in the groin, he screamed and fell writhing in pain. But before she fired her gun - almost simultaneously - she heard another shot. The other man who had been on her left holding her down fell dead beside her.

Mark realized that Analise had saved him. Because of her he had not failed her again. He looked at her victim, still writhing on the ground, then over at the commotion where the Moroccan soldiers were. Fueled by terror, their captives had grabbed their tormentors' weapons in the split second of confusion caused by Mark's charge, and shot them. They were seizing the Moroccans' horses; Mark bent and dragged the dead officer off Analise's ankles and helped her up. She was hobbling. "My pants!" she said.

She was hampered while she fastened them because she would not let go of her gun. Meanwhile, Mark selected the motorcycle that held a spare can of gas in the sidecar. He cushioned it with his blanket and helped her into it.

"My bag!" she cried, preparing to get out. He dashed back, retrieved her bag, kicked the cycle into motion and roared off. Half an hour later, he pulled off the road. The ride had been bumpy, especially for Analise in the side car. He dismounted and came to her side.

"Are you all right?" he asked.

She nodded but did not look at him. She still clutched the pistol.

"– Do you want to get out and stretch your legs?"

She nodded but did not move or say anything. After a while he knelt beside her. "Thanks. You saved my life. When I heard that shot I thought...."

She shouted, "Don't you realize I just killed a man! *Do you?*" She glared with thin lipped anger, her eyes green marbles.

He was stunned. "– No, Analise, what I realize is you saved me from being shot. I wouldn't be here now if it weren't for you. - Would you rather they raped you?"

She refused to look at him or say anything. Some time passed with him kneeling beside her before she said in a broken voice, "I'm sorry, Mark, but I didn't come here to kill people." She buried her face, still clutching the gun, her shoulders heaving with sobs. She did not tell him, but it disturbed her to think that her mother had also killed a man; it did not matter how or why, it only mattered that she and her mother had killed someone – they had both committed murder.

He did not know how to comfort her. He wanted to hug her but if he touched her, would she angrily wrench away? "Don't forget," he said softly, "I killed someone, too and I'm not sorry for saving myself and you. We escaped, Analise – we survived. Willie didn't. Nothing's your fault. What were you supposed to do? You told them you were a nurse; that should have been enough for any sane person. You were attacked in every sense of the word! Hell, you're allowed to protect yourself. Your body's sacred."

She offered no response but sat hugging herself, looking miserable and staring into the middle distance at things she did not see, remembering the shots, but mostly the man between her legs trying to force them apart. And Decius who had.

Mark had saved her, but that could not erase the memory of multiple horrors. Later she got out of the sidecar and they walked among the olive trees. "I'm sorry," she said. "I mean about our dreams and blaming you. I guess I'm a mess."

"*No you're not!* You have every right to feel that way! Do you realize you've been through hell and you're still standing? Almost being murdered on the ship, being abandoned on the road and then this and I don't know what else. We're living in this life, and one from a thousand years ago! Let's just try to get back to civilization and go from there…What do you say?"

The pounding she had taken in the side car was aggravating her back, a reminder of having been thrown over the side of the ship. She mounted the cycle behind him. They roared away determined not to worry about reconnaissance planes or patrols. They knew it would be risky but they fled in the general direction of the Ebro.

***

The nights were colder the farther north they went; the roads twisted and turned following the path of least resistance through the rocky surface. They saw villages clustered at the foot of the mountain range and avoiding them was difficult. They were sure to be patrolled by Civil Guards who were pro Fascist. At some point she asked him how he learned to ride a motorcycle.

"A friend in college, Bobby Evans, had a motorcycle. We both lived in Philadelphia so on school breaks he'd let me ride back with him; we'd take turns driving. I never knew what became of him. That's the way it is a lot of the time; you graduate and everybody scatters and disappears."

The refugees on the road, at the sound of their approach, either shrank back or left the road altogether. In the distance, whitewashed houses of farmers and the huts of peasants appeared on hillsides. One particular farmhouse was not far from where the road and an ancient footpath intersected. Faded whitewash flaked from the wooden sides of the house; gray smoke drifted from the chimney.

He stopped and dismounted. He took out his pistol and walked cautiously toward the house. She watched, tense with apprehension. She got off the cycle and took her pistol from her pocket and as he approached the house, she looked warily about for signs of movement.

The bare, warped wooden door was ajar. He knocked. Meeting no response, he pushed it open and entered. He was met with the smell of animal urine. Food was cooking in a pot in the fireplace. A roasted chicken sat on a chipped plate on a bare wooden table. Cautiously he searched the two rooms. The occupants had evidently fled at the sound of their approach. He went to the door and motioned to Analise to come in.

She wrinkled her nose. "What's that smell?"

He shrugged. They found earthen bowls. She took them from him and set them in the fireplace. When she was satisfied that they had been purified, she used the poker to remove them. She repeated the process with the spoons that they found. The food in the pot did not look like anything they had ever seen before but it tasted savory.

There was a large loaf of bread wrapped in a faded blue cloth sitting next to the chicken.

They broke off pieces. It was golden brown, crusty and good. They ate their fill standing by the table, pistols in hand, watching the door. They wrapped the chicken and the rest of the bread in the cloth, and then they replenished their canteens from the pitcher of water that sat on the floor next to the table. He dug in his pocket and placed twenty pesetas on the table.

"Is that going to be enough?" she asked.

"It's two days' pay."

"It may not be enough. I'd leave more. We must have frightened them badly."

He left five days' pay. Once they had to stop and push the cycle along a narrow road blocked by the skeletons of battle - rusted and burned out vehicles amid a scattering of bones of decomposed bodies. Seats and tires had long since been scavenged from the vehicles. A lone tank sat beside the road with its armor twisted and rusted. The hatch was bent into an immovable "V" shape.

"Guys are probably still in there," he guessed, approaching the hulk.

"Look how rusty it is. I wonder how long it's been here."

"Hard to say. There was a big battle before we got here. I think that's when the army got pushed back across the river."

At their elevation they could see in the distance what appeared to be rooftops along the Ebro River. From their height, the olive groves appeared to be green cotton balls lined up in neat rows. They would reach the Ebro in a matter of hours. But twenty minutes after they resumed their journey, they ran out of gas. They pushed the cycle as far off the road as they could and proceeded on foot.

They had only taken fifteen or twenty steps before she stopped. Her eyes were thoughtful.

"– I wonder - could there be any gas left in that tank? It didn't look like it burned."

Without hesitation they retraced their steps. The tank held gas. "What made you remember the tank?"

"I never saw one before."

"We'll need a siphon to get the gas out." He looked to her for a suggestion.

"– I've got two catheters in my bag. Will that work?"

They joined them together with adhesive tape. Then they pushed the motorcycle back to the tank.

The catheters were too short to reach from gas tank to gas tank. They were reluctant to abandon their pot of gold. "We could fill one of our canteens," she suggested, "and fill the tank that way." He proceeded to suck on the end to get the gas moving but nothing happened. She looked sympathetic as he tried repeatedly.

"I'll try," she said.

His instinct was to say no, but it was as fleeting as the wink of an eye. He shrugged and she tried. Nothing happened. Reluctantly they concluded that short of tilting the armored tank on its side, they could not get the gas out. They would have to walk the rest of the way. But at about the same spot where they had stopped before, Analise had yet another idea. When she explained it, his face lit up. "I think that'll work!"

She cut off a strip of his blanket with her surgical scissors. He lowered most of the strip into the tank. Like a wick, the material soaked up the gas. He then held the strip over the tank of the motorcycle with one hand and with his free hand squeezed the strip down so that the gas flowed into the tank. She suggested it might work better if she held the strip of cloth and he used both his hands to squeeze the gas into the tank. And she gave him a pair of gloves. They wrung out enough gas to partly fill the tank. She rubbed his hand with lotion as he looked at her fondly. "You know," he said, "you're quite an engineer."

"No," she smiled. "I remembered when I went to summer camp. At night, we'd see how the wicks in oil lamps soaked up the oil. They never put in enough oil to last as long as we wanted to stay up."

***

They reached the vicinity of the Ebro in the evening. They hid the motorcycle in a grove and waited until nightfall. Shielded by the dark, they crept along a road, alert for the slightest sight or sound of the Civil Guard. They skirted a village where light shone in many of the windows. In the distance they saw the outline of a boat pulled up on the river bank next to a rickety dock. Guns drawn, they crept closer. The oars were missing.

"I think I saw a house farther back," she whispered. "Some olive trees are in front of it."

Cautiously, they drew near the house. The window was too high to see into it. There was another structure about fifty feet away. He picked up a piece of wood and hurled it against the side of the structure. Soon, the door of the house opened. A stocky man came out to investigate. He appeared to be in his fifties. Mark, who was pressed against the house, stepped forward and pointed his gun in the man's face. His eyes widened and then focused on the gun.

A woman followed him out, wiping her hands on her apron. Seeing the danger, she shouted something excitedly in Spanish, waving her hands as she rushed toward them.

Analise blocked her way, holding up her palm and brandishing her gun. All four of them froze. Mark pointed to the river. Turning to his side, carefully keeping the gun away from the man, he made a rowing motion with his arms and pointed to the far river bank. The woman crept closer, speaking and gesturing all the while. Mark repeated the rowing motion. The man shook his head, staring at the gun.

While holding her gun on the woman, Analise dug in her pocket and produced a number of pesetas that she offered to the boatman. He eyed the money but made no move to take it. The woman by gestures wanted to speak with her husband. After they conferred, he again firmly shook his head.

"Wait for me by the boat," Mark said. "We'll figure something out."

Analise looked uncertain. "– You're not going to hurt them are you?"

He refused to lie to her. "– Maybe scare them a little."

She shook her head. "No. I'll look around for the oars. I know how to row a boat."

She gingerly felt her way around the house in the dark. He was getting anxious when she reappeared. "They're leaning against the house."

He prodded the couple ahead of him. The oars were much longer than he had imagined. He lifted them to his shoulder and said, "We have to at least pretend we'll shoot or we'll never get across the river. Hold them here until I get to the boat and then leave them."

It took both of them to push the boat into the water. They knew that the oars were much too heavy for her to manage and he had never been in a boat before. He would have to row. She showed him how to sit with his back facing the direction he wanted to go. They put the oars in the oarlocks and were on the point of leaving when they saw the couple hurrying through the dark toward them.

They took out their guns and held them at the ready. The boatman paused. His hands were empty. He motioned to himself and made a sign of rowing. He got into the boat and when they were on the point of leaving, the woman splashed into the water with her hand held out to Analise. Analise gave her a number of pesetas and the woman withdrew with an expression that reminded Analise of Juanita's ill-concealed hostility.

When they were safely across, they watched the man row slowly back across the river before throwing themselves on a grassy slope with a sigh of relief.

"I wonder what changed his mind?" Mark mused. "You think his wife got after him for turning down the money?"

"He wanted his boat back. It may have been a bit of both, but if we left without him, how would he get his boat back? - Are we safe now?"

"Almost. We still have to worry about the Civil Guard and the Assault Guard. They're like the cops. The Civil Guard's mostly rural; the Assaults are in the cities. They're the ones who'll be watching the border. If we get stopped we'll need a reason for why we're here. If we're stopped crossing the border – we don't have a story that'll mean anything."

She drew her knees up and wrapped her arms around them. She looked at the haze above the river for some time before she spoke in a calm, assured voice. "We've been here before. Many times. We can find our way." She looked at him and smiled. "This is our country, Hanno, remember?"

He reached for her hand and they sat close together in silence. Later she searched in her nurse's bag and found the Red Cross arm band that she had never worn and without a word, tied it around his arm. "There," she said. "You were an ambulance driver if anyone asks."

He removed the binoculars and tossed it and his rifle among the trees.

CHAPTER 38

They walked toward the mountains under the blanket that they shared as a buffer against the wind. "Do you hear that?" she asked, glancing around. "It sounds like a car."

She always heard things before he did. He peered up and down the empty winding road. Soon a vehicle appeared quickly closing the distance between them. "Uh oh! Probably Civil Guard," he warned. "We may have to shoot."

She took out her gun; they moved to the shoulder of the road, guns concealed under the blanket and watched the vehicle approach. The automobile rushed toward them and sped past in a dull green wall of dust and wind. Relieved, they stared after it. Suddenly the taillights glowed red. The vehicle stopped. It backed up a distance and stopped again.

They watched a heavyset man emerge from the passenger side and lumber back towards them with a fixed stare. The driver got out and with one elbow resting on the roof, watched. Both wore civilian clothes. When the heavyset man was near enough, Mark smiled, surprised.

Tank Maynard returned the smile, waving a greeting. Mark holstered his gun. They shook hands with evident pleasure, their eyes alive with curiosity. Tank tipped his hat to Analise. "I don't believe we've met," he said, "but I think you were the damsel in distress on the ship." Turning to Mark he asked, "What the hell are you two doing here?"

"It's a long story, Tank, but to make it short – trapped behind enemy lines, escaped yesterday."

Tank's eyes rested on Mark's Red Cross armband.

"A little extra insurance. That's supposed to be our safe haven. What about you? Where are you off to?"

"Ripoll. This is the quickest way. All the roads are wall to wall with refugees and soldiers. – Something tells me you haven't heard."

"– No. Heard what? What's with Ripoll?"

"Prime Minister Negrin dismissed all the International Brigades. They're all being sent home. You're no longer needed or wanted. Take your pick."

They were stunned. "- When was this?" she asked. "Are you sure?"

"Why would he do that?" Mark asked.

"Negrin's been making peace overtures to Franco for weeks. By sending the Internationals home, he's expecting Franco to reciprocate and pull his German and Italian "volunteers" back, too. Fat chance. War's been over for months. Franco won.

"Truth be told, all you internationals have been a pain in the butt – pardon me saying so, but they have been. The Spanish soldiers resent them. Not only because they can't understand them, but they don't want foreigners giving them orders, especially since over half the Internationals have been killed or wounded."

Mark and Analise looked at each other. The other man in the car drew near. He was tall, lean and had a longish, serious face. He fixed grey eyes on Mark.

"What about Ripoll?" Analise asked. "Where's that?"

"It's the end of the line for anybody trying to escape. From there it's Perpignan in France."

"They have concentration camps there," Mark warned her. "We're not going there."

The tall man spoke. "You two been actually *travelling* together?"

Sensing hostility in his tone, neither answered. Tank hastened to interpose. "What're you planning to do?" he asked Mark.

"Leave, especially since you say the Internationals are being kicked out."

"It's a nightmare leaving or staying. What's left of the Army is trapped across the river down by Fayon and Cherta. They got whipped at Sierra Pandols and you got 70, 80 thousand refugees and soldiers up in Catalonia trying to squeeze across the International Bridge into France...."

"C'mon, Tank," the other man growled, "we don't have all day. Give the lady a ride and let's get the hell outa here."

"If it's as bad as Tank says it is," Mark told him, "what's she supposed to do in Ripoll, stand in line without food or water with a million strangers?"

"You shut your mouth!" the tall man snarled. "We'll take care of her!"

Tank gently put his hand on the man's back and tried to make light of the situation. "The man's got a gun, Joe," he chuckled, "been killing people...."

"I don't give a goddamn!" Joe barked, brushing Tank's hand away. "No way in *hell* I'm leaving a white woman alone, in the middle of *nowhere*, with a goddamn *nigger*. Let's go!" he ordered, grabbing Analise by her arm and starting to move off.

The second he grabbed her arm she gave a frightened scream, wrenched free and he was left holding the blanket while she stood pointing her gun at him -

The second he grabbed Analise's arm Mark whipped his gun from its holster, lunged forward, and with his left hand pushing against Joe's chest fired at his head -

The moment Joe grabbed her arm Tank lunged toward him roaring, "Stop it!" He pushed against Mark with just enough force to spoil his aim. The gun discharged inches over Joe's head. Joe felt the heat from the explosion and smelled the gun powder that touched them all. He blinked away the smoke that stung his eyes.

They froze for a startled count of three.

Joe was ashen, torn between outrage and disbelief. He stared at Mark's murderous brown eyes and lips curled in anger. It dawned on Joe that Mark meant to kill him. Analise was standing by Mark, his right shoulder covering her left. Her gun was still pointed at him; her slender face still hard with anger.

Tank shouted, "Get back in the goddamn, freaking car and *stay there!*"

"Hell, no! He can kill me but I'm not leaving!"

"You touch me again," she warned with rigid lips, "he won't have to. I will. *Keep your hands off me!* I'll go where I want when I want." Then near tears and in a quavering voice she said, "Everybody who's tried to harm me ever since I left home has been white. Go find somebody else to 'protect.' Mark'll protect me."

Several seconds passed. Finally Joe wheeled and strode angrily back to the car.

"- Sorry about that," Tank said quietly. "Look, here's my advice. Keep going north. Try to get out through Andorra. It's a tiny country the size of a pinprick but it's been a smuggler's paradise for centuries.

"If you can meet up with a smuggler, he'll have you in France in less than a day. Of course, you have to have money. I can give you a lift to within striking distance."

***

Analise and Mark sat in the back of the car in total silence. Their heads touched occasionally as they dozed. As evening approached, they reached a village inn near the Segre River.

"Now's a good time," Tank said. "Did you keep your passport like I told you? Good. People with money and on Franco's list are getting out that way."

"- What kind of money?" Analise asked.

He shook his head. "Can't say but I'll soon find out."

Tank had them wait in the car. He took Joe with him and they were gone for nearly an hour. Children appeared. They stood at a respectful distance and discussed the green vehicle.

"I don't know what we'll use for money," Mark said quietly. "We may have to try getting out through the mountain but I don't think we'd survive."

She looked at the snowcapped mountains in the distance. "We wouldn't. It's cold just sitting here. I have some money, but I don't know if it's enough. My mother always said no matter what, you need money in Europe. Lots of it."

"I have a couple hundred," he offered, "and a pocket full of *pesetas*. With the exchange rate, a dollar might be worth 20 times as much. What do you think?"

She opened her nurse's bag. "My mother had me line it with money. That's why I never let my bag out of my sight."

He looked at her and said frankly, "I think you're the one doing the rescuing rather than the other way around."

She smiled, closing the bag. "We're rescuing each other."

Tank returned accompanied by a thin man with large, curious brown eyes. He gripped a pipe between his teeth. He did not approach the car. Tank leaned his head in the window and spoke quietly. "That's Alvaro. He'll help you. Listen – no matter what they ask for, offer half or less. Walk away if you have to. All you have to do is show a British pound or an American dollar and somebody will show up. The dollar's worth about 35 francs; a British pound is five times that. You think you have enough?"

"We're rich by those standards," she said."

"You'll probably need about two or three hundred; that'd give you ten thousand their money. That should do it."

They got out of the car. Mark shook his hand and then impulsively gave him a quick hug to their mutual embarrassment.

"Thank you," Analise murmured, and she gave him a hug that embarrassed no one.

Joe came out of the inn and got behind the wheel. He glared at Mark. "I hope to God I see you back in the States!"

Mark leaned toward the open window. "Do you know that if it wasn't for Tank, I'd blow your worthless brains out. Look at me – do you think I'm kidding? Hate's a two-way street, buddy. If you can spare the time, thank him for saving your worthless life because I'd love to kill you for Willie."

They watched the car drive angrily away. Joe wondered – *who the hell's Willie?*

CHAPTER 39

They were on their way to France.

They exchanged their uniforms for ill-fitting second-hand clothes that had a damp, moldy smell. Their guide used hand motions to lead them through the stinging cold night into a forest to a waiting truck. Clutching blankets, they were directed to sit on the floor in the back.

Ten minutes later four other people wordlessly entered the truck – a family of three and a silver haired man. The husband was a stern looking man in his fifties. He had a dismissive air about him. His taller, thin wife and their adult daughter were each dressed in black. The family bore mournful expressions which did not disguise their disdainful glances at Mark and Analise. They sat as far away as space permitted. The silver haired man also bore a haughty demeanor. Their guide warned them never to speak or make a sound unless the truck was in full motion.

Some moments later the guide came back with a bucket which he deposited at their feet without a word. He also gave each of them a loaf of bread and a slab of cheese. After he left, men loaded boxes of merchandise into the remaining space filling it from top to bottom and from side to side until the only light was a faint suggestion at the ceiling of the truck. The doors of the truck were slammed shut. They were left in darkness.

An hour into their lurching, stop and go escape, the silver haired man, who sat next to Analise, made several attempts to engage the father of the family in conversation. He ignored him. Ten minutes or so later, he directed his voice in the darkness toward the disreputable couple.

Speaking barely above a whisper, Analise replied, "*La norteamericana.*"

"Ah, Americans!" he rejoiced. He revealed that he had friends in America. He had taught both at Harvard and at Yale and, yes – he had briefly served as a Socialist Deputy in the Cortes in 1936. But why that was now a crime punishable by death, only a madman could answer. And was it a crime….

"Shhhh!" Analise cautioned. The truck was slowing to a stop.

After the truck picked up speed again – "…. Is it a crime," he whispered passionately, "that my name is Azana, the same as Manual Azana, the Republican president? I am a professor, not a politician! And though men may differ, why is there no room for compromise and courtesy?"

His grievance simmered in the darkness but to help pass the time, he spoke of his time in America to which he planned to return once he got to France. He seemed compelled to talk either from nervousness or from habit. Sometime later, someone made use of the bucket. The stench was overpowering but there was no escape from the heavy, clinging sulfurous gas. Azana fell silent when the truck began to slow again.

The truck stopped. A door opened and closed. Voices outside began arguing. Abruptly the back doors of the truck were flung open and a glimmer of light flowed along the ceiling. The argument grew louder. Not long after, they heard the merchandise being removed. Analise and Mark squeezed each other's hand, their heads touching and their hearts racing.

More light appeared until they could see apprehension in the anxious eyes of each other. Mark mourned the mandatory surrender of their weapons. How could he possibly protect Analise now? He felt her draw closer to him. What desperate sacrifice could he make for her that would not simply end in his death and her being brutalized as had happened in the distant past and almost repeated mere days ago?

Then the boxes of merchandise were being reloaded. The light in the truck gradually diminished to their relief. The doors slammed shut again and the truck gave a jerk and resumed its journey. Still they clung to each other for the comfort it gave. He buried his face in her hair and she pressed her face against his neck and they felt safe.

Sleeping was difficult because they grew tense each time the truck slowed. "– Do you know much about Spanish history?" she asked Azana softly.

His reply was unexpectedly terse. "Why shouldn't I?"

Mark spoke for the first time. "She means that you may be a physicist or an engineer, not a historian."

"That offers no excuse for being ignorant of one's own history," he countered stiffly.

Nothing further was said. The truck labored up one steep incline after another. Analise and Mark shivered in the unheated compartment with their inadequate blankets drawn about them and their bodies pressed together for warmth. Finally the professor, mastering his indignation, deigned to speak. "Why do you ask?"

"I was curious – who were the Iberians? Were they the original people of Spain?"

After a long pause his voice came out of the darkness – "Yes, until the Carthaginians, the Romans, the Moors and the Visigoths took turns destroying not only them but also their language, their history and their culture. The name Iberia comes from Iber and that meant the Ebro River. The culture of Spain is now a mixture of Christian and Muslim. There's still a lot of evidence of Moorish or Muslim culture. Cynics will tell you, 'Scratch a Spaniard and there bleeds a Moor.' Rubbish!"

"Isn't there any evidence at all about the Iberians?" she persisted. "There must be monuments, records...."

He snorted a cynical laugh. "What there was has been lost, stolen, destroyed or merged into somebody else's culture. – You must remember one thing about history, young lady, and it will explain it all: conquered people never get to write their own history; they become part of the conqueror's history and what is left is dismissed as 'folklore,' 'myth' or 'superstition.' The conqueror is always good and the vanquished always bad.

"Those who conquer will appropriate your language, your customs, your food, and by taking your women, he will erase all trace of you. The Iberians mastered copper, tin, gold, silver; they forged arms – any race that does that also develops records, but...." He left the rest unsaid.

They lurched and swayed a while in silence. Analise was not satisfied. "Did – I think I read somewhere that the women actually fought in their armies. Did they?"

He expressed astonishment. "– Why, yes! But how on earth did you know? We've only just discovered that. – Yes, they fought alongside the men and they participated in councils and were even priestesses. Who told you?"

"Oh, I don't know. I must have read it somewhere. Do you know what Iberians looked like?"

He was amused. "After thousands of years? Dragons, if you believe their conquerors. As I mentioned, conquerors erase the features of those they conquer. Some say Iberians came from Africa because you can practically see Africa across the Mediterranean; others say Asia or the Caucasus....I, for one, say the last of the Iberians are the Basques but my colleagues laugh at me."

She was a little depressed at what seemed to be the total destruction of the Iberians whom she now believed were her and Mark's ancestors. Azana continued and innocently banished them further into invisibility.

"Even now," he said, "this miserable war will be written by Franco. People like you won't even be a footnote. Your nation's own history is no exception. When I taught at Yale, one of the professors took umbrage when I reminded him that it was the French, not George Washington, who won Americans their independence at the Battle of Yorktown. The French suffered grave losses, the Americans – maybe 60 or 70. The French fleet destroyed the British forts and prevented British ships from landing reinforcements. But... 'history' ignores it all."

"The Iberians," Analise began," how long ago was that? I mean Hannibal, the Romans...?"

"Exact dates anyone can guess. Two hundred B.C would not be wrong."

Analise murmured to Mark, "That's two thousand years ago!"

***

The journey ended among trees. Snow lay on the ground. They kept their blankets and were led several shivering miles on foot to an open truck. Huddled on the cold bed of the truck under the open sky, they had to lie down and a tarpaulin was pulled over them. It offered some protection from the elements as they commenced a long, bumpy, cold, uncomfortable journey into the night.

Some hours later they arrived at a farm in France.

Others had arrived before them. Everyone slept on hay in a large barn, but no one complained. On the second day, a black sedan appeared and the family of three got in and vanished. It was only then that Azana confided that the man was a well-known Republican general fleeing for his life, but he would not divulge the general's name. Over several days they were moved, always at night, from one way station to another. One guide always kept his face concealed behind a large red handkerchief.

CHAPTER 40

Once in Paris they found their way to the Hotel Les Saisons where they had first met. It was one of the "friendly" places for the Internationals. They engaged separate rooms and for the first time felt free from the tensions of anger and the sounds of death. They stood by the window of her room with an arm around the other and looked down into the street. "So much in so short a time," she mused.

"Maybe we can stay here forever," he said hopefully.

It had been a short time. He remembered Ben and Svetlana and Harold in the room above the print shop and the unexpected passion that the three of them had shown when speaking of the war. And the woman who was angry because she wanted to fight in the war and not tend to sick soldiers. Walter and his corny jokes. Danny and Willie and the bastard blond officer.

So much in so short a time.

She wondered whether or not Clara and Irene had made it out; she remembered the soldier who was paralyzed and had taught her humanity. Commissar Juanita Aquilas taught her the color of hatred. Where was Jacob? And Iberia - Was the future an extension of the past?

> *Dear Mom,*
>
> *I'm in Paris, I'm safe and I just want to rest, rest, rest and bathe, bathe, bathe and wash my hair and my underwear every day until I feel clean again. I enjoy feeling in control of my life once more.*
>
> *I'm sorry I couldn't call you or write. There were no phones and even here the phone is virtually useless. I hear people screaming to be heard when they are just calling England which is a lot closer than America. I am not destitute. Even though we had to bribe our way past border guards, with the exchange rate we're in good shape. I've missed you terribly and I can't wait to get home and tell you all about Spain until your ears drop off.*

I guess you read that Prime Minister Negrin discharged all of the International Brigades. A lot of them feel betrayed, and they were. Many had escaped from Germany, Poland, Romania, Italy; the list goes on. The Spanish government had promised them citizenship but under Franco they can't stay in Spain without being shot and they can't go home without being shot. Now they have nowhere to go.

Even Americans are in trouble. Our State Department won't give them papers to return to America. The Spanish government took their passports so the men can't prove who they are and our government considers them Communists and not worth helping. The only help they are getting is from two men, Bernard Baruch and Frederick Thompson who put up $10,000 to help get some of them home. That will only cover about 80 men. The Nation *magazine is also asking for donations. The whole thing is a disgrace. Those men were fighting for democracy.*

I found Jacob in Spain. He was beyond exhausted, going days on end without proper sleep. We were not able to have anything approaching a real conversation. We were both exhausted and because he is an officer and I am not, it is supposed to be against the rules for us to associate!

But I don't think we feel as we once did. The truth is I have fallen in love with Mark. I have not told him that. I don't feel it is right as long as there is a possible chance that Jacob and I can make it. I feel I owe it to Jacob to go forward.

I will have to tell you about Mark when I see you. He saved my life on the ship and he later saved me from being raped in Spain. But things between us go far beyond that.

Mom – I may as well tell you – Mark is colored and I can see the shock on your face.

I know that if I said he was as rich as Rockefeller and as handsome as Clark Gable and as smart as Einstein, everyone would simply say – "But he's a Negro.*" Can you see how utterly absurd that is? You also said that Europe is no place for love. For Mark and me – neither is any other place, so I have a pretty good idea of what I'm getting into. France may be the best bet but with Hitler and the Nazis everything is too jumbled up now to make any decisions.*

I will have to tell you in person how Mark and I came to meet each other. You will not believe me and I do not expect you to. No one would. Maybe nothing will come of this. Maybe Jacob will decide after all that I am worthy of his attention and maybe I will still care. Who can say?

I just hope you will not disown me the way the Braunsteins disowned Ruth because she got pregnant. Dad may eventually, but neither Clara nor Irene have a real mother and I can see now that every girl needs one.

Love, Analise

***

In Spain they had grown accustomed to seeing each other unwashed, unkempt, dirty, smelling from waves of acrid body odor and having to advertise their need to answer nature's call. In Paris the first things they did were bathe and buy decent clothes. After that they arranged to have their first dinner together. When she opened her door, he saw her as he had on the ship; slender in a pale blue, calf length dress belted at the waist. Her hair was twisted in a chignon and when she smiled he wanted to sweep her up in his arms and hold her forever, but he dared not.

She saw the same look of wonder in his eyes that she had seen the day they were finally able to sit together at the outdoor café and speak to one another without fear. She had felt valued and treasured.

And beneath it all, she had felt in control, equal to him and not an appendage to be yelled at and dominated. They had never kissed nor embraced though in Spain they had lain with her back pressed against his chest, each sharing the warmth and assurance of the other's body. At times his arm crept tentatively around her, but if she moved slightly he drew it back.

Mark had considered it presumptuous to attempt to embrace her or to kiss her.

Not only was she engaged to be married, he recognized the reality of her being white and him being black in America. Far more, his own mystical and inexplicable love for her did not mean that she either appreciated his feelings or reciprocated them. So he dared not misinterpret her smile for consent or her welcoming voice for encouragement.

As they fled together across Spain and into France, they came to know how intimately they were joined together by time. But neither of them were hostages of Yesterday which was invisible in the bright glare of Today.

She became dependent on him in Spain just as she had when he held on to her at the side of the ship to keep her from falling into the sea. But because of her trust in him and her dependence on him, it became, in his mind, an unforgivable extortion to act on his feelings for her. It would be tantamount to holding a gun at her head while she was alone in the middle of an alien land.

To love Analise was to do what was best for Analise and to applaud and amplify her sense of being. They needed to stride the earth together as they had in Spain and not have her walk one subservient step behind him simply because his physical strength was greater than hers.

So dressed in a blue double breasted suit with faint pinstripes, he went to her room and knocked softly on her door and saw her in a pale blue dress. As he closed the door behind him, there was a question in his eyes – May I?

He leaned toward her intending to touch her lips lightly with his but she drew back.

"…I'm sorry," she murmured looking way. After a moment, "It's not you, Mark…I'm still engaged. I don't want you to think…."

"Shhhh. It's all right, Analise. I'm the one who forgot, not you. As for what I think, I think you are who you are."

Then without a word and despite the things they had just said, they came together and hugged each other, swaying slightly as though dancing. They relished the warmth from their bodies that gave their souls nourishment after the long years. They parted, holding hands, looking at each other and for the first time they kissed.

Their kiss was without lust or urgency; it was a gentle kiss that said, *"I love you"* rather than *"I want you."* It was a kiss of love that asked for nothing in return. They felt, more than they knew, that they had kissed before in that long distant past.

**

They left the hotel and he offered her his arm and she took it and it was a thrill walking arm in arm to the café where they had first gone. Their table was by a window looking out onto the street and they had dinner together again after all those days lost to time.

She spoke to the waiter in French. "*Encore deux cafes crème, si'l vous plait.*"

"What did you say?"

She laughed. "Two more coffees with cream, please."

She taught him to say *s'il vous plait* by writing it out as "sill voo play" and she taught him other common expressions as they waited for their coffee.

"It's hard to believe we were in a truck freezing to death only a week ago," she said after they had their coffee.

"I was thinking the same thing."

"It may sound crazy," she said," but I almost miss the uncertainty, the tension, the danger. It was such a different and new experience."

"It's not crazy. I feel the same way. Even though we were running, I felt more in control. We had each other in a way we don't anymore. Maybe we were freer; I think we were a complete world together."

"Yes, I think that's it. But in life, there's always that 'but.'"

There followed a long, thoughtful silence.

"– I wrote to my mother today," she said. "I told her about us."

It took him a moment to answer. "That's a bridge we had to cross sooner or later. Nothing's going to be easy for us, Analise. The war was easy compared to this. I feel like those Internationals who can't stay in Spain and can't go home and can't stay here, either. I can go back but I don't want to go back to being just a pile of shit. There are too many Joes back home and only one or two Tanks or Professor Millers; it's like the war where we had to fight with rifles against tanks, artillery and airplanes."

"You make it sound so grim, Mark, like we might as well call it quits." She sounded a little annoyed.

"After two thousand years? Never. You're still Elissayah and I'm still Hanno. We're just not fighting the Romans, that's all; but there's a lot to be frustrated about, Analise. If I go back, the second I step off the ship, I'll be nothing no matter who I am. I can't *ever* let you see me like that – helpless.

"I know lots of people have it just as bad. Immigrants go to America to escape getting slapped in the face and kicked in the ass only to get slapped in the face anyway. The slap may not be as hard but you'd never get Catholics to believe that when they see their church burned down or a Chinese man when he's shot for nothing. Everybody's got somebody else standing with a foot on his throat; I understand that. Willie told me once that I was 'spoiled' because I never lived in Mississippi where he'd seen people lynched...."

She placed her hand over his mouth. Her eyes brimmed with tears. "Let's wait to hear from my mother and let's not talk about this anymore. And we won't ever say *never*, do you hear!"

They left the café and each put an arm around the other and they matched their strides and remembered Spain and knew then that they must return one day and retrace their steps from two thousand years ago and see who once they were.

CHAPTER 41

By an unspoken agreement, Analise's room was where they removed their shoes and sat on her bed with their backs against the headboard and their thighs and shoulders pressed together and read the English language newspapers and magazines. They shared little secrets of their lives as they waited to hear from her mother. They often held hands because it gave them a sudden unexplained sense of comfort and when they did, it was like shutting the door against the storm. They felt safe and more complete and often they shared the intimacy of silence.

They would have breakfast in the morning in an alcove in the hotel dining room as Paris was stirring. Sometimes they discussed what they remembered of their dreams and they noticed that their dreams were no longer as clear or as real as they had been in Spain. One thing was constant - the sense that they were both in the same place at the same time, but neither ever saw the other's face to know what they looked like thousands of years ago.

She told him of her girlhood and going into the woods with Saul to search for stones and canoeing on a lake though she was afraid because she could not swim. He smiled and told her that only a brave girl would have done that or gone to Spain all alone. Emboldened, she told him with clear green eyes she would never have intimate relations with anyone unless she were married to him.

"Be honest – do you think I'm 'cold?'"

"'Cold?' Where'd that come from?" He shook his head and reminded her of what had happened to her in the distant past and that she had no way of knowing whether or not Decius had scarred her soul in some way making "relations" a problem. In the end, what did it matter? She was who she was and he loved who she was and, anyway, he wouldn't know because he did not think of her sexually, only that she was Analise and he had found her again after a million years.

"...I think my soul may have been scarred, though – yours, too. That's probably why you had those nightmares."

After that as they lay together on her bed with their bodies touching, she gradually began to hope that he would turn to her and hold her and kiss her in a gentle way until she was immersed in a flood of feeling. She was growing curious to know how it would feel to have him penetrate her.

With Jacob, she had never felt that urge. She had let him feel her, but she had never been a partner and worse - he had clumsily forced her to think - to almost examine - what was happening to her. She did not want to think or to know; she wanted to awaken as from a dream and wonder how it had happened.

Eventually, while they were having breakfast, she said wistfully after setting down her coffee cup, "I don't think we can lie on the bed together anymore, Mark. I think we have to keep both our feet on the floor."

He presented a sad little smile and nodded. She knew from his expression that he understood she might not be able to say, "No." And that he respected her decision.

***

Occasionally they sent each other letters because they discovered that speech was not always adequate. Speech was often coded and guarded. But if they wrote, they could construct and rewrite and burnish their thoughts until they were certain their language flowed like molten silver shimmering in the sunlight. Their letters could be organ voices bestriding their world without stuttering or embarrassment or wondering whether or not they sounded foolish or needy.

They would slip their letters under each other's door as things to be discovered, not presented. By unspoken agreement, neither answered the other's letters. They were not meant as correspondence, but as revelations. Their warmth and promise and naked frankness colored their moments together in hues they could never have imagined.

> Dear Mark -
>
> I never said I love you but you knew that I did. Because I could not say it with Jacob still beside me, nor could I renounce the things I said to him until they did not matter anymore. "I love you" seemed more precious left unsaid. But now I believe my life with Jacob has ended,

and if somehow, it hasn't, I do not know what I can say to you or to myself that would make sense. We must wait for the other shoe to drop.

I cherish our quiet times together in the cafes on the Left Bank and on my bed discussing bits and pieces of our secret lives. Being together is all we need. Can you believe that? And just holding hands and feeling a wonderful freedom to do so gives newness to life. And when you raise my fingers to your lips and kiss them, I always feel a silent thrill.

Do you know that you never once made me feel as though you wanted my body more than you wanted me? This is the love I cherish. It is to feel and to know that I am precious and the most important thing in your life.

I want a true friend because I believe no one can truly love you who isn't first your friend. But I'm still a girl so I want to be first in all things no matter how that sounds. After all is said, in the end, we are different than men; the only issue is our <u>right</u> to be. So I want to feel I am precious.

So yes, Mark – I love you.
Me

***

Dear Analise -
Sometimes I feel like a bird that flaps its wings like other birds but cannot leave the ground. I believe other people go through something like that. Our dreams are crushed so we never become who we really want to be. Think of all of the "I-should-have-beens" in the world. Society decides things for you and if you don't agree you end up depressed, in jail, dead or in an asylum - a failure or misfit.

Society has decided I cannot love you. If I do, I cannot be with you. Society can kiss-my-you know what. And yes, I know society can hunt me down like a dog and dispose of me like offal. It seems strange, but like we both said, at times it felt better in Spain even while hiding from the

Civil and Assault Guard because we could master our own destiny.

But tomorrow and tomorrow and the day after, we will cross the Seine to the Left Bank and we will sit in cafes and later walk hand in hand along the boulevards and look for the ghosts of Hemingway and Fitzgerald in the Montparnasse and we will stare at paintings in art galleries that we will never buy. And I will tell you again that love is beauty and beauty is love just as music is beauty and these are ends in themselves. Only beauty and love move us to tears and nobody ever wonders – why.

I do love that something within your slender body that makes me want desperately to protect you. Did you know that when we walk we match our stride together? And may I say I love you again?

Mark

***

Dear Mark,

Once my only goal was to get married and be a housewife, but now if marriage means surrendering who I am - <u>no</u>. I won't be something that defines me as dumb, helpless and essentially ignorant of anything in life that matters as though I were just another child in the family to be scolded.

Why is it so difficult to be me as I have a right to be simply because I am a woman? And why are you in chains simply because of your color when I know you are every bit as good as anyone I have ever known? If King Edward can surrender his throne because he will be who he wants to be – why can't I have someone who loves me as I want to be loved?

Yet I want someone to take care of me. But not by putting food on the table. I want someone to care for me the way we were in Spain and now France. In some way, Spain seems more the life we should lead. We became intertwined. We needed each other. We must and we will go back to Spain.

Elissayah

***

Dear Elissayah,

Yes, we will return to Spain someday. I heard you from thousands of years ago and what I heard is what I heard yesterday and the day before that and what I want to hear tomorrow and the day after tomorrow. But today, who will hear us and understand?

Love in this world has become focused on sexual coupling, a thing that any dog, cat or roach can do. You and I are not allowed to be together simply because the thought of sexual coupling between us is insupportable. Sex is incidental, and not love itself. If you were dead, I would still love you. We have proven this, you and I. Like beauty, love brings a sense of awe and wonder just as music does, and a sunset or a dawn or a new born child. It is the surrender of the soul; love is the soul speaking. We will not be denied, you and I.

Hanno

CHAPTER 42

Her mother's reply came as they were preparing to leave the hotel to climb the steep streets of Montmartre.

> *Dear Analise,*
> *Thank God you are safe. Not to hear from you –*
> *terrible. Jacob sent cable you were missing. Told him you*
> *are in France. Will meet you there.*
> *Your father worried. Will come. Provide passage home.*
> *Hurry. Cannot wait to see you.*
> *Great love, Mom*

Her heart sank.

No mention of Mark. Just Jacob. As though Mark existed only as a child's imaginary friend. She alternated between anger and despair.

Later that day, Jacob left a message for her at the switchboard asking her to please meet him for seven o'clock reservations at the Hotel Ritz. "Reply if cannot." She re-read the message several times. It did not indicate where he was staying. She was a little disturbed that he had not called on her at her hotel.

When Mark came to her room, she asked him to hug her and then told him, "My father's coming to get me. I don't know why I suddenly can't get on a ship by myself. My mother said she heard from Jacob. He's in England and he's coming to Paris. He left a message at the switchboard that he wants to meet me at the Hotel Ritz for dinner."

He made himself look noncommittal but felt tension rising in his chest. "- You have to go...You're still engaged...."

"Sort of, I guess...."

"All the more reason to go, Analise...We both know about elephants in the living room. He's one and I'm the other."

She laughed. "I've never been good at taming elephants."

"I'm not used to being one."

She knew the Ritz on the Place Vendome was one of Paris' most exclusive hotels. She smiled to herself when it occurred to her that a place known for its wealthy clientele was the last place a dedicated Socialist or Communist should patronize.

Jacob was waiting in the lobby. He was dressed in a gray flannel suit with a white handkerchief in the breast pocket; he looked far more rested than when she had seen him last. He smiled and came to meet her. They presented each other with happy faces but they did not embrace as though agreeing it would be unseemly in a place like the Ritz. Their eyes examined the other for scratches and bruises.

"Gee," he exclaimed softly, "you have no idea how relieved I was when your mother told me you were safe! Everything was pure *chaos*. Nobody knew where half the people were. We were lucky to get out."

They were promptly seated and she asked him how he got to England.

"The English navy evacuated the British medical staff and us along with them."

"Do you remember Clara and Irene? Are they all right?"

He could not say for sure, but he thought they were evacuated. She was thoughtful for a moment. "Were they able to evacuate any of the patients?"

He looked down briefly and shook his head. Before she could pursue the question, he asked, "What happened to your medical unit, Ana? The major ordered it evacuated, and then you just seemed to disappear."

Over wine she told him about Juanita. He was stunned. He stared at her as though she had more to tell. Finally, he shook his head, cursing silently. "I'll make sure the major hears about this. Not that it'll do any good. She's probably in Russia by now."

She told him that Mark had appeared and helped her escape.

"–Is that the fellow your mother said might be a 'rival?'"

"Did she say that? I suppose so - Yes."

They ate their dinner in silence for a count of ten.

"None of this monkey business," he remarked, "would ever have happened had you stayed at home, Ana."

Angry lightning flashed through her. Then the brightness was gone. Nor did thunder follow. "None of 'this monkey business' would ever have happened, Jacob," she pointed out gently, holding his eyes, "if you had married me instead of trying to screw me in a hotel room."

His eyes widened briefly either because she used the word "screw" or at her unexpected reply.

"We didn't come here to quarrel," he said, maintaining a pleasant demeanor and glancing around at the other diners.

"I agree, but why did we come here? If it was to talk, you should have come to the hotel."

"I'd rather see you without somebody else standing in the background. Anyway, it's obvious you're angry with me. Why, I don't know. But be fair; I tried to warn you that a war is no place for romance or any kind of normal relationship. Be honest with yourself, Ana – isn't that what you were expecting?"

She said nothing for a while then, "– Probably. But it all goes back to your pretending you were going to marry me instead of breaking off the engagement. Maybe I *was* foolish – stupid actually – chasing all the way to Europe after you like all I had to do was pick up a telephone and arrange a date.

"Sure, it was stupid. Romantic foolishness – but I think the thing we have to admit is we don't feel the same way about each other and you haven't since before you left. – Wouldn't you agree? My mother warned me never to chase after a man, but I think my coming was the best thing that could have happened. I've learned a lot, I did a lot and I changed a lot.

"I believe love is something grander than anything you can imagine, Jacob – far, far grander than…than just intercourse and if you knew what love was, I think that when the major relieved you, you would have taken me with you."

He paused over his dinner plate and regarded her with an amused expression. "Like you said, 'romantic foolishness.' But go on - please."

"You should have told him - no, you should have *insisted* that yes, you'd stay longer to help with the wounded, but only if your fiancée could come with you because I'd travelled all the way to Spain just to be by your side. Your future wife and future mother of your children and you couldn't just leave her behind! That's a fair exchange. That's what I think. You were volunteering to stay. It wasn't an order."

He shook his head, his lips pressed in a knowing smile as though pitying her ignorance. "I took it as an order, Ana. You expected me to disobey orders just like that? Orders are not suggestions or compromises. You do as you're told or face a firing squad. Obeying orders is what you, me and everybody else has been doing all along. This is the military not a civilian hospital or college. Orders are orders. *Period.* I shouldn't have to tell you that."

"It didn't sound that way to me. Anyway, you never even made the effort. Orders may be orders but love is love, Jacob. *Period.*"

After a while, to change the subject, she told him about being attacked on the ship and thrown over the side because – as Clara had suggested – she was considered a Communist and too friendly with one of the volunteers. She was alive only because of Mark.

He sat back, incredulous. "Why...why didn't you tell me any of this before?"

"When, Jacob? We've hardly spoken a word to each other. And after all – you're an *officer* and I'm not. Remember? I was on that ship because of love. And after that thing with Juanita, I was nearly raped so don't sit there and tell me I should have stayed home and just let you screw me."

He opened his mouth, looked around to see if they were making a scene. He decided to look properly troubled and say nothing and wait for her flashing eyes and high color to subside.

She lowered her voice. "Do you know who saved me from being raped? *Someone who disobeyed 'orders.'* They shoot soldiers for what he did. But when we retreated, Mark was worried that I wouldn't survive and to him – my survival was far more important than 'orders.' He was willing to trade his life...."

She felt herself tearing up and took a deep breath and a diversionary sip of water. "I was abandoned by that bitch because I disobeyed *'orders'* to save a brave, brutalized woman who was going to be left behind because she wasn't the right kind of Communist. I hate the word, *'orders.'* It's a disguise for cowardice and inhumanity."

He expected her to tell him the name of the woman of whom she was speaking but she did not. They finished their meal in silence. She refused dessert and he asked for the check.

"I can only suppose," he began, "that this fellow, Mark, is the one you prefer. We're calling it off, right?"

"Be a man, Jacob, and admit you called it off long ago. That's what you were going to tell me, isn't it? Are you in contact with the blonde nurse, Giselle? I'm sure she wasn't left behind."

His difficulty in replying gave him away. Finally he gave an elaborate shrug but did not reply.

After she quietly returned his ring, he saw her to a cab, and before she shut the door he asked, "What does this Mark look like? - Just curious."

She smiled, "He's not tall, dark and handsome – just dark and handsome."

***

Once the cab was in motion, she fumbled in her bag for her handkerchief and dabbed at her eyes. Breaking off her engagement had not been a triumphant, ringing and satisfying declaration of her worth as a person, nor was it an act of revenge. She had not intended anything of the sort; she had not even known what she would say nor how she would feel when she saw Jacob again in quiet, civilized circumstances.

She thought they had known each other for far too long to be blown apart by a casual, summer breeze. Their life had been lived in the future and she had often looked forward to joining all of her friends who were already married with a husband of her very own. Then she could live the life her mother had lived. That would have been the triumph.

Giselle?

Who was she beyond a glimpse of blonde hair boarding the ship with Jacob and the others? Or a glimpse at the medical station when Jacob had appeared looking bewildered that his betrothed had actually come to Spain.

Only intuition led her to mention Giselle's name. It found its mark. But it meant that even had she stayed in America or given her body to Jacob, Giselle would still have been in Spain and the engagement broken. She had not caught the platter. It had slipped from her fingers and had shattered into a thousand pieces long ago.

But was any of this avoidable?

Was Jacob's accusation that she was "cold" tinged with truth? It was possible that she was reticent about sex because of what had happened in the distant past, but she had never been persuaded that there was anything romantic about surrendering herself to sexual penetration. It had made her wonder about her life after marriage.

Throughout college when the other girls discussed sex, she had tried to hide her sense of shame and embarrassment behind bland smiles. Though the girls giggled a lot from nervousness, they obliquely tried to discover who among them had actually "done it" or done anything to evoke oohs and ahs. Amid wide eyed pretended ignorance, they laid bait to tempt confessions.

During sophomore year Miranda confided that she he had not only had her breasts fondled by a boy but also he had *sucked* them! Oohs and aahs! With hands covering open mouths, eyes wide with manifest satisfaction, they circled around Miranda and smothered her with attention. Someone asked what they all desperately wanted to know.

"How did it feel?"

"Oh, God – I'm waiting for him to do it again! It was *swell!* It's something you have to experience for yourself!"

Evelyn regarded her with a hint of envy. "It didn't feel that way to me," she informed them with a superior air. "I didn't like it."

Analise edged out of the circle, marking them down as bad girls.

From time to time she heard other verbal indiscretions and she could never reconcile why anyone would voluntarily admit to such shameful conduct. How could that other girl, whose name she had forgotten, tell everyone that she given her boyfriend a "hand job" and then have the nerve to describe the volcanic explosion of his ejaculation? During junior year, Josephine, a quiet girl with chubby cheeks, admitted that last summer in Maine she had "done it."

"But I didn't like it," she added a moment later as though that would take away her confession. "It hurt – After that we sort of stopped seeing each other...."

Analise wondered what Josephine's husband would say when he discovered that she was not a virgin. When someone asked, "What made you do it?" Analise slipped out of the room.

Her sense of shame was discovered after she made a face when Inez let it be known that George's cock was bigger than Alfred's and amid giggles, offered a detailed tutorial on the differences during intercourse.

With raucous laughter, someone pointed to Analise's pink faced embarrassment and went on to declare that she guessed, "Everybody in a skirt's not a woman."

Stung, Analise replied, "Meaning what?"

"Meaning what I said," replied Ruth, a tall, thin girl with short hair.

"Then I guess that means that everybody in a skirt is not a whore."

There was a period of silence. Analise hated confrontation, still she plunged on. "I always go by what my mother said…."

"*My mother said?*" Ruth hooted. "Mommy?"

"…that the most a girl has to give is her body, and the most a man has to give is his name and unless you exchange one for the other you're just his whore."

Five faces stared at her in the silence that followed. It was a spring day and the windows were open. A fly buzzed somewhere in the room. The fly found a place to settle before anyone mounted a reply. What was said always remained fuzzy to her because she had closed her mind.

A coolness followed her until the day she graduated. But she refused to relinquish her belief that an invasion of her body was akin to having a poker thrust up into her and if that be the case, it would have to be for something grand and significant. If there must be sexual intercourse before marriage, it must be for something sacred though she had no notion at all what constituted such a union.

She started to knock on Mark's door to let him know she had returned from the Ritz but hesitated. No. Let a little more time massage away any lingering emotional pain she might feel; she needed time to separate out the colors of her emotions into disappointment, embarrassment, anger, betrayal and relief. She would tell Mark, but not now; she needed time to put Giselle in a dark corner of her mind. After that she would tell him the elephants were gone.

CHAPTER 43

It was her father on the phone.

After her ordeal in Spain, her mother had sent him to Paris to rescue her. Her parents, despite their divorce, were always agreeable where their daughter was concerned.

But Analise did not need to be rescued.

She needed to be understood. And Mark needed to be understood. And Spain needed to be understood. Yet both she and Mark knew that neither her parents nor anyone else would ever understand or sympathize with them. Still it was good to hear her father's voice. He always spoke with a youthful eagerness that lent persuasiveness to whatever he said.

"Is that you, Ana? - Thank God, you're safe! Listen, do you want to meet me here? I'm at the Ritz, or do you want me to come there? Anything you say's fine with me."

The Ritz again and unwelcome memories of Jacob. "- I'll meet you at your hotel, Papa. You can buy me lunch."

Her father's lavishly furnished room reduced hers to little more than four walls and a bed.

He greeted her at the door with a big grin and outstretched arms and she went to him and he hugged her. He always smelled of cigars and Bay Rum shaving lotion. He held her at arm's length to look at her. There was a certain air about her now that he could not quite identify. What had happened to her in Spain?

"- So thin!" he declared. "They don't feed you? You'll get sick. Have you seen a doctor?"

"Papa - I'm fine. I'll gain it back. Everybody's thin. It's the war. – How have you been? I still haven't had a chance to see your last picture...."

"You gotta see it. I'll get you tickets. Got Academy written all over it. The people in Washington want to see me and some of the other producers. They want us to make war pictures - you know, help explain the craziness in China with the Japanese. I got people in Washington now I can call anytime if I need something. You ought to know, your old man's got influence."

He had ordered room service. While they waited he led her over to a small couch and studied her face as they sat. She smiled and gave him an account of her experiences in Spain. Her recital was sketchy because neither he nor anyone else would ever believe what had really happened so why bother. Nevertheless, she braced herself for his onslaught of questions.

Instead he reached into his suit coat pocket and produced an envelope. "Here," he said, handing it to her, "that's your passage on the *Ile de France.* We can leave France tomorrow afternoon. I have to be in Washington. They want we should get into production as soon as possible. War pictures."

Her mother used to joke about her father. He wanted to be seen as an American and tried to avoid Jewish idioms and expressions that set him apart. Like now, saying *'They want we should.'*

Before she could respond, there was a knock on the door. It was the waiter with their lunch. While the waiter set it up, she pretended interest in her ticket and the brochure that came with it. As soon as the waiter closed the door, she laid the ticket on the luncheon table.

"- I can't take this, Papa. Didn't Mom tell you? About Mark?"

He stared at her. The stare used to reduce her to rebellious outbursts and occasional tears. Now she stared back. Neither had touched the food. He was of middle height, tanned and youthful looking with a mouth that always suggested a friendly smile.

"- You're not a child, Ana. I shouldn't have to explain it to you. For God's sake, think of your mother tearing her heart out with worry all these months. Did you get bombed? Shot? Dead? No letters, nothing but worry, now this. Such a daughter no one should have. This doctor you're engaged to – Jacob - he's a nice boy...."

"I didn't come here to quarrel with you, Papa, "she said quietly but firmly. "I'm not leaving Mark and that's all there is to it. This isn't one of your movies where everything is nice and tidy at the end. Your daughter wouldn't be alive today it hadn't been for Mark and she'd have been raped and scarred for life if it hadn't been for him.

"Twice he saved my life. *Twice.* And all anyone can say is 'that's nice but he's a Negro' like somebody's dog that you pat on the head because he barked and woke you up from a fire in the middle of the night!"

He saw she was determined. After a moment: "- So alright. Alright, I'll give this Mark money, what he wants. What else can I do? I'll buy him a ticket home but please, listen to me, don't destroy your life, *and his.* Yes, *his*, don't forget. America is what it is, Ana. Germany is what it is. Better maybe he should stay here. The French treat those people well, but us - Jews?" He shook his head – "You can't stay here with war coming, Hitler and Fascists here like the Cross of Fire and the French Popular party! Do you even realize what you're saying?"

"Yes, I know what I'm saying, Papa, Do you? If you're concerned that Jews are treated worse than rats, what about Mark? Can't you see that one's no different than the other and that a lot of us, maybe even you, are the ones doing the dirt?"

"The difference is you're my daughter, Ana, my flesh and blood. I'm concerned about you, no one else. A sinking ship, everyone saves his own. Safe, then maybe others."

"And what if Mark is my own, Papa?"

He offered her a reproachful look and got up from the table, the lunch untouched. With a heavy sigh, he walked over to the window and stared at the column in the square with Napoleon standing on top of it. She stood and walked over to him. She touched his arm. He turned and she gave a little smile. "I'm not a little girl anymore, Papa, and this isn't some silly lark like white people going up to some Harlem night club to mess around with people they wouldn't spit on anywhere else.

"And please don't mention Jacob. He found a blonde in Spain and even before he left to go there, he expected me to sleep with him. I refused, of course. I insisted on a silly little thing like marriage first."

After a moment, he put his arm around her; he kissed her on the cheek. They both stared into the square of the Place Vendome. Aware of a new, defiant change in her, he spoke quietly, almost as though he were speaking to himself, "What do you expect, Ana? A man saves your life and the world changes? You'll say, 'But he's different.' So's a two-headed monkey but it's still a monkey.

"Hate. In Germany, Poland, Austria – everywhere. The Cross of Fire here, Black Shirts in England, Blue Shirts in Ireland, Brown in Germany, Green in Brazil, the Bund in America – everywhere it's a crime to be a Jew. In America it's also a crime to be a Negro. It's a fact. California, they lynched a Negro just last year, *1937*. Clyde Johnson. I knew him. Used to work for one of the men. What he did wrong, if anything, who can say. But just last year."

He turned from the window, shaking his head, watching her face. "When people hate, Ana, love is not enough, believe me, I know and not from movies. Your friends – what would they say? Relatives, people on the street? You live a life of cops stopping him, angry stares, insults, threats. And not just from whites, Negroes, too. Did you know that? Negroes hate, too. And you go out to dinner, they won't let him in. Movies, theaters the same. Like he has a terrible, contagious disease.

"Even if he was white, you know how we Jews are. - 'He's not Jewish?' - Everybody finds fault. This one's shanty Irish, that one's a dago, another one's not Catholic, somebody else didn't come on the Mayflower. We make movies about that stuff. Even the *King of England* can't marry who he wants. They kicked him out.

"I'll take care of him, I promise. He saved my daughter's life. A bank account, a car, a job. What work does he do? I have an idea what maybe he can do. Write a story about Spain and the war. I'll buy it but it has to be good, not junk, and my people can clean it up for maybe a movie."

She felt devastated.

It was as though she could not breathe. "…Papa …*he killed a man to save me*. Three, I keep forgetting the other ones - his commander and…I think that after all of that, I'd rather die than live in a world where love is forbidden. A world of yesterday.

"I know you love me and Mom does, too. But I love Mark, Papa. Not because he saved my life. Even before that we fell in love. That's why he saved me; because he treasures me above anything else, not because he was being a good Samaritan. It goes beyond that but nobody would believe us so it's not worth discussing."

"…Do you mind if I talk to him, Ana? It can't hurt."

She sighed. "- I suppose. I'll ask him. But I think you'd better get a refund on the ticket just in case. And Papa, if you don't want to offend him, please speak to him as though he were Jacob or somebody you respect."

When Mark saw her later that afternoon, he could tell from her expression that the meeting with her father had not gone well. He took her in his arms and held her to comfort her.

"Not good?"

She shook her head. She told him what her father had said and what she had said. "He asked to talk to you."

He sighed, still holding her, his face nestled in her hair. "When?"

"I guess today's as good as any. I'll go with you and wait in the lobby, and then we can have lunch together."

***

Mort Stern was waiting for him in the open door of his room and offered a cautious smile. "Mark? Come in; I'm Mr. Stern, Analise's father." Mark offered his hand but Stern did not shake it. "Please," he said, "have a seat."

They sat in arm chairs with a small table between them. Mark saw a trim, sun tanned man with a pleasant face who did not look at all like Analise. He had a full head of silver hair and light brown eyes. Mort Stern saw a Negro who did not look any different from any other Negro he had ever seen. Apart from his courteous smile when he first came in the door, he had not smiled. He did not appear to be nervous; he sat back, crossed his legs and looked attentive. He was not sure whether or not he liked him.

Mort began. "We're both adults, Mark, so I'll be frank. Did my daughter tell you what we discussed? Good. So you know how very concerned I am for her well-being. Yours, too. First, I am deeply grateful to you for saving my daughter's life; she said *three times?* There's no price a parent can put on that. I'll never forget that. Thanks and thanks again." He leaned forward and offered his hand and they shook.

Mark smiled, "Actually, Analise saved my life, too. I think she forgets that sometimes."

"–Really? I see you two had quite an adventure... Do you mind telling me how you met? Ana left a good bit out. Was she attacked because - well, because she was too friendly?"

"– Probably. - We sat at the same table and spoke for maybe ten or fifteen minutes. That evidently became a crime punishable by death. I guess it would have been me if I'd been there instead of her."

Mort furrowed his brow. "Let me get this straight; you only had a ten or fifteen-minute conversation on a five day cruise…?"

"Well, we saw each other in Paris for about an hour before she had to leave for Spain."

Mort's lips tightened. His face colored beneath the tan. "I produce motion pictures – I come across maybe a hundred movie scripts a year. - People don't meet for an hour and ten minutes and then decide to throw their lives away come hell or high water. *People don't do that!* I can understand you want to keep some things personal, especially where I or her mother are concerned, but don't take me for a fool!"

"Nobody's taking you for a fool, Mr. Stern. You asked me a question and I answered it. An hour and ten minutes, ten hours – what's it matter? It happened or else we wouldn't be here. And I'll tell you something else. I felt ashamed of myself because she was white. After all the stuff white people had done to us, I felt like I should spit in my own face!

"How would you feel if you fell in love with a Nazi. Think about it. A lot of stuff has happened between us including *déjà vu* and reincarnation, but you probably wouldn't believe any of it so maybe you'd better ask her about it."

Exasperated, Mort stood up and ran a hand through his hair. "I think I'm sophisticated enough to know about 'love-at-first-sight' but this this crazy. What chance would she have married to you? Don't talk to me about sacrifice and love; if you love her – walk away! Be a man. *Save her.*"

His face was etched in agony. His eyes looked down on Mark as though trying to decide what to do next. The phone rang and he walked across the room to answer it. He turned to Mark, his voice was flat. "It's my daughter. She said do you want her to come up?"

"If it's all right with you."

He hung up the phone but did not come back to his chair. He moved over to the window and looked out with his hands clasped behind his back. As the seconds passed, the silence grew louder. They were both relieved to hear her knock on the door. Mort opened the door and Mark stood to greet her. She entered with a faint smile on her lips, looking from one to the other.

"Did I interrupt something?" she asked, removing her hat and gloves. Her father gave her a peck on the cheek. "You didn't tell me about the *déjà vu*," he said in a mock accusatory tone.

"Do you believe it?" When he did not answer she said, "That's why."

"So you intend going back home and acting like everything is perfectly normal?"

"We really haven't decided." She looked to Mark for affirmation.

"We know what we're up against, Mr. Stern. France may be our best bet right now."

He exploded, his face purple. "What's the matter with you two! Don't you read the papers! France is no place for Jews; it never was! Everybody in Europe is getting to be just like Hitler. Even the United States turned away a ship carrying a thousand Jews trying to escape from that bastard. Nobody from Canada to South America would take them - They had to go back to Germany and that son of a bitch, Hitler! That's like turning a woman over to the man who just raped her!

"Don't you know what that means, Ana? You have to come home *now* while there's time. You can't wait and wait until there's a panic and everybody's rushing for one door and nobody gets out. Even Holland bars Jews now. You've got to leave!" He turned blazing eyes on Mark. "You want to protect her? So protect her. Make her go home!"

She moved close to Mark and reached for his hand They held hands. "I mean no disrespect, Mr. Stern, but Analise is not going to let anybody 'make' her do anything. She almost shot the last guy who tried it. And like I said, I didn't just save her life, she also saved mine and she had to kill somebody to do it."

Mort looked startled, scrutinizing his daughter with new interest.

Mark said, "I've no intention of going back to be a pile of shit. I've got a college degree and I end up operating an elevator. You came to America, no college degree, yet you're a millionaire. Sure, you had brains, ability, a vision, and with the *opportunity* you made it. But back where you came from – be honest, what would you be now? - A peasant, a drunk, a bitter old man? Here you had opportunity.

"Me? Opportunity? I'm not allowed to do 'white man's work.' Know why? They'd feel like I'm equal to them, and that *lowers* them in the eyes of other white men. That'd be the end of the world as we know it. We can't have that now, can we?

"Analise said you offered me a job. I appreciate the gesture, Mr. Stern, but doing what? Sweeping floors? Any job matching my abilities would cause a strike or they'd try to make my life hell. Try it and see. What do you think I was doing back home?

"I'm not going back and I'm not a writer but I appreciate the offer. I don't know where I'm going or what I'm going to do but nobody's going to tell me that simply because I'm black I'm worthless when I know I'm not. Somebody told you that, and you told them to go to hell. I'm tired of being treated like a monkey in a tuxedo by every ignorant Tom, Dick and Harry who can barely spell his own name!"

"We need time to decide, Papa. Mark and I met for a reason. Neither of us knows what it is, but we can't let go, not even if you disown me. And I hope you won't."

"Of course not, don't talk silly, but do me a favor. Talk to your mother before you make any decision. Will you do that for me?"

"Will you let Mark and me talk it over and let you know later?"

"I'm afraid you'd shoot me if I said no."

CHAPTER 44

After they left, they felt protective of each other. They had little to say that could speak more eloquently than the warmth of their intertwined fingers.

At the restaurant she told him about Jacob. She was free of yesterday and suggested softly, "Let's not go back. Let's stay here and be regular people. We can do that here. We can be free. We'll only have this once and after all those years – let's stay forever and whatever will be will be."

She watched his vulnerable eyes caress her face and felt a flush on her cheeks because she knew he idolized her and she liked the warm feeling it invoked.

"I'd like that. A whole new world and when spring comes we can see all the things we've read about. I want to see light reflected from wet cobblestones and orange light from shop windows. I want to see you striding down the street toward me just as evening comes and we can have dinner in warm places and talk over wine of the little things that comprise our day. It's important that we know and care that I spilled coffee on my desk and you accomplished another engineering feat."

They laughed. She said, "First we'll have to get you a desk while I find a feat."

They kept reality, like snarling dogs lunging behind a fence, at bay throughout lunch. When they were through, he said soberly, "I don't know if we can live here like we want to forever, Analise. I damn sure want to."

"Why can't we? We're not children. We know we'll have to pay for things and wash clothes and dirty dishes, but that's just like the weather or the seasons. It doesn't matter. All that matters is how we feel about each other, how we help each other, how we watch out for the other and how we share every minute of every day like we did in Spain. We were alive."

He remembered the hunger, the fear, the dirt, the filth and the cold but above all, their discovery of Iberia and who they had been. It validated their existence both yesterday and today. And he remembered how glorious it had been, that when she most needed him - he had been there. Such impossibilities could not be dismissed.

He took her hand in both of his and said "yes" to preserve the lyrical music of the moment and the soft but steel determination in her face. Only later, would he remind her of her father's warning of anti-Semitism in France and the spread of Hitler's hatred.

After two thousand years, they still faced the Romans and the Carthaginians. But as Shakespeare said, "What's in a name?"

They drew occasional stares on their long walk back to their hotel. He told her that it was because she was so pretty. She laughed and said no, it was because he looked so grim. By the time they walked through the doors of their hotel, their brave new world of romance and dreams was drowned in the frigid water of reality. They were taking off their coats in her room when she turned to him, concern on her face.

"Mark, no matter what, I'll have to go home sooner or later. I have to see my mother. I can't simply disappear from her life. I don't want to, and I couldn't do that to her."

"I understand. I'm surprised you didn't say it sooner."

"…But I don't want to leave you. I think something will happen and we'll lose each other again. We have to go together. I don't mean permanently, but…."

He shook his head adamantly and pleaded with her. "I can't go back. I remember coming here on the ship - I'd look at you and it was painful, simply wanting to just talk to you, to hear your voice, and watch the way your lips moved, like you were whispering, and yet I couldn't even speak your name like one human being to another! I'll never go through that perverse shit again. I'll never pretend I don't love you. That's not the color of love, Analise. You're new to this, but I've heard of women pretending that their boyfriends or husbands were their chauffeurs or servants. That makes shit out of love."

She was embarrassed by the intensity of his emotions, yet felt stimulated by the love it expressed and her stomach did an unfamiliar flip flop. "Listen to me, Mark. We're going back together. *Together.* This is something we'll always have to face - stares, sneers, insults, avoidance, even here sometimes. I already had a dose of it on the way over here so I know what's in store for us. Maybe not as well as you do, but I know what it'll be like. We'll just look straight ahead, past the little people."

He was not convinced; he wanted to stay forever like they had fantasized they would but the cold water of reality, echoing her father's voice, said no. She made him look at her and examined his face. She meant to hug away his apprehension and disappointment like one does a child afraid of the dark. She put her arms around him and rested her head on his chest.

"What choice do we have, Mark? You free here and me free in America makes no sense. It'll mean the end of us and everything we believe. And here, in the end, people like Hitler will win anyway. You'll be my sword and I'll be your shield; maybe it's the other way around, but who cares. Do you understand? *We're going back!*"

He drew her closer in wonder at her audacity. They stood together, embraced, for a long moment. Finally, he sighed. " - Can I have a little time to think it over? Tomorrow. Tomorrow I'll know."

The next day she cabled her mother - *Bringing Mark* - and nothing more.

***

Olga Stern met them at the pier on an overcast day in October. Mark saw a slender woman with an erect, commanding posture looking this way and that for sight of her daughter. She was fashionably dressed and wore a dark purple hat that slanted a little to one side with pale lavender gloves to match.

Analise saw her first and rushing to her, flung herself into her arms. Olga's face glowed with happiness and she pressed her daughter's head against her shoulder and held it there. They remained embraced for long moments savoring the warmth of reunion.

Eventually, Analise disengaged herself and wiped her eyes with the back of her hand. She pulled Mark closer to her mother and smiling, introduced him. He removed his hat and said he was pleased to meet her. She presented a polite smile and examined his face with curious green eyes that put a wall between them.

Mort had given her his impression of him. A Negro with superior airs; educated at some rinky dink college; maybe a little loony with some cock-and-bull story about how they met that was not worth repeating, but he was headed for trouble if he ever came back to America. Olga should encourage their daughter to leave him in France and she must avoid Europe altogether; it was too dangerous for Jews.

Olga was disappointed when she saw him. He was not tall, or light skinned or especially handsome. She had imagined someone like Cab Calloway or Paul Robeson or maybe even Joe Louis. Someone recognizable and imposing enough to be able to turn her daughter's head. Especially since she was engaged to a doctor.

But she abandoned all thought of Mark the moment she saw her daughter. So thin! She only wanted to mother and nourish her. Mark helped the cab driver load their luggage into the trunk while glancing solicitously at Analise.

Olga and Analise sat in the back of the cab; he sat up front with the driver. He heard Analise, between quiet sobs, give her mother glimpses of some of the trauma that she had endured in Spain. She had held her anguish in and now she could release it. Though he understood the near rape, he never knew how devastating it had been for her to be abandoned first by Jacob and then by Juanita. Analise told it all in capital letters with a lot of the smaller print left out; it was a dead recitation of fear, of cold, of hunger and more fear with only Mark beside her.

When they arrived at their house, Olga, with her arm around her daughter, whispered, "The spare bedroom? You will show him?"

She nodded. As they went into the house Olga asked, "At dinner, you will tell the rest?"

With a faint smile, Analise nodded again.

Olga watched Mark come into the house with their luggage. He looked taller than he had seemed at the pier. He had a nice smile but it seemed a little reserved. She had not noticed before that his chin was square and strong.

Analise led him up the carpeted staircase to the spare bedroom. Her eyes were puffy from crying. He took her hands in his. "I know you need time to talk to your mother. If you can find something for me to read, I'll be fine."

She left to see what she could find. He noticed the floors were carpeted and not covered with linoleum. He walked over to the window and looked out at neat row houses with green shades facing the quiet street. He could hear a trolley car pass an intersection several blocks away. He wondered about Olga Stern's polite smile and her searching eyes.

Analise returned shortly with the day's newspaper and several old magazines. She handed them to him but seemed hesitant. "Are you sure you'll be all right? - You have to give my mother a chance to know you."

"I'll be fine. Right now your mom's biggest concern is you. That's only natural."

She closed the door softly behind her. He removed his shoes, propped himself up on the pillows and lay on the bed with the magazines and newspaper.

What had Analise's father told her mother about him, especially concerning how he and Analise had met? It obviously had made little impression on her. She would probably ask him to stay for dinner and maybe stay the night. After that life would be an adventure. And he would have to write to his father and let him know he had survived.

CHAPTER 45

She sat by her mother at the kitchen table with glasses of tea and a dish of sweet biscuits. Olga wanted a calmer explanation than the one she had received in the cab ride home. That had been like Swiss cheese; now she wanted the holes filled in. First - "How did you meet? Your father was not clear."

Analise brightened and with glowing eyes told her mother what had happened when her body first touched Mark's on the ship. And then there was the outdoor café in Paris when they first spoke to each other like normal people and discovered their attraction to each other. In Spain Mark had suddenly appeared at the hospital and promised to look after her and they both knew they had been in Spain before but could not explain where or when.

Finally they knew. It was the night they had spent together on the ledge and shared the same dream about Iberia - there was no way to say why or how - but they, both of them, knew *the when* of their lives together and the truth that they shared together.

Even though she half expected to be met with disbelief, she was crestfallen at her mother's response.

"- For this you left Jacob?"

The joy went out of Analise like the sun going behind a cloud. "Mama, *please!* I didn't leave Jacob. He left me. I told you that already. Anyway, Mark and I belong together, you just have to believe that, there's nothing else either of us can say."

Olga had great difficulty believing that *déjà vu* or dreams or nightmares or reincarnation had the slightest connection to reality. Analise had always been so level headed. How could this be? Holding her daughter's hand she explained gently, "We live, Ana, we die – heaven maybe, no more. We die, no more. Never. Not for any of us."

"– But, Mama, every religion on earth believes in an existence after death and…."

She shook her head gently but firmly. "*Religion* – maybe yes; dreams, no."

She felt a twinge of anger. It was an emotion toward her mother that she had not felt since childhood. She needed validation and affirmation and perhaps wide eyed astonishment. She had turned to a safe harbor only to find it closed. Following a long pause she took a deep breath and said, almost defiantly, "Well, our dreams have been good to us. We'll live by them."

Understanding her disappointment, Olga let a little time elapse before she admitted she had had misgivings about Jacob from the moment he announced that he had volunteered to go to Spain without once confiding his intentions. "And your father told me he was 'improper'?"

She nodded. "Yes, and I refused."

Olga took both her hands in hers and squeezed them and looked in her eyes and examined her face. She saw disappointment in the set of her mouth because she did not believe her. Still Olga wanted to know the details of the horrors Analise had endured, aware that it was here at this table, some months ago, that she herself had confessed her own horror.

When Analise described the near rape and almost in a whisper confided, "I shot him," anger ridged Olga face. "*Good for you!*" she flared, "Good for you! The thing that they wanted to do, *forever* you remember! Forever. After that, women shun men. They fear….they – you know…."

"Intercourse? You can say it, Mama; I'm a nurse."

"Better you shoot." Satisfied, she got up to start preparing dinner.

Analise rose to help. "Papa seemed to have a hard time appreciating that I wouldn't be alive if it hadn't been for Mark. I was disappointed. I know Papa loves me but does he think money is the answer for everything?"

"More than money, Ana. - Prestige. To be one of the best. Recognized. All you hear, 'Washington this,' 'Washington that.' Such a man with a daughter involved with a Negro?" She shook her head. "He should know love is lightening. Here it strikes, there. Who can tell? Still, it can harm. Then a terrible price to pay."

She was pounding the steaks; Analise was peeling potatoes. Olga said, "I told you of Boris and me. Boris was Russian upper class and I was a Jew and after…well, after we were forced to flee, that is when I discovered we would never marry because his family could not bear the 'shame.'

She stopped pounding and looked at her daughter with a severe expression. "And yet for politics - *at forfeit of his life even* - go challenge the Czar and the secret police, but to marry a Jew, only a ballerina? – No. To be his whore – yes!"

Analise put her arm around her mother, and then in silence they went about preparing dinner at the kitchen counter.

"I can bear the 'shame,' Mama, but it's not just that anymore. I only wanted to be Jacob's wife; I wanted to be like you and Mrs. Arnold and Mrs. Muller and now I don't. I apologize, Mama, but...."

"Shhh. No. You must talk now. I did once."

"I mean, how can you see people dying, young boys even...and I saw all of those women and children running from war with only a little of what they owned, their entire lives in bundles and bags; tired, hungry, scared and the old people too crippled to keep up. This was their reward for the lives they had lived. – I tried to help...." She paused to control her emotions.

"I can't feel the same about anything anymore. I can't watch houses around me burn to the ground and think it's all right because mine isn't on fire... It's how Jacob felt. I hate to say it, but now I think life is ugly. All anyone wants to do is kill, kill, kill! They kill you unless you go down on your knees! And they kill you if you don't follow *orders* to kill.

"I won't let anyone tell me I can't love, Mama, that I have to hate someone else in order to win society's approval. Because that's what it means."

They continued preparing dinner in the pause that followed. When Olga spoke her voice was soft with sympathy. "Many years ago we said, 'Those who love war – go fight each other. The sons of others, leave alone.' But those who speak, even think such things, they hunt down. Prison. Execution. It is the way, Ana. They are stronger, more determined, ruthless.... You, me – just to survive is to win."

Things were left unsaid, hanging in the air. They moved about the kitchen and set the dining room table for dinner. Finally Analise said, "Men control everything because they're physically stronger and they bully us to get their way. We're just cows whose only purpose is to give milk and have calves and shut up. Know what Mark told me? If you look at all the things slaves aren't allowed to do, the same things apply to women. Women in France still can't vote. Can you believe that?

"I'm going to do something with my life, Mama, besides just take care of myself. We can't sit by and let men tear up the earth whenever they please as though we have no say in it. They act as though it belongs to them and they're just tolerating us. And we're the ones who suffer. I saw those refugees and it's even worse now for the ones who escaped into France. What had they done? Nothing, except 'get in the way.'"

Olga shook her head, a sad smile on her lips. "Like you I was, Ana. So angry, furious. 'Things must change!' 'Start a revolution!' But you learn, pick battles you can win, others ignore. Don't become a victim, Ana, soon forgotten like dust. Mark is a battle. Maybe you win, maybe you lose. Who can say?"

Analise finished setting the table and stood beside her mother. – "What should I do, Mama? I may disagree, but...."

"Here you cannot live together and you will not surrender love. What is left between? You must decide. We are women; we always find a way."

"– How long can Mark stay here?"

"Three days too much. People see him – they stare. They knock on the door, pretend to visit...."

***

Olga took her place at the head of the table. Mark and Analise sat next to each other. They found things to say as they helped themselves to steak and carrots and potatoes. Mark expressed surprise that a hurricane had struck New England and killed 700 people. Olga informed them that of all the states in the union, New York was the only one that now required a blood test before people could get married. It was silly. The American Rocket Society had tried to launch a seven-foot-long interplanetary rocket; it never left the ground. The Germans had launched one years before that went almost a mile high. On a more somber note Olga informed them that Italy had passed an anti-Semitic law. What could you expect? Mussolini was another Hitler, and no, Analise, she had still not heard the song "Where or When."

The pause in the conversation was becoming loud when Olga said, "Ana tells me you refuse to live here. Then where? You plan what with my daughter?"

He smiled while he framed an answer. "Actually, Mrs. Stern, it's not just my decision. We have to plan things together. She helped me to escape as much as I helped her. We took turns doing whatever needed to be done. I want to go on living," - he held one hand up and folded into a fist- "like that, together. We both do. But I'm not certain where I'll go; maybe Canada."

Analise added, "We'll get married and we believe that somehow things will turn out all right and one day we'll return to Paris to celebrate at the outdoor café where we first were able to speak to each other without being afraid."

"I'll love Analise no matter what we decide because...I guess that's just the way it is."

Analise reached over and took his hand in hers. "On the ship back," she said, "we were ostracized, and know what? We didn't care. We know that life is only a passing moment and we'll have other passing moments together in another time and place. We'll be together throughout eternity. I know it's hard for anyone to believe it, but we do."

Olga regarded him for long moment. "Forgive me," she said. "I never thanked you for giving me back my daughter. And when you know more, you will tell me. For now, this is home."

THE END

CPSIA information can be obtained
at www.ICGtesting.com
Printed in the USA
BVHW030505090622
639222BV00006B/731